Torn

a novel

Kara Householder

www.KaraHouseholder.com

Acknowledgements

There are not words great enough to express the gratitude I feel toward those involved in bringing this book to life, but I will try my best.

To my mother and copy editor, Donna McDaniel. This book would not possible without your expertise and wisdom. It is better because of you. To my first readers, Laura Jayne and Phillip Abbott for your guidance through suggestion and excitement. To Lisa Bush and Phillip Abbott for taking the visions in my head and making them real. To all my friends and family who've lent their ear and given support for this project. To my husband, Travis for your hard work, dedication and continual support, encouragement and prodding and for not letting me quit when it felt too hard to keep going. You deserve as much credit for this book as I do. I love you.

Chapter 1

The alarm sounded; 5:04 AM. What station was that? The Latin music station was playing today, thanks to Jack, her 18 month old. He loved to play with the radio so it was always a surprise in the morning as to which genre of music would be starting the day. Christina Hampton quickly rolled over and hit the snooze button. Her body begged for five more minutes, but she knew that was an extravagance she couldn't afford this morning. She sat up and swung her legs over the side of the bed, groaning as she did. How had the night passed so quickly?

She looked over at her husband Todd as she wiped the sleep from her eyes. His sleep apnea machine whirred quietly as he slept. That machine was the only reason her marriage had survived as long as it had. Todd's snoring was unbearably loud. Before the machine they had been sleeping in separate bedrooms. That unfortunate arrangement had started within the first year of their marriage. However, she knew it wasn't his fault that he sounded like a heavy duty buzz saw.

She smiled as she gazed at him. Even after all this time she still found him as handsome as she had the first day they met. She still remembered how her eyes had widened and she'd done a double take when she initially saw him. A tingle had traveled up her spine then and occasionally that still happened after nearly ten years together. The machine may have altered his appearance while they slept, but in every other way he had not aged. He was naturally lean and tan. Even in the dead of winter his olive complexion gave him a healthy glow of color. He had not been as active since taking his current position with his accounting firm, but he still worked out enough to maintain his firm athletic build. She was the envy of all her friends with a husband as handsome as he.

Ah, the life of the accountant, she thought to herself as she stood up. She let her eyes drift over his sleeping form. His bare chest rose and fell lightly and one arm was thrown overhead. Sleeping in was such a treat. However, it had been so long since Christina had had that luxury she really couldn't remember what it was like. With two small children, a full time job with somewhat unpredictable hours, and a passion for running, she was lucky to squeeze in five or six hours a night. She was usually up before the sun.

Stretching her arms high overhead, Christina walked into the bathroom. The dim beam from the wall mounted nightlight cast a soft violet glow around the room. In full light the walls were two-toned, periwinkle and lettuce green. The color combination had been Todd's idea. He'd picked them from a design he'd seen on a box from Target when they'd purchased medicine cabinets. He called it quirky-chic, kind of like him. She grinned at the funkiness of the room every time she entered the space. It was definitely an unexpected, yet pleasant surprise. She splashed water on her face and headed for the closet. Within five minutes she was dressed and ready for her morning run. With such a busy morning ahead, she decided to do a three mile route instead of her regular six mile course. The three mile course was definitely a more challenging run, with inclines varying in difficulty, despite its being half the length to which she was accustomed. She pulled her long brown hair into a ponytail and grabbed her I-Pod. The music for the morning needed to be fast and hard in order to sustain her speed on the hills. The Red Jumpsuits, Jet, Fall Out Boy and The All American Rejects would get her through the next half hour.

Her dog Max, a sturdy, Golden Retriever mix, met her at the door, tail wagging in anticipation. Max shed like crazy! Everywhere he went he left a trail of yellow fur in his wake. Christina hooked up his leash and gave his head a quick pat. "You ready for this run, Max? We're going fast today, even on the hills." Max panted as if to say, "Bring it on!" She looped the running leash around her shoulders and off they went.

The neighborhood was quite hilly and even a seasoned athlete would find it challenging. After a moderately flat warm up, Christina hit hill number one and chugged along. With every step energy flooded her body until there was no trace of the sleepiness she had felt just fifteen minutes before. Rounding the initial turn, she thought back to the first and only time she had taken Todd jogging with her. He had been a trooper and tried desperately to keep up, but he'd ended up collapsing in the grass gasping for breath. She was afraid he was coughing up a lung. When she'd checked to see if he was really as sick as he sounded, he looked up at her from his sprawling position and said, "Yes, I know I'm dead sexy and no, I will not make out with you right now. I don't care how much you beg." She had laughed so hard she'd nearly fallen down in the grass beside him. He told her to go on and to pick him up on her way back. When she'd returned, he was still lying in the grass staring at the sky panting as if he'd just finished a marathon. She smiled to herself thinking of his goofiness as she ran along.

The loop took her through her middle class suburban neighborhood. Most of the porch lights were still out, but a few were starting to flicker on. The early dawn sunlight was just peeking over the edge of the horizon, painting the eastern sky with soft oranges, violets and pinks. This was her favorite time of day. Things were still quiet and peaceful; something that didn't last long once Atlanta woke up and began the cacophony of horn-honking that signaled the beginning of every morning rush hour. She passed her neighbor John as he pulled out of his driveway. John, an executive at Atlanta Gas Light Company, liked to beat the traffic in the mornings. Even leaving at 5:30 it wasn't going to be great. Atlanta's brutal traffic made it one of the worst places in the country to drive. She waved to him as he backed out. Waving back, he greeted her through his open window.

"Lookin' good today Christina. Man, if I only had your energy!"

"Thanks, John!" Christina replied laughingly. He was a good neighbor, she thought as she continued her jog. John was a night runner. They often passed each other coming or going. She had no doubt that when she returned home this evening, he'd be the one hitting the pavement.

As Christina jogged she pictured her two kids sleeping at home: Kate, her five year old and Jack, the baby with the radio fetish. She picked up her pace, remembering that she would have to drop Kate off early so she could get downtown for her meeting. She was hoping to spend a little time with them this morning as the day's schedule would make it a long one. On a normal day she could be home no later than 4:00 PM, even with the commute time factored in. However, most days in her industry were not all that normal. She would probably not be home until after 6:00 that evening. By most standards this didn't qualify as late, but by "mom standards" it was an eternity! Her kids went to sleep at 8:00, and spending less than two hours a day just didn't seem like enough. Christina loved her job, but she loved her kids more. Any extra time spent away from them was too much.

Moving into a sharp incline, Christina's breathing became more labored, and looking down at Max, she saw that he was panting much harder too. His jowl dripped with saliva as he pushed ahead. It made her a little sad to see the flecks of white that were beginning to replace the yellow in his coat. The area around his eyes and nose looked like a fawn's dappled coat. There were so many white speckles that they were starting to override his youthful golden hue. She probably shouldn't run him so hard. He was, after all, ten years old and beginning to suffer from arthritis in his hips. It didn't help that Todd had hit him with the golf cart this past summer.

Todd was fun and goofy, but this sometimes made him a bit careless. She'd been really angry when she found out about the accident. Max had limped for over a week, and he'd cried whenever he had to lie down. Plus, it had been very difficult to lift a 70 pound dog into the back of an SUV to take him to the vet, or the park, or anywhere. He'd eventually recovered, but the memory just gave her pause to stop and think. She knew Max would go crazy if she went jogging without him; he seemed to love it so much. Besides, their morning jogs were all the time they had together and she wouldn't trade that for the world. She'd keep running him until the vet said absolutely no more.

He was a great jogging partner. He kept up the pace, not allowing her to stop when she was sure she couldn't run another step. In many instances he helped move her along against her will. Max kept her jogging honest. She really couldn't exaggerate the amount of work they did because Max could really do a lot of work. He didn't pull her though. He stayed right by her side, but he would nudge her leg with his nose if he felt she was slowing down before it was time. Sometimes she wondered if she'd still be at this if it weren't for ole Max.

As she crested the last hill and headed home, Christina thought about today's agenda. She had a ton of work to do to prepare for meeting her newest client this morning at 9:00. Christina was an executive at Mastermind Records, one of the top record companies in the world. Headquartered in Atlanta, Mastermind, had started as a very small recording company for independent artists. Decatur and nearby Athens were brimming with local talent that had needed representation. A few affluent people had joined forces to create a production house for these local musicians. Twenty-five years later Mastermind Records was one of the most sought after record labels in the industry. As a tribute to its beginning, Mastermind always treated local talent like royalty. The company, along with big name producers, had literally put Atlanta on the map in terms of the music business.

Christina worked in the A&R management division of Mastermind. Her job was to help new signers adapt to the fast-paced lifestyle of large scale recording artists. She assisted them with everything from hiring their band, cutting the first CD, scheduling and promoting the first major tour, to choosing their wardrobes for their public appearances. She had even accompanied some of her artists to their first Grammy and MTV Award shows. She also worked closely with the record promotion team to ensure the album's advertisement was in line with the image set for her respective clients.

She stayed with a client from signing through the first major tour, usually six months to a year, until their feet were firmly planted and their first project was successfully launched. Then she moved on, normally while the artist took a break before beginning a sophomore project, at which time a different type A&R representative would take over. It was her job to make sure the artist was happy, productive and flourishing, which in turn made money for the company. She kept in touch with many of her former clients, but fame and the glitzy lifestyle usually proved to be too much of an aphrodisiac for them to continue a close relationship with her.

This new client was local singer/songwriter, Steven Lily. She had heard his demo CD and liked it very much. It was a blend of soulful ballads and alternative rock; Dave Matthews meets Def Tones. The album title that he chose, A Little Chunk of My Soul, was a perfect fit. The lyrics spoke of a past riddled with the pain of forgotten loves, lost opportunities, drug abuse and the tough road to recovery. Steven's music was honest and heart-wrenching, but held a hint of hope and a chance for better things to come. He spoke of real issues and used his words to bring the voiced thoughts of many out in the open. There was a familiarity about his work, something she couldn't explain. It touched her deep inside her soul.

The signing had been so quick that she hadn't even had a chance to see a picture of Steven, let alone meet him. Recording had already begun, the acoustic sessions anyway, and were currently being overseen by Ed Sills. Ed worked as a talent scout within the A&R department. He'd discovered Steven, wooed him and fast tracked him into recording. The buzz around the office was that the higher ups wanted to see his album on the shelves by the holidays, and they wanted Steven Lily to become a household name.

His success would be almost guaranteed. Mastermind was willing to put forth any and all resources necessary to make that happen. It always struck her as odd that some artists were given virtual assurance of success while many others were doomed to struggle and claw their way to the top, even after getting a record deal. Favoritism was a big issue in the music industry. Artists with great commercial and economic potential were usually treated better than those with their own unique, but untested, style. It was something that bothered her a bit, but it wasn't her job to do the picking and choosing. Obviously Steven Lily had impressed the right people. His style was distinctive, and she could see its appeal to a wide range of audiences.

Christina was excited to finally meet Steven and anxious to get his promotion underway. This was the part of the job that she looked forward to the most. She liked getting to know the artists, learning their likes and dislikes, and really helping their career take off. After their introduction this morning, they would meet with the style consultants before his first photo shoot at 1:00 this afternoon. Then they would begin the tedious, yet absolutely necessary, process of hiring the band for the remainder of the CD and for the touring sessions.

Although these decisions were mostly up to the artist, Mastermind would have the final say. Studio musicians were easy to find, but putting together a band to tour with was an entirely different story. Personalities had to gel in order to have a properly functioning tour band. If at all possible, she would like to only have to hire one band. As wearisome and prolonged as it was her input here was essential and this phase would require more time than usual. She really found a lot of satisfaction in the intricacies of putting together a good band for her client, but it definitely took time away from her family. That part wasn't so satisfying.

Christina returned home sweaty but rejuvenated. After giving Max a big bowl of water, and downing a glass herself, she jumped into the shower. Cool water cascaded down her shoulders as she quickly shaved her legs and decided on her wardrobe choice for the day. Her black Jessica McClintock pants and long white Dolce and Gabbana button down shirt that emphasized her curves would be the best bet for the day, comfortable and stylish at the same time. She'd finish it off with black boots. The outfit had to say, "I am a professional, but I'm still stylish and cool enough to hang out with rock stars."

She dried off quickly, dressed, and subjected her dark tresses to the hair dryer and straightening iron. Taming the wild waves and frizz was a daily battle. Todd joined her in the bathroom as she pulled the flat iron over a front section.

"Morning, babe," he said groggily as he bent down and kissed her on the cheek. He stood behind her and wrapped his arms around her waist and hugged her lightly, his bare chest brushing her back. She breathed in his earthy aroma. She had once told him she always knew he was near because of his natural scent, which always enticed her. She was pretty sure all that talk about pheromones was exactly true. Todd's people smell, as Kate like to call it, was extremely alluring. Christina never tired of it and tried very hard not to get used to it.

"Morning, yourself. Did you sleep well?" she asked as she finished her hair and began to put on her jewelry. She held her arm out for Todd to clasp her bracelet as he headed toward the shower.

"Like a baby. Speaking of...love the station this morning."

"Don't you though? I like it better than the Republican talk radio that greeted us yesterday morning. Hey, don't forget that you're picking the kids up this afternoon. I'm not sure how long the photo shoot will take. New clients can be tricky sometimes. Then we start band interviews, and you know how that goes."

"Sure, no problem. Kate's taking the bus to sitter's house, right?" He turned on the water and hot steam once again began to fill the small space. He pulled off his pajama bottoms and caught her eye in the mirror. "I see you checking me out. You'd better cut it out or you'll end up in here with me." He grinned slyly.

"Yeah, you wish. Thanks, babe. I'll call you about dinner. Hopefully I'll be home in plenty of time for that this evening. If not, you guys are on your own." She clasped her earrings and put on her wedding ring set.

"Well, seeing that I cook most of the time anyway, I don't think that'll be an issue," Todd said as he got in the shower. "By the way, Kate's already dressed and eating her breakfast."

"You're the best husband I've ever had!" Christina said over the shower. "I'll see you tonight!"

"I know. I'm the greatest! Good luck with the new client. Love you!"

"Love you, too. Have a great day."

Christina entered the kitchen to find Kate eating cereal and reading the back of the box. She was only five, but had already mastered writing the whole alphabet, many words and short sentences.

"Good morning, sweetie. Are you almost ready to go?" Christina kissed the top of her little girl's dark hair. Her kids could not have been more different. Kate had the dark waves of her mother and Jack had the blond locks of his father. They barely looked alike at all. Sometimes it seemed to Christina that Kate was her exact clone, but she had just provided a warm place for Jack to grow.

"Yes, Mommy, I'm done. I want to kiss Jack before we go. Don't forget it's my teacher's birthday and you promised you'd give her the autographed CD from Blue Streak." Kate said as she slid out of her chair and ran to Jack's room.

"I didn't forget. In fact, I put it in your backpack already." They both kissed the little boy who was sleeping in the yoga position called child's pose, butt in the air and knees underneath his body. Then they quickly piled into the car. No need to wake him up if he was sleeping soundly. A cranky toddler wouldn't be a terrific start to the day. So much for spending time with them both, Christina thought. But now she'd be even more motivated to get home as fast as she could after work.

Less than ten minutes later they pulled up in front of the school.

"Okay, sweetie, we're here. Your teacher's present is in the front pocket of your book bag and your math worksheet is in your homework folder. Good luck on your quiz today. I'll see you tonight." Christina said as her daughter hopped out of the backseat. A quiz for a class of five year olds! A lot had changed since she'd been in the education industry.

When Christina had been teaching, there were no such things as quizzes for first graders. She had been an elementary school teacher for a few years before changing careers altogether and joining the Mastermind team. With the current changes in the field of education, she wasn't sure she'd be able to keep up if she ever did decide to return to the classroom. She had thought about it, but a few things held her back. One, her certificate had lapsed and would need to be renewed. Two, while the vacation time couldn't be beat, the money sure could and three, she really loved working in the music industry. She felt connected to a bigger world, held a position of importance, found immense satisfaction in helping new artists succeed, and kept her appearance fashionable and youthful. In today's world, where major corporations were run by kids barely out of college, a youthful appearance was a necessity. She'd gotten over the star-struck phase pretty quickly and realized early on that celebrities were, for the most part, ordinary people with extraordinary jobs.

Kate came to the open window for a kiss. "Bye Mommy. I love you very much!" she said in her sing-song little girl voice.

"Bye-bye. I love you very much too!" Christina kissed her daughter goodbye and watched as she pranced up the stairs to the building. At the top of the stairs, Kate turned around and gave a little wave. That was the cue for Christina to drive away. She gave a last quick wave and headed out. With any luck she would still beat most of the traffic downtown.

Chapter 2

Just as she expected, I-75 was backing up before Delk Road. Getting inside the perimeter was always the trickiest part. Once past I-285 she could find back roads to avoid the congestion around Brookwood. Her office was located in Buckhead in a high rise called Tower Place. Mastermind Records dominated the top three floors of the building. The A&R department was on the second of those floors. The first of the floors occupied by Mastermind housed the various recording studios. Many artists chose to use the in-house studios as opposed to private ones because they got better scheduling and they could retain more profits from their sales. The top floor housed the offices of the top executives and the department heads.

Christina finally swung her black Toyota Highlander onto West Paces Road. This was part of the scenic route. Passing the governor's mansion every morning was just one perk to using this shortcut. The road had some of the largest and most beautiful homes in Atlanta on it. Christina loved looking at those homes to gather ideas for the planned renovations of her own home. Unfortunately, not many of the ideas from these houses would work on hers. If she tried to tile her roof in adobe and put up a high brick wall around her property without being a member of the nearest country club, it would stand out quite a bit.

Nevertheless, each morning she'd pick out a different one to study for the few brief seconds she passed it. Today she chose the two-story Spanish style home on the left. The terra cotta tiled roof perfectly accentuated the peachy stucco. The sprawling lawn was lush and healthy despite the drought restrictions currently in place. The porch came winding down with two sets of steps on either side meeting at a central circular driveway. Christina often wondered what kind of jobs the people who owned these homes had. She and Todd made quite a bit of money between the two of them, but there was no way they could ever afford one of the homes on this street. Old money was definitely part of the fabric of life down here.

She was still shaking her head at the decadence of it all when she pulled into the parking deck at ten past eight. She had less than an hour to make sure everything was ready for the day and to reconfirm tomorrow's appointments. If her client was on time this morning, she would hopefully be able to wrap everything up by 6:00 and beat the majority of the traffic home, leaving time to take the kids to the playground before dinner. She checked her makeup in the mirror one last time before getting out of her car and starting for the building.

"Hola, Jorge!" she greeted the doorman as he held open the glass front doors for her. Jorge was a Hispanic gentleman in his mid-sixties.

"Hola, Miss Christina! Busy day ahead?"

"I have a new client coming in this morning. Local guy who lives over in Tucker I believe. Should be interesting. I'll keep you posted. Have a great day."

"Yes ma'am. Good luck. I know new clients can be complicated. Have a great day too."

Christina smiled and gave him a little wave as she entered the elevator. When the doors opened on her floor, she exited and turned to the left. Her office was near the back of the floor facing the downtown area. She was one of the few Mastermind employees with a window, much less a view. Being the lead A&R rep for her division had more perks than just attending star-studded bashes and award shows. Being able to look out over the Buckhead skyline and watch the day come to life was really a nice touch to her office, especially since she had started off in a cubical just five years ago. Her assistant Andrea had not yet arrived, but that was not atypical. Andrea was often late but was excellent at her job, so Christina mostly overlooked the tardiness.

She sat down at her desk and logged on to her computer. She reviewed the list of appointments for the day and began making contacts to confirm tomorrow's appointments. This was normally Andrea's job, but as she had still not arrived, Christina went ahead and took care of the calls on her own. She would be accompanying Steven Lily to his first radio interview tomorrow morning. She had arranged an interview and a live performance on Q101's The Morning Burn, a radio program that aired from 5:00-10:00 each morning. Being friends with the DJ's really was a plus. Over the years she had nurtured a relationship that allowed The Morning Burn to be the first to introduce many of her new artists, and this in turn gave her an in whenever she wanted a new artist played. It was a win-win situation. With Steven, this was the first method of getting his name out there and his first single recognized. She confirmed for 9:15.

As she reviewed the remaining notes for the day, the fingers of her right hand slipped mindlessly over the charms on her bracelet. She'd had the bracelet since high school. It was pretty cheesy, she knew, but it held great sentimental value.

The first charm she'd received was from her mom on her 16th birthday. It was a small music note. While she couldn't sing a lick, she'd always been interested in music. She'd learned to read music and joined the school band, and studied musical trends throughout history as a hobby. The second charm was a gift from her first love, a Christmas present her freshman year of college. It was a small circle with a star cut from the middle. Engraved around the star were the words, "Love Much, Live Well". Even though the relationship had ended poorly, the sentiment was nice and the words had always held an inspirational message for her. Next she'd received a small scroll charm, which had once been on a necklace that had belonged to her dad, when she graduated from college. Her grandmother had saved it for her, and it was one of the best gifts she'd ever received. The last three charms she got after she met Todd. The first was for their one year anniversary. It was two silver hearts linked together. The other two were birthstone angels for Kate and Jack.

The bracelet served as a daily reminder of her life, where she'd been, and where she was now. It kept her focused on the important things and people in her life. She wore it every day, taking it off only for her morning runs and special functions. It held more value to her than any of the expensive tennis bracelets she'd received from Todd over the years. She appreciated those and wore them to industry dinners, release parties, or award shows, but their material value held no candle to the sterling silver charm bracelet she'd had for nearly half her life now.

Andrea stuck her head in the door when she arrived. Her assistant was tall with long flowing red hair. She wore it in loose curls that had a very sensuous quality. She was naturally slender, evidenced by the fact that she ate food of the poorest nutritional value, lots of it, and still maintained a size six. Christina hadn't wanted to like her. Andrea was the kind of woman that most other women despised. Beautiful, built and smart! Andrea had it all. She was also one of the nicest, most caring people Christina had ever met, and that had convinced her that the two should be friends.

"Hey, there! Sorry I'm late." The two women smiled at each other because they both knew Andrea really didn't care if she was late or not. Neither did Christina for that matter, "Do you want me to ring you when Mr. Lily arrives?"

"That'd be great, thanks. I have just a few more things to wrap up for tomorrow before we get started this morning. Hey Andrea, what have you heard about this guy? Everything's been pretty mysterious so far. I was just given his demo CD and told to fast track him. Nothing else though."

Andrea leaned against the door frame. "Apparently he was playing at some hole in the wall club that Mr. Sills just happened to pop into some weeks back. You know how he likes to explore the dive bars. Anyway, this Steven Lily guy was playing a set with a mediocre band. Sills loved the voice and the guitar, but hated the rest of them. So after their set ended, he arranged a meeting with Steven and got him to sign as a solo artist."

"Well, I know that already, and that Steven has already started his acoustic recordings. But, why was he moved to us? Especially this early?"

"Word has it he's pretty rough around the edges. That's probably why you were called in. You know, to polish him up."

"Andrea, how do you know EVERYTHING that goes on in this place?" Christina asked, lacing her hands behind her head. "That's why I keep you around. I'd be totally clueless if you weren't here."

"You're right, you would be pretty much clueless," Andrea joked. "People generally tell the assistants everything. They underestimate the power of our knowledge. Why do you think the higher ups are so nice to us on Administrative Professionals Day? They don't want us to spill all their secrets!"

"That's funny because it's true!"

"I'll let you know when he's here."

"Thanks a bunch." Christina said as she looked back down at her calendar. After the meeting with the style consultants this morning, she would begin putting together a shopping list for Steven Lily. They would have to assess how much of the reported "rough edges" could remain and how much smoothing actually had to be done. She was usually assigned to the edgier clients. She'd proved to the company that she could handle the temperamental attitude and behavior of many musicians. Her teaching background came in handy here. Sometimes it still amazed her that adult musicians could behave so much like fourth graders when they didn't get what they wanted. At times, she swore her students had been far more mature than her clients.

Her intercom buzzed. "Mr. Lily is here to see you Christina."

"Thanks. Send him in."

Christina stood and readied herself, but nothing could have prepared her for what was about to walk through the door. A slight knock sounded. "Please come in," she said. The door opened and Steven Lily walked in.

Christina froze in place as her eyes met his. They were familiar eyes, but she knew them by a different name. "Oh my god," she gasped, "Alex!"

Chapter 3

She was instantly transported back eleven years. Back to the time when she knew Alex Lily, her walk-on-the-wild-side, her first love. She was 20 years old, naïve and not nearly seasoned enough to handle the relationship. He was a musician, and unlike anyone she'd ever been with. His creative spirit, his energy and his eyes pulled her in and held her transfixed. His voice and the way he made his guitar resonate drew her like a moth to a flame. Theirs had been a brief, but superbly passionate affair. One that lingered on even years after it ended.

In the end though, things had been bad. The drugs, the late nights talking him through scary trips, the fury, and the lies had ultimately proved to be too much for her to handle and they had parted ways in anger. She and Alex had been a disastrous match from the beginning, but she had ignored her instinct. She had wanted him more than any other man and she'd paid the price for her indulgence.

Now, a lifetime later, he was standing in her office and she had to maintain a professional composure. Inside, her heart beat rapidly and she held on to the edge of her desk to steady herself. She had never even known his first name was Steven. She should have made the connection though. There weren't that many people with the last name

Lily, and even fewer were musicians. His voice had matured so much over the past decade that she hadn't recognized it when she'd listened to his CD. The familiarity of the music made sense once she realized who was behind it. She had lived through part of it with him.

He broke the silence first. "Well, this is a surprise."

"I would say so. What are you doing here? Well, that's a stupid question. Of course I know why you're here. I guess I mean, oh I don't know what I mean," she babbled on like a damn teenager faced with her first crush.

"I can see you still jabber when you're nervous," he smiled, trying to ease the awkwardness.

"Yes, unfortunately it's one of my annoying traits that haven't gotten better with age." She tried to recover her composure. "Come in, please," she said as she moved to close the door behind him. Andrea was looking in, not even trying to hide her interest in her boss's reaction to the new client. Christina gave her a look that said, "I'll tell you later," and turned her attention back to him.

He'd changed a lot over the past eleven years. His hair had receded somewhat, but it worked for him. However, the bleached blond made him look slightly wan. He'd put on weight that comes with leaving the twenties behind, but he was still solidly built and she could see the outline of muscle through his faded T-shirt. His face was lined a bit more with age, in a way that made him look even more dangerously handsome than he had before, but his eyes remained the same. They were the dark green she remembered and had the same intensity. The same piercing stare, that had at one time driven her mad with desire and then later driven her to pieces with grief, was still there, looking right at her. He had a full sleeve arm tattoo, a tribal pattern. The tattoo suited him. The eyebrow stud, however, did not. He had on worn blue jeans that were frayed along the bottom and scuffed black Doc Martens that had seen better days.

She could see the rough edges Andrea had mentioned. He still looked like the guy from the wrong side of the tracks that all mothers warned their daughters about, the very ones the daughters could not get enough of. Honestly though, she wouldn't change much about him. The roughness worked for him: it always had. She turned and went back to her desk.

"So, you're going by Steven these days? What happened to Alex?" she asked with a genuine interest, grateful for something to say to get the conversation started.

"Alex is my middle name. I still go by that in personal circles, but I started performing under Steven. I thought it had a better ring to it." He gazed upon her with intensity. "It's great to see you again. I take it you're married now. I would have recognized Christina Malone, but not Hampton. You look amazing." He smiled again and she looked up into his olive eyes, the identical eyes that had at one time looked upon her with desire and then later in rage. She looked away before she spoke.

"Thanks. I'd say it's good to see you too, but I'm still in too much shock to know if that is true or not."

"It's been a long time, Christina. Haven't you forgiven me yet?"

"I forgave you a long time ago, but I haven't forgotten."

"I know, but to be fair, you did say you never wanted to see me again."

"This is not the time or the place," she said. "Why don't we start over for today? I can explain to you what my role is here at Mastermind and we can get started."

"Okay, let's ignore the purple elephant in the room and maybe it will go away," he said with a smile. "Hey, I thought you were teacher. What are you doing at Mastermind?"

"I'm sure there will be plenty of time later for us to catch up. Right now, we're actually on a schedule," Christina said as she sat down. She motioned for him to take a seat as well. Once he was settled she began to speak.

"My job, Mr. Lily, is to assist you in becoming acclimated to the life of a Mastermind recording artist. I will pretty much be by your side, professionally speaking, for the next six months or so. I'll be there through the recording process and the promotion that follows. I work for Mastermind, and so do you. I earn my pay by making you look good and making you successful. I will be with you when you interview and audition your band members, through the recording the remainder of the CD, and through the first tour. I will showcase your assets, but also identify your areas that need some refinement and help improve them. I represent your interests to the company. However, it's important to remember that Mastermind has certain standards for its artists to live up to. It's my job to make sure you meet or exceed those expectations."

"Whoa, hold on," Alex interrupted, "what is this? You have to approve everything I do?" His temper was beginning to flare. The thought of having his every move approved was ridiculous and he planned to let her know it.

"Before you freak out, just hold on a minute," she broke in hoping to defuse the situation before it got out of hand. He was not the first client to feel this way. Oftentimes, artists came in and felt that Christina was censoring them, or stifling their true nature. She was ready for this reaction.

"I am here to help you, not hinder you. I will not schedule you for anything that you don't approve of first. While there will be professionals who can suggest ways to style your hair and what type of clothing to wear, I will not try to change you. We want *you* to shine through and be yourself. We just want to make sure that if you go on national television, you appropriately represent the company. You have a great deal of input in all matters, and in many cases you'll have full approval. It's my job to present you with as many options as I find necessary. Does that make a little more sense?" she asked.

"A little, I guess. What I don't understand is why any of this is necessary. Can't my regular manager take care of these things for me? Or Ed. Why can't Ed handle this?"

"Well, first of all, your manager's main job is to assist you with contractual matters. He's done a good job of making sure you received a very nice advance and a good percentage of the profits from album sales and ticket sales from concerts. Ed serves mainly as a talent scout. He finds the talent, presents the talent to the company, gets the ball rolling, and then moves on to find the next big thing.

"This division of A&R is much more intricate and involved with the development of the record and the artist. Besides, it's in your contract that you use our services until you are well established in the music industry. Also, we help ease the culture shock and the overwhelming feeling that can come with 'instant' stardom. Would you want to go on TRL without someone to run answers to potential questions by? Would you know how to deal with paparazzi hounding your every move? We want you to feel comfortable with the drastic changes that will occur in your life. That's my job."

Christina managed a smile. She was beginning to feel a little more like herself. If she could just keep a professional facade, the day would be okay.

"So, how long will I be in your service?" Alex asked, still projecting a hint of sarcasm.

"Probably until your first tour wraps up, sometimes a little past that if you want my help with award shows and other appearances like that. Then you'll move to the next division that will take over and get you ready for your next project. Your manager will work closely with you on this as well."

"Do all new artists get this service?"

"That's a fair question," she answered. "The answer is yes, but in varying degrees. All new artists and their managers get a representative who works with their producer and promotion team. The promotion team gets the word out there. The rep tries to make sure the artists don't make asses of themselves on the red carpet or on Saturday Night Live. Of course, the Ashlee Simpson debacle proved that can still occur!

"Then, there are clients like you who are being fast-tracked, if you will, because Mastermind sees a huge future in store. I work directly with the promotion team and your producer to make sure things are fair and balanced for you. I also have contacts that will directly benefit both you and the company. I won't let them schedule you for more than you think you can handle, although I may push you to do more than you assume you can do. You will rise faster and go farther by working with me. Hopefully, you will also feel more at ease."

"Do you have other clients besides me, or am I your sole responsibility?"

'Right now, I have three other clients besides you. However, they are all three finishing up their work with me within the next couple of weeks. Are you familiar with Travis Johnson, Michelle Norris or Tawney Blount?" she asked.

"Yes! They're your clients? I love their work," Alex replied.

"Yep, they're mine. Michelle signed first, about six months ago. She was pretty shy and it took a while for her to come out of her shell. She goes on her first tour in two weeks, and then she and her team will be on their own. Travis and Tawney signed around the same time and have really embraced their lives in the spotlight. Travis needed very little help. He already had his image down and just needed brief coaching with interview answers, schedule adjustments and such.

"Tawney was the same. We spent the majority of our time on scheduling and promotion. Their CD's took very little time to cut and they were off and running. From listening to your demo, I'd say that same thing will apply with you. Your work is very good."

She had always loved his music. Even when things were at their worst, she still respected and admired his talent. She'd hated to see him throwing it away back then and was glad he was finally making a name for himself.

"Thanks. Alright, I'm sold. If you can get the same results that you got with them with a loser like me, I'll do anything you want," Alex said.

"Well, I can see your negative self-talk hasn't changed. That's the first thing we'll work on. It's good to appear humble, but you must also display a sense of confidence or this business will eat you for breakfast!"

"Okay, so noted. So, what do we do first?" he asked. Overcoming his self-imposed negativity would be hard, but he'd do it, she thought.

"We meet with a team of stylists first. Then, you have a photo shoot for your CD. After that, we start interviewing band mates and then complete recording. You'll also be given a list of items to shop for."

"Wait, you don't go shopping with me?" he joked. "What if I need someone to tell me if I look like an ass?"

"I can send my assistant with you if you'd like. She has an excellent eye, or I can send an intern," she replied not playing into his comments.

"What if I don't want your assistant or an intern? What if I want your opinion?"

"Then, bring your clothes in tomorrow and I'll go through them. I have to get home tonight though. My daughter has a project for school that I'll have to help her with," Christina lied. Damn, she hated using her kids as excuses, but they sure were convenient.

"You have kids? I see you got over your maternal issues. Yes, I remember everything," he said, noticing the blush that had risen in her cheeks. She had held firm for years that having kids was out of the question. She couldn't see bringing children into a scary, hateful world.

But that was years ago, before she met Todd who had changed her life and outlook completely.

She smiled. "I have two kids. Kate is five and in first grade. Jack is 18 months old. What about you; girlfriend, fiancé, wife, kids?" Christina asked with sincere curiosity. What had this man who had caused her such heartache been doing with his life?

"None of the above. My significant other is my music," he said with a shrug. Christina sensed dangerous territory and steered the conversation in a safer direction.

"Okay, let's get going then. It's nearly 10:00 and we need to have you out of the stylists by noon. There will be food at the studio for lunch, but it will take us a while to get there. Are you ready, Steven Alex Lily, for your first official assignment as a Mastermind artist?" she smiled as she stood. He stood as well, following her cue.

"I'm as ready as I'll ever be."

He held the door for her as she passed. He did have a lot to explain to her, but had no idea where to start. Should he even try?

"Andrea, we're off. You can forward any calls to my cell," Christina said as they left. She gave her curious assistant a look that said, "Don't ask".

"Of course. It was nice to meet you, Mr. Lily. I'm sure we'll be seeing a lot of you around here," Andrea said to Alex as they passed.

"Nice to meet you too, Andrea," he replied. "Nice girl," he said as they reached the bank of elevators.

"Yes, but she's nosy. I'd appreciate it if you didn't tell her how we used to know each other," Christina said. "She will ask, and you probably won't know even realize it until you've told her the whole story. She's really good at getting people to talk, sometimes against their will."

"You mean you don't want your assistant to know that eleven years ago you used to sleep with your brand new client? I think I can manage that," he said with a smirk. "Thing is, can you?"

"I can manage lots of things, Alex," she said curtly, looking him directly in the eye. Damn, after all this time he could still piss her off!

Chapter 4

When they reached the lobby, George opened the door for them and bade them good day. Christina led Alex to a black Lincoln Town Car, a company vehicle, and opened the doors with the remote.

"Nice ride. Yours?" he asked.

"Hardly! I drive this for clients and company use."

"Let me guess, you drive a small sedan that gets excellent gas mileage and has been paid off for years," he ventured, remembering her frugality and environmentalist nature. He used to kid her about being a hippy in disguise. From the outside she never looked much like a flower child, but she definitely had the heart and soul of one. He did remember a lot. More than she would have guessed.

"You would have been right up until three months ago when I got my oversized SUV. It's roomy, but has a pretty nice sized payment to go along with the 20 gallon gas tank. Luckily, it gets decent gas mileage for a vehicle of its size. That, and the extra room for traveling with two kids, is the only way I could justify it," she replied. She had always hated when people got new cars every two years and drove vehicles much bigger than they ever really needed.

The drive to the stylists' studio lasted nearly twenty minutes. The first few minutes were awkwardly silent. Christina was afraid to say too much for fear of losing whatever professional dignity she had managed to recoup from her initial shock. Alex sat motionless taking it all in, still a bit stunned that he was here, on his way to his first professional photo shoot for *his* CD. Not too long ago he'd been a graphic artist in a dead end job with no possibility of advancement, living with his mom and spending most nights playing his guitar and writing music. He'd finally been able to save enough money to put a down payment on a small house and was at least able to get out on his own. His fifteen years of hard work and not giving up on his passion were finally starting to pay off.

And she was here to share it with him. Obviously, it had come as a surprise to both of them. She showed it more, he thought. But then again, she'd always been the one who wore her heart on her sleeve. He had become a master at pushing everyone away and living behind a mask of numbness. Inside, however, he died a little more each day. His music was the only thing that kept him going in life and sustained him through the really bad days.

He stole a glance at Christina as she drove. Her hair was longer than it had been in college, but still the same rich mahogany color. When the light hit her hair, it shone with great intensity and glinted with natural red highlights. His eyes traced its path as it cascaded over her shoulders and down her back. She had been shapely in college and still was, but now she was leaner. Her curves were still there, just in smaller proportion. She had changed in many ways. She seemed harder, a bit cold and methodical. He wondered how much of that had been his fault. When he'd pushed her away he hit rock bottom. She was the one person in the world who had been unconditionally kind to him and he had treated her like shit. He had told himself he didn't care about her tears or that he'd said hateful things to the only person who had ever given a damn about him. It wasn't until she'd said she never wanted to see him or hear his voice again with steel behind her words that he realized what he'd done. She was beautiful, brilliant, and tough as nails. But at the same time more loving and tender than anyone he'd ever met. He knew what he'd given up and regretted it every day since.

It was painful to think about her back then. He could remember seeing her on campus and walking the other way so he could honor her desire not to see him. He'd watched her reading on park benches, writing by the lake and cry in the moonlight. He'd left school shortly after everything ended for good. He'd come to realize what a mistake he'd made by pushing her away and couldn't stand to be that near to her yet not be with her.

Two years later he'd attempted to move forward with his life and moved in with Nicole. One day, about a year into their relationship, she'd found Christina's picture in his notebook where he wrote his lyrics. "Who's this?" she'd asked. He told her with no emotion behind his voice. "Did you love her?" she'd asked. He replied with yes, very much. "Do you still love her?" she'd asked. He replied with yes, very much. Nicole moved out the next day. He had never told Christina any of this; he'd never had the opportunity to. Now, he didn't know how he could, given their working arrangement and the fact that she was happily married with a family.

"So Chris, tell me about yourself. What have you been doing all these years?" he asked, hoping a normal conversation would ease the awkwardness between them.

"Well, I'm married and I have kids, as we've already established." She talked as she changed lanes and checked her mirrors, not allowing her eyes to meet his. "I've been married for eight years. My husband's name is Todd. I did teach school for about four years and then decided it was time for a change. I had a friend who had a contact at Mastermind. I found a use for all those public relations, journalism and broadcasting classes I took in college, and now I'm here. That's the short version. What about you? Fill me in on your life for the past eleven years."

"Not much to tell really. I left school after we…" he paused not really knowing how to finish, "split up, I guess. I moved back home, eventually got into a recovery program, found a job and wrote music. Pretty much the same old same old, day in and day out. The first few years were pretty tough, trying to clean up and all. The past seven have been as normal as I guess they could be. Go to work, go home, write music, play, repeat."

"I'm glad to know you cleaned up," was all she could think to say right then.

"Yeah, it took losing something really important for me to realize it was time for a change."

"Oh yeah, what was that?"

"You Chris, it was you."

She felt a chill spread through her body. Her heart was physically starting to hurt. It was a feeling, an ache, she hadn't experienced in a long time. They rode the rest of the way in silence, absorbed by the strangeness of the situation. She didn't know how to respond to him, and he didn't know what to say to her.

He knew what he wanted to say, but how could he? She was married, and had moved on years ago. He wanted to tell her everything, that it was her face he saw when he fell asleep at night, that she was behind the majority of the songs he'd written, that even after all this time he still loved her. He was afraid he always would.

When they arrived, she led him into a studio where he met a wardrobe consultant and hair stylist. He didn't have much hair left to style, but whatever this guy could do to help, Alex was up for.

"The tattoos are wonderful," Jillian, the wardrobe consultant, gushed.

In additional to the arm sleeve he also had several tattoos across his chest and his back. The one on his back was a phoenix draped in blue flames. It symbolized his rebirth and the recovery from his drug abuse. He'd gotten it on his one year anniversary of sobriety.

"We really must find a way to showcase them the majority of the time. But honestly, we'll have to lose the eyebrow stud. It just doesn't work on someone your age," Jillian continued.

"Okay, so this won't be as bad as I thought. We may have to fight over the stud though," he said removing it from his brow. Alex laughed, looking over at Christina who smiled in spite of herself. She's still in there, he thought, despite the stony front she was putting up. He wondered how much it would take to bring her out of her shell.

After an hour of trying on what seemed like a thousand pairs of jeans, sweaters, long sleeved and short sleeved T-shirts, the team agreed on a forest green long sleeved button front shirt, white T-shirt and slightly grungy designer jeans. Alex gasped for breath when he heard the price of the jeans. He couldn't figure out why someone would spend $125.00 on jeans that were made to look dirty. He could get an old pair of Levi's from Goodwill and traipse through the woods behind his house and get the same effect. The shirt brought out the green in his eyes and made them appear even more vivid. The sleeves were rolled up to show his tattoo and the front was left unbuttoned to reveal his form.

Lawrence, the hair stylist, gave him a quick shave, leaving just a thin goatee and razored his cut to enhance his natural curls. A toner was use to remove the fake blond and he was taken back to a more natural shade, a light chestnut brown. Alex turned to Christina for approval.

"Excellent," was her only response. Even at thirty-three he looked so much like he had eleven years ago. He had taken her breath away then and the same was proving true now. She had to lean on a chair to keep from losing her balance. How on earth was she going to be able to do this?

Armed with printed digital photos of what to look for on future shopping expeditions, they left for the photographer's studio. Makeup, which was done on site, was an interesting experience for Alex since he'd never worn makeup in his life. Christina told him to get used to it because it would happen a lot. His guitar had been delivered already in preparation for the CD cover shot. Lunch had also been delivered and was set out for them. Christina picked at her food, too afraid to eat for fear of not keeping it down.

"You're not eating."

"I guess I'm a little uneasy still," she said with a sigh dropping her sandwich back on the plate. "This really is a lot to digest, no pun intended, for one day. I mean, it's been eleven years, Alex. It's just strange."

"I know. It's pretty weird. But, in a way, I'm glad you're the one working with me on this. It's nice to see a familiar face in this unfamiliar world." He gave her a sheepish grin and met her eyes. She quickly looked away, trying not to be drawn in by his gaze.

"Things are going to change a lot for you. But this was the life you were meant to lead. I've always known that. You'll adapt quickly." She put her plate to the side and wiped her hands on her napkin. She had always believed his gifts should be shared with the world. The same slightly fearful flutter of excitement she'd felt back then had resurfaced, but this time the stakes were higher. Career and family were on the line, not just her personal well-being.

"So, when can we sit down and actually talk? You've barely said ten words since we left your office. I want to know everything about your life now. Anything you want to tell me, anything at all."

"I don't know if talking about personal stuff is such a good idea. It'll lead to our lives in the past. Perhaps we should just let it lie," she ventured.

"That's fine, if that's really what you want. I do have things to say though. An apology for one, but I've waited this long. I guess I can wait until you're ready."

"Thank you, I appreciate that. Well, it looks like Micah and his team are ready. Time to get started. It'll be weird at first if you're not used to taking direction, but it does get easier. Remember to work with the photographer, not the camera lens," she said as they got up to meet the photographer.

She was right. It was weird at first. But Micah was an excellent photographer, one of the best in the business, and pretty soon Alex felt more at ease. Micah shot him in a variety of different poses; both shirts on, one off, both off, sitting, standing, lying down. Alex focused on his guitar, on his music, and then he focused on her. He began to play and then sing one of the songs he'd written for her years ago.

"Beautiful Sadness" was still one of the most personal, emotional songs he'd ever written. He'd written it one night after things had ended for good. He'd watched her from the shadows as she sat by the lake on campus. The moon had reflected in her eyes and made the tears that fell, shimmer. She had been the picture of bittersweet perfection, so sad yet so beautiful. Now, his green eyes locked in on her blue ones and held them. God, she's breathtaking, he thought. Neither of them looked away as he sang.

"That's it!" Micah shouted. "That's the shot! I don't know what just happened, but that was *the* look!" The photographer jumped up and made his way over to Alex.

The spell was broken and she averted her eyes. Micah shook hands with Alex and kissed Christina on the cheek as the crew began to break down the set. This was not going to work, she thought. It was already too personal. She had to get out of this.

It was barely 3:00 when they left the studio. Micah said he'd get the photos to her and the design team as soon as possible. They drove back in complete silence, both lost in their own worlds that were revolving around each other.

When they arrived back at Mastermind headquarters, Alex reached out and touched her hand before she could open the door. The feel of her soft skin on his fingertips sent shivers through his body. He caught her looking at his hands, large with calloused fingers. Those same hands he'd used to caress her so sweetly. The same hands that also used needles to shoot up and smoke the drugs that had once ruined his life. The same hands that created the music that helped him deal with the pain of life. He felt her body flinch at his touch. The memories of her almost overwhelmed him.

"Christina, look at me please," he said softly.

"Alex, I can't," she whispered and got out of the car. Gathering her composure, she smoothed her blouse and turned toward him. "I have some musicians in the studio waiting to audition with you. We need to get going."

He followed her reluctantly. She didn't see him hang his head regretting that he had sung that song too soon. He needed her to be open and he was afraid he'd just helped her nail the door shut. They spent the afternoon listening to and interviewing musicians from all walks of life, from a kid barely out of high school to a man in his late fifties. He watched her work and she was amazing. She was all business, yet she knew how to conduct the interviews in a personal but effective way. She was very respectful to all the musicians who auditioned even when it was clear they had no shot. The nervous girl in the car had disappeared and a competent business woman had taken her place. During several auditions they made eye contact, speaking without words. They were almost completely in sync with regards as to who should stay and who should go. Most of their responses were communicated nonverbally. It was a connection they had shared that still held true.

He asked several questions as well and together they began making the call back list. By 6:00 they had narrowed the list down. The final selections would be made the next day when the remaining candidates would play with him and with each other. All the hopefuls had been given copies of his music to learn. It was weird seeing his songs on sheet music. He hadn't even been able to formally read music until recently and now his songs were printed for other musicians to learn.

Christina stepped out to make a phone call while the sound techs broke down and packed up equipment. He sat there absently strumming his guitar. It's what he did when he was uneasy. Some of his best songs were begun just by random strumming. He caught himself staring at her long legs as she walked purposefully back in the studio.

"Well, that's it for today. Good work for your full first day. How do you feel?"

"Not bad, a little overwhelmed, but pretty good. You're great with the whole interview thing."

"Thanks, I've had a lot of practice," she smiled. She waved to the techs as they finished up, "See you tomorrow guys. Thanks!" She turned her attention back to Alex. "Please be here tomorrow morning by 8:15. You'll be playing live on the radio so go home and rest your voice."

"Okay. So, I guess this is good night then." It was his turn to feel uncomfortable. He was afraid if he let her walk out the door that she'd never come back, that all of this would disappear and he'd be right back where he started, still making T-shirts for 4-H camping programs and family reunions.

"I'll see you in the morning." She turned and walked away leaving him there to watch her go. She returned to her floor, but didn't go to her office. First, she went to pay a visit to Joe, her boss.

Chapter 5

"I can't do this, Joe. You have to give Steven Lily to someone else."

Joe Delucci looked surprised at Christina's abrupt and rather unexpected entrance.

"Why on earth would I give him to someone else? Was he offensive? Should we reconsider our level of commitment to him?" Joe asked. Christina and Joe had known each other a long time. He looked very much like Joe Pesci. Barely 5'7, he had a little round paunch and a head full of thick dark hair that tended to wave in the wrong direction. He was Italian and looked stereotypically like a Brooklyn mobster would look. He'd moved to Atlanta from New York ten years ago, but the accent had not faded in the slightest. He had trained her when she first came to Mastermind, and as he had moved up in the company, he'd brought her with him. They had been through a lot together. She'd comforted him through the breakup of his marriage, and he'd celebrated the birth of both her kids. They were friends as well as colleagues and he deserved to know what was really going on.

"No, he's remarkably talented. It's just that… well, we have a history together," she stammered. "It didn't end on a good note and I honestly don't know if I can separate my professional life from my personal baggage on this one, Joe". She sank into a chair and dropped her head into her hands.

"Christina, you're the best I've got. Steven Lily needs a lot of coaching and you're the one who's going to do it. I'm going to tell you what you tell the other reps in your division; suck it up and do your job. You are a professional. Now act like one! Whatever happened was a long time ago and you've moved on," he said in a stern tone that meant business.

"You're right, Joe. You are absolutely right. I'm sure I can hold it together at work, but I'm afraid working with him every day will complicate things on a personal level."

"How long ago was it?"

"Eleven years, and before you say it, yes it was a long time ago. Things are very different now. But, I don't know. There was no closure I guess," Christina explained.

"So close it and move on. You have a great family that you'd never risk *and* you're a professional who would never risk her job either. Am I right?"

"Yes, you're right," she said resigned. She knew the company policy about reps getting involved with clients. She'd seen several good reps fired because they broke the policy and couldn't handle the relationship fallout. Most musicians were not known for their long-term stable relationship potential. When they moved on to someone else, many reps who gave in to the temptation got burned. Mastermind was quick to let them go.

"Chris," he softened a little, "you've been by my side through a lot of tough times. I can tell this guy has you rattled, but I need you on this one," he said a bit more tenderly. He'd never seen her like this. She was usually so strong when it came to work matters. It made him more than a little nervous. She was the best in the business and he'd hate to see her fall apart.

"Okay, so I'll suck it up and get it done. I'll just try to fast track the fast track and move along. In the meantime, once I turn my other three loose, I'll get someone new to work with too, right?" Christina was eager to have another client to diffuse the pressure of working with Steven Alex Lily.

"Of course you'll get someone else. However, I can't say how soon. Nothing promising has turned up yet. I'll let you know though. You have a lot going on right now just closing out three clients," Joe responded. "Go home Chris, and enjoy being with your family. Try to focus on what's important now, not what's in the past."

"Thanks, Joe. I'll see you tomorrow." She left his office feeling a little deflated, but their talk had helped put things in perspective. She did love her family and her career, and Joe was right. She would risk neither of them. But, confronting her mixed feelings about Alex was going to be really tough.

Andrea had already left for the day when she returned to her office. There were a few messages on her desk that she would return in the morning. One was a note from Andrea. Christina smiled at the thought of the interrogation she'd face in the morning. "We will talk and you will spill!" Still, staying busy had helped her forget him before. It would have to help now.

At 7:00 she left for home. Later than she planned, but at least traffic wouldn't be such a mess. The day had gone remarkably well, professionally speaking. Alex took direction well, was open to suggestions, and had a pleasant demeanor around the crew. If he remained this way, things would be relatively easy. When other people were around, it was not very different from working with other clients. It was the alone times that were uncomfortable. She didn't know why she was kidding herself. He was Alex, and things had never been easy with him.

Alex left the studio not long after she left. He waited by the bus stop, taking in the day. His first photo shoot, a whole bunch advice for clothes to buy, auditioning musicians, seeing Christina. It felt like too much to take in. He'd get his sister to help with the shopping. Mastermind had cut him an advance so the money wasn't an issue. He would get a car eventually, but right now he actually welcomed the time on the bus. It was a great place to think and create. In fact, he'd written some of his best songs on a bus. *Alone*, the first single on the album, was written on a MARTA bus one sad, lonely evening. He'd been in the process of ending a relationship that had no meaning. They were both still there simply to not hurt the other. This song had served its purpose and helped them both move on.

Now, Christina Malone had come back into his life. He sighed as he collapsed into the seat and stared out the window. How could he tell her that he thought of her all the time? That he kicked himself in the ass at least once a week for not going after her, not chasing her the way she deserved to be chased and loving her with his whole heart? That it had been eleven years and still, the only way he could withstand the unrelenting pain of being without her was to be numb. He had tried to move on, and thought himself successful a few times, but her memory haunted him. She was married now. No use in stirring up old emotions. But how could they work together, share these moments of importance, and not have emotions re-emerge? He was glad she was happy. If anyone in the world deserved happiness it was her. He'd caused her enough pain and he wouldn't do it anymore. They would maintain a professional working relationship. He'd not mention the past again, would not sing to her again, would not get lost in her eyes again. Well, at least not on purpose anyway.

He called his sister and asked her to meet him at Lenox Mall. With the help of the photos and a list of stores they put together quite an ensemble of clothes. He eventually stopped looking at the price tags because he thought he'd become ill. What was wrong with Target or even Good Will? Afterwards they sat in the food court sipping milkshakes, surrounded by bags of assorted clothing for every conceivable occasion. He had never spent so much money on clothes in his entire life. The most he'd paid for an outfit before was $35.00, and that included shoes.

Sarah Thomas was his baby sister. Despite the age difference they looked remarkably alike. She had the same chestnut hair that was styled in natural ringlet curls. Their hair was not the only similarity. She had striking green eyes as well, only more of a hunter green, while his were olive. He filled her in on the day, especially on Chris.

"I remember her," Sarah said slurping her strawberry shake. "She was so nice. She helped me with my biology homework one night when you guys came home for the weekend."

"I know. She *was* really nice. I'm sure she still is, although she didn't show it much today. She was very professional." He sucked some of the chocolate mush through his straw. "I remember coming home that weekend and watching her help you. I was thinking I'd never be able to do that; I barely got through biology myself. I remember thinking, what am *I* doing with someone who knows everything about biology? I couldn't figure out why someone like her was wasting her time with a dill hole like me."

"Alex, you are not a waste of time. If you're going to make it in the music industry, you need to start believing in yourself."

"That's what Chris said too. I think that was part of the problem back then as well. The more she tried to show me she believed in me, the more I doubted myself. The more I doubted myself, the more drugs I did."

"I also remember that she talked me through one of your worst drug trips, Alex."

"Yeah, I know. Did I ever apologize for that night? I had no right to subject you to that. You were only fifteen," he looked down at his cup.

"Yeah, you apologized the next day after Mom raked you over the coals for it." They were quiet for a few moments. Then she continued. "You know, Mom called Chris about a year after you guys split up."

"She what?!" Alex was totally shocked. "Why on earth did she call her?"

"Well, Mom saw the drastic changes you went through after you left Chris. She was frightened for you. She was afraid that you'd never have another chance at the happiness you had with Chris. She was also afraid you'd never get clean without Chris's forgiveness. So, she called Chris to tell her what was going on and to see what the chances were of you two ever getting back together."

"I'm guessing the response wasn't good. I mean, we didn't get back together. In fact, she made it very clear she never wanted to see or hear from me again."

"No, it wasn't good, Alex, but could you really blame her? Mom told me the horrible things you said to her. She said Chris was really frank about it and made no effort to sugar coat the messages she'd been sent. You lied about her, you lied to her and then you blamed everything on her. I'd never want to talk to you again either if I were in her shoes."

"Thanks, Sarah. You're making things so much better," he replied sarcastically. "Did Mom ask her anything else?"

"Well, Mom asked her if she was seeing anyone and she said yes, and that she was happy. Mom told her that she was the only one who could pull you out of the depressive state you were in, but Chris said she couldn't help. Supporting you was too painful for her. It made Mom really sad, but she understood."

"Yeah, I understood too. That's why I left school. Chris might have helped lift me back up, but I burned that bridge completely down and there was no way I could repair the damage I'd done. I didn't even know how to apologize right. I tried, but," he let his head and shoulders droop as he spoke. Eleven years had gone by and the pain was almost as fresh as if it'd happened yesterday.

"Honestly, I don't think you were in the right place to be with her then. You were pretty messed up. But looks like you've been given a chance to make things right after all," Sarah nudged his shoulder.

"Sarah, she's married now, with kids. I don't want to go messing things up for her."

"Who said anything about messing things up? You've lived without her for eleven years, but your guilt and regret is still eating you alive. You need to get everything out in the open. Clear the air, get some closure. It'd be best for both of you. It'll probably be painful at first, but it beats walking on eggshells like you both did today."

"You're right. I'll tell her tomorrow that we need some time to talk. I'll get it all out in the open and we'll start over."

Armed with a new confidence Alex stood up and offered his sister an arm. She took it and they began to walk. Sarah, his kid sister, had grown up and was giving him advice. He still remembered her as the dorky teenage kid he'd left at home when he went to college. In his mind she'd never fully grown up. They left the mall and she gave him a ride home.

"So, what's on my rock star brother's agenda for tomorrow?" she asked as they drove.

"I have my first radio interview in the morning and then I finish up auditions. That will probably take all day. Afterward, we start recording the tracks with the band. That will take a while I'm sure," he said as they turned onto his street. "My acoustic tracks are almost done, but we have to put it all together." Sarah stopped in front of his house. "Tell Dave I said hi when you get home."

"Okay, big brother," she said hugging him hard. "Don't worry about it. Things will work out the way they are meant to. You'll see." She kissed his cheek and he got out of the car.

Alex waved as she drove off. He needed to have a talk with his mother. As he closed the door behind him, he was already dialing his cell phone.

Chapter 6

Christina sat in her car grid locked in traffic. Apparently, an appliance truck had slammed into a guard rail, causing a massive back up. The traffic reporter announced a "yard sale alert"- washers and dryers were strewn all over the roadway. "Last Tears" by the Indigo Girls played on the radio. She couldn't think of a more appropriate song for the moment. She'd spent months recovering from the damage Alex had inflicted upon her, and years trying not to blame Todd for mistakes Alex had made.

Even though she and Alex had only been together a few months, the intensity had been so great it had overwhelmed her life. The quarter the firestorm had occurred, she'd struggled with her classes, almost failing one. The only thing she'd ever really been good at was school and when her grades started falling, she knew she needed a drastic life change. She developed the art of thought-blocking when it came to Alex, literally blocking him out by envisioning a big black wall every time thoughts of him entered her mind. It had been the only thing to get her through. She would have to do the same thing now.

The difference was that back then she had been able to avoid seeing him. Now she would have to see him on a regular basis, and for a while every day. Building that wall again would be tough. She thought she could try picturing her husband whenever things got difficult to manage. He was very even-keeled and helped balance out her nervous tendencies. But would picturing another man help her forget Alex? She seriously doubted it. Even if that man was her husband.

She'd met Todd her senior year of college. She was completing her student teaching in a small school in the north metro area. Todd was the accountant who handled the school system's finances. She met him at the school's career day and they hit it off right away. They were engaged in less than a year and married a few months later. Kate came along at the beginning of their third year of marriage.

Todd was an amazing guy. He was funny and adventurous and never let her take life too seriously. He always knew exactly what to say to make her feel better if she was down, and he knew how to make everyone in a room laugh when he told stories. On top of being classically handsome, he was smart, goal-oriented, and one of the kindest people she'd met in her life. She had ignored the warning instinct about Alex and had paid a heavy price. When she met Todd her instinct practically screamed, "Don't let this one go!" This time she'd listened. It hadn't been easy though. She'd felt so damaged from her previous relationship that, at times, she behaved very unfairly toward Todd. He was strong though and stood by her side through every decision she made, no matter how irrational it was.

Over the years they had settled into a routine. Their lives were safe, stable and secure. She had everything she needed, or wanted for that matter. When she decided to leave teaching to work at Mastermind, Todd was completely supportive. He knew it meant traveling and no more summers free, but he also knew that if he said no or even voiced his reservations about the change, Christina would have resented him.

Todd was everything Alex wasn't. He loved unconditionally. He rarely said unkind words. He was the best father she'd ever seen. He was just as comfortable being with a crowd of people as he was being alone, and he made her laugh. His loyalty, tenderness, and humor were good medicine for her broken heart, and over the years together most of the pain had subsided. She loved her husband tremendously. She felt things for him that she'd never felt for anyone before, including Alex.

But sometimes she wondered if she had been so quick to start a life with Todd because he was the antithesis of Alex.

Todd wasn't much into music other than listening to it on the way to work or joining Christina at the concert of one of her clients. He found no emotional pull in the lyrics of songs. He'd never felt his heart break with the sad strumming of a guitar or the key strokes on a piano. He loved the outdoors, rafting, hiking, and camping, but found no bond to music. He liked to hear it, but that was about it. Her reaction to music was totally different.

Music was where she found her passion. She loved the way lyrics blended with melodies to create priceless works of art that could make a person weep or laugh, or even both at the same time. That's part of the reason she'd taken the job at Mastermind, to be more connected to music. She knew she didn't have what it took to be a musician. She was probably the worst singer ever and was not gifted in song writing. But she loved getting lost in the music. She had an ear for talent and for matching musicians together. She had carved a nice little niche for herself in the industry. She just never imagined that this previously comfortable niche would become a quagmire with Alex at the center of it.

When Christina finally made it through the Cobb Cloverleaf, a nationally recognized traffic hotspot, she began to think about how to bring this up with her husband. He needed to know, at least the basics. Fortunately, Todd was trusting, and not the jealous type, because she had to do her job and couldn't let any marital issues distract her from the task she had in promoting Steven Lily, the rock star. She tried to convince herself that the two could remain separate. Her husband normally had very little interaction with her work. He didn't know much about it and really didn't care as long as she was happy. He enjoyed going to the concerts and parties, but other than that he pretty much stayed out of her work. Since business and personal lives rarely mix well, she wanted to keep it that way. So far it hadn't been too hard since she was no more interested in accounting than he was in music. However, under these circumstances, she was unsure if she could or should keep them separate.

She pulled into her driveway a little after 8:00. John, her neighbor, was now completing his daily run. She waved, shouted a friendly hello through her open window, and marveled at his energy level for being able to run at this late hour. She parked in the garage and went upstairs to find her family waiting for her.

Before she even opened the door from the garage she heard Jack shouting, "Mommy, Mommy, Mommy!" It was one of his new words and of the twenty he knew, this was clearly the one he loved to say the most right now. Christina had been disappointed when "Mommy" hadn't been his first word, but now she sometimes wished he'd pick a different word to shout over and over. Still, he was her baby and she was always incredibly happy to see him. Being with her kids made the stress of the day melt away. She was always able to forget, or at least delay dealing with, a difficult situation by playing with Kate and Jack.

"Mommy, my teacher *loved* her present! She said you're getting the Parent of the Year award," Kate said running to hug her mother. Christina scooped her up and gave her a great swinging hug.

"I'm so glad, sweetie! How was your quiz today?" she asked, planting a kiss on the little girl's nose. It was only a first grade quiz, but Kate was very serious about school, serious about everything really. She was so much like her mother.

"It was good. I think I got an A. We'll know tomorrow. Mommy, can I go over to Lila's house after school tomorrow? Her mom is taking her to Fired Up and asked if I could come," Kate smiled sweetly at her mom, batting her long dark lashes.

"Well, I suppose you can go *if* you get all your homework done first," Christina bargained. A chance for Kate to go paint pottery with her friend was great. That meant Christina could hopefully spend some one on one time with Jack.

Christina put her daughter down and sat down on the couch. Jack climbed up beside her and started making the ticking noises he made when he was trying to tickle her. She laughed and scooped him up in a warm embrace. "Hey, mister! How was your day? Was it the best day ever?"

Jack giggled and jumped down to go ride his big wheel. His legs weren't quite long enough to reach the pedals, so he used it more as a scooter. Todd came out of the kitchen and gave her a kiss hello. They never hid their affection in front of the kids. They wanted the kids to know how much they loved each other. She noticed Kate making a face, but Jack wasn't fazed in the least.

"Welcome home. I was beginning to worry about you. So, how's the new guy?" Todd asked drying his hands on a dish cloth.

"Well, he's pretty agreeable so far," she answered honestly. "The crazy thing is that I already know him."

"Oh yeah, how?"

"Well, we actually dated back in college for a little while. He was going by his middle name then. Now he's working under his first name. That's why I didn't know who he was," Christina left the kids playing in the living room and ran upstairs to the bedroom where she quickly changed clothes into sweatpants and a pink tank. Padding back downstairs and into the kitchen, she saw Todd giving her a quizzical glance. "What?" she asked as she pulled her hair back.

"So, is it weird? Working with him?" Todd asked.

"Yeah, of course it is, a little. I mean, it's been over a decade and then all of a sudden this guy I haven't seen or spoken to in a very long time shows up in my office, and I have to help promote him and turn him into the next big star."

She left out the part about her heart dropping into her stomach when she first saw him, and the fact that during the photo shoot he'd sung that breathtaking song she was pretty sure was meant for her. She didn't mention any of the really important things, telling herself that she didn't want Todd to feel uncomfortable. It was bad enough to deal with tension at work; she didn't want to bring it home too.

"Okay, well behave yourself. Don't go postal on him for something that happened such a long time ago."

"You have a point," she said, sitting down the help Jack to stack his blocks. "There's no sense in harboring any old feelings of resentment." Christina looked up at him and forced a smile. She drew on her high school acting lessons to help her pull off an air of indifference. "What's for dinner, babe?"

"We already ate, but I saved you a plate. We had grilled pork tenderloin, baby carrots and fresh green beans. For dessert I have a nice sweet potato pie, made from fresh sweet potatoes."

"Ooh, sound delicious! You really know how to spoil me." Todd was a fabulous cook, and this was something she really appreciated since she was not much better at cooking than she was at singing. In fact, even basic things like boxed macaroni and cheese proved to be too much to handle at times. She was a huge fan of take-out and delivery when it was up to her to prepare dinner.

The rest of the night passed smoothly. It was too late to take their evening walk so she put both kids into the tub for a quick bath. Jack was ready to go to sleep first and gave her a huge hug after getting his PJ's on. As she rocked him, the little boy smiled at her and said, "Missed Mommy". She snuggled him close and kissed his baby soft cheeks as she told him she missed him too. Turning off his light she tiptoed across the hall to her daughter's room. Kate was already lying in bed with her book ready to read when Christina walked in.

"Hey sweetie, what are we reading tonight?" Christina greeted her daughter quietly as she opened the door and stepped in.

"I want to read Polar Babies. I got it at the book fair last week and haven't read it yet," Kate replied as she snuggled close to her mother.

"Okay, well let's get reading."

Christina let Kate read as many of the words as she could, and only stepped in to supply an unfamiliar word here and there. After she finished what she could, Christina read it again from start to finish. It was their thing. They had seen a significant an improvement in Kate's reading over the past few months.

When the story was over, Christina tucked her daughter in and brushed a kiss across her forehead. "Sleep well, my little princess. See you in the morning."

"Okay Mommy. Love you!" Kate returned, hugging her teddy bear tightly. The little girl immediately rolled over on her side, the same position she'd wake up in the next morning.

"Love you too." Christina slipped from the room leaving the door cracked just a bit.

She went into the living to find Todd watching "The Office". She sat down beside him and watched until the end of the episode. "I think I'll turn in early tonight. We have the first radio interview in the morning and then final call back auditions."

"Another long one?" Todd asked looking over at his wife. He brushed a strand of hair that had slipped out of her ponytail away from her face and tucked it behind her ear.

"Yeah, looks that way. Hopefully I'll be home earlier than tonight though. Goodnight, sweetie. See you in the morning," Christina quickly kissed her husband before walking to the bathroom. There had once been a time when that kiss would have lingered and led to something else. But the days of wild abandon had given way to schedules, toddlers and trying to catch a few extra minutes of rest.

She quickly got ready for bed and climbed under the covers. She decided to wait until morning to pick out the clothes she would wear the next day. Reluctantly, she took an Ambien. She tried not to take them very often, but she was pretty sure sleep wouldn't come naturally this evening. As she drifted off, she was transported back to a time she had tried to forget for the better part of a decade.

Chapter 7

She was reliving the first time they met. She walked into government class and sat down in the second row. A geek to the core, she chose the second row only because all the front row seats were taken. She took out her notebook and tape recorder. Her professor was Chinese and it had been difficult sometimes to understand him during class so she'd replay the lesson later on in her dorm. She heard the door shut with an unexpected thud and she looked up.

She'd never noticed him before until this day. Maybe because he was the last one to come in the room, or maybe she'd looked up at just the right time, but when she saw him, she was sure her heart must have skipped at least five beats. He was about 6'1. He was wearing a green baseball cap, a grey T-shirt and jeans. Taken apart, the pieces were ordinary. Put together, they formed a spectacular work of art. He was not the clean cut fraternity type she'd dated in the past. He had a dangerous quality about him that she detected immediately. He was the kind of guy her mom had told her to stay away from.

Her eyes met his and she froze. He gave her a quick smile and passed her to sit in the back row. She felt him watching her the entire class period. She wondered if he'd watched her before or if this was the first time. The quarter was nearly halfway over. She couldn't believe she hadn't noticed him until now. Once during the hour long class, she pretended to have an itch on her shoulder and turned slightly to scratch it. She dared a quick glance to find his eyes staring straight at her, mischievous grin upon his lips. She turned back to the front quickly, blushing furiously. She felt her temperature rise at least ten degrees and fought the urge to fan herself with her notebook.

She remembered nothing of the lesson that day. Thank goodness she's taped it. Her notes made absolutely no sense and she honestly couldn't bring to mind one thing that had been discussed. As she packed up to go she felt nervous. Would she speak to him, or would he approach her? What if they said nothing and just ignored the electricity between them? Could she do that? She knew she probably should stay away from him. The bad boy types were never a good thing for very long. The last bad boy type she'd dated had even fooled her mother at first! He'd stolen both of their hearts before stealing quite a bit of jewelry as well. What a disaster that had turned out to be!

As she stood to leave, she saw he'd already left. Feeling more than a little disappointed, she let out the breath she didn't realize she'd been holding. Oh well, she thought, time for algebra anyway. She walked out of the classroom and across the hall to her next class. Algebra was difficult for her to understand so she actually managed to stay focused through the whole lesson. After class she lingered to discuss a problem with her professor. She'd almost forgotten about the mysterious guy from government by the time she walked into the hallway.

But there he stood, leaning against the wall, with arms folded across his chest and one foot propped up behind him. She stopped in her tracks when she saw him. He smiled the same playful grin he'd given her earlier.

"Hi," he said as he approached her.

"Hello," she stammered in surprise.

"I'm Alex. Alex Lily."

"Christina Malone."

"Well, Christina Malone, it's very nice to meet you," he extended his hand. She shook his hand, feeling a bit sheepish.

"Very nice to meet you too," she cocked her head to one side and furrowed her brow. "How did you know I was here?" she asked with real curiosity. She had never noticed him before class today, but was it possible that this deadly handsome guy had been watching her all this time?

"Well, we've shared the same classroom for nearly two months and I've seen you walk across the hall every day. You're usually lost in your own world. That's why I haven't approached you before."

She blushed as he spoke. He'd been watching her for two months and she'd never noticed! "I guess I get deep into concentration when I'm in class." What a lame response! It was almost as bad as that line from Dirty Dancing when Baby says, 'I carried a watermelon.' She'd never been this nervous around a guy before. She prayed for the ground to open and swallow her whole.

"Yeah, I can tell. I've been trying to get your attention since the quarter started. You're the only reason I haven't dropped Government yet."

"Oh," she looked down at her feet trying to will away the furious color from her cheeks. "So, what have you done before? To get my attention, I mean."

"Well, I've dropped my book on the floor and you didn't even stir. I had a coughing fit once and that only got a sidewise scornful look. I figured that was probably not the way to go. So, today I decided to make sure I came in after you in and I banged the door loud enough to make sure you'd look up."

"It worked. So, you've actually been hanging out here until my algebra class was over?" she asked with disbelief.

"Yeah, and then you stayed even longer to talk to your professor," he grinned as he spoke, clearly flirting with her. "I don't usually hang around campus when I don't have to. Busy now?" he asked.

Something in her gut told her to say yes, she was very, very busy. Turn and go, it said. She forced that little voice down. She couldn't believe that someone like *him* had any interest in a bookworm like her. He was so strikingly handsome, with eyes that could melt butter. There was no way he could want her.

"No, I'm not busy. Well, I was going to go back to the dorm and put my stuff away before grabbing some dinner. But, besides that I'm not busy," she tried not to sound too pathetic. He already knew she was a serious student who was very involved in her studies. She didn't want to look like any more of a nerd than she already did.

"Mind if I tag along? I could walk you home and we could go have dinner together. I have a meal plan card with your name on it," Alex winked.

She laughed out loud and the ice was broken. "What a romantic guy you are, and such a big spender!" she flirted back a little more freely. "You know, it's a policy of mine to always go Dutch on the first date. I have my own meal plan card, thank you very much."

They both laughed and started to walk. "Okay, have it your way! Can I carry your bag for you?" he asked. She handed over her bag and their hands brushed. Electricity shot through her entire body. She imagined that must be what being struck by lightning felt like. God, she was going to regret this, she knew it. But there was no way she wasn't going on this ride. She tried to contain the bubbles in her stomach and keep from smiling like a complete idiot.

They ate at Lakeside Café out on the balcony. The main dinner rush hadn't started yet so they had some time to talk before it got too noisy. He told her about his family, about his dad who had left when he was young leaving him, and his mother and sister alone. Then he told her about his music. He played the guitar and had performed at some local clubs in the area.

She shared her love of music as well, though confessing she couldn't sing worth a lick. She told him a little bit about her family also. She'd been raised by her mom since the age of twelve. Her dad had died from a rapidly spreading cancer, leaving them on their own too. She didn't tell him much more right away because her father's death was an issue that was still hard for her to bring up. But he'd asked so she revealed what she thought she could for a first meeting. Out of nervousness she hardly ate anything, and she talked too much with her hands. She felt edgy, but also excited. It'd been a really long time since she'd felt anything like this, if she'd ever felt it before. His eyes were amazing. They drew her in and she felt hypnotized by them. The olive green swirls flecked with brown and gold were mesmerizing.

After dinner he walked her back home and asked if she'd like to meet for dinner the following night and maybe come back to his place to watch a movie. She said sure and they made plans to meet the next evening after her last class.

The next evening they walked hand in hand to his small apartment. They never made it to the movie part. He picked up his guitar once they returned and played for her. His voice and the melodies he played paralyzed her. She barely heard the words, but as he played, she felt an energy surge through her body as the guitar spoke directly to her heart. The music cast a spell over her and she felt herself give in to every desire she knew she should avoid. At the end of the song he leaned in and kissed her.

At first it was tender, gentle and longing. As the time slipped slowly by the kiss grew hungrier and more demanding. He threaded his hands through her long dark hair and pulled slightly. She gasped with surprise. She helped him slip his shirt easily over his head. His chest was smooth and she traced the outline of his muscles with her finger tips, ending over his washboard stomach. He took care of himself, but apparently wasn't obsessive about it. He helped her with the buttons of her blouse while never taking his mouth away from hers. He slipped the shirt over her bare white shoulders. Her skin prickled and shivered as he did.

He moved his mouth down to her bra strap leaving a trail of warmth behind. His teeth tugged the strap and he pulled it down her arm with his mouth. She was quivering as much on the inside as she was on the outside. She tried to control the feelings that were surging through her body, but his essence overwhelmed her. He reached around and unclasped the back, and let the filmy material fall to the floor. She wondered if he could see her heart beating fast in her chest, as her breathing became deeper and slightly labored.

He buried his head in the valley between her breasts and traced circles with his tongue. Her breath caught in her throat and her mind reeled slightly as she wrapped her arms around him, fingers pressing into his bare back. What was she doing? This was not like her. She had never been one to jump into something physical so fast, but she couldn't help herself. She couldn't believe this was really happening. The little voice was arguing with her to turn and run and not look back. She knew the voice was probably right, but this felt so good and there was something irresistible about him. She forced it from her mind and focused instead on the feel of his hands across her skin. She made no move to stop him and wasn't sure she could even if she tried.

He picked her up and carried her to the bedroom and laid her down on jumbled sheets of his unmade bed. He fumbled with his belt and then the button of his jeans. She slid them down over his hips and he kicked them away. God, she thought, he's magnificent! He unbuttoned her jeans and pulled them off both legs together. She giggled a little as he did this. She raised her hips so he could slide her panties off, and the pink satin floated to the floor. As he lowered himself down on her, he caressed every inch of her alabaster skin. She felt the shiver of yearning follow the path his hands took.

He rubbed against her, slowly, languidly, and she was sure her head would spin out of control. The pounding in her chest increased until she was sure her heart was going to explode. Unable to tell whether she was scared or excited, she let herself succumb to the desire that built inside her. It had been so long, and she'd never felt like this before. Her legs parted as she welcomed him, hard and long, inside of her. The pressure surprised her and her fingers clenched in reflex. She closed her eyes and let the feeling envelop her. Don't think, she told herself, just enjoy.

"Open your eyes," he said huskily. "Look at me." Their eyes locked and in that moment she saw everything; his heart, his soul, his potential, his entire being. It was like floating and falling at the same time. Their hearts and their bodies were one. The realization, the power of what they could be to each other was frightening, but she was unwilling to back away. In that one moment she was granted a brief look into whom he really was and she learned all that she needed to know. Everything of value to her had crystallized and she knew that nothing else mattered.

They moved slowly at first, seeking each other's rhythm. Once found, they moved in sync, gaining strength and speed with each thrust. Her nails gripped his back. Her head swirled as their bodies dampened with sweat. His body glistened as he pinned her hands behind her head. His mouth found hers, and then traveled to the curve of her neck. He moved in her and with her at the same time. She cried out in ecstasy as the waves rolled through her, her body shivering and convulsing under his as he gained momentum.

He pulled back slightly, letting her recover and trying to pace himself at the same time. Her cries encouraged him to drive deeper and she felt she could take it no more. Deeper, harder, faster until at last her body released the passion that had taken them both over. He came with her this time, and their bodies trembled for a few moments more.

He collapsed on top of her, their breathing rough and ragged. She clasped him tightly, afraid to let go. When he rolled away he stayed close, moving only far enough to reach for a cigarette. It took some time for her heart rate to return to normal. He covered them both with a sheet. They lay together in silence for what seemed like hours. If he hadn't been smoking she would have almost thought he'd fallen asleep. The ecstasy of the night lingered around them. Both felt the command of the other, yet their spirits were free. They had been able to speak with no words. Their eyes, their bodies communicated all that was necessary.

Unsure she could even find her voice, she started to speak, "I just want you to know that I don't do this with everyone. Especially not after having dinner only twice."

"I kinda figured that," he answered draping his arm around her and bringing her head to rest upon his chest. "Just so you know though, I do."

"What?" she asked, a bit taken aback.

"Just kidding. What time is your first class tomorrow?" He stroked her hair with his cigarette free his and she noted the tingle that accompanied each touch.

"I have English at 8:00," she groaned.

"Stay tonight," he turned toward her, looking her straight in the eye. She thought she detected a bit of uncertainty behind his intense stare, but it was fleeting. "I'll get you back to your dorm in time to get ready tomorrow."

"Oh, I can't! I *have* to finish a stupid response to literature assignment that's due tomorrow," she covered her face with one arm.

All she wanted to do was fall asleep in his arms and stay there for as long as possible. She feared he wouldn't speak to her again once she left his apartment. She was letting her insecurities get the better of her. But then she remembered the honesty she'd seen in his eyes and tried to push her fears away. The fear was two pronged; one of losing this amazing gift she'd just been given, and two of being able to keep the same gift. She wasn't sure she was ready to handle this, but she was going to find out if she could.

"Okay, then. I guess you'd better get up and going before I am forced to make you stay. If you lie here naked in my bed too much longer, it may not be possible for you leave." He helped her gather her clothes before slipping out of bed. He pulled his jeans on and then his T-shirt, then walked into the bathroom and closed the door. She heard water running. The spell shifted, breaking its hold and allowing her to get up.

She was dressed and had slipped her flip flops on by the time he returned. She smiled at him as he approached her. They walked through the apartment and he picked up his keys. The drive to her dorm was quiet, but not awkward. A satisfied silence settled around them. When they arrived, she turned to face him to say thank you for the evening. He caught her and kissed her gently.

"*You* are why songs are written," he whispered against her cheek. "I'll see you in class tomorrow."

"Okay," she sighed breathlessly. "Thank you for a most fantastic night. You are amazing, in more ways than one." She pulled away and reached for her door handle. He waited out front until she waved that she had gotten in okay. She watched him drive away and leaned her back against the door. The butterflies reemerged a bit as she watched his tail lights fade into the distance. She touched her cheek where his words left their mark. Oh my god, she thought as she exhaled slowly, what was happening?

Chapter 8

Christina awoke from her dream damp with perspiration. She rolled over and looked at the clock. It was only 3:37 AM. There was no way she was going back to sleep so she carefully moved to the side of the bed and slid out. She went into the bathroom and looked in the mirror. Her cornflower blue eyes had a hazy look about them. She couldn't tell if it was from the ungodly hour, the Ambien, or the memory she'd just experienced. Either way, she needed to push it as far from her mind as possible.

Sighing, she changed clothes and made her way to the basement and climbed on the elliptical glider. An hour of hard work and sweat would hopefully help her forget. She could hear the rain tinkling on the gutters as she popped in her ear bud headphones. Damn, she thought, traffic would be a nightmare. One drop of rain falls in Atlanta and everyone suddenly forgets how to drive. She pushed herself hard on the machine. She'd rather be running, but at this time of morning, coupled with the rain, she'd be a great fool to get out on the road. Finger Eleven, Public Enemy, Kid Rock, and Limp Bizkit helped keep her tempo up and stride fast.

Upon finishing her exhausting workout, Christina showered, letting the hot water run over her body. She immersed her face and head under the cascading stream, willing herself to repress the memories stirred up by her dream. She wrapped herself in her comfy white robe and padded to the kitchen to make some tea. It was barely 5:00, and she had some time to kill before starting the day. Read a magazine, look over some proposals for club tours, do *anything* to keep your mind off of him, she thought to herself.

Unfortunately, that didn't happen. She thought back to the time after their first night together. She had been a book worm in college and had always stressed about her grades. It was an issue that had plagued her ever since she started school. Alex had asked her once why she pushed herself so hard. She said she honestly didn't know, that her dad had asked her the same thing when she was in second grade. It was the first time she had been open to sharing about life with her dad. "He used to say I came out of the womb worried," she once joked to Alex. "I guess I've always been serious."

She hadn't shared with him then that her dad had tried so hard to get her to be more like him. He was a risk taker and was never afraid to experience new, exciting things. That wasn't her at all. She had played it safe for as long as she could remember. He had tried to convince her to throw caution to the wind and just have fun with life. She'd tried really hard, for him, but it was like trying to jam a square peg into a round hole. It fit if pushed hard enough, but it didn't really belong. Taking a chance on Alex was the first risky thing she'd done in a long time. It felt good, but scary at the same time.

What she'd forgotten was that Todd was so much like her dad in that respect. He was also adventurous and loved trying new things. She had gone bungee jumping with Todd by her side, something she had sworn only crazy people did. Sky diving had followed, along with rock climbing and white water rafting. Over the years Todd had helped her break out of her shell in a way that was so natural she didn't even realize it was happening. He made taking a risk feel exciting and fun, not scary. After ten years together it had become so natural that she failed to recognize that element of her husband and that that was part of the reason she'd fallen for him in the first place.

At 6:00 she got dressed and woke up the kids. Todd got them dressed as she finished her hair and makeup. Christina stared at herself in the mirror. She realized how habitual her life had become. Granted, she thrived on routine and stability, but other than that there didn't seem to be much of her old self left. She loved her job - helping rock stars launch their careers was a blast. She got to travel all over the world, hear great music and literally watch them blossom. It was more difficult now with the kids. Before Kate was born Christina had no problem staying gone for a 10 day road tour, but now when those trips came up, she was quick to pass them off to someone else. She felt torn between her desire to help her clients and her dedication to her family. Of course, her kids came first, no matter what. But sometimes she really missed the spur of the moment events. Kind of hard to be spontaneous and eccentric with two young kids, she thought shrugging as she left the bathroom.

Outside of the excitement of her job, she found herself living a predictable life. She woke up, ran, got the kids ready, went to work, came home, spent some time with them and Todd, went to sleep and repeated the same things the next day. There had been a time when she and Todd would take off on a Friday to travel anywhere that they felt led to go. They would go rock climbing on a random Wednesday, or stay out until 3:00 in the morning on a Thursday night. Now the kids were their lives, and despite how much she loved them, it seemed like a part of her had disappeared when they were born. Her job, she supposed, was her way to keep that part of her alive. This is why she worked so hard and had advanced so far. She missed the old times with Todd though and sometimes wished they could find their way back to each other as a couple, and not just through Kate and Jack.

Todd was in the kitchen putting the breakfast dishes in the sink when she walked through, ready to leave for the day. How could she let herself be dragged back into the past when she had such a great man right in front of her? He was a wonderful husband and father. She couldn't ask for anyone more loyal and loving. He was home every night, even during tax season. He took care of her and the kids when they were sick. He was playful, kind and considerate. It would seem she had it all.

Watching her husband dressed in his business suit, with the kitchen almost clean and their kids completely ready to go, she knew how lucky she was. Most women prayed for a man to be just half as helpful. She would just have to put the past back where it belonged. Alex had definitely brought out a side of her that she hadn't experienced before, but it had hurt so badly in the end. The problem was, now that he was her client, it didn't seem possible to forget a time she'd worked so hard to quash.

"The kids have eaten and are ready to go," Todd announced as he helped her put on her jacket.

"Awesome. Then I guess we'll hit the road!" she smiled at Kate and Jack. She lifted Jack into her arms as they moved toward the door. "See you tonight. Tell Daddy bye-bye, kids." Both kids echoed their mother as they waved goodbye. "I'll call if I think I'll be late."

"No problem. Love you!" Todd said over his shoulder as they headed down the basement stairs to the garage.

"Love you too!" they all chorused as they left. Christina noticed the kiss that didn't come. She quickly shrugged it off and prepared for the day ahead.

After dropping off Jack at his sitter and Kate at school, Christina made her way to the office. Maintain a professional attitude, she thought. Stay cordial and polite, and do not get into a personal discussion with him. She mentally coached herself all the way through the traffic back up that always came with bad weather.

When she arrived, fifteen minutes late, she was surprised to see Andrea already there. "Well, what's the occasion? You're actually early, for you. And on a rainy day!" Christina smiled as she crossed her arms and glared playfully at her assistant. She already knew the answer.

"Okay Chris, you need to come clean with me about Steven Lily. I have been *dying* all night and morning to get the scoop," Andrea's eyes flickered with excitement and curiosity. She followed Christina into the office and closed the door behind them.

"Well, you know how you said assistants get the good gifts so they won't tell all the boss's secrets?" Andrea nodded. "I don't have the money to buy you anything *that* expensive, so let's just say we used to know each other in college," Christina said as she sat behind her desk.

"That's it? That's all you're going to give me when I got up super early to be here?" Andrea was a bit put out.

"Well, since you did come in early," Christina chided, "I guess I can share a few details with you. I've already told you most of the story. He's the musician I dated in college. The one with the drug problem and the really violent mood swings."

"Oh my god, really!" Andrea gasped as she sat down across the desk from Christina. "What kind of luck is that that you're his rep now? Have you told Todd?"

"Sort of. I did tell him we used to date each other at school, but I didn't go into full detail. There are some things I just don't think my husband needs to know about, not right now. Plus, I'm pretty sure Todd would insist I drop him as a client."

"Is that an option?" Andrea asked.

"Unfortunately, no, I've already tried to get him switched. Joe said absolutely not. Alex, or Steven, to those unfamiliar with him, obviously impressed the right people. Regardless of what happened between us, Joe said no. And he doesn't know if he's going to give me anyone else for a while either. He says there's no one promising on the horizon right now so I may be stuck for a while."

"Well," Andrea leaned back in her chair, hands crossed over her torso in thought, "you could always get the interns to handle the majority of the interactions. They could work with him to get sets arranged and stuff while you confirm club dates and interview schedules. I know they can't handle the big stuff, but some of the smaller interactions could occupy his time. If you don't think they're ready to handle things on their own, at least have one or two of them with you at every meeting with him."

"That's a great idea, Andrea! I hadn't thought of that. The interns need to learn and I need someone there to keep things professional. Perfect! The interns will be with us every step of the way," Christina smiled as she looked at her assistant. Andrea really was a good planner. She should move beyond being an office assistant. "You know Andrea, you should consider applying for a position within the department that goes above scheduling meetings and answering phones. You're much smarter than your job description allows you to be."

"Thanks for the confidence there boss, but honestly, who would keep you in line if I left?" Andrea joked as she got up and walked toward the office door. "I think he'll be here pretty soon. I'll see if I can get you an intern for the trip to the radio station this morning."

"Thanks, Andrea. You're the best!" Christina looked back at the paperwork on her desk. She had to schedule the recording session dates as soon as they had the band put together. Watching the jam sessions today would be fun. It was always interesting to see how the front man interacted with the potential band members. She was unsure how she'd handle seeing him play live though. The song he played at the photo shoot was pretty deep. She was almost positive it was about her. It had to have been, as personal as it sounded, and that scared her more than a little. Maybe she could get them to stick to songs that were less intense. Looking at the demo and song titles though, there didn't seem to be many songs that weren't intense.

Once the recording was done, the public relations part of her job would come into play. She would have to schedule radio appearances and cities for the tour and find groups for which Alex and his band could be the opening act. Promotions would help with those decisions. Her next decision would be which club dates she'd have to attend, and which ones she could get out of. Touring should start before the holidays and would continue well into February.

She was not looking forward to being on the road, away from home and with someone who could both make her blood boil *and* ignite a passionate firestorm in her heart! Eleven years was a long time, but somehow the left over garbage still lingered. She prayed that by the time the tour started she would be assigned another artist and could get out of most of the travel.

She was reluctant about traveling with the tour for two reasons. The main one, she told herself, was being away from her kids for so much of the time. Every time she left they seemed to grow three inches each. The second- one she was trying not to acknowledge- was the idea of spending so much time with Alex. She loved Todd, and she wanted to be loyal to him. She just wasn't sure if that could be maintained if she and Alex were alone for even a small amount of time. Of course, the band and crew would be there, so that alone time could be limited. But things had a way of happening around Alex that she had never been able to explain. Was she strong enough to resist if anything were to emerge? She hoped so, but... with Alex there was always a 'but'. Even more reason to keep everything as professional as possible, she told herself.

Alex arrived shortly before 8:30. She felt his presence before she actually saw him. Andrea buzzed him in and he opened the door hurriedly. She knew that look on his face. She'd seen it before. He thought he'd disappointed her because he was late. When they were dating, he'd always hated disappointing her. It was like he'd failed somehow if he couldn't provide her exactly what he thought she needed. However, he never asked her what she needed. It was one thing she never really understood. She didn't need any more than he offered, yet he always thought she required more from him. In the end, however, disappointment hadn't been the problem.

"I'm sorry I'm late," he said as he bustled in. "Traffic is a mess and the bus was late. I got here as fast as I could."

"Hey, it's fine. I completely understand. It took me a long time to get here today too." She smiled as she stood to greet him. "I think we got off on the wrong foot yesterday, Alex. I was in complete shock that you were my new client and I am afraid I behaved rather inappropriately. Why don't we start over?"

She had decided that the best way to handle the situation was to make it as professional, yet personable, as possible. She needed to treat him like her other clients. With them she would ordinarily make small talk and get to know more about them. She needed to do this with him. She and Alex were basically strangers, just strangers with a history. Getting comfortable with each other was the only way to make this situation work. This was even more important today since no interns were available on such short notice. Andrea had tried her best to find someone, but they all had been assigned tasks with the other reps in her department. She thought about grabbing an intern from promotions, but hadn't had a chance. She would behave as if she had no history with Alex and rebuff any attempts to discuss the difficult part of their past.

"Okay," he replied slowly as he gave her a sideways glance. "What does that mean?"

"Well, I think it's best for everyone involved that we maintain a totally professional relationship. No good can come of dredging up old feelings from a hundred years ago. I've moved on, you've moved on and our paths have brought us together in an unusual way neither of us expected. Let's just keep it simple, get to know the basics about each other and focus on the music, okay?"

Alex mulled her words over in his head. "Okay, if that's what you want, I guess I'll play by your rules. You are, after all, my foremost link to this company and my career." He gave a slight shrug and a little smile. Wow, she had completely changed. The Christina he knew from before was not afraid to confront things head on. This new Christina would rather push things away and pretend they didn't exist. But, he reminded himself, her life was utterly different than it was when he'd known her.

Hell, he was utterly different, he told himself. In actuality, he thought of himself as pretty much the same guy he'd been back then, minus the drugs. He'd given those up once he realized they had been the reason he'd lost everything good in his life. He'd lost her, dropped out of college and had become pretty much a useless bum barely getting by, living with his mom until he'd finally kicked the habit, got a job and focused on his future. Until recently, he'd been an older, more sober version of his younger self. This new lifestyle, the fact that he'd actually been discovered, signed by a major label and was finally going somewhere in life, was so foreign to him.

He still couldn't fully believe it was real. He kept waiting for someone to jump out and shout, "Just kidding, you fool!" There was no way a jackass like him was really becoming a successful recording artist. But, there *she* was and it was her job to make sure he became that super star. He couldn't think of a better person to have on his side through this. Her energy was infectious, her optimism was what he needed, and her drive for perfection would propel him forward whether he thought he could do it or not. That's how he remembered her. If she wanted to pretend that nothing had happened between them all those years ago, he would certainly oblige her, for a little while at least. It was the least he could do for her after all she'd done and would do for him.

"So, the interview this morning, do you know what to expect?" she asked.

"No, not really. I've listened to radio interviews before but don't have a clue how they work or what'll happen."

"Okay, well let me start by saying that this radio show has helped launch the careers of many new artists. You'll be part of their ongoing segment that introduces fresh talent to their listeners. The fact that you're a local will help you a lot here. They'll want to know about your life before you got signed; how you started, where you played, your reaction to being discovered, things like that. You'll be asked to play a song and if they really like you, they'll ask you to play at least two. You'll start with the first single that's being released next week. This is very important because we want to start creating buzz about the album so when it's released it will sell. If they ask for another song, play another cut from the album. If you get a third request you can choose whatever song you want, from the album or not. The more airtime you get, the better. Got it?"

"Wow," he said, "I can tell you've done this before."

"I helped create the segment, so yeah I've done it a few times."

"You helped create the segment?" he was impressed. He'd heard this segment before and had always wondered what it would be like to be part of it.

"Yeah, I'm friends with the DJ's. I met Jane and Mel when we co-hosted a charity auction and we struck up a friendship. They came to me soon afterward about creating a segment to help recognize unknown musicians, and since I represent new talent, I was the perfect person for the job. So, with the help of Kevin and Brad, the other two DJ's, we came up with this interview segment and now I am a regular fixture around the station," she explained.

"That's cool. Are all the artists featured your clients?"

"No, of course not. There are hundreds of new artists that sign with other recording companies. A lot of them are from other states. Some do phone interviews and the radio station just plays tracks that have been sent to them. Many of the artists I promote go on live. It's better to hear the songs performed in person as opposed to a recording. It's more personal. That's one of the traits I like to emphasize with my artists, personal contact."

"You'll be there the whole time, right?"

"Absolutely."

"Are there any questions I should avoid answering?" he asked.

"At this point, probably not. You're too new for them to have done much digging into your past yet. You want to be accessible. You want to be open and honest about your struggles to make it through the ranks and you want people to know how hard you're going to work to get your music heard. When you're starting out in this career, open is good. Just remember, everything will be taped and there will be evidence if you say something later that can be contradicted. Only share what you don't mind coming back to haunt you once you've made it big. Select your answers carefully, but try not to sound like you're crafting your responses."

"What if I blow it? What if I totally fuck up the whole thing?" His nervousness was starting to get to him.

"Well, first of all you won't. This is really informal and laid back. Besides, you have too much riding on this to let your insecurity get it the way, Alex. Second, if you have any problems we'll practice more before your next interview. I'll get a copy of the interview transcript and we'll go over your responses together to see where improvements need to be made. You're local and you're brand new. Try not to be too hard on yourself. You're bound to make a few mistakes along the way. That's why I'm here, to help you through them and to move forward." She smiled at him, her eyes flashing with excitement. Those eyes could melt ice, and they were already melting his heart.

"Okay then. Let's do this," he said standing up. He already felt more comfortable. She was there. The one person who'd always believed in him was there. He could do this. Her smile was all he needed.

As they left the office Andrea wished him luck. She was cute, he thought. He wondered if it would be too weird to ask her out for a drink. He instantly decided that yes, it would be too weird and dismissed the thought from his mind. Not only was Chris just getting comfortable with representing him, even if it was under somewhat awkward circumstances, he was pretty sure Andrea already knew about their past. That would just make things intensely strange. He didn't want there to be any reason for Christina to feel uncomfortable again.

If she only knew, he thought, how much her approval meant to him. He was sure that she still thought of him as selfish. She had no idea how he'd put her needs before his own when he'd agreed to stay away, how it had almost killed him to avoid her when he really wanted her and needed her back then. It was one of the only times he'd put someone else's needs before his own.

He wanted to think he'd changed. That he was no longer a completely self-centered asshole. Andrea was cute, but nothing would come of it. She was ultimately not the one he wanted. But the one he wanted was not available, and hadn't been in a very long time. Not worth the risk, he thought to himself, even if there was no shot at having her back in his life.

Chapter 9

They arrived at the radio station a little before 9:00. She introduced him to the DJ's, producers and interns. It was obvious she was in her element. He watched her work the room. She moved warmly from person to person asking them about their personal lives. How was Ryan doing? Still traveling as much? How's the baby? Getting bigger every day? The birthday card was so sweet! They had to get the kids together to play soon. He wondered if she was like this with all the radio DJ's in Atlanta, or just these. He guessed he'd find out soon enough.

The producer, a slightly OCD girl named Stacey, set him up with headphones and a microphone. She had one of the interns set up a microphone for his guitar as well. As the interview began he could feel his muscles tense and the urge to throw up coming on. He lifted his eyes to meet Christina's gaze. With a slight nod and an encouraging smile, she conveyed the only message he needed to hear; you'll do great! He nodded and smiled back, then geared up for the first question.

The interview went exactly as Christina said it would go. He played the first single from his album, a song entitled *Alone*. Jane asked for the story behind the song and he answered honestly. He'd ended a relationship with someone he knew was only staying with him because she had been afraid of what he'd do if left alone. She'd wanted to love him, and he'd wanted to love her, but it just wasn't working for either of them. They asked a few more questions and asked for a second song. He played the second song scheduled to be released from the album entitled *All A Mother's Tears*. This song was about his mother and the nights he'd hear her crying in her room when she thought the kids were asleep. His father's leaving had been hard on them all, but mostly on her. He'd been eight years old when his father left. He didn't remember his mom genuinely smiling until he was nearly eighteen. All four DJ's were touched by the story and the song.

A third song was requested "real quick" before he had to go, which was funny because he wasn't in a particular hurry to go anywhere for a while. He made a risky move, but he chose his favorite song of all time, the song he'd written for her after she'd said she never wanted to hear from him again. It was called *If Only She Knew*. It was his favorite because it was raw and divulged more of his true self than he'd ever let out before. It had taken several years to perfect the tone and the rhythm of the song. After a year or so he'd been able to play it without welling up himself and had added it to his set when he played clubs.

Christina didn't know this, but this song was the one that ended his set the night he'd been approached by Ed Sills from Mastermind. The song spoke of the tremendous mistakes he'd made in their relationship: the lies, the drugs, the cheating, and how he'd give everything up to tell her how sorry he was.

When the song ended he chanced meeting her eye. There were tears streaming down her face. He looked at the other DJ's. Jane and Mel, the two female DJ's, were also teary-eyed, as well as Stacey, the producer, and all the female interns. Even one of the guys in the room had glistening eyes. Good, he sighed to himself. At least her tears won't seem unusual here. He knew she'd be upset with him for singing this song, but he had to let her know how he'd felt and if talking about it was off limits, he had to express himself through the only method he could, his music.

The DJ's asked for the story on the song and he said he thought it spoke for itself. They asked if the girl knew how he'd felt afterward. He said he was pretty sure she didn't know before now, but if she'd been listening she did. He was careful not to look at her through this.

They took phone calls from listeners, all positive reviews. People wanted to see him play, wanted to buy the album, wanted to download the songs. Some women said a "Mascara Alert" should have been issued because now their makeup was ruined. Alex gave the slated month of release for the album again and said people could come out and see him Friday night at the Tabernacle where he was opening for Butch Walker, a well established local artist. Christina and Alex left the station with nearly 45 minutes of air time and a lot of valuable exposure.

Once they were outside he stopped and met her eyes full on. What he saw was a myriad of emotions. She was angry, he could tell, but he also saw sadness and surprise. "Chris, tell me what you're thinking," he said gripping her shoulders.

She decided not to struggle; it would only make him hold tighter. That was the last thing she needed, or wanted. She looked down at her feet trying to collect her thoughts. She couldn't keep the color from her cheeks. It was a problem that plagued her whenever she became emotional.

What was she thinking? She'd never known what happened to him after their final meeting. She'd always wondered, but had known finding out would be a bad idea. She'd stayed away for her own sake. Her heart couldn't take anymore of the "love" Alex Lily had had to offer. She hadn't known that telling him that she never wanted to see or hear from him again had torn *him* up so badly, maybe as much as it had torn her up to say it. She looked up and met his gaze. His eyes were searching for some kind of clue to how she was feeling, what her reaction was. She sighed and simply said, "I never knew."

"I know," he said releasing her shoulders. "I wasn't very good at being honest about my feelings. Hurting you was the worst thing I've ever done. You need to know that. You need to know how sorry I am, for everything."

"Alex," she paused, "I don't know what to say."

"Don't say anything. You already told me you forgave me. That's enough for me. I know you think talking about what happened between us back then is a bad idea now. I can respect your decision. You're married and you have a family, and you're right. Stirring up old emotions is not a good idea. But, when you *are* ready to clear the air, let me know. There are things I need to say."

"Okay." That was all she said. She'd never been at such a loss for words before. They both turned and headed for the car. They drove directly to the sound studio entrance. The rain had started up again. When they arrived she turned to face him and finally spoke.

"So, we'll spend the rest of the day with the callbacks from yesterday. We have them grouped and you'll play with each group. In between sessions we'll compare notes. What I'd like to accomplish by the end of the day are the final selections with some alternates. Then we can get all the musicians together tomorrow and see what it sounds like. There will be some other execs around as well when we have the final session. Hopefully, everything will be fine. We may need to change out one or two members so we'll have the alternate list on standby."

Alex nodded. She was all business right now. He knew this was how she coped with things. He'd forgotten that she threw herself into whatever work she was doing in order to push a problem from her mind.

He'd watched her work intensely on a research study back in college when her mom had been falling apart. Her father's death haunted her and Christina really didn't know how to help. She was only open to discussing it with him after she'd spent hours and hours on the study.

While never afraid to face a direct problem head on, she tended to shy away from issues involving others that she felt helpless to control, or that made her feel distraught. It was like she wanted to take care of everything else first; sometimes things that didn't even need to be addressed, before she could take care of herself. He could see that element in her had not changed. He wondered how it affected the rest of her life.

Did she push problems with her husband aside and obscure them with work issues? Did she put her needs on the back burner to care for her family or get her work done? Almost certainly she did. But, back then she would eventually deal with the issues that plagued her. She would delve in and analyze whatever was happening and search for solutions. She wasn't afraid of the problems; she just needed a clear head to handle them. Maybe that meant she would eventually come around and take care of the issues from their past, when she had a clear head. It needed to be on her time, and he knew he couldn't force her before she was ready.

The day passed almost exactly as she said it would. Sound techs had the studio ready to go and the musician ensembles were brought in to play the songs they'd learned overnight. Christina took meticulous notes on each musician who entered the studio. When they sat down to compare responses to the first group, Alex was very amused when he reviewed what she'd written down.

Under the name of the bassist who had performed, she'd simply written the word NO! in all caps and underlined. Alex had felt the same way. The guy was more suited for a jazz ensemble than a rock band. The auditions with the remaining groups progressed the same way. The familiar NO! was written for at least three other musicians they'd heard.

By the end of the day they had a list. Alex had picked a drummer, bassist, second guitarist and keyboardist. Christina had approved of them all. They'd also assembled an alternate list. It was one thing to like the musicians individually, but quite another to hear them all together. She called the first choices and the alternates in and told them to be ready at 8:00 a.m. the following morning.

It was after 4:00 when they finished the auditions. Alex had an appointment at 5:00 to lay down some more acoustic tracks. His fingers were a bit sore from playing most of the day already, but it was the satisfying pain that followed doing what he loved the most. He was dying for a cigarette, but knew that it would have to wait. He looked over at Chris who was on the phone deep in conversation. He couldn't tell from her body language whether she was talking to another colleague or to her husband. Although he'd never even met him, he was already resentful of the man who had taken a permanent place in her life. Alex knew he wasn't good enough for Chris, but he seriously doubted the guy she'd married was either.

As she finished up her phone call, Christina walked over to him and smiled. "Good work today. I really think we have the makings of a great band here."

"Yeah, that was pretty cool. It's nice to have the choice of who to play with. Before I was really just playing with whomever I could get." He rubbed his fingers against the palms of his hands to relieve a bit of the tenderness.

"Hands hurt?" she asked.

"Yeah, a little. I have some more recording to do today though."

"Do you want me to reschedule it?"

"No, I'll get by. I've played longer than this before and I've been okay."

"Here, let me see your right hand," she said and reached out. He extended his hand as instructed and she took it in both of hers. She rubbed the knots from his palms and slowly massaged each finger. It felt heavenly and he closed his eyes as she dissolved the tension that had built up from the day. Tingles spread from his hand throughout his entire body. Somehow he felt the gentle pressure of her hands all the way to his toes. He'd missed this. In college after he'd played for hours and his hands hurt like this, she had done the same thing. When she finished with his right hand, she took his left. He never wanted her to stop. It was as if God was giving him a small glimpse of what he could have had after every show if he hadn't been such a fool.

"I should hire you to do this after every long day," he said with a smile, eyes still closed. "I think you missed your calling as a massage therapist."

"Thanks," she replied as she dropped his left hand, "but I think the gig I have is much better. I hope your hands are okay. That should get you through your sessions tonight."

"I think I'll survive. Are you staying for the recordings?" He knew the answer, but secretly hoped she would say yes.

"No, I have some boring office work to do before going home. I'll see you tomorrow morning for final call." As she turned to go, he reached for her hand to stop her.

"Chris," he began but didn't know how to finish. He held her hand, afraid to let go. She was so soft. He couldn't help sensing her vulnerable femininity under her steely façade. He knew he couldn't hold on to her for long without pulling her to him and pressing his lips against her full luscious ones. Then, for the first time, he noticed her bracelet. His brow creased together as he realized she was still wearing the charm he'd given her all those years ago. "Thanks," was all he could manage.

"For what?" she asked as she pulled her hand away. She noticed he'd seen the charm. 'Love much, live well' was engraved on the charm he'd given her on their first and only Christmas together.

"For everything," he finished. She smiled, "I'll see you in the morning." She turned and walked out of the studio. He was left standing there speechless. He put his hands on top of his head and breathed out slowly. What was he doing? She was married now. But why was she still wearing the charm? He couldn't let her know how he still felt, but it was eating him alive.

Christina stood outside the studio door and leaned against it hoping to absorb some of the strength from the building. She had massaged the hands of countless artists in the past, but she shouldn't have massaged his. With every touch she felt herself longing to feel more of him. With every note he sang she was being pulled closer and closer to that dangerous curve she'd slipped on before. She'd nearly lost herself the first time. This time there was much more at stake. She steadied herself, smoothed her clothes and went to her office.

Christina had returned several phone calls and was beginning to put together a tour calendar when she realized how late it was. Wanting to leave, she quickly packed her things up for the evening, grabbed her purse and left the building. She didn't want to be around when Alex finished recording for the night. She wanted to be at home where things were familiar, ordinary and safe.

Chapter 10

Alex climbed on the bus and made his way toward home. Exhaustion was setting in. It had only been two days, but man was it different from his old life. Abruptly, his reverie was interrupted by the ringing of his cell phone. He didn't really want to answer it, but went ahead anyway. It was his friend Josh wanting to meet up later for a bite to eat. The evening was still warm. Late September in Atlanta usually had a nip in the air, but this year summer was still holding on.

Alex agreed to meet Josh at Fiesta Bar and Grill. The patio would be open and they could still see any ball games that were being shown. He and Josh had been friends for a long time. They'd met at the graphic design studio where Alex had found work after leaving school. Josh had been the one friend who supported his decision to get clean. The other guys were in just as deep as Alex. Josh had seen first-hand the damage the drugs were doing to his friend and had convinced Alex's family to do an intervention. He'd even convinced their boss to hold Alex's position until his stint in rehab was over.

Strains of a mariachi band filled the autumn night as Alex greeted Josh. They sat down on the festively decorated patio and ordered hot wings. Josh ordered a pint of beer. Alex filled Josh in on the past few weeks, emphasizing how drastically everything had changed for him.

Josh told Alex about his new son who was just learning to army crawl, arms propelling him forward and legs motionless, at seven months old as well as the latest news about the guys from the studio.

The two friends couldn't have been more different. Josh had settled down, moved as high as he could in the company, married a nice Rhode Island girl, and started his family. Alex was still chasing the rock and roll dream with no prospects of settling down in his future. Both in their early thirties, Alex had been pretty sure Josh had come away with the reward. It wasn't for a lack of trying on Alex's part though. He wanted to find someone and have a family, but his heart hadn't been open to anyone he'd met. He found companionship in his music, and up until recently, he'd convinced himself that was enough. Alex really needed the advice of his oldest friend who had been with him through the toughest times of his life. He decided to bring up Christina and see what Josh's take was.

"Hey, do you remember the girl from college that I told you about?" Alex ventured, knowing full well that Josh would know exactly who he was talking about.

"How could I forget her? You talked about her nonstop for the first two years I knew you." Josh replied biting into a wing while their waitress brought him another beer.

"Well, here's the funny thing. She's actually my rep at Mastermind." Alex said.

"No shit!" Josh's eyes were wide. "How's that going?"

"It's weird. She's married now and has kids, but she seems really uncomfortable around me."

"Well, can you blame her?"

"No, I can't blame her. But it's been eleven years. If she were truly over it, it wouldn't stay weird, right?" Alex asked.

"You're probably right. But, it's only been two days. Besides, didn't you say you guys had a really bad break up?"

"Yeah, we did. I was totally strung out then."

"So, what's it like working with her?" Josh asked. He'd known Alex a long time and had never seen him as torn up by anything as he was by this girl. Josh knew it wasn't her fault, but he'd watched his friend being eaten up by guilt and regret for years and then watched him spend several more years yearning to get that same feeling back with someone else. Every relationship Alex had fell short compared to

Christina. Josh didn't think it was healthy to still be pining for someone after all this time.

"Well," Alex said, finishing a wing, "she's really good at her job. She's very professional. When she's in her work zone, she's totally there. She focuses totally on the task at hand. That's great for me. She gave me some names of her other clients. I've seen how she's turned around new talent before and I am very glad to have her working on me. Thing is though, if the conversation ever turns to anything other than work, she turns into a stone wall. It's like she wants to pretend nothing ever happened with us."

"Maybe that's her way of letting you know she's moved on." Josh ventured, sipping his beer. He hated seeing his friend still obsessed with this girl, especially if there was no chance of their getting back together. He wondered if the company had a policy about reps and artists getting involved. From the stories he'd heard though, he was pretty sure if such a policy existed it wasn't enforced.

"Yeah, maybe. Except she's still wearing the charm I gave her back then. Why would she still wear it if she's moved on?"

"Did you ask her about that?"

"No. I just noticed it tonight. I haven't been able to be alone with her yet to ask," Alex sighed as he drained his water glass and motioned to their waitress for a refill. "Anyway, let's change the subject. How's life at the print shop? Anyone miss me yet?"

"Dude, you're totally missed. There's no one there who can design quite like you. We get calls all the time about when we are going to woo you back," Josh answered sarcastically. "We keep trying to tell them that you're off about to become the next John Mayer, but they don't believe us."

"Thanks, smart ass. Hey listen, I have final band auditions tomorrow morning so I need to take off. You and Becky are coming to the show on Friday right?"

"We wouldn't miss it for the world, man. Hey, is your girl going to be there?"

"I assume so."

"Cool, I'll finally get to meet the woman who's held you captive all these years."

"Please don't phrase it like that when you meet her, dude," Alex scoffed.

"No worries friend. I'll be perfectly discreet. I can't say the same for Becky." Becky was Josh's wife. As they were both from Rhode Island, they had a tendency to be pretty blunt. Becky was especially straight forward.

"Thanks, dude. Hey, food and drinks on me tonight," Alex said as he picked up the check and they moved to pay. "Don't get used to it though. I'm not going to let my friends mooch off me once I'm rich and famous."

"You mean we can't come live in your pool house?" Josh joked back.

"Not a chance man! I'll see you Friday. Be there by 8:00, okay?"

"Cool, see you then. Hey, do you want a ride home?" Josh replied and headed toward his car. Alex declined and Josh watched his friend catch the bus that had just pulled up to the corner.

Chapter 11

Alex woke early the next morning. He showered, shaved and dressed quickly. He wanted to get to her office before they had their final auditions. The sound techs and producers would be in the way of any conversation he hoped to have with Chris. He knew she wouldn't want to talk about it, but he couldn't go on pretending that nothing had happened. He wanted, no needed, to get some things cleared up. He now realized he wanted to start with the charm on her bracelet. Why would she still be wearing it after all this time if she truly was over him? It was a question he couldn't reconcile in his mind.

The bus dropped him off in front of the building at half past 7:00. No one would be there yet, but he thought he'd go on up and wait. Jorge, the doorman, opened the door and greeted him. He returned the greeting warmly and took the elevator to her floor. He was all ready to take a seat in the waiting room when he noticed her office door already ajar. He took a chance and stuck his head in. She was deep in concentration staring intently at the papers in front of her. Her hair was pulled back in a twist revealing her long slender neck. He ached to brush her neck with kisses. He watched her for a bit as she checked her files against the computer screen. Then he gave a small knock on the door and chuckled as she practically jumped out of her seat.

"Alex, you frightened me! How long have you been there?" Christina gasped as her hand flew to her chest covering her heart. He noticed her breath was shallower than it usually was.

"Not long. You were concentrating so hard I didn't want to bother you," he replied. "Sorry if I scared you." He'd always found her the sexiest when she was deep in thought.

"No, it's fine. Just next time, please make a little more noise when you come down the hall so I know someone is here. Come on in and have a seat. What are you doing here so early?" she asked. She stacked the papers and gave them a tap on the desk before placing them back in the empty file folder beside her.

"Just thought I'd get an early start to the day. What about you? Do you always get to work before anyone else in the building?"

"Well, not normally. Todd dropped the kids off this morning so I thought I'd come in early and get some work done. He's got a late meeting tonight so I need to pick them up," she said leaning back in her chair.

"Oh," he said as he looked at the photos on her wall. She'd been photographed alongside some of the top artists in the industry. Many were Mastermind artists, but there were photos of other music celebrities as well including Snoop Dogg, Britney Spears, Gwen Stefani and Justin Timberlake. "Do you know all these people?" he asked.

"Well, yes in a way. I mean, I don't go to their houses for dinner parties, but I know them. That photo with Maroon 5 was taken at the Vanity Fair party after the Grammies. That was a fun night."

"So, can you like call them up and set up events and stuff?" It was a stupid question, but he was more than slightly awed by her presence in the industry.

"I would probably set it up through their managers, but yeah pretty much. I organized a silent auction for Kate's school last year and was able to get tons of autographed stuff donated. I even got Aly and AJ to perform for the kids. It was a great night," she said. She could tell he was thoroughly impressed.

"So, what does he do? Your husband. What kind of meeting does he have tonight?" Alex asked still perusing the photos.

"He's an accountant with Portman Kindle Morgan."

Alex turned and gave her a quizzical glance. "You married an accountant?"

"Yeah, I married an accountant. Why?" She raised her eyebrow, returning his glance and sitting back in her chair.

"Just seems so…not you. I mean, here you are with Steve Tyler's arm draped around your shoulder, yet you spend your life married to an accountant. Just doesn't seem to fit very well, that's all."

"I tried dating a musician once. It didn't end well, or don't you remember?" her voice had gone flat. He knew he'd pushed the limit.

"I'm sorry. That was rude of me. I'm sure your husband is a great guy."

"He *is* a great guy, thank you. He's very vibrant, especially for an accountant. Alex, why are you really here?" she asked with her arms folded across her chest.

He decided to just be up front with her. "I want to know why you still wear the charm I gave you."

She sat there for a moment thinking of the best way to answer. She honestly wasn't sure why she still wore it. She told herself it was because she liked the message on the charm. That was part of it, sure, but that's not really why she kept it. She was afraid of the real answer. She was afraid she kept it as a way to maintain some kind of attachment to the past, to him. Even if she went months, or years without thinking of him, the charm gave her memory a foundation.

"I don't know," she replied with a small shrug, "I guess it reminds me of where I've been." It was a pretty dumb response, but it was the best she could come up with on the spur of the moment.

Alex thought about her answer and wasn't sure how to take it. It reminded her of where she'd been? What did that mean? He decided not to push it anymore. He'd already rubbed her the wrong way with the comment about her husband. "So, what were you working on before I interrupted you?"

"Well, I was looking at possible itineraries and locations for a tour and trying to match them up with bands that need opening acts," she said glad that he steered the conversation back to work matters.

"Tour? For who?" he asked.

"For you. We're starting to set up your club tour and radio spots today at the promotions meeting. I'm actually glad you stopped by. I need you to let me know if you have any specific towns you want to play or any specific clubs you'd like to play and I'll try my best to work them into the schedule. I already have a list of the towns and clubs that I work with regularly. I just need to get the order straightened out. I also went ahead and put your hometown on the list. You do want to play your hometown, right? It's a really small town, but I think we can work in a stop after Charlotte and before Raleigh. You'll be the headliner there. There aren't too many big name groups that go through Mt. Pleasant, North Carolina."

"Yes, I'd love to play Mt. Pleasant." She remembered where he was from. He was touched. "When do you need the rest of the list by?"

"Friday would be great if you can get it to me. My fax number is on my card, as well as my email address," she motioned to the front of her desk where her cards were placed. "You can send it to me either way. I know you'll be in the studio pretty much the rest of the week. There's no need to come to the office. Just get it to me when you can."

"That's cool," he said. He picked up a card from the card holder on her desk and slid it into the back pocket of his jeans.

"I'll see you on Friday at 5:00 at the Tabernacle. We'll meet so I can review your set list. Your first club appearance as a Mastermind artist needs to be different than your other club spots. If you want, I'll have Jillian send over some of the clothes from the shoot, or you can bring your own. The press will be there. The first impression is important."

"Today's Wednesday. I won't see you the rest of the week?"

"You'll be fine, and we're both going to be very busy," she checked her watch. It was approaching 8:00. "We'd better get going and finish up this last round of auditions," she said, giving him shaky smile.

"Chris, are you okay?" he asked. "Are we okay?"

"Yes, Alex. We're fine, professionally speaking. I just have a lot to think about right now. Let's get down to the studio and get your band put together. Shall we?"

As they left the office, they passed Andrea who was trying to look as if she hadn't been listening to the whole conversation. Christina gave her a look that said, "None of your business". The assistant smiled and put on her very guilty innocent face that said, 'What did I do?'

The rest of the day went by amazingly fast. The schedule kept them extremely busy. Usually this is how Chris liked to work, especially when her mind was stuck on something. Staying busy kept her focused and in control. The final auditions went well. They ended up with three of their first picks and two of the alternates. The band jammed well together. Alex was very personable and easy to work with, and his easy-going attitude was reflected in the other musicians. So far, so good.

She left them shortly before lunch time. Now that the band was chosen, the managers needed to approve contracts. This was a point in the process where she could step back from the front line for a little while. Besides, Micah had sent the disk from the photo shoot over. She'd let promotions choose the top three pictures and then email them to Alex so he could decide which one would be used for the CD's cover. The company wanted the CD on the shelves by mid-November. That didn't give them much time for recording, editing and production. She'd have Micah go over and take some shots of the band as well for the inside jacket.

She was actually glad for the break from working with Alex. It was hard to stay focused when the person she wanted to forget was the person she was working with the closest. Relieved, she turned her attention to her other clients.

Michelle Norris was embracing her new found stardom a little too much. She'd been involved in some situations that were definitely not approved by Mastermind, including some unsavory photos snapped by the paparazzi. Not uncommon in the industry, but these were overly scandalous and could hinder Michelle's image and reputation. Christina needed to get on the phone and do some damage control. By the time she left at 4:00, she felt almost back to normal.

It was a beautiful afternoon with just a hint of fall in the air. She picked up Kate and Jack and they headed over to the park. The time would change soon and it would be too dark for them to go there except on weekends. And, once winter came it would often be too cold. After their play time she took them to Goldilocks Café for dinner. Anthony, the owner, was one of Todd's clients. The food was great, and very healthy. The kids actually loved the sweet potato fries. So did everyone else for that matter.

Anthony put Jack on his shoulders and made the rounds of the restaurant. The toddler squealed with delight as he moved through the restaurant pretending to take orders. Christina and Kate laughed right along with him.

She loved times like these. It was part of what kept her grounded in her rock star world. The glamorous life could be addictive if there wasn't something that refocused her on the things that really mattered. Listening to the delighted giggles of her kids kept her head where it needed to be. Their laughter also happened to be her favorite sound in the world. It was better than any song ever recorded.

After getting them both to sleep that night, she lay down in bed with a book. She was two chapters in when she heard the garage door open a little past 9:00. Todd looked exhausted as he loosened his tie and took off his shoes. He lay down on the bed next to her and snuggled in close.

"Long day, sweetie?" She stroked his hair and felt his breath rise and fall matching hers.

"Yes, very. I'm beat," Todd answered with his head on her chest.

"What was the meeting about?" she asked trying to take an interest in his work.

"We're putting in a bid to represent the Center for Disease Control. It's amazing how much stuff we have to sort through," he continued to talk but Christina was no longer listening. She just stroked his head and murmured "Uh, huh" every once in a while. Accounting work really was boring and she didn't understand a lot of it. She often wondered how someone with her husband's vitality had found his way to such a dull career.

"You know what would make you feel better?" she asked him.

"What's that?"

"A nice hot bubble bath with your wife would probably do wonders for your tired, aching bones. Are you up for it?" she really hoped he'd say yes. She missed her husband, missed the intimacy they had been forgetting lately.

"Maybe not the bath, but how about we share some wine?" he asked as he took off his tie and began to unbutton his shirt. She watched him take off the blue silk material and hang it in its place in the closet. She noticed the ripple of muscle along his back even through his undershirt.

Christina sighed quietly as she went into the kitchen and poured two glasses of chardonnay. She remembered the days when he would have raced her to the bathroom to start the water. When she returned he was already under the covers. She let her night gown fall into a puddle around her feet and climbed in. They made love in the bed they'd shared for eight years. It was sweet and sensual. He moved over her slowly and rhythmically. Todd was a very considerate lover, always making sure she was satisfied before meeting his own needs. Afterwards, they lay in bed tangled in each other's arms. Christina was content. Todd was always so tender when they made love. But things *had* changed since their early days together. He had always been gentle, but there was a time when they hadn't been able to keep their hands away from one another.

In those days they would have made love right in the tub and then again in their bed. Their love making was still wonderful, but sometimes she missed the intensity she'd had with Alex. This was one of those times. She couldn't help feeling a little let down. She'd wanted Todd to rip the nightgown from her body and take her ferociously. She wanted to feel the strength in his arms and the heat from his body. Over the last five years that hadn't happened very often. She was beginning to think it never would again. Having Kate had drained a certain amount of passion from their relationship, and Jack's arrival hadn't helped the situation either. Wrapped in his strong arms, she forced her eyes to close, diligently trying to keep her mind focused on her husband and family. She loved Todd very much. She knew had a great life together, and the night had been great. She didn't want to spoil it with thoughts of *him*.

Chapter 12

Alex lay on his bed and stared at the ceiling. God, he was exhausted. He had been in the studio all week. Editing, interviewing, auditioning, rehearsing- he hadn't realized there was so much involved. He knew he'd adjust to the pace, but damn! He'd never wanted to just sleep so much in his life. Christina had become a fleeting thought with so much going on after the final auditions, but now, it was Thursday night. He'd see her tomorrow.

The thought made his heart flutter nervously. It excited him, but at the same time it filled him with apprehension. All business, that's what she wanted. But he wanted to tell her everything. How unfair he'd been to her, how he'd changed because of her, how sorry he was that he'd hurt her so many times. The song was a start, but there was so much more to say.

Once again, he began to replay their relationship in his head, something he'd done a thousand times before. They had been doomed from the start. He hadn't been honest with her and his lies continued to grow. She never knew about Audrey, about how messed up he'd been because of her when he met Christina. He'd taken out his anger and frustration toward Audrey on Chris, a deal she never signed up for.

Audrey had gotten into his head and under his skin. She'd made him believe he'd be nowhere and no one without her. She'd introduced him to drugs, and soon he was hooked physically and mentally, but not just on the drugs. Every decision he made, every thought he had, every emotion he felt had to be approved by her. She'd torn him away from his family, and made him think only she could love him. Then she'd leave, for months at a time, only to return begging him to take her back, swearing she'd changed. He had fallen for it every time. Each time she left he'd break apart, and it seemed that just when he was getting himself back together, she'd return and his whole world would come crashing down again. She was his ultimate drug. Just a taste and he was hooked again.

He'd met Chris during one of Audrey's disappearances. She'd been gone for four months, the longest stretch ever, and Alex was pretty sure, or at least hopeful, that she was gone for good. His life was getting back on track. He was attending class regularly and seeing improvements in his grades. He'd learned to celebrate the small successes.

He'd also backed off on the drugs. The hard stuff had started to get to him in weird ways and he needed a break. He stuck to weed when he needed to unwind, but mostly he focused on his music.

He even tried to study, and succeeded a bit. The quarter before he met Christina he'd pulled two B's and only one C. Not bad considering a C was the highest grade he'd made the quarter before that. He'd been skirting academic probation for the past two years, since Audrey had arrived on scene. With a solid quarter behind him and this one looking even better, the threat of being forced out of school was becoming less ominous.

Then he met Christina Malone. She was different from anyone he'd ever met. She was brilliant and beautiful, and surprisingly optimistic. She looked for and found the best in everything and everyone. Her energy was refreshing. She saw the potential in him and tried really hard to help him see it too. He'd wanted desperately to believe she was genuine, but there was no way that *she* could see potential in *him*. She was strong, stronger than she should have been he later realized, considering what she'd been through.

At first she had seemed totally together, but after a short time she'd opened up to him and revealed a vulnerability she'd kept well hidden.

She told him her high school boyfriend who'd robbed her. She'd talked about her dad's illness and how watching him die was the hardest thing she'd ever been through. Through these trials she should have become tough as nails, and on the surface, she appeared to be that way. But on the inside, she maintained a softness he'd never known before.

Christina and Alex had a lot in common, coming from similar backgrounds, both growing up without their fathers. That was one thing that really made him connect with her. She knew what it was like to hear her mother cry all night, then watch her get up in the morning, put on a smile and face the day like she was fine. Still, they had turned out quite differently. This was likely because his father had walked out, while her father had died. Neither was ever coming back, but at least she'd had closure.

They were different in almost every other way. Christina was serious about her schoolwork; he was serious about music. She wanted to change the world; he wanted a cigarette. She was resilient; he was fragile. She looked at her past as something to triumph over. He saw it as a well he could not pull himself out of. Alex appeared self-confident outwardly while she seemed self-conscious and a little shy, but inwardly was very sure of herself.

He realized early on that she didn't realize how beautiful she truly was. Christina took his breath away and made his heart skip a beat every time she smiled, which was a lot. No doubt, she was out of his league and he should have stayed away, but he couldn't. For once in his life, he wanted to have something stable, solid and true. She was all that and much more, but he hadn't really been ready for it all. It scared him to death to admit that he was falling in love with her, and fast. It terrified him to know that at the age of twenty two he'd found the one person he was meant to be with for the rest of his life. He had no idea how to handle that.

They'd been dating pretty seriously for over a month before things started to crack. After their first night together they'd been inseparable. In the beginning, she'd meet him after her last class and they would spend their evenings together. They would make love for hours and then they would drag themselves out for food. Sometimes they never made it out for the food. They lived off each other on those nights.

After the first month or so, they even began studying together. He never knew studying could be so enjoyable. He would watch her chew on the end of her pen with her brow furrowed, deep in concentration. She looked so adorable he found it difficult to keep his hands off her, but if he tried to distract her while she was studying, she would get serious and the message was clear. She took school very seriously; everything else was secondary. There would be time for play after the work was complete.

Christina was a really good tutor too. She could explain things to him in a way that he could actually understand. He began getting A's for the first time in his life. He thought her chosen career as a teacher would be perfect for her. If he'd had teachers like her when he was growing up, he might have turned out differently.

Always the loner, he'd been seen as a troubled youth, a lost cause. She saw past all that. She was able to see good things in him that no one else could, or didn't bother, to see. She often saw things in him he didn't even realize were there. She saw the possibilities that he had and often told him he had a special kind of intelligence that wasn't measured in school. Words like that had never been spoken to him before. She seemed to have a sixth sense about when he needed encouragement because it came when he needed it the most.

That sixth sense scared him immensely too. Even without his telling her what he was feeling, she seemed to know. And she could calm him in a way that he'd never experienced. What they had felt good. Alex had never met someone with so pure a heart. With his dad taking off, and his experience with Audrey, he was doubtful that such a person actually existed. The fact that she did, and she was with him, was something he never could quite grasp. Why would someone so sweet and caring and good waste time on a low-down loser like him? It frightened the hell out of him. He had seriously considered calling it quits and walking away. Better to strike first and get out before the iron gets too hot, he thought to himself. But the thought of going back to a life without her radiant smile, her encouraging words, the feel of her skin, the taste of her breath and the smell of her hair, made him almost physically ill.

For months, he kept waiting for the rug to be pulled out from under him, for her to pull an "Audrey move" and just disappear. Every afternoon that he waited for her was like waiting for the verdict in a high profile case. What if she didn't come back to the apartment? What if she left him for someone else or for no reason at all? He hated the hour between their class together and her algebra class. But then part of him wanted her to not come back.

He found it hard to accept that she selflessly gave her heart to him; he felt he didn't deserve it. She expected nothing in return, and that made him want to give her more. But he had nothing to give her except himself, and he didn't even know if *that* was possible. If he didn't know who he was, how could he give himself to her? One minute he was elated that she had chosen him; the next, he feared he'd be a disappointment to her. No matter how much he wanted to, he believed he could never love her the way she deserved to be loved. He was frightened to be with her yet terrified to be without her. If this was what real love was like, he wasn't sure he could handle it.

Christina was everything Audrey wasn't. Trying to compare the two was like trying to compare an apple to an orangutan. It just couldn't be done! But Audrey was all he had known for so long. She was poisonous, and he knew that, but he wasn't sure he would ever get used to being with anyone else. Audrey felt normal. Christina did not.

He recalled one of their first fights. One day she'd been late from class. Looking back, it was probably only half an hour, but it had seemed like forever. He'd decided to go to campus to make sure everything was okay. He stopped by her dorm first. Her roommate had answered the callbox sounding bored and annoyed, as usual. After ascertaining that she was not there, he made his way to Hayes Hall where they had government and then she had algebra. No luck there either. He told himself he was concerned for her safety, but honestly he was scared for himself. The insecurities from the past were sweeping over him.

Feeling panicky, he headed to the library where he found her, head lowered over a book in deep conversation with a guy he'd never seen before. He saw the guy touch her arm lightly and she laughed. That was when lost it. He stormed over to the table with fury in his eyes. She was cheating on him, he was sure of it. She looked up when she saw him starting to smile until she saw the look on his face. "Hey…" she said uncertainly.

"Where have you been!? Who is this?" Alex's voice was loud enough to draw attention from several nearby tables.

Her eyes registered shock and her mouth gaped slightly opened. "Alex, what are you talking about? I told you this morning I had a study session this afternoon. This is Doug, from my algebra class," she tried to whisper calmly, but her face showed fear and confusion.

"Get your things. You're leaving," he grabbed her arm and forcefully pulled her out of the chair.

"Dude, get your hands off of her!" Doug rose from his seat and grabbed Alex's arm. "Chill out. We're just studying."

Alex didn't hear a word. He felt the hand on his arm and reacted. Before he realized what he'd done, he'd punched the other guy in the mouth. Doug fell backwards into the table behind them. Books, paper and pens flew into the air. People scattered out of the way and there were gasps of surprise. Blood trickled from his lip and Doug used his hand to wipe the blood from his chin.

"Alex! What is wrong with you?" Christina yelled, running to Doug's side. Now the entire floor of the library was watching and security was on the way. "Are you okay?" she asked trying to help Doug up. Alex turned and stormed out of the library. He made it to the bottom of the outside stairs by the time she caught up to him. "Alex, what is wrong with you!" she shouted putting her hand on his arm. He shrugged her off. "Alex, talk to me, please!"

"Are you sleeping with him?" he demanded spinning around to face her. His face was red with anger; hers was white with fear. She looked completely terrified.

"What? No. I'm not sleeping with Doug! He's the teacher's assistant! He's helping me in algebra! I told you this morning I had tutoring after class!"

"You lying little bitch! Do you really expect me to believe that you're getting help in algebra? You're the smartest person I know. You don't need help in algebra!"

"Yes, I do! You know that! I am not sleeping with anyone but you! I can't believe you don't believe me. What has gotten into you?" she was trying to speak low to keep the whole campus from hearing their business, but the anger was starting to rise in her voice. He was attacking her for no reason. He knew that, but couldn't stop himself.

"Don't fuck with me Christina! What has gotten into me?! Nothing! I'm just seeing things clearly for the first time. You're just like the rest of them! Why don't you just go back in there, clean Doug up, take him home and screw him? Do you leave my house and go straight to his for another round, you stupid slut!"

She smacked him hard across the face. Stunned, he stepped back, his hand touching the side of his cheek seared by her hand. He hadn't expected the response but he should have.

"How dare you talk to me like that?" She was furious now.

Her entire body trembled with anger. Her eyes blazed and he saw in them a fury he didn't know she was capable of.

"I have only been with you since we met and I do not deserve to be attacked and insulted for no reason! I have nothing more to say to you, Alex!"

She moved to walk around him, but he caught her by the arm and spun her around hard.

"You make me sick!" he shouted in her face.

"Then let go of me, asshole!" She wrenched free from his grip and stormed off.

He was left standing there alone. For the first time he noticed the crowd of people who were watching. Embarrassed and angry, he turned and quickly made his way back to his car. When he got back to his apartment, he dug through his drawers and closet looking for something to help him cool down. Seeing nothing strong enough, he made a phone call he hadn't made in several months.

While he waited he paced around his apartment. He smoked a joint trying to calm himself down, but it didn't help. What was happening? What was wrong with him? Less than an hour later he prepared the drug and syringe. He hesitated only briefly before sticking the needle in his arm and depressing the plunger. He didn't care about the months he'd stayed clean. Everything disappeared and he was floating. Nirvana was the word often used to describe the feel of a heroin high. He didn't even remember passing out.

He woke up several hours later on the floor of his bedroom, drenched in sweat. His head was pounding and his skin itched horrendously. What had he done? Suddenly, it all came flooding back to him. God, he was such a fucking idiot! First, he'd attacked Christina for no reason at all. She *had* told him about the tutoring session. He remembered now.

Then, he'd shot up! He'd been off heroin for nearly five months! What was going on with him? He replayed the fight in his head and realized that through the whole thing, it wasn't Christina's face he'd seen. He'd seen Audrey the whole time. Even when she was out of his life she was still there ruining any happiness that he felt.

He had to see Christina! He rolled over and sat up. He groaned loudly as he held his head in his hands. The pain was almost unbearable. He looked at the clock. 12:44 AM. It had been nearly eight hours since their fight. He stumbled into the bathroom, caught himself on the countertop to keep from falling, and swallowed four Advil. His eyes were bloodshot making the green stand out even more. They were also dry and it hurt to blink.

He took his time cleaning himself up. He took a long shower trying to will the hot water to wash away everything that had happened. His hands twitched slightly as he rubbed the soap across his body. There was no way he could let her know he'd shot up. He was fairly sure she didn't know about the drugs at all.

He dressed slowly because moving too suddenly would make his head feel like it was about to explode. Once he felt semi-human and thought he looked presentable enough, he cleaned up the remnants of the heroin, flushed the rest of it down the toilet, and threw the needle in the garbage. He took the trash bag to the dumpster on his way out. He needed to get rid of every trace immediately.

When he got to her dorm he buzzed her room from the call box. Her roommate answered and refused to buzz him in. Her tone had altered from perpetually bored to extremely angry. Please, he begged, he just needed to talk to Chris, to apologize. No answer. He stood in the lobby, unsure of what to do next.

He went to the side of the building and yelled her name. Nothing. He sat down on the curb and started to sob. He'd blown it. The best thing to ever happen to him and he'd blown it. God, what a fucking loser he was! He'd known it was too good to be true, but he had been the cause of this. Losing her was his fault. She had been nothing but kind to him, shown him more tenderness than he'd ever known from anyone. And he had pushed her away. It wouldn't surprise him if she never talked to him again. Those horrible things he said to her! He hadn't meant a word of it. How could he make her understand?

Then, he heard the outside door creak open. He raised his head slightly and stood up quickly. She was standing there, eyes swollen from crying, face streaked with tears. Her hair was disheveled and her clothes wrinkled.

"Christina," he whispered as he approached her, "I'm so sorry." He broke down in gut wrenching sobs. "I'm so sorry. I didn't mean it. I didn't mean any of it."

He sank to his knees in front of her and reached out. To his relief she let him wrap his arms around her waist.

"Please forgive me," he said, kissing her hands. "Please forgive me. I never meant to hurt you. I never wanted to make you cry. I hate it that I caused you pain. Don't leave me, Christina, please don't leave me," he sobbed against her abdomen. She lifted her hands and ran them through his hair unable to speak, but unable to move away.

They stayed that way for a long time, sobbing in each other's arms. When she finally pulled away, she brought him to his feet and looked him dead in the eye. Her eyes were serious beneath the dark circles and puffiness. Any trace of makeup had been washed away by her tears and what he saw was raw and tough. Her eyes looked even bluer, if that was possible, against the redness of her face.

"You hurt me today."

"I know."

"You embarrassed me and called me horrible names."

"I know and I'm so sorry," he hung his head. He was not worthy to meet her eyes. Seeing the hurt he'd caused was too much for him to bear.

"Don't do it again," she said flatly. That was all she said.

His eyes flew to hers. He drew her into his arms once again and brushed his lips against hers. They remained in each other's arms for a long while before he led her to his car and took her back to his apartment. They made love gingerly that night. He nursed her wounds; wounds that he'd caused. He kissed her eyes trying to take away the tears. He stroked her cheeks and ran his fingers through her hair. He tried to memorize every part of her body, her face, because he was terrified that in the morning she'd be gone. She held him tightly in her arms while he cried. Being held by her was all he needed.

She skipped her morning classes the next day, something totally out of character for her. When he awoke she was sipping tea on the couch. There was another cup sitting on the coffee table made from milk crates and a piece of dark stained plywood. He came out and sat beside her, taking the steaming cup. She asked him if he wanted to talk about what had happened. He said no. He knew he was totally wrong and she had to understand that it would never happen again.

"Then all you need to do is listen," she'd said. "Alex, you are very special. I can see the goodness radiating from inside you, just dying to be set free. I know that wasn't you yelling at me yesterday. You are harboring some pretty scary demons, and you are the only one who can deal with them. I can't make them go away; no matter how hard I try, especially if you won't let me get close enough. You can trust me with your secrets when you're ready. I won't push you to open up, but you need to know that I'm here for you." She took his face in her hands and looked deep into his eyes before she continued.

"I know you are tortured. I hear it in your music. I hear it when you dream at night. Sometimes I just hold you while you're sleeping and will your pain to come into my body so I can do something to make you feel better. I see it in your eyes when you think I'm not looking. You are unlike anyone I've ever known. You're not who you present yourself to be on the outside. But I don't know if I've seen the real Alex either. I think I've seen pieces of him, but I'd like to see it all.

"I was scared yesterday. What I saw staring back at me by the library was not the same person I've spent the last month with. Everything about you was different, even your eyes changed color. I don't ever want to see that person again. He was not the tender, passionate person I've come to care so deeply for. You've promised it will never happen again. If it does, I'm gone," she stroked his cheeks and his forehead.

He closed his eyes as tears slid down through her fingers.

"I'm so sorry, Chris. You have no idea how bad I feel right now."

"Alex, I feel things for you I've never felt for anyone before and I am afraid to lose it. I'm afraid to lose you, but I will give you up if you ever speak to me like that again. Do you understand?"

He said yes, and embraced her with a strength he didn't know he possessed. "Thank you," was all he could say. They stayed that way on the couch for what seemed like hours. When she finally broke away, she told him she was going to class and that she'd see him later that evening. He said okay, and nothing more was said about the incident. The tension between them remained thick for quite a while though and things were never quite the same between them after that. She became more guarded and appeared slightly afraid of him. He couldn't stand to see her hold her breath, waiting for his reaction when she told him she was going to be late. He pretended not to notice when it happened.

Weeks went by and gradually they became comfortable with each other again. He'd noticed she didn't talk about her friends as much as before. When he asked why, she'd said they thought she was nuts to stay with him. She finally stopped talking about them altogether. She could tell it upset him whenever she mentioned their feelings about him. Once he'd asked why she stayed, knowing how much they disapproved. Her answer shouldn't have shocked him, but it did. "They don't know you like I know you. They don't see how great you are."

The holidays came and went. They spent Thanksgiving at school with just a few friends over. Things had gone well that day. They were almost like the perfect couple. He'd given her the charm for Christmas. They celebrated New Years Eve at his family's house. Things were good, and they were happy. They fell back into their routine; loving-making, studying, repeat, and went on with their lives. They were together, that's all that mattered to him. He would change for her, he told himself. He would become a better man, one who could trust and love openly without fear. Determined, he vowed to kick the drugs for good. But no matter how hard he tried, no matter how much she demonstrated her loyalty, no matter how much she said she believed in him, he'd never felt worthy of her. He tried to fake it, but he could tell his demons were returning. He began smoking more weed to keep himself calm. Unfamiliar and scary feeling he'd never felt before were threatening a take-over, and it frightened him. Needing a way to deal with it all, he smoked weed only when she wasn't around. She barely tolerated the cigarettes, and he knew she'd never approve of the drugs. He didn't want her to know because she would be ashamed of him the way he was ashamed of himself.

One day in early February one of his demons returned, literally. Christina had left for class already that morning. He was getting out of the shower when he heard the door open.

"Hey, did you forget something?" he shouted through the bathroom into the bedroom.

"Yeah," a familiar voice said, "I forgot how damned sexy you look right after a shower."

He froze and looked up. Audrey was leaning against the door frame, arms folded, grinning at him. He stood there glued to the spot, towel midways wrapped around him.

"Miss me?" she asked.

Chapter 13

At 5:00 sharp Alex walked into the back stage area of the Tabernacle. Christina was on the phone, but waved him in. He sat down on the sofa in the dressing room and pretended to read a magazine while she finished up.

"No, the outfit for the last number is all wrong, Joel." There was a pause while the guy on the other end responded. "Look, this is her first world tour. We've set up her image as the All-American Girl Next Door. If she goes out in that outfit the whole image will be blown. This outfit says, 'Look at me! I'm a tramp who's trying too hard'".

Pause.

"Yes, I know she wants to wear it but the answer is no. She can find something in the wardrobe selection that was sent over that is seductive without being sluttish. Remember that horrible phase Christina Aguilera went through where she died her hair black and pretty much performed in her underwear? It took her years to overcome that whorish image. Email me the new choices once you've made them."

Pause.

"Well, considering the first leg of the tour starts in two days this decision needs to be made fast. You are her manager Joel. Do your job and *manage* your client."

Another pause.

"Yeah, I know. She'll be fine. I'll be looking for the wardrobe picks by tomorrow midday. Talk to you soon."

She hung up the phone and gave him an apologetic smile. "Sorry about that," she said.

"Wardrobe crisis?" he asked.

"Yes. Although I don't know if I'd call it a crisis. Michelle's tour starts in a few days and we're still trying to nail down the wardrobe of all things. Sets and pyrotechnic schemes are all done. Choreography is excellent and dancers are trained and have been rehearsing. But we are dealing with wardrobe selection. God, I like working with men so much more than women. Women are way too complicated." She gave him a smile and rolled her eyes. "Anyway, how was the rest of your week? Get everything taken care of?"

"We got some of the tracks laid down. There's still a lot of polishing to be done, but overall it's coming along nicely. I'm glad the auditions are over. I'm still a little shaky about how the bassist will gel with the rest of the guys, but so far it's good." The truth was he'd hated the audition process. Some guys were really good, but others were just awful. He really didn't want to have to try finding someone to replace the iffy bassist.

"Okay then. Let me see your set list. Afterward I'm going to send you down to get set up and start sound checks," she said as she walked over to a closet. She pulled out a rack of clothes with a row of shoes at the bottom. "My intern Nick is going to help with this, okay? How's your voice?"

"My voice is fine," he said looking up as Nick walked in the room. "Where did you get these?" he asked walking over to the rack.

"I had Jillian send over some pieces that fit in with the style we chose for your photo shoot. I wasn't sure what you'd bring for yourself. Do you like them? If you don't, what you have on is great."

"I love them. Do I have to give them back?"

"Well, yes. At least the pieces you don't choose. I think I can swing letting you keep the things you wear tonight, shoes included. By the way, Butch Walker is warming up right now and said you're welcome to come hang out afterward. How cool is that?"

"Awesome. How'd you swing that?"

"Butch and I are old friends. The kind where he comes over for dinner, not just 'call the manager' friend."

"Wow. That's really cool." She was completely fascinating. She was friends with rock stars on top of everything else. "You're staying tonight right?"

"Of course I'll be here. I wouldn't miss this for the world. This is a really big night for you. Have you ever played the Tabernacle before?"

"No, I haven't. I'm really excited about it. My mom and sister are probably more ecstatic than I am," he smiled as he said it. His mom had been planning for weeks and had told just about everyone she knew.

"They always were very proud of you, Alex. I hope I get to say hi during the evening. Oh hey, you'll get to meet my husband tonight too. We got a sitter so he could join me. He says it's one of the fringe benefits, getting to come to gigs with me and see some really great shows."

"Chris, does he know about us?" Alex asked with concern, his voice at a whisper so Nick wouldn't hear. He didn't want a scene for either of them.

"No. Well, not really." She turned her attention to Nick and asked him to make sure the rest of the band had arrived and was getting ready for their sound checks. As Nick left the room she said, "He knows we used to date in college, but he doesn't know any of the details. At this point, I'd really like to keep it that way. On that subject, I need you to do me a favor."

"Sure, anything. What is it?"

"Don't play the song you played on Tuesday. I've got your set list, but please don't add it. I don't think I could hold it together in front of him and that would raise a lot of questions once we got home."

"Okay, done. You know, I'm really glad to finally meet him. He can see how harmless I truly am, and I get to see the man who swept you off your feet and took you off the market once and for all."

"Nothing about you is harmless, Alex." She rolled her eyes at him and left the dressing room so she could take care of some other business.

A couple hours later Alex had finished his sound checks and was gearing up for the show. He'd changed clothes and run some gel through his hair to keep his curls in check. Spending time with Butch had been amazing. No wonder Chris had become friends with him. He was funny and smart. He'd shared some great insights to the business with Alex; advice Alex would really benefit from. He was sitting back stage strumming his guitar when Christina walked in. She had changed clothes during the time he'd been rehearsing. She was wearing a black leather pencil skirt and a blue, fitted sweater that made her eyes stand out even more than they normally did. He stood as she approached setting his guitar on the floor beside him.

"Wow," was all he could manage.

"Thank you," she smiled coyly.

"Where is your husband? I've been looking forward to meeting this handsome beau of yours." Nothing could actually be farther from the truth, he thought.

"He's parking the car. You're playing for 45 minutes, maybe an hour. Afterward you'll have time to sign copies of your single. Limit that time to no more than 30 minutes after Butch finishes his set. You need to be out of the building within three hours of your start time."

"Why is that?"

"You need to give the impression that you're a star. If you hang around with the crowd you're just one of them. Being average doesn't sell records. You have to maintain some mystery."

"But, don't I want to appear as the down to earth musician?"

"Yes, you do, but you also want to *look* like a star. There will be plenty of time for after show parties later." She turned her head and glanced at the door that had just opened. "Here's my husband."

Alex immediately realized what she saw in him, from a physical standpoint anyway. He was tall, about 6'4 with blond hair that appeared sun-bleached. He had deep brown eyes and a fairly athletic build. He looked as if he belonged on a surf board in southern California. Not bad for an accountant, he thought to himself. She could've done worse.

"Steven, meet my husband Todd Hampton. Todd, this is my client Steven Lily," she introduced them rather formally. The two men shook hands and greeted each other properly.

"Hey, man. Nice to meet you," Alex said.

"Nice to meet you too. I hear you and Chris used to know each other in college,"

"Yeah, small world huh?"

Small talk was awkward so Alex was relieved when Christina told him to go back to his dressing room. She kissed her husband and followed Alex behind the curtain.

"He seems nice," Alex ventured.

"Yeah, he is nice," she answered with a sidewise smile. "What is that look for?" She knew him too well.

"It's just that he's an accountant, Chris. Isn't he a little on the boring side for you?"

"Look, maybe I like boring. But for the record, he's not. He's pretty fun, especially for an accountant."

"Why on earth would you like boring?" he asked playfully.

"Oh, I don't know. I guess it hurts less." She smiled crookedly and averted her eyes. "Go get ready. You go on in half an hour. Hey, I think you have company."

Alex turned and saw his that mom, sister and Josh were all there. It was supremely comforting to Alex to see Josh. They shook hands and did the "guy hug" as his sister Sarah called it. There wasn't much time for chit chat. Christina greeted his mom and sister as if they were old friends. His mom was so happy to see Chris that she sort of clapped her hands together. It was a move she'd always done when Alex was younger. Chuckling under his breath, he quickly introduced Christina to Josh. They shook hands and exchanged "Nice to meet yous" before she moved along to check on the final preparations.

"Dude, I can see why she's held your attention all these years," Josh whispered to Alex after she'd left. "How are things going?"

"I've honestly been too busy to give it much thought. I asked her about the charm though. She gave me some odd answer about it reminding her where she'd been, whatever that means. Hey, where's Becky?"

"She's out front. I'd better go join her. There's a line of people waiting to storm the stage. Standing room only is great, but it's a pain to thread through. Good luck man. You'll do great."

"Hey, big brother. Got a hug for your sister before you go out there to get mauled by all the beautiful groupies?" Sarah asked as she embraced her brother.

"I always have time for you," he said, hugging her back. Turning to his mom he said, "Mom, I couldn't have done this without you."

"I know, sweetie. I know," his mother said as she let her oldest son put his forehead to hers. Theirs had been a tumultuous relationship that definitely had its ups and downs. Alex had the temperament of his father and her stubbornness. It had proved a difficult combination to live with. But, he knew she was very proud of him. He'd come so far, especially from where he'd once been.

When the time came for his set to start, Alex felt his nerves beginning to fray. He'd played small clubs hundreds of times, but this one was different. People had come to see him, had paid for a ticket, not just to enjoy free music. Granted, Butch Walker was the main pull, but there were people he didn't know here, interested in *his* music. The band was ready and he nervously awaited his introduction. Just before he took the stage, he felt a hand on his shoulder. He turned and looked deep into the blue eyes he'd dreamed about for many years. For a brief moment he saw the old Christina. The one who'd loved him without question. Was it possible she still felt the same? He brushed the thought away as quickly as it came to him.

"You're going to be great, Alex. Enjoy every moment of tonight. You deserve it all," she said with a smile and gave him a quick kiss on the cheek. "I'll be out front after the show."

"Okay. Hey, thanks Chris. It means a lot to me that you're here, even if you're only here because it's your job," he smiled as she walked away. The place on his cheek where her lips had been still tingled.

The show went perfectly. He played a full hour, performing three additional songs for an encore. The rush was better than any drug he'd ever taken. This was a high he could get used to. Butch gave his accolades when Alex was done. After watching Butch's performance which was awesome, he was ushered to a table near the exit of the club for his meet and greet. Copies of the first single had been given to everyone who'd purchased a ticket. He signed what seemed like a million autographs. Many girls slipped him their phone numbers as well. Temptation was everywhere. He could totally give in too. He had no commitments weighing him down. If he could just overcome the feelings that had resurfaced for someone he could never have.

Christina appeared about a half hour after the show ended. He was again ushered out, this time through the back door of the club where several cabs were waiting. The band and crew were all going for drinks at Tin Lizzy's. Josh and Becky caught up with them, along with Sarah. Lynda, Alex's mom, had decided it was time to call it a night.

"Are you and Todd coming with us?" he asked Chris, trying to appear nonchalant.

"Yes, I suppose I can go for a little while. Todd's going on home though. He has an early tee time tomorrow. Don't give me that look Alex!" she swatted his arm as he rolled his eyes.

"Tee time! That doesn't surprise me at all!" he laughed as he got in to one of the cabs and drove away. He rode with Josh, Becky and Sarah. She rode with Nick and the crew.

As they rode Becky said, "That's her?" in her nasally Rhode Island voice, "Wow, she's pretty. Too bad she's married. You guys would be a great pair."

Josh elbowed her slightly to get her to shut up.

"What? What'd I say?" Becky replied rolling her eyes at her husband.

"You were great tonight, Alex. You really look like you belong on the stage," Sarah chimed in trying to divert the conversation from Chris.

Alex knew she wanted him to be happy. She'd liked Chris back then, but had wondered aloud if working with her would ultimately do Alex more harm than good.

"Thanks, sis. It was awesome. There's no other word to describe it." The rest of the way they talked about what they liked about the show. Which songs were their favorites and which ones they thought the crowd like most? Alex was still floating on a cloud when they arrived.

"So, how did you like it? Your first performance as a Mastermind artist?" Christina asked as they sat at the bar. Josh and Becky were playing darts, and Sarah had gone to the restroom.

"It was awesome! I've never felt anything like that before. It's totally different from playing the dives for tips. I can't wait for the tour to start," he replied enthusiastically.

"Touring has its perks. I saw the hotties passing their digits to you. But, be mindful that it can be lonely sometimes too. Choose carefully which groupies you take back to the tour bus with you. Some of them may turn out to be psychos!" she laughed. "Make friends with your band. That will help." Things were okay. Conversation was easy and appropriate. Perhaps this wouldn't be so hard after all.

The band and crew joined him in toasting a successful first show and many of them drank more than they should have, although Alex stuck to Coca-Cola. The group started to thin out around 1:00 AM. Josh and Becky left first needing to pick up their son before heading home. Sarah left shortly after they did, claiming an early shift at the hospital where she worked. Pretty soon it was obvious that the party was over and everyone started making their way home.

"Hey Alex, how are you getting home?" Christina asked as they stumbled out of the door. High fives were given as various band members and crew made their way to cabs or waiting rides.

"I figured I'd take the bus. I don't have a car and I think my ride has had too much to drink," he poked her on the arm.

"Very funny, especially since I took a cab like the rest of you. I've already called a cab for me. Want me to call one for you too?"

"No, I like the bus. It gives me time to think."

"Okay, suit yourself. We'll talk soon. Congratulations on tonight!" She hugged him hard. His arms embraced her and he felt like holding on for the rest of his life. The hug lasted only a few seconds, and he wished it had gone on forever. He could smell the lavender shampoo she'd used that morning mixed with the smoky residue from the bar.

She broke the embrace just as her cab pulled to the curb. When she turned to leave, he called her name. When she looked back, he pulled her in and kissed her, right on the mouth. He didn't mean to, but couldn't stop himself. She lingered, briefly pressing her lips against his, before pulling away. Then she quickly backed away and got into the cab. As it pulled away from the curb, she wouldn't even look at him.

Alex watched her cab leave and cursed himself for his stupidity. She probably would have him reassigned to another rep. He'd kissed her, in public! How stupid could he be? But, he thought to himself, she didn't fight it, at least not at first. He looked around to see if anyone they knew was still there. No one seemed to have noticed the kiss, thankfully. As the new kid the last thing he wanted was to cause trouble.

There was no way he could go home alone with the taste of her lips still on his mouth. He needed to forget that and fast. He was feeling the urge to return to the old ways of dealing with issues. He knew where he could pick up just about any drug he wanted. But that was something he really didn't want to happen, so he fell back on his second strategy. He dug in his pocket and pulled out a random phone number. Brittney, whoever she was, he couldn't remember and didn't care. He dialed the number.

"Hey, this is Steven Lily from the show tonight," he said into the receiver of his cell. "Wanna meet me at the Westin in an hour?" Pause. "Great, ask the front desk for the room number when you get there."

Brittney Whoever would be treated to a luxurious room and great sex with an up and coming rock star, but she was not going back to his home. He decided to skip the bus and hailed a passing cab that took him to the hotel. He checked in and waited for Brittney to get there. He needed to erase Christina from his mind and he couldn't think of a better way to do it.

Christina got out of the cab in front of her house. Before she could make it to the stairs though, she vomited in the bushes. She'd feared this was going to happen, but thankfully, for her and the cab driver, she had been able to wait until she was home. After wiping the vomit from her mouth she went inside and tiptoed to the bathroom. She ran the shower and stepped into the hot water.

It was the alcohol, she tried to convince herself. She only let him kiss her because she'd been drinking. The alcohol and the euphoria of the evening had affected them both. She figured if she kept repeating the mantra enough eventually she'd believe it. She would go in her room, lie down next to her fantastic husband and try desperately to forget the fact that Alex had kissed her, and that for a second she'd let him. She grabbed a wash cloth and scrubbed her mouth trying to wash away the sensation that had been burned on her lips and into her memory. Nevertheless, it was back in full force.

This was not happening. She would not let it happen. She had a wonderful husband, terrific kids, and a great career. She would not be stupidly selfish and throw away everything she'd worked so hard for on a ghost from her past. This ghost was not just haunting her though. It had come back to life and now she would have to find a way to deal with it. This was unfamiliar territory for her.

Unsure of what to do, or how to handle the situation, she racked her brain for a solution. There was nothing she could do about it right now, except go to bed. After getting out of the shower and drying off she reached into the medicine cabinet and grabbed her Ambien. Two were in order tonight. These would allow her to forget everything, at least temporarily. She would deal with it all later. Right now she just wanted to sleep.

Chapter 14

Sleep didn't come though. Hours later she was still wide awake. She tried to stop replaying the kiss in her head, but she couldn't. She tried to forget the feel of his lips against hers. Her knees had weakened at his touch. That hadn't happened in years, not since the early years with Todd. It had felt natural, thrilling and completely wrong. That's how it'd always felt for her when it came to Alex. She'd known before the first blow up that things were too good to be true. The blistering fight about her algebra tutor had brought the façade crashing down.

For a few weeks after the fight, things had almost seemed normal, except Alex had started acting funny. There were times he would space out for hours, forgetting things they'd talked about. Then he'd seem to pull himself together and be the self-confident guy she'd first met. She noticed he'd become extremely self-conscious about his music and about how he was perceived by other people. He'd asked her once why she stayed with him knowing her friends didn't approve. She'd been honest. He was wonderful and had potential for greatness. She loved his music, and she loved the parts of himself he'd let her see. The confident lover and musician drew her in, but the tortured, vulnerable soul kept her there.

Alex and Chris had never said the words 'I love you' to each other. But she knew she had fallen head over heels for him. However, when things began to get heavy and deep between them, Alex had seemed to distance himself from her. She assumed he had some issues from the past he was dealing with, and figured when he was ready he'd talk about it. She had walked on eggshells since the fight, confused about what had set him off and not wanting to give him any reason for another blowup. He'd been true to his word though; it hadn't happened again.

By the middle of February, things became drastically different. She'd returned from class one afternoon to find him almost comatose. Next to him was a needle attached to an empty syringe. The harsh reality finally set in. Alex was on drugs. The meaning of the recent signs became clear- the forgetfulness, the spacey behavior, the paranoia, the agitation. They were all signs of drug abuse. The evidence before her was unmistakable! The syringe, the spoon, the lighter- he was using heroin. She got him into the shower and tried to revive him. Afterward he'd cried and begged for help. She'd had no idea what to do so once he was asleep, she'd called his mom and Lynda came to take him back home to Tucker for a while.

A few days later his sister called hysterical. Sarah was only 15 years old and had never seen her brother in this shape. Christina remembered the phone call vividly. It was close to 3:00 AM when her phone rang.

"Hello," she'd answered groggily.

"Chris? It's Sarah," she was crying and barely able to speak.

"Sarah? What's wrong?" She sat up in bed and turned the light on.

"I woke up because I heard Alex freaking out in the kitchen. He's railing on and on about the walls melting around him. He's just lying on the floor. He's really messed up!"

"Sarah, where is your mom?"

"She's not home. I don't know where she is. Chris, what should I do? He's scaring me! He keeps going on and on about how he's messed everything up and now that she's back, he doesn't know what to do."

Christina had no idea what that meant. Who was back? She refocused her attention. "Sarah, ask him what he took."

"Mescaline. He took mescaline. He said it was about an hour ago."

"I don't know what to do Sarah, but let's try water. Try to get him to drink some water. Maybe we can flush it out."

There was a pause for a long while. When Sarah came back she said he was sipping water but finding it difficult to keep the cup in his hands. They stayed on the phone for a while. Then Christina told Sarah to ask him about what was happening now. Sarah reported that the floor was no longer trying to swallow him, but the walls were still melting. Sarah asked him if he wanted to speak to her and he said no. He couldn't talk to her now. He started crying. He was a failure, she heard him scream. Why was she wasting her time with him? She should just go and leave him alone. Sarah cried harder. An hour went by, mostly in silence, when Sarah said he was sweating heavily. Christina suggested Sarah go and run a cool bath for him. She'd have to get him into the tub, fully clothed would be fine.

Christina heard the water running and then she heard him ask, "What if the drain tries to suck me down?"

"Tell him you won't let that happen, Sarah. Tell him you'll stay right there with him the whole time." By the time Alex had calmed down, dried off and Sarah got him to bed, it was after 5:00 AM. Christina hung up the phone and started crying. She was five hours away from Tucker, and there was nothing she could do to help him right now. She didn't know if she could ever help him, and she definitely knew that now was not the time to tell him she was pregnant.

It was at the end of this memory that she fell into a tortured, uneasy sleep.

Chapter 15

A couple of weeks went by before Alex gathered the nerve to talk to Christina again. He'd decided it was best to wait for the dust to settle and let her make the first move, but he was beginning to think she never would. They worked together pretty much every day, but she always made sure she came in after he did, with an intern attached to her hip, or with sound techs all around. They'd been busy too. They were finalizing the recordings and beginning the editing process.

It was now pushing mid-October, and the mid-November deadline for release was looming in his mind. The tour dates were nearly all in place. Twenty shows in two months. He'd okayed the list that Nick, one of the interns, had emailed him.

Alex had also been interviewed on a couple more local radio stations. Nick had accompanied them to all the interviews. Andrea made sure he got the recording schedule adjustments and kept him in the loop from the company's end. Alex understood why there were suddenly so many people around and why Chris kept her conversations brisk and strictly about the job. It was how it should be, he knew that, but it didn't feel right.

When his cell rang and registered her office number, his heart jumped. Okay Alex, the moment of truth, he thought. Follow her lead;

let her decide what happens from here. But it was just Andrea though, filling him in on the details of the first leg of the tour and the details for the CD release party that would be happening within the next month. He asked if he could speak to Christina to talk about some touring concerns. Andrea reluctantly put him through. She knows, he thought.

"Christina Hampton," she answered the phone.

"Hey, it's me," he replied not knowing what else to say.

"Hey Alex," she replied awkwardly. "What can I do for you?"

"Well, I was wondering what I needed to be aware of for this CD release party and if I could bring a date." Damn he sounded pathetic! Bring a date? What was wrong with him?

"Well, be prepared to perform at least two or three songs from the CD. I'll be in touch soon with wardrobe choices from Jillian and we'll probably bring Lawrence and his team in for styling. And, it's your party so of course you can bring a date. Anything else?"

"Chris, you can't keep pawning me off on other people. Eventually we're going to have to talk about what happened."

"I know," she sighed. "Just to let you know though, Nick is very capable and will be graduating at the end of this semester. I am most likely hiring him to do the very same job he's been doing with you now so you're in really good hands when he's there."

"Okay great, but you're my rep and I need to work with you. Will you be coming down to the studio soon? I think you need to hear some of the final cuts," he said.

"Yes, I'll come down to the studio whenever you need me to. I know you've been busy trying to get things finished. I didn't want to be in your way."

"You're never in the way, Chris. Hey, I think I've chosen the twelve tracks I want for the CD. I think we'll save the others for the next one," he paused for a moment. "I guess I need to apologize for the other night."

"No worries. We'd been drinking and got caught up in the moment, that's all." She sounded like she was trying to convince herself as well as him. He didn't have the heart to tell her he'd been completely sober when he kissed her. "Do you need me to come down today?" she asked.

"Well, no, I'm not in studio today. They're just editing what's already been recorded. I have another show this Saturday at the Roxy. Are you coming?"

"I'll be there to get the ball rolling, sure."

"Okay. I guess I'll see you there. I'll talk to you soon then?" he asked.

"Of course. Hey, by the way, Micah sent over the shots that he took with the band and the pictures from the Tabernacle. You'll want to see them and decide which ones to put in the CD jacket. I'll bring them with me on Saturday, okay."

"Okay, Chris. I'll see you then. Take care."

"Take care, Alex," she said as he hung up the phone.

It was true. She had been postponing any private contact between them that she could. She'd pretty much taken Nick as her own personal intern and kept him with her at all times when they worked on Steven Lily projects. Andrea had also been given more to do than just answer the phone and make copies. Christina told herself it was because she was busy with her other clients.

Michelle had been moved to the third tier A&R division now that her tour was well under way. Christina kept in touch with her manager and the team on the road in case there were any issues she needed to take care of, but for the most part she was done. Travis and Tawney were well on their way to release as well. The sooner she cut them loose, the sooner Joe would give her another client to work with.

In all honesty though, she was just trying to avoid a messy situation with Alex, who unfortunately, would still need a lot of work before he could be moved on. She was grooming Nick to step in and take her place as much as possible. Joe had made it clear that no other rep could take on this project, but he hadn't said she couldn't assign an able intern, under the guise of training, to assist her.

Alex leaned back against the cushions of his couch. He was actually home in the middle of the afternoon and didn't know what to do with himself. He'd written no new songs lately due to all the promotional activities and the exhaustion that engulfed him at the end of the day. Part of him really wanted to pick up his guitar and compose some new songs; he needed to sort out his feelings.

It wasn't only Chris, although she was a big part of it. It was also the adjustment to the lifestyle. He hadn't even had that much national exposure yet, other than the single that had been played in select markets, but he was already being recognized around town. He'd also met up with several of the girls who'd left their phone numbers at the Tabernacle show. Having girls at his disposal at a moment's notice was a rush at first, but one night stands only took his mind off things for that short time. It was nice to be recognized and given the kind of respect that had previously eluded him. But it was a lot to take in. Everyone had told him it would be a huge adjustment, but he had no idea. He knew more was to come once the tour started.

He decided it was time to buy a car. He'd hardly used any of his advance money. While he did love the bus and taking cabs, it made getting around to the studio, radio stations, and clubs a little difficult, especially when the schedule was tight. It was also much less impressive to the girls he met up with to show up on the bus, or stepping out of a cab. He didn't really care what they thought, after all he'd never see them again after that night, but he was ready for his lifestyle to match his position.

He called Josh and they met at 4:00 when Josh got off work. They hit several dealerships before walking out of the Acura dealership with the keys to a brand new RDX SUV. Alex had paid cash for it, something he never dreamed possible. He never thought he'd own a brand new car, much less a really nice one, and being able to walk away with no monthly payments was even more unbelievable.

Josh's phone rang; it was Becky trying to find out when he'd be home. When she heard Alex was there as well, she invited him over for dinner. An hour later, the three friends were enjoying grilled hamburgers and baked potatoes on Josh's deck. It was the most normal night Alex had experienced in a long time. He hadn't realized how much he missed just hanging out with his friends until now.

Chapter 16

Saturday's show at the Roxy came and went with much fanfare. Chris brought the photos and Alex gave his input on which ones he'd like to see in the CD jacket. He was interviewed by a reporter for the metro section of the Atlanta Journal and Constitution. The AJC photographer took photos of him, the band, the show, just about everything. The write up in the Sunday entertainment section of the paper gave an extremely positive review of his show and his music.

His phone started blowing up after people read the article. His mom, sister, friends, and former co-workers called to give their congratulations. Neighbors stopped by for a chat or shouted kudos as they passed him in the neighborhood. He was floating on cloud nine. He decided to throw a spur of the moment cookout to celebrate. Everyone who'd called or stopped by recently was invited. By 4:00 in the afternoon the party was in full swing.

Alex was flipping burgers and shooting the breeze with friends and neighbors when the phone rang. Sarah answered it and called him to take it. He handed the spatula off to his neighbor Russ and instructed him when to turn the burgers and chicken. He wiped the sweat from his brow as he walked into the house. His eyes took a moment to adjust to the darkness of the living room from the brightness outside. After blinking a few times, he moved to where Sarah had left the phone on the counter.

"Hello," he said brightly.

"Hey there!" It was Chris. "I just read the article. It's fantastic! Congratulations!"

"Thanks, it *was* pretty amazing," Alex said.

"This reporter is notorious for tough reviews, so to get one this good is awesome! I couldn't be any prouder of you, Alex."

He was momentarily stunned. She was proud of him. The feeling flooded through his body wrapping him in a warm blanket. He needed nothing more in life. "Hey, I'm having a little gathering to celebrate last night's success. Why don't you and your family come on over?" he asked. He really did want to celebrate with her. After all, she was the reason behind his success.

"Oh, thanks for the invitation, but we can't. Maybe some other time though. Hey listen, can you come by the office tomorrow? I have some exciting news to share with you."

"Yeah, I can come by, but can't you just tell me now?"

"I'd rather wait. It's about your tour," she paused. "But I guess I can tell you now. It'll fuel your euphoria a little more," she said.

"Okay, tell me already!" he said laughingly.

"We've added a stop on your tour. When you're in New York you'll be performing on Letterman on Thursday before your Saturday show."

"I'm doing Letterman?" he practically shouted. "That wasn't in my itinerary. How did you swing that?"

"I didn't want to tell you until I knew for sure. Confirmation just came in Friday and I had some details to work out."

"How did you get me on Letterman so fast?"

"I know people, Alex. Things are going to move fast. You've done great on your radio interviews around town and the single is getting a lot of air time. I heard it on XM radio a few times as well. That's national exposure. Once the tour starts, that exposure is really going to expand. You have a radio circuit in almost every city."

"I don't know what to say, or how to thank you enough," he was almost gushing, but he couldn't help himself.

"Hey, just doing my job. Get back to your party. Will you be in studio tomorrow? I have a few documents I need you to sign."

"Yeah, I'll be in around noon. I can come up before then if you'd like. Maybe take you to lunch to say thank you."

"I'll say maybe to lunch, but please stop by before you go in studio," she said. "Now, get back to your friends. You deserve it. See you tomorrow."

"Alright, see you then. Bye, Chris." Alex said, still giddy with the thought of being on Letterman.

"Bye, Alex."

He hung up the phone and practically skipped to the back yard.

"I'm going to be on Letterman!" he shouted.

A loud roar went up from the crowd gathered in his yard. There was clapping, shouting, whistles, pats on the back, and hugs all around. Alex had never felt more exhilarated in his life. His only regret was that Chris wasn't there to share it with him.

The next day he got to her office a little before 11:00. He greeted Andrea who told him to go on in; she was expecting him. He walked in and was pleased to see that she was alone. He liked Nick, but the kid was sometimes in the way. At his small knock on the door, she looked up from her computer. She took her glasses off as she greeted him.

"Hey!" she said brightly. "I was just printing all the documents that need to be signed. I also need you to make a list of items you'd like to have in your dressing room while on tour."

"Wow, you are all business aren't you?" he asked teasingly.

"Well, it's my job after all," she replied smiling. "Just look these over and sign at the bottom. You can get the list back to me later," she said handing him the forms.

He sat down and read through the documents signing them quickly at the bottom. He'd work on the dressing room list this afternoon. "So, are you going to go to lunch with me voluntarily, or am I going to have to carry you against your will?"

She checked her watch and looked at her day planner. "I guess I have time for a quick bite. Sure why not? Where do you want to go?"

"How about RuSan's? I'm in the mood for some sushi," he suggested. He'd never actually eaten sushi, but was willing to give it a try.

"Sounds great. I'll get my purse and my jacket. We can walk if that's okay with you. It's such a pretty day," she said.

"A walk it is then," he said as he moved to the side to let her pass. She stopped to speak briefly with Andrea so he waited for her by the elevator.

They exited the building and turned left. The day was bright and the air was crisp. Late fall days were probably his favorite in Atlanta. The sky was bluer than any other time of the year. The air was warm in the sun, but slightly nippy in the shade. They walked in silence for a moment just soaking up the gloriousness of the day. He broke the silence first.

"If you weren't working today, what would you be doing?" he asked.

"I'd be at Piedmont Park with my kids. Probably playing Frisbee. Jack's just learning how to handle the Frisbee. Kate's pretty good at it. What about you? If you weren't working today, what would you be doing?"

"I'd be at Piedmont Park too. Probably playing my guitar and writing new songs. I'd probably see you and your kids romping around having a good time. I might even write a song about it," he answered.

"Sounds like fun. If you had your case open, I'd probably give the kids a few dollars to throw in," she said playfully.

"Thanks! A few dollars. A big time record executive like you?" he teased sarcastically.

"Hey, you said we weren't working. I'd give you my card and tell you to call me if I was working," she smiled.

They reached the restaurant and were seated on the patio. The server brought them each glasses of water. Chris ordered hot tea as well. While they waited for their food they continued the light banter they'd had during the walk over.

"So, why did you leave teaching?" Alex asked.

"Well, honestly it was a little overwhelming. I mean, there's a lot of pressure when you're responsible for shaping the future of kids. It's not as scary as knowing I have to shape the lives of my own children, but still. I went into teaching thinking I could make a difference in the world. What I realized was that the obstacles were way too powerful for me to handle.

"In the school I worked at we had a lot of kids who were in pretty disadvantaged situations. Dads in jail, moms strung out on crack, a lot of grandmas raising their grandkids, a lot of poverty. Some kids were resilient and were able to succeed in school in spite of their circumstances. Others, well, they were too worried about how they'd eat after school, or if they'd get beat when mom's new boyfriend came home. It was too much for me. I did it for four years and that was enough," she paused contemplatively.

"The really sad part is that school is literally five miles from this restaurant. I took some of my students to Phipp's Plaza one day for a movie and they were in complete awe of the surroundings."

"I'm a little awed by Phipp's myself," he broke in.

"Me too, at least I used to be. But these girls had never been past the Varsity. I remember we passed Ann Taylor and one of the girls said I should buy the shirt in the window. When I told her it was $55.00 and I couldn't afford it, her eyes nearly bugged out of her head. She couldn't believe that *anyone* would pay that much for a shirt. I remember that moment every time I pass by Ann Taylor."

"That's crazy," was all he could say. He hadn't seen her this open and exposed in years. It was nice to see the realness.

"People think teaching is easy. Summers off, vacation time for Thanksgiving, Christmas and spring break. Working 7:30-3:30. They don't see what's really involved. They've never tried to be a teacher, a mother, a father, a doctor, a lawyer, a psychologist, and a conflict resolution expert all at the same time.

"At some point in the day, which never really ended at 3:30, between dealing with DFACS, health issues, fights and tears, and temper tantrums, I was supposed to teach my kids how to read and do math. Many of my kids came to me in August at least four grade levels below where they should have been and I was expected to get them to pass a grade level test by mid-April. One year I had everything from Pre-Primer reading to a kid reading at a 12th grade level in one 5th grade class. I was provided a curriculum that taught to the middle, but pretty much ignored the top and the bottom. I just felt ineffective and burned out. So I left."

"Do you miss it? Any part of it?" he asked.

"Yeah, I do. I don't miss giving every standardized test known to man, or dealing with arguments over stupid things, or being cursed out by parents. Yes, that happened a lot," she said at the look on his face. "I even had a girl throw a chair at me once. I don't miss that stuff or the mountain of paperwork.

"But I do miss the kids. I never had a boring day at work. They would tell interesting and entertaining stories, and if I ever gave them a group project that involved some kind of performance, I'd always get the funniest rap song and usually a dance to go with it. One time there was a dance after school and I stayed to chaperone. The kids had me out on the dance floor trying to teach me some of their moves. It was hysterical! I looked like such an idiot, but it was awesome." Her eyes glistened. "I do miss it, a lot actually."

"Do you keep in touch with any of your former students?" he asked. He wanted this to go on forever. She was finally opening up to him, telling him about her life. It was more conversation than they'd had since they'd been reintroduced.

"I keep in touch with a few of them. One boy's mom started a mobile dog grooming business, and we hired her to take care of Max, our dog. Another student actually has an aunt who works for Columbia Records so we keep in touch through work. The one I talk to the most though is a girl whose mom died while she was in my class."

"What happened to her mom?"

"We'd gone our end of the year field trip that day. We had to leave early so they could have plenty of time to see all the exhibits at the zoo and enjoy the cookout in Grant Park. This girl was tardy a lot so I made it clear that she had to be at school no later than 7:30. So, she and her sister spent the night at their grandmother's house down the street from the school. During the night the apartment she lived in with her mother caught fire and her mother was killed. My principal found out as the bus was pulling out of the parking lot that morning. She let us go so the girl could have one more normal day. We were told when we returned. It was so sad."

She welled up with tears even now. Alex couldn't help himself either as a tear escaped his eye.

"I wanted to take her in, her and her sister. Todd was on board with it. Our house was big enough. We didn't have our own kids yet. But they went to live with their mother's sister in Athens. We talk on the phone about once a month. She's doing great. She's one of the resilient ones." Chris fell quiet and breathed deeply with memory.

"So, how did you get into this business? It's a big leap from teaching 5th grade."

"Honestly, I knew someone who knew someone. I was looking for a change and my friend Wes, who knows everyone under the sun it seems, asked me a very good question. He asked, 'What would you do for free?' I thought back to college, and how I loved being involved with the music scene, about the months I volunteered at the radio station. My answer was something with music where I didn't have to perform. He said he'd make some calls.

"Wes introduced me to Joe, who is now my boss at Mastermind. Joe taught me the aspects of the business, and as he moved up, he brought me along with him. Along the way, I've cultivated great working relationships that have proved to be beneficial for me and my clients. I met Butch through this job and he's become a great friend. He even golfs with Todd every once in a while."

"You're really good at your job. I know I've told you that before, but it bears repeating," he said as he sipped his Miso soup.

"Thanks, it's easy to do when the talent is there. That's one great thing about Mastermind. They are really selective about who they sign. Some artists, if you can call them that, only sound good when their voices are completely digitized. Hell, I even sound good when my voice is layered and digitally enhanced."

"You are a pretty bad singer, I remember. You're lucky you're pretty because you couldn't carry a tune in a bucket," he said and they laughed together.

"That's only funny because it's true!" she said, feigning irritation.

Their food arrived and Alex followed her lead. He filled the little bowl with soy sauce and used the chop sticks to pick up what looked like something he might use for bait while fishing tied to a ball of rice. He dipped it in the soy sauce and then popped the whole thing in his mouth, just as she did. As he started to chew the slimy fish he almost choked. His eyes began to water as he sputtered and tried diligently to swallow the piece. She eyed him suspiciously.

"You've never eaten sushi before, have you?" she asked.

He coughed as the tears rolled down his face. He grabbed his glass of water and took a long swig. "Is it that obvious?"

She laughed freely and melodiously. "Then why did you want to come here?"

"I thought I'd try something new. Perhaps a burger is more my style," he admitted laughing at himself. The harder she laughed, the more he laughed, and soon tears of sheer joy were streaming down his face.

"Hey, it's an acquired taste. Come on, I'll get this wrapped up and we'll go over to the Tower Café to get your burger. It's almost time for your studio appointment anyway." She motioned for the check.

"Let me get this, Chris," he said reaching for his wallet after wiping away the last of the drops on his face.

"But you didn't even eat it," she protested.

"I don't care. It was just great to spend some time with you outside of the office, or clubs or studios. Come on, friends let friends pay for their lunch sometimes," he smiled.

"Okay, fine. But just this once…as friends," she said, smiling back.

"Friends then?" he asked.

"Friends," she answered.

As they walked back to the office building, he told her a funny story about trying to fix the brakes on his friend's truck. They'd been testing the brakes at midnight when they realized neither one of them had reconnected the cables. They ended up crashing into the bushes in a neighbor's yard. Luckily, no one was hurt. They had to pay the neighbor for landscaping repairs, but other than the damage to their wallets they were fine. They stopped by the corner café and he ordered his burger to go. She walked with him to the studio and said hello to the techs and sound engineers.

"Thanks for a fun afternoon," she said extending her hand. "I'm glad we did this."

"Thanks for joining me," he said taking her hand. They shook and then he pulled her in for a quick hug. "I'm happy we did this today."

"I'm glad we're friends, Alex," she whispered.

"Me, too."

"If I don't see you before then, I'll see you at the release party. I have a surprise in store for you," She winked as she turned to go.

"Oh, and I guess I'm just going to be left to wonder what it is for the next week, huh?"

"You got it!" she waved from the elevator.

"That's mean, you know!" he shouted after her.

"I know!" was all he heard as the doors shut behind her.

She returned to her office to find Andrea pretending to be working on something. It was obvious that she was waiting for Christina's return to get the inside scoop on the unexpected lunch date.

"So, how was your lunch?" the assistant questioned.

"It was fine, thank you," Christina said turning into her office.

Andrea followed, not about to be put off so fast. "Hold on there, missy. The one guy you've avoided being alone with like the plague for the past month asks you to lunch and you just up and go? With no intern to chaperone you? What gives?"

Christina sat at her desk and flipped her Rolodex to the M's. "It was fine. We talked, as friends. Nothing inappropriate came up and nothing inappropriate happened. We finally did some much needed catching up."

"So, that's it? You go on one lunch date and everything is forgiven and forgotten?" Andrea looked disappointed there wasn't more. She was unabashedly nosy, but could be trusted with most secrets.

"I forgave him a long time ago, Andrea. I don't think I'll ever forget what happened back then, but it's time to move past it. He's my client, and I need to give him a shot. It was nice to talk about things other than work or relationships. I guess we're just getting to know each other again. Now, if you'll excuse me, I have a *huge* favor to call in for the release party next week." Andrea shrugged her shoulders and went back to her desk. Christina shook her head as she dialed. She hoped she could work enough magic to make a miracle happen. It was very short notice, but there was someone she wanted to come to the party. Hopefully, she could persuade this person to do a guest performance with Alex.

Chapter 17

The CD was officially released on Tuesday, November 18. Alex and Christina didn't talk much before the CD release party. She was working furiously monitoring the charts and radio air times during the week. The single had been out for over a month and had broken into the top twenty. That was unheard of for a previously unknown artist. By Friday afternoon "A Little Chunk of My Soul" had placed in the top ten on the local charts. Alex was a hit in the Atlanta area.

Nationally, he was climbing as well. From Wednesday to Friday he jumped five spaces to number 45. Not bad for someone with limited national exposure. After his tour got under way, and especially after the Letterman appearance, they were guaranteed a top ten spot.

She, Nick and Andrea spent the rest of the week following up with contacts for the party. They reconfirmed guests scheduled to attend, finalized details with the caterer, made sure Micah and his team were set, along with Jillian, Lawrence and their teams. By Friday evening they were exhausted. The last call of the day was to Alex. Nick confirmed that he'd be at Center Stage by 5:00 for sound checks and wardrobe.

This was the first time she'd ever held a CD release party at Center Stage. Usually they held them at the Variety Playhouse, or the Cotton

Club. But Alex had been adamant about holding it at Center Stage. It was a very historic theater in Atlanta, hosting artists like Etta James, the Donnas, BB King and Santana to name a meager few.

Alex said the first concert he ever saw in Atlanta had been at Center Stage, although it was called something else way back when. He remembered the cool vibe he'd felt in the place and how he'd gotten swept away by the atmosphere. Ever since then, he'd wanted to perform there. What better time than his first release party?

The venue was cool, and Christina loved its historical flavor, but trying to figure out the parking situation was a nightmare! Industry guests would be shuttled in by limos that would then be parked in a nearby lot. She made sure the other nearby lots regulated what they were charging for parking. It was ridiculous to expect people to pay $20.00 for parking to attend a party they'd been *invited* to.

She went home and collapsed on the sofa. It was after 9:00 when she woke up. Her family was nowhere to be seen. She sat up groggily and stretched. She padded upstairs and found the kids sleeping soundly and Todd reading.

"Hey there, sleeping beauty," he said when she entered the bedroom. "Have a nice nap?"

"Yeah," she said climbing into bed next to him. "I didn't even hear you guys come in. How long was I out?"

"About four hours, I guess. We got home around 5:30 and you were sacked out. I took the kids to Pizza Hut for dinner. You were sleeping so soundly I hated to wake you."

"Thanks, honey. Things will calm down soon and I'll be back to normal. We're still having the party on Sunday, right?" she asked as she got up to change into her pajamas. She brushed her long dark hair and pulled it into a low braid to keep it from getting tangled during the night.

"Yeah," Todd said rolling on his side to face her. "I've taken care of everything. Have I told you how beautiful you are?"

"Not today," she smiled as she rubbed cleansing gel on her face. "Still think I'm beautiful?" she asked turning toward him with green goop on her face. She held her hands up in hooks and growled, pretending to be a scary monster. It was something she did with Jack every day, minus the face cream.

He laughed, "How could I not find that face lovely?"

She rinsed her face, brushed her teeth and climbed back in bed. "I'm sorry I haven't been able to help you plan your birthday party. I promise I won't stay too late at the party tomorrow night. Are you going to come?" she asked as she snuggled down under the covers.

"No, I think I'll skip this one if it's okay with you. I'm going to pack tomorrow and start getting ready for the trip next week."

"Oh, I forgot that was coming up. Todd, there is no way I can take a week off work right now to go to Michigan for Thanksgiving."

"I know. That's why I asked my mom to ride with us. She'll be able to help with the kids and the driving. We'll celebrate Thanksgiving as a family when we get back. Hey, it's okay," he said hugging her close when he saw her frown. "It's just one Thanksgiving. You don't like Michigan anyway. Don't feel bad."

"I'm just starting to wonder if this job is worth missing out on family stuff like this," she said pensively.

"Well, that's something you have to decide for yourself, sweetie. If you want to take a leave of absence after this project, I'd be okay with it. It would be nice to see you more. But it's completely up to you. Let's go to sleep. We both have busy days ahead of us," he said as he rolled to turn off the light.

"I don't deserve you, you know," she said in the dark, nuzzling against his chest.

"Yes, you do," he said.

Center Stage was decked out to the nines. Alex stood mesmerized as he looked around the ancient club. The venue had been draped in white and deep red fabric. Round tables had been strategically placed in the area near the stage. Tables were covered in alternating white and ruby linens. White tables had dark red rose center pieces while red tables were graced with pristine white rose arrangements. It was a breathtaking sight. He completed his sound checks with the band and went back stage to get ready for the festivities. Jillian had chosen an all black ensemble for him for the evening. The Armani suit was definitely not his normal style, but he liked it. It wasn't overly formal, and it allowed him to move freely while he was on stage. At 8:30 he joined the party.

There were all sorts of people at the party. Other Mastermind recording artists were there, high level executives, and the recording crew as well. But then there were regular people there. His mom Lynda, his sister and her husband Dave, Josh and Becky, his friends from the graphics studio he'd worked at before signing, his band members. He'd brought another groupie to the party, Vicki Whoever. He knew it was wrong to treat these women like objects, but they would never have given him a second look if he didn't have a major label recording contract. He justified his using them by thinking they were just using his him for a fame buzz.

Amid the glamorous surroundings, his glance kept returning to Chris. She looked stunning tonight. Her long dark hair glistened under the theater's lights. She was wearing a red halter dress with a very low cut back. She was laughing with some of the artists who were there and hadn't seen him come in. As he gazed at her, she turned to look straight at him. It was as if she knew he was watching her. She smiled and excused herself from the group she was talking with. She made her way over to Alex and Vicki.

"Hi there!" she said brightly. She turned to Vicki and introduced herself. Alex heard none of it. His heart was beating out of his chest. The two women exchanged pleasantries. An AJC photographer asked Alex and Christina to pose for a picture for the article to be printed in the following Monday's Peach Buzz section. He moved to stand next to her with a slightly uneasy smile. "What's wrong?" she asked.

"Guys, act like you like each other, will ya?" the photographer called out. "Move in closer please."

They moved together and he put his arm around her waist. They posed for the photos, but he held on even after the photographer had moved on. She politely removed his arm.

"This is not the time or place, Alex," she said looking at him hard.

"I know, but you're so beautiful. I just can't take my eyes off you."

"Try," she said walking away.

A few moments later she climbed the stairs to the stage and introduced herself, thanked everyone for coming and then gave them an introduction of the artist everyone had come to see. The band took the stage and the music began. Alex came out and performed his set. The set combined a nice blend of ballads and more up-tempo songs that kept the crowd singing along. As the set ended, and the crowd applauded, she came back on stage.

"Ladies and gentlemen, I hope you enjoyed that as much as I did. Now, I have a special surprise for you, Alex," she said turning to address him. "Please welcome to the stage Chino Moreno from Deftones!"

Alex's eyes flew to the other side of the stage. Chino Moreno was one of his favorite artists. He moved to her side as the crowd roared with approval. "How did you…?"

"I called in a pretty big favor," she said next to his ear. "Enjoy." She moved off stage as Chino took up a guitar. Together he and Alex played, alternating between Alex's songs and Deftones songs. She smiled at him knowing he was obviously in heaven. She appeared pleased, and he saw her make her way to the back of the room and prepared to leave.

Near the end of the last song he saw her slip out. As soon as it was done he hugged Chino and hurried after her, ignoring the calls for more and the beckoning of those wanting to mingle with him. He reached the door just in time to see her car pulling away. He stood, disappointed and breathless, at the doorway watching her taillights fade into the darkness.

Reluctantly, he rejoined the party and Vicki Whoever. His mom and sister rushed to him with congratulatory kisses and hugs. Josh greeted him shouting about how cool it was to see him play with Chino Moreno. Noting the tight smile and distance in his eyes, Lynda asked him what was wrong. Sarah could see it too. He shrugged it off and told them nothing was wrong. The party was still going strong.

Sarah leaned in and whispered to him, "Don't do it big brother. Don't fall for her now. It won't do either of you any good."

"It's too late, sis. I fell a long time ago and never got up. But hey, this is a party. Let's have a good time."

The party ended a few hours later and he took Vicki Whoever back to his hotel room. He did not invite her to stay the night. After she left he took a shower and sat on the couch wrapped in the hotel robe, staring out at the city below. What was he going to do? He was completely and irretrievably in love with the one woman he could never have.

Chapter 18

Alex sat there, reflecting back to the first time he realized how much he loved her. And to the time when things had started to go terribly wrong. After that first horrible explosion he'd had toward her, she had forgiven him, no questions asked. She was completely accepting of him, faults and all. At least what she knew of him anyway. He loved her for that. He loved her for her unwavering positive nature. She always saw the good in everyone, especially him. It had scared the hell out of him.

He had begun to feel the urge to pull away, but desperately wanted, no needed, to stay. The drugs had helped him cope with the two warring sides of his mind, and he stayed. That all changed though when Audrey showed back up, standing in his bedroom, after his shower.

"What are you doing here, Audrey?" he questioned as he walked past her into the bedroom.

"I had to see you, Alex. I want you back, I need you back," she replied following him.

"Too late, I have a girlfriend now. You need to leave," he said returning to the bathroom with his clothes and shutting the door behind him. He leaned on the sink and breathed deeply.

This wasn't happening; it was just a bad hallucination. He put on jeans over his boxers and then pulled a blue t-shirt over his head. He could cast her out for good this time, he thought. He had Chris now. There was no way he was going to let a manipulative crack head like Audrey screw things up.

After taking one more deep breath and arming himself with a belly full of resolve, he opened the bathroom door ready to face the most destructive person who'd ever been in his life. The problem was that Audrey was like a train wreck; he didn't want to look at it, or even want to know what happened, but he could never stop himself from peeking. Before he knew it he'd be helping with the debris removal.

She was sitting on his bed when he came out. He stood by the wall and waited, not saying anything for a moment. He felt his pulse quicken and heat rising in his cheeks. He was angry. Angry at her for leaving, angry at her for coming back, angry at himself for never being strong enough to turn her away.

"I told you to leave, Audrey."

"I know you did, but I'm not going. I need to talk to you."

"I don't have anything to say to you. You need to leave before my girlfriend comes back."

"You can't be serious about her. She's a little too goody-goody for you, don't you think?' she asked as she stood to face him.

Audrey was the polar opposite of Christina. She was petite with blond streaked hair that fell to her shoulders. Audrey had a much curvier figure than Christina. Her shape was full hourglass. Christina had a longer, leaner frame that had a sweet softness to it. Audrey, though more buxom, had a hard edge to her look. What was it about her that refused to release its hold on him?

"My girlfriend is great. Don't say anything negative about her. She's been better for me than you ever were." He steeled his eyes against hers.

"That's harsh, Alex." She moved in a little closer to him. "I just want to make you happy. I know I've done you wrong in the past, more than once, but you know I love you. You know no one else can love you like I do."

She trailed her fingers up his forearms lightly and tilted her head slightly so that she met his eye through her upturned lashes.

"Don't, Audrey. You need to stop now." He gritted his teeth as he spoke and closed his eyes. He missed her sly smile. He knew she had almost accomplished what she'd set out to do, and he tried with all his might to withstand her temptation.

"You might need me to stop, Alex, but do you want me to stop?" She slid her hand down his neck as she exhaled gently against his lips.

He broke away seconds before the kiss came. He moved to the other side of the room putting as much distant between the two of them as he could.

"Why are you back? Why now? You've been gone nearly eight months."

"I know it's been a long time. I need to apologize for that Alex, but I was trying to clean myself up. I went to rehab. I've been sober for months now. I also got a job at Eastern States Bank and have been working really hard. I'm trying to better myself so that I can be someone you'd be proud of."

She spoke with a tone of genuine sincerity. Alex was hesitant to believe her, but she sounded so real.

"It's too late. I've moved on and so should you," he sighed as he sat on his bed with his head in his hands. Damn it, not now! Not when things were almost perfect!

"It's never too late for us, Alex," she said as she slid across the floor to stand right in front of him. "We're supposed to be together. Didn't you miss me, even a little bit?" she teased as she stroked his hair.

"I missed you every day for four months! But I'm different now. I can't do this again." He turned his head and looked directly in her eyes. He grabbed her forearms to stop her from touching him. "Please leave before something happens that we can't take back." His eyes were almost pleading with hers.

"Okay, I'll go," she backed away and made a move toward the door. "But, can I have one small kiss for the road? I mean, if this is truly the end of us, I need something to remember you by."

She straddled his lap before he could respond. She draped her arms around his neck and placed her lips gently on his. He resisted for only a moment. Then his lips parted and welcomed her tongue. He wrapped his arms around her and pulled her in. He couldn't stop himself.

It was the same feeling he experienced before shooting up. He knew he shouldn't do it, knew he'd regret it the minute the high ended, but he had to have the high "just one last time". She tugged on his earlobe with her teeth and he felt a shudder go through him. She pulled his shirt up and ran her tongue up his chest as she pulled the shirt away from his body. She moved his hands to her pants and guided them to pull down the zipper.

What they did wasn't making love. It was hard, raw and edgy. It felt wrong the entire time, but he couldn't make himself stop. His ultimate drug had retuned and taken full hold of him again.

An hour later she left smiling as if she'd just gotten away with murder. He was lying in his bed naked, smoking a cigarette. What the hell had he done?! What would he say to Chris? Audrey would be back. They had said it wouldn't happen again, but that's what they always said. Chris didn't deserve this. She deserved someone who could love her as fully as she loved in return. She deserved someone who wasn't haunted by a demon who kept showing up. She deserved someone who could be loyal to and honest with her.

He began to cry as he lay there knowing he was about to lose the best thing that had ever happened to him. He didn't know what else to do, so he made the call. He needed to forget everything, forget the pain he still felt from Audrey and forget the pain he was going to cause Christina. He shot up more heroin than normal, but this was a desperate circumstance.

Christina found him later that afternoon. He was passed out on the floor of his room, barely able to move or talk, wearing only his boxers. She was terrified and began to cry silent tears, but she tried to remain strong. She helped him to the shower, and stood in the water, fully clothed, with him.

Unable to stand fully on his own, he held on to her for dear life. His body shook all over and he was sure that any minute his legs would give way, but the surprisingly strong arms wrapped around him and held him steady. He sobbed heaving, gulping sobs as he came to enough to realize she was caring for him. Once again, she was there, no questions, no blame. He couldn't take it anymore. He'd tell her everything as soon as he was sober.

After they'd dried off, she made him some ramen noodles and helped him eat. They'd said nothing of substance to each other. A couple of "I've got yous" as she was getting him out of the shower and into bed. One "Here, you need to eat," as she fed him the noodles. He responded with mumbled thanks. He grasped her wrist as she held the spoon for him. The tears stung his eyes again and for the first time he noticed the worry behind her eyes. When he was done with the noodles she climbed in bed with him and held him as he fell asleep.

In the morning she was gone, and so was the remainder of his stash and everything that went with it. She'd cleaned out his closet and drawers, gathering everything she could find that had to do with drugs. He went into the living area expecting to see her eating cereal and watching the news. He was ready to come clean with her. He wanted to tell her everything, thank her for taking care of him and thank her for getting rid of everything in the apartment. He was ready to get help, and with her by his side, he was sure it would stick this time. He was even ready to tell her about Audrey. Instead, he saw his mom sitting on the couch holding an envelope.

"Hey ma," he said a bit surprised. "What are you doing here?"

Lynda Lily looked up at her oldest son with a serious expression. "Christina called me last night. She told me what happened."

Alex sat down on the couch next to his mother, head drooped down. "Ma, I'm so sorry. You have no idea how sorry I am."

"You need to read this while I'm packing up some of your things. I'm taking you home for a while until you can get yourself straightened out," Lynda handed him the envelope and went into his room.

Alex slowly opened the envelope terrified of what he already knew the letter said. He read it slowly, not once but twice before breaking down into gut wrenching sobs.

Dear Alex,

    I don't know what's going on with you right now, but I do know it's more than I know how to handle. I wish you felt comfortable enough with me to talk about what's bothering you instead of turning to drugs. I know things have been awkward with us since our fight. I have tried to let you know I forgive you, but I don't know what else to do. The drugs scare me, and looking back now I can see that you've been using for a while, and that I missed it. Obviously it's not something you're proud of doing or you wouldn't have hid it from me.

That's why I called your mom. She said she'd helped you through this before and I honestly think she can help you much more now than I can.

She's going to take you home for a while and get you cleaned up. I'll be here when you get back and I'll be ready to do anything I can to help you stay clean. I have faith that you will come through this and you'll be a stronger, better person because of it. I'm only sorry that I am not strong enough to take this journey with you.

I'll understand if you are mad at me and don't want to talk for a while. But, if you can find it in your heart to forgive me, and you want to talk, you know how to reach me. I'll talk to your professors and see what needs to be done about the rest of the quarter. I'll take care of what I can down here. You take care of yourself at home.

I am so sorry I had to do this. Please know that I love you with all my heart and will always be here for you. I miss you already.

Love,
Christina

He moved across the hotel room and he pulled the letter out of his guitar case and read it again. She'd really had no idea what had been going on with him. She'd tried her best to understand, but he'd given her nothing. This letter was the first time she'd said she loved him. It hurt just as much to read it now as it had back then. He kept the letter in his guitar case so it would always be with him. It was his one real connection to love, to knowing that someone in the world once loved him enough to get him the help he'd so desperately needed.

He took another quick shower to get the remaining smell of Vicky Whoever off his body. Tomorrow was Sunday. He had to talk to Chris and it couldn't wait until Monday. He would find her house and go for a visit. It would be hard with her husband and kids there, but he needed to talk to her, and at least clear the air about the whole Audrey situation. It had plagued him for long enough. He'd pick up his car first thing in the morning. He didn't want to take a cab to the suburbs. It would cost a fortune. Besides he didn't want to look like a complete loser in front Todd. Somehow he couldn't shake the need to compete with Todd, but for what? Todd had already won.

Chapter 19

At noon Alex drove away from the hotel. The valet had been slow in bringing his car around, but now he was on his way before he could change his mind. He had gotten her address from Mapquest and headed toward the Northwest metro area. He had no idea what he was going to say, or what he could say with her family there. He just knew that it was time to do some explaining and trying to do that in her office with phones ringing, people interrupting and fax machines blaring would not do. He'd never been much of a planner so he decided to stick with what had worked for him up till now. He would just wing it and see where things led.

He rang the doorbell at 12:30. Not a bad drive from the city, not next door, but not terribly far away. Still, he was a bit surprised that she lived this far out. He remembered her eagerness to move into the heart of the city and teach in an underserved urban school. Wow, he thought, her life turned out so different from what she'd planned. A bit to his surprise, Todd answered the door.

"Steven, hey man. You're a little early, but come on in," Todd greeted him shaking his hand heartily. Early? Early for what? "Christina's in the kitchen getting the food ready."

"Call me Alex, please. Steven is really just my performance name," he said as they walked through the foyer.

Todd led him through a large entryway. On one side was a room that was probably supposed to be a formal dining room, but had been turned into an office/den area. It was paneled in a deep wood. A dark cherry desk took up much of one corner. A green desk lamp sat on the edge of the desk giving it a very businesslike look. The seriousness of the room was tempered by crayon and marker drawings taped to the sides of the desk. It was easy to distinguish between Kate's drawings and Jack's scribbles. He couldn't help smiling when he saw them.

On the other side was a semi-formal sitting room decorated in whites and pastel blues. He noticed the baby gate blocking the entrance to the room, probably not the place to be scrubbing crayon and marker from the walls or upholstery. It reminded him of a room from Better Homes and Garden, not exactly the carefree, mish mash décor Christina had liked in college. Her dorm room had been decorated in a myriad of colors amid antiques and garage sale bests.

They passed a flight of stairs and went into the large family room, kitchen, dining area space. Christina was at the sink washing vegetables. She was wearing light blue Capri pants and a white long sleeved T-shirt. Her feet were bare exposing her bright red toenails. She'd always hated wearing shoes. He remembered how she always kicked them off the minute she walked in a door, got in a car, even during class. Her dark hair was pulled back into a low ponytail. She was wearing her glasses and her face was scrubbed clean. She looked exactly as she did in college, fresh faced, and serious. He loved a girl in glasses and she looked damn good in hers. She was scrubbing those vegetables as if she were a surgeon about to perform open heart surgery with them. He'd never seen someone wash vegetables like they'd just cussed at her. She looked up in total shock to see him standing there.

"Alex, what are you doing here?" she asked surprised. "So early, I mean," she tried to cover before Todd could become suspicious. She didn't want him to know Alex hadn't been invited to the celebration. That he'd just shown up at their house.

"Well, I just thought I'd come out early and see what I could do to help," he played along. He caught on fast. He knew she would explain as soon as Todd left the room.

"I'm going to start setting up the tables outside. Hey Alex, mind giving me a hand in the backyard? There're tables and chairs to move." Todd asked.

"Not at all, I'll be out in a bit. I do need to talk shop with Chris for a moment though."

"Cool. Christina will show you how to get out through the basement," Todd replied walking toward a door Alex assumed led to the basement. "Hon, mom's bringing the kids back after Jack wakes up from his nap."

"Okay, thanks. Let me know when you're ready for the food," she spoke her words to his back, her eyes never leaving Alex's face. They heard the door shut and she waited a few seconds before she spoke. "What are you doing here?" she asked in almost a hiss.

"I needed to talk to you and didn't want to wait until Monday. What's going on here today? What am I early for?"

He smiled inwardly. She looked so cute when she was flustered. He remembered doing things on purpose just to watch the color rise in her cheeks. One time he'd replaced all the door knobs in the apartment so they locked from the other side. It had really confused her when he locked her in the bathroom from the bedroom and then later locked her in the bedroom from the living room. She had not been that amused, but he couldn't help it. She just looked so damn sexy with those red cheeks.

"It's Todd's birthday. We're having people over this afternoon."

"I wasn't invited."

"You're right, you weren't. But, since you're here now I guess you should stay for a while," she returned her attention to the vegetables and scoured them voraciously.

"Is Butch coming?" he asked, remembering her friendship with the local rock star.

"What do you want Alex?"

"You left pretty suddenly last night." He was no good at direct conversation. There had to be a way to ease into this.

"My job was done and I needed to get home."

"Todd wasn't there last night."

"He took the kids to his mom's house to spend the night. They're going on a trip for Thanksgiving and he needed to get some packing done."

"So, you left early to come back to a practically empty house?"

"Yes, Alex I did. What are you expecting me to say?"

"Are you mad at me about something?" he asked. 'I mean, I know I probably should have called today, but…"

"Well, I'm not thrilled with you just showing up, but no I'm not mad at you." She returned her attention to the carrots.

"Chris, I wanted to say thank you for last night. It was a great honor and privilege to play with Chino. I don't know how you pulled that off."

"I told you, I called in a favor." She looked up, relaxed a little and smiled at him. "A pretty big favor too. I can't ask anyone at Warner Brothers anything for a long time now."

"Well, I don't know how to tell you how much I appreciate what you did for me. I know I owe you big time now too. But, I actually wanted to talk to you about something else."

He didn't want to wear out his welcome or make her any more uncomfortable than she already was.

"I saved that letter you wrote me," he said as she looked up at him, lips slightly parted in surprise. "I keep it in my guitar case and reread it now and then. I read it last night and I wanted to explain how I ended up in that situation." He was going to come clean on everything. But the conversation took a slightly different turn.

"I know. Well, I know most of it anyway. I talked to your mom a lot that night. She told me that you'd been using for a couple of years, that it started when you met some girl named Audrey and that it usually got worse whenever she showed back up. She told me how Audrey would disappear for long stretches just to reappear out of the blue. She said it just tore you up when Audrey returned. She suspected that that relapse was because of her."

"Wow, why didn't you ever tell me this?" Now it was his turn to be shocked. She'd known about Audrey already. He'd never even contemplated his mother telling her.

"I figured it was something you'd talk about when you were ready. I didn't want to push you. You seemed so fragile then. I was afraid that…" she couldn't finish her sentence. "I was just afraid. Let's leave it at that."

He stood there in silence, leaning against the beige Corian countertop. The only sound heard was the peeler gently scraping the outer layer off the potato she'd picked up. She turned on the water and rinsed each potato before putting them in a huge pot. She finally broke the silence.

"She called me once. Audrey did."

"What?! Why?" his eyes opened wide as he jerked his head up.

"She told me who she was and introduced herself as your girlfriend. She told me she'd been away at rehab and that she'd spent time bettering herself for you. Now that she was back it was time for me to let you go. She said you two were soul mates and that you told her I was just a 'filler'. She said she knew I was probably a really nice girl, who hadn't signed up for this, but she loved you and you loved her and that it would be easier for everyone if I left quietly. She even thanked me for calling your mom to try to get you help."

Alex leaned back on the counter. His legs felt weak and his knees practically became jelly. This explained so much. Not only was she trying to protect herself, but she was trying to let him go so he could be happy with Audrey. Of course his behavior toward her had not helped the situation either. He'd been so hateful about her having him sent home. Audrey was back and filling his head with lies about how she'd changed and how this new girl was not what he needed. She had turned on the manipulative charm and he'd fallen for it again. He'd lied about Christina too in order to not lose Audrey again. Eventually caving in, saying that he didn't love Chris, that he wanted and needed Audrey back. Inside he was dying because he didn't know what he wanted or who he loved anymore. He had had no idea which end was up by the end of the whole debacle.

He had been such a moron. As soon as Chris was out of the picture Audrey had encouraged his using and tried to pull him back into the lifestyle he was desperately trying to leave behind. It took losing the best thing that ever happened to him to see Audrey for who she really was. He remembered the day he'd kicked her out instead of watching her leave. It was a great feeling. He slammed the door right in her face and had never looked back. It was too late though. He'd contacted Christina shortly thereafter, asked to meet her, and that's when she told him to never call or see her again. After that his drug use began to spiral out of control and the bottom looming closer every day. Through all of it though, he managed to keep away from Audrey.

"Did she tell you…" he began.

"That you slept together that same day I found you? Yes." She looked down at the sink. Her hands were shaking so badly now that he didn't think she should chopping the vegetables she'd just peeled. She dropped the peeler and held on to the edge of the sink.

"Chris, I'm so sorry. I never meant for any of that to happen. I never in a million years wanted to drag you into that situation." He moved behind her and put his hands lightly on her shoulders and ran them down her arms. Her skin was still as smooth as it had been all those years ago. Despite the heat in the kitchen, she was cool to the touch.

"Hey, it was a long time ago, right?" she tried to brush it off but the raw pain was back. She must have felt sucker punched when Audrey had called her. Now, the same feeling had returned.

"It doesn't matter. You didn't deserve any of that. I never told her you were just a 'filler'. You don't know what it was like with her. I knew she was bad news, knew she would just fuck up my life again. But every time she came back, I caved." He turned her to face him. "I did lie to you, and I lied about you, and I am so sorry. She was like the drugs, and I needed the high. I wanted to tell you so many times, about her and our past, but I was too afraid. I didn't want to risk letting you get that close. What I failed to realize was that the harder I tried to keep you out, the more you got in. Pushing you away is what I regret more than anything."

"More than sleeping with her a few hours after I left?" Her voice was gritty with emotion. She was trying valiantly to keep it under control, her arms crossed over her body. She was involuntarily trying to protect her heart from having to relive the agony she'd experienced before.

"I regret that for sure. But, what I regret more is not being strong enough to push her away altogether. I regret not being strong enough to resist something so horrific. The drugs always increased when Audrey was around. I regret letting her mess me up so much that it ruined any chance we had at happiness. I was stupid, Chris. I was scared, strung out and stupid." He cupped her face tenderly in his hands. "I had perfection, I had the love I had always craved, and I let it go because of a very manipulative bitch and a high I thought I couldn't do without."

She pulled away from him and turned back to the sink. She picked up the knife and continued chopping the vegetables. "I wasn't perfect

Alex. Don't kid yourself about that. I just wanted you to be happy. I thought I could do that for you, but I was wrong."

"Are you kidding? I was never happier in my life than when I was with you. I was just really screwed up back then." He brushed his knuckles over her arms. She recoiled instantly.

"You'd better go help Todd with the tables. People will be arriving soon." She focused her attention on the potatoes and tried to steady her breathing.

"Okay, you're right. That's enough. I'll leave if you want me to, after I help set up tables of course."

"No, stay. You're already here, and Todd's already asked to put you to work. I'm sure you'll be asked to play later. You can say no if you want." Her voice was so fragile she was afraid it would break at any second.

"I'll play all night if that's what you want." He turned toward to basement door. "Thanks for letting me stay. I want to know more about your life now. You've been pretty mysterious up until lately."

"There's a good reason for that."

"I know, but I just want to know you again," he put his hand on the knob and pulled the door toward him. "It's ironic, isn't it?"

"What's that?"

"I finally have something to offer you. I can finally give you the life you deserve and you're already taken."

"Alex," she whispered, "I never wanted or needed anything more. You were enough, just you."

He said nothing, but went through the open door. He closed the door behind him and leaned against it for a moment. He felt his heart hammer with grief. It felt good to clear the air, but damn did it hurt. The wave of anger at Audrey for calling Chris had swept over him quickly, but faded just as fast. There was no use rehashing the actions of a cracked-out tramp who'd say and do anything to get her way. He needed to stay focused on Chris and what he could do to make it up to her. He walked down the basement stairs and into the backyard where he helped the man who was married to the love of his life set up tables and chairs.

Christina leaned on the kitchen sink and let out a very shaky breath. Why now? Why today of all days? What on earth had he been thinking coming to her house? She couldn't deal with this right now. In less than an hour she had 50 people coming over for her husband's birthday party. Her husband! Her wonderfully sweet husband. She couldn't do this to him. She couldn't betray the one man who had been her anchor for so long. She looked out the kitchen window and brushed a strand of hair out of her face with the back of her hand. Todd and Alex were hauling tables and laughing together. She wondered what they were talking about. They were getting along pretty well from the looks of it.

She couldn't let herself fall back in love with the one man who had made her cry more than anyone else. She had never felt the kind of pain she had felt with Alex. True, things had never been more passionate either, but passion wasn't enough. She'd never doubted herself more or cried as hard and long. Now some of that pain was back, and fresh. However, things were different now. He was coming clean and feeling remorse, something she hadn't experienced with him since that first fight. She was falling though, falling hard for the man Alex Lily had become; the man she always knew he could and would become. A single tear escaped from her eye before she hurriedly wiped it away. She would not have today ruined. She could cry later. Steeling herself, she resumed chopping the vegetables.

"Stay busy," she said out loud to herself. "Stay busy and look happy. It's always worked in the past."

When the vegetables were gently simmering to form what would later become her semi-famous potato salad, the only thing she could cook well, she went upstairs and got ready for the afternoon. She washed her face again and put on a little bit of makeup. It was late November, and while it was still pretty warm, it would be cold once the sun went down. She replaced her capri pants with blue jeans, slipped on her sneakers and checked her appearance. So far, she thought to herself, so good. She headed back downstairs to become a hostess.

Within minutes, the guests began to arrive: friends, family members, neighbors, co-workers. The kids all played together on the swing set while the adults mingled. The women talked about the normal things women talk about. They discussed everything from baby care to husband stories to the best new skin care products to shopping deals. The men took turns at the grill and talked about sports. Alex was quite a hit. He indulged them by playing a few songs. Many of the women were eyeing him conspicuously. He was, after all, a rising rock star who was very good looking. Christina was sure she'd have calls the next day from her single friends asking for the set up.

Christina watched as Alex played with Kate and Jack and the other kids. He was really good with them. He pushed them on the swings and slid down the slide about a hundred times. He even gave piggy back rides across the lawn. She began to feel the tug of wonder that often came to her when she watched children play. She wondered what their child would have been like.

She'd never told him she was pregnant. The secret was a bit easier to keep after she'd miscarried. She was 12 weeks along when she'd awakened with terrible pain in her abdomen. She'd gone straight to the hospital and seven hours later was no longer expecting a baby. The pregnancy had not come at a good time and part of her was relieved that she would not be a 21 year old single mother. But still she wondered what that child would have looked like. Would the child have been book smart like her, musically talented like Alex, or athletic or artistic? Her two children reminded her everyday how fortunate she was to be able to get to know them.

She watched her husband with his friends. She glimpsed in him what had attracted her to him in the first place. He was telling jokes and doing imitations and making everyone laugh. Besides being considerate and kind, he was a hopeless romantic and had a very adventurous spirit. He had never been afraid to try something new. She remembered the first time he asked her to go white water rafting with him. She had been terrified. Todd had said that she could feel safe taking a chance with him. He wouldn't let any harm come to her. "Yes, there is a danger in it," he'd said, "but if we lived our lives doing everything safe, we'd never have any fun." He'd sounded so much like her dad then that she agreed to go. They had had a blast and for years they took rafting trips at least twice a year.

She looked over at Alex and then back at Todd. They were as opposite as two people could be. She saw qualities in both of them that she loved. The one was brooding with an air of danger. He was creative and knew ways to express his passion. The other was fun-loving, kind, affectionate and adventurous. He encouraged her to come out of her shell and take a chance. He was also the best father she had ever known. If only they could be one person who had everything, life would be so much easier. She loved them both for very different reasons and didn't know what to do about it.

The party began to fizzle around 6:00. Kids were getting tired and whiny. Some of the men were suffering from the combination of too much beer and too much sun. The mothers rolled their eyes when a few of Todd's friends suggested taking the remainder of the party to a local sports bar to watch the college football games. Still they acquiesced; they loaded their kids in car seats and went home while the guys carpooled to the bar. Alex was invited, but politely declined. Christina got Kate and Jack bathed and changed into their PJ's. She settled them down in the play room to watch Happy Feet. When she came back downstairs Alex was loading the last of the dishes into her dishwasher.

"What are you still doing here?" she asked while she picked up Solo cups to throw away.

"I thought I'd help you get everything cleaned up," he said. He opened the cabinet under the sink and found the detergent.

"That's nice of you, but you don't have to. Don't you have some sort of pressing engagement tonight?"

"Well, it's Sunday night and my rep thought I should have a free day after the party last night." He glanced up with a grin. Christina smiled in spite of herself.

"She sounds like a smart woman. She must know how grueling the upcoming tour will be for you."

"Yeah, she's pretty great. There," he said closing the dishwasher and pressing start, "no more dirty dishes to worry about." He turned to face her and slipped his hands in his back pockets. For a while they stood there and stared at each other. An uncomfortable silence began to creep in around them. After their talk earlier they were both too afraid to say anymore.

The silence was broken by Max who began to scratch on the door to come in. Christina cleared her throat and moved to open the door. Max came bounding in trailing fur behind him as he scurried to his hiding place in the family room. He ran two laps around the table and then hunkered down to climb underneath it. When she turned back from the door Alex was making his way toward the front hall.

"I should get going," he said nervously.

"Yeah, you really should."

"I had a great time this afternoon. Thanks for letting me crash the party."

"Hey, no problem. I wish you had called first though. It would have saved me quite a shock."

"I'll remember that for next time." He opened the door and stepped onto the porch. "I really am sorry about all that stuff from before. Audrey, the drugs, I was in a really bad place."

"I know. I'm sorry too. Thank you for apologizing. It makes things a little better."

"Don't hate me anymore?" he asked.

"Never did."

"Maybe one day soon I can explain everything that went on. I'd like to get it all out on the table."

"I think we've cleared just about everything up, Alex. I don't know if I can take much more," she said as they stood by her front door.

He turned to leave and then reversed his direction. He spoke hesitantly, "Todd seems like a great guy. I'm sorry I made fun of him the other week. Tell him thanks for letting me hang out today."

"I will. Good night Alex," she said softly as she started closing the door.

"Hey, Chris?" he asked.

"Yeah?" she said reopening the door.

"You said you earlier that Todd was packing. Are you guys going on a trip?"

"He and his mom are taking the kids to Michigan for Thanksgiving to visit his family."

"You're not going?"

"No. There's too much to settle before your tour begins. So, I'll be here."

"When are they leaving?"

"Wednesday morning. They'll be back sometime on Saturday or Sunday."

"Do you have plans for Thanksgiving?"

"Not yet, why?" she asked resting her face gently against the door.

"You're more than welcome to join us, my family and me, for dinner," he said as he moved down the front stairs. "We'll be eating around 6:00. Just let me know if you want to join us."

"I'll think about it. Good night."

"Good night Chris."

The door shut and Alex was left on the porch. They both waited on either side of the door. It took all her strength not to open the door and fall into his arms. She could almost feel the hunger of his kiss.

He wondered if she had any idea how he felt about her, how he'd always felt. His heart was gripped with a sensation he didn't recognize. On his side of the door he was having the same battle, but he would not disrespect her home or her marriage by acting on his impulses. The old Alex wouldn't have cared. *He* only thought of himself. The new Alex was different. He didn't want to do anything she wasn't comfortable with, and he certainly didn't want to hurt her anymore. She had been through enough, he thought.

Chapter 20

Christina went upstairs to her bathroom and stood against the counter. She looked up at herself, and then down at her bottle of Ambien. She decided against taking a pill although the need for one seemed very apparent. Instead, she changed into her workout clothes.

After moving the sleeping kids to their rooms and turning off the DVD, she went down to the basement. There would be no need for music to sustain her through this workout. She had enough natural drive to sweat out all the frustrations and old feelings to keep her going. She could not let herself think of the good times, or the times that could be. She needed to keep the memory of the angry, irrational Alex fresh so that she could keep her distance.

She climbed onto the elliptical glider and pressed start. The machine was set to automatically adjust itself to the pre-determined program. As she started pedaling she let her mind travel back to the night when her world changed forever.

Alex had been gone for a few weeks. They'd talked on the phone a few times, but he seemed distant and cold. She thought that was because he was angry with her for calling his mother and sending him home. That was part of it, but she didn't know that Audrey had followed and was undoing all the good his family was trying to do. In fact, the longer Alex stayed at home the more damage Audrey did.

Christina was returning back to her dorm from the on campus fitness center. It was the dead of winter and even in South Georgia it was cold. It was only 4:30 in the afternoon, but dusk was already starting to set in. Her breath blew out in smoky clouds that huddled around her as she rode. She parked her bike and wrapped the chain around the bike rack and the front wheel. She hoisted her back pack higher on her shoulders and began walking up the path to the building. She remembered vividly what she was wearing that night; pink sweatpants with a white T-shirt. Her T-shirt was layered with a white hoodie. A white scarf draped around her neck and covered her mouth. Her gloved hands rubbed together as she entered the lobby of her dorm.

She climbed the stairs to the second floor. It was Saturday and most of the residents had gone home for the weekend. Not having a car made it difficult for her to go anywhere off campus. As she approached her door she saw him sitting in front of the door, legs stretched out in front of him, crossed at the ankle. He looked thinner, and paler than before he left. He turned his head toward her as she came closer.

"Hey," he said in a distant voice.

"Hey. What are you doing here?" she asked.

"I had to come back to school or risk being kicked out."

"Oh, I see." She looked at her feet not knowing what else to say. "Want to come in?"

"Sure," he answered.

She unlocked the door and they walked inside. The dorm suite consisted of a common area kitchen and living room. On either side of the common area were the two bedrooms each with a private bathroom. It was set up and looked pretty much like a two-bedroom apartment. She dropped her back pack on the barstool and began to unwind the scarf. He didn't move from the entry way.

"So, how have you been?" she ventured.

"Pretty much shitty, you?" he asked in return. He stood near the door, barely over the threshold with his hands in his pockets.

"I've been worried and I've missed you."

She put the scarf on top of the back pack and took a deep breath. She stood facing him with her hands resting lightly on her hips. Her first instinct was to embrace him and tell him how terribly lonely she'd been while he was gone, but his body language kept her at a distance. He was radiating tension and it scared her. She had no idea how to tell him about the baby. She didn't know if this was the right time or not. So far it didn't feel like it.

"What happens now?"

"I want to know why you sent me home," he said with a hard edge in his voice.

"I didn't want to send you home, but I was scared, Alex. I didn't know what else to do," she said putting her right hand in the middle of her chest like she was trying to hold her heart in. "I called your mom because I thought she could help," she said, her voice trembling with trepidation.

"You thought she could help?! Sending me back there was the worst thing that could have happened!" He backed out of the door and began to move down the hallway.

"Why? Because it got you away from whatever it was that was messing you up so bad?" Christina was not one to shrink away in the face of anger. She met him head on and followed him back out of the apartment.

"Messed up! That's what you think, I'm messed up." He turned to face her. She knew he was rapidly losing control.

"Alex, I came over to find you passed out with a heroin needle next to you. You *were* messed up!"

"No, the only thing that messed me up was you! You've done nothing but fuck things up since I met you! You're the problem Christina, not me. I was fine until I met you."

She physically flinched from his words. He knew he was hurting her. That was the aim of his words. He wanted her to feel the kind of pain he'd been feeling. He tried to step around her and leave, but she moved to stand in front of him.

"Then, why in the hell did you come back here? To see me?" Her voice was shaking, a mix of anger and pain.

"Because I wanted you to know that it's over. You called my mom and had me sent away. Now I'm facing expulsion. You couldn't leave well enough alone, could you? You couldn't just let me handle things my way. You were definitely not worth the fucking trouble you caused."

"Trouble? I'm the one who's causing trouble? I have done nothing but try to be supportive of you since the first day I met you! I helped you study, I listened to your music, and I've taken verbal battery and stood by your side through the fallout. I have also picked your strung out ass up off the floor and literally nursed you back to health. You were not handling things, you were escaping into a dangerous place and it scared the shit out of me.

"I did the only thing I could think of to do that night. I'm sorry if you were unhappy with what I did, but I didn't know what else to do. I have done nothing but try to love you, but you won't let me! And through it all I have asked for nothing in return. I only wanted you to love me the same way that I love you." She had walked right up to him, close enough to touch, and met his fiery stare. Her blue eyes had turned to ice.

"Here's a news flash, Chris. I don't love you, I never did. And here's a bonus round, could I have learned to love you? Probably not. You were just another girl to add to the collection."

Her eyes went dead and her jaw was set firm.

"Go. Away," she said in the most even, monotone voice he'd ever heard.

"Gladly," he sneered and stepped around her.

She jumped as the door leading to the stairs slammed behind him. She waited a few moments, afraid to move. She was afraid she'd run to him, or that he'd be back. She used the wall as a support as she moved back into her apartment. Closing the door behind her she covered her mouth and sank to her knees, one arm hugged around her middle. She stifled a scream.

Somehow she managed to crawl to her bathroom where she vomited. She had no idea how long she sat on the bathroom floor crying and shaking with her back against the tub. She finally laid down right on the bathroom floor, grabbed her towel and fell asleep out of sheer self-defense. She couldn't stand to feel the pain any longer.

She woke up hours later. It was pitch black and cold. The bathroom tile had left an imprint on her cheek. She pulled herself to standing, hung her towel back on the rack and stumbled into the kitchen.

What had just happened? Who was that person who'd been here? That wasn't the man she loved, the father of the child she was carrying.

It was over, he didn't love her. She didn't want to believe him, but the hatred and anger she'd seen in his eyes convinced her. She made a decision standing there in her small college kitchen. He would never know about the baby. She would not inflict that kind of wrath on a small, defenseless child whose greatest need in life was to be loved.

It wasn't as late as she thought, only 8:30. Her roommate had gone home for the weekend, as had most of her friends. February was a lonely time on the college campus. It was cold, and got dark very early. She had no appetite, but tried to force down some food. She choked down a cup of yogurt and part of an apple. It all came back up in a matter of minutes. She was pregnant and alone and scared to death.

As she finished reliving the memory she looked down to see that over an hour had gone by. No wonder she was tired. The Alex who lost his temper and yelled and said horrible things, that's who she needed to keep front and center. But that wasn't really him, one of her inner voices said. You know he's not really like that. "Yes, but that's who you need to see," she said aloud.

Steadying herself she climbed off the machine and wiped the sweat from her brow. She left the basement and stopped in the kitchen for some water. She gulped down a big glass before dragging herself upstairs to the shower. It was after 10:00 by the time she finally climbed into bed. Todd was still out with his friends. Just as well, she thought. She didn't want to have to pretend that everything was fine right now. She decided to call in sick tomorrow. While there were things that seemed extremely pressing to do, the staff could get along without her for one day.

The next morning after she dropped Kate off at school, she took Jack to Monkey Joe's. It was a facility with huge inflatable bouncy slides and play equipment. Jack loved it. He was such a little daredevil. After being helped only once or twice, he was climbing to the top of the tallest slide all by himself. She decided that this would be where they'd hold his second birthday party.

His first birthday party had been at their house. He'd come down with a 102 degree fever the morning of the party. They couldn't cancel it that late. Her mom and her new husband had already left North Carolina to be there.

She remembered lying in bed looking at the picture of Jack resting on her shoulder when he was barely a few hours old. It was hard to believe an entire year had gone by. She'd cried more on his birthday than on hers and she'd turned 30!

She'd given Jack a cool bath and tried to coax the fever away with Baby Tylenol. There had been too many people in the house. Everything scared him, the kids, the presents, the streamers, just about everything. He spent the entire party either in her arms, Todd's arms or her mom's arms. He was, however, fascinated by the cake. He forgot he was scared and dug in. There was blue icing everywhere. The pictures were priceless.

They played together at Monkey Joe's for two hours before it was time for his mid-afternoon nap. They drove home, ate some lunch and then she rocked her little boy to sleep. She sat with him asleep on her chest for a long time. Something told her to hold on tight to her little man, and she did just that. She finally put him down in his crib and sat down in the living room. In a rare moment of self-indulgence, she watched TV for about an hour before falling asleep herself. When Jack woke up it was nearing 2:15. She called Kate's school and told the office Kate would need to come through the car rider line that afternoon. Christina loaded Jack into his car seat and picked her daughter up from school.

The three of them spent the afternoon making the biggest mess she'd ever seen in her kitchen. She rolled out cookie dough and let Kate show Jack how to use the cookie cutters. The attempted stars, hearts and bunnies ended up looking more like shapeless lumps than anything else. But, she baked them and once they were cooled they all sat down to frost the cookies. Chocolate, strawberry and vanilla frosting coated every crevice of the breakfast table, both kids and her.

She called Thai Coon and placed an order for delivery. Todd loved curry, so she made sure to order two different kinds, along with orders of teriyaki chicken for the kids. Then, the three of them tromped upstairs for a much needed bath.

With both kids in the bath, she stood at the sink and washed the frosting from her arms and face. She used a wet comb to remove as much from her hair as possible, before stripping her clothes and tossing them into the hamper. She pulled on the bathrobe that hung on the inside of the door and sat on the edge of the tub singing all their favorite bath time songs.

"Boop, boop choo", Jack crowed singing the fishy song. Kate piled bubbles on top of her brother's head and then her own. She loved to make 'snow hats' as she called them. Chris hadn't laughed that purely in a long time. She looked at her kids playing together in the bathtub and thought, "This is what life is about, the little sweet moments."

Once they were good and pruny, she got them out and dressed them in their best PJ's. They sat in the playroom coloring while she finished cleaning up the mess in the kitchen. She hurriedly pulled on a pink T-shirt and jeans just as the delivery guy arrived. She paid for the food and set it out on the dining room table. She arranged the cookies, baked and decorated with love, nicely on a plate for dessert. Hearing the garage door open, she called for the kids to come down for dinner.

Todd walked upstairs and into the kitchen from the basement. The three of them yelled, "Surprise!" as he walked through the door.

He looked up astonished, and then smiled broadly at them. "What's all this?" he asked as Kate and Jack ran to him. He picked Jack up with one arm and hugged Kate with the other. He looked at Christina and then to the table. "You guys made me a gourmet dinner, huh?" he asked teasingly.

"No, Daddy. We *ordered* the food, but we did make the cookies," Kate answered him not catching the sarcasm behind Todd's question. Besides the potato salad, Christina couldn't really cook much of anything except frozen chicken nuggets and French fries. Her motto had always been that take out existed for a reason. Kate dragged him over to the table and showed him the plate full of lumps and bumps that were destined to be their dessert.

"Hi," he said as he kissed Christina. "Enjoyed your day off, I see?"

"It was great," she said as he put Jack into his high chair. She dipped small spoonfuls of rice and chicken onto Kate's and Jack's plates. "We spent the afternoon making these lovely cookies and then getting all the frosting cleaned up. It was one of the best days I've had in a long time."

She spooned some rice and green curry with chicken onto her own plate. Todd poured them each a glass of wine before he sat down to serve his own plate.

"How was your day?" she asked.

"Oh, the same old thing. Budgets, audits, receipts, the regular stuff," he replied taking a bite of his red curry. "This is great! What a treat."

After they finished the food, they gave the kids each a cookie of their choice. Christina allowed herself to have two, one chocolate frosted and one strawberry frosted. Todd launched a tickling attack on Kate who quickly turned it around on him. Lying on the floor with Kate sitting on his stomach, Todd was pretty defenseless to Jack's jumping in on the action too. With both kids ticking him, Christina felt compelled to join them too. By the end of it, they had all been tickled breathless. They all collapsed together on the floor, laughing and too exhausted to move.

Eventually, they moved the kids to their rooms, read the perfunctory good night stories and met back in the bedroom. Todd had the drawers of his dresser open and was packing clothes into his suitcase. He smiled at her when she walked in.

"Almost done packing?" she asked with her head resting on his back.

"Almost," he said.

"Think I could persuade you to take a break for the night?" she asked as he put a sweater in the case before turning around. He smoothed her hair back from her face with his hands. His fingers found some missed frosting and pulled it down the strand of hair. He brought his mouth down to hers and kissed her tenderly. She ran her hands down his back and untucked his shirt. He stopped her hands in mid caress.

"I really need to get this done, sweetie. Perhaps if you're still awake, and in the mood when I'm done, we can fool around a little."

"Ok," she sighed. "I'll go get ready for bed." She walked to the bathroom a little disappointed. With the dinner and the cookies, she was hoping for a little more passion. Unfortunately, it didn't look like it was coming that night.

Chapter 21

Alex unlocked the door and let himself into his small bungalow style house. The front hall was dark, but there was enough light streaming in the window from the street light that he was able to make out the basic shapes in his living room. He tossed his keys on the small counter to his left. To his right he could see his kitchen, the sink piled high with dirty dishes. He'd let his cleaning go for a while and it showed. That's what he would do in the morning, clean his house from top to bottom. He'd be gone for a month, better to get it done before leaving.

He walked to the couch and lay down. What had he been thinking, showing up at her house yesterday? What had he expected to happen? He had told himself he just wanted to explain some things and apologize. He'd done just that so why did he feel so empty still? Because he loved her; he had never stopped and didn't know if he ever would.

Had he expected her to accept his apology, profess her love and leave her family? No, of course not. But a small part of him hoped she'd admit that she'd thought of him the way he thought of her. Of course she wouldn't have said if she did or not though, not in her home, not at her husband's birthday party.

Damn! He'd crashed her husband's birthday party! He felt like such an asshole.

She hadn't gone into the office today either. He'd called under the guise of wanting to discuss a scheduling issue on the tour. Andrea said she'd taken the day off, but he could talk to Nick if he wanted. He's said okay, just to not seem like a complete loser. He discussed his issue, which really wasn't an issue at all, with Nick and asked him to have Chris call him the next day.

He'd have to carve out some time during the tour to finish the conversation he'd started yesterday. He still wanted to tell her about how he'd finally got rid of Audrey and stopped using. Eventually he hoped to tell her that he still loved her. He didn't know if he'd ever get to the last part.

She *was* married, and to a guy who was actually pretty cool. He wasn't the uptight boring stiff Alex thought he'd be. Todd had a great sense of humor, could hold a conversation about anything that came up, and it was obvious he loved his wife and children profusely. Alex thought that under different circumstances he and Todd probably could have been friends. Christina did deserve someone who could give her whatever she needed and wanted. Regardless of what she'd said, there was no way he could provide her with what Todd could. Even now, with a career that was taking off, Alex couldn't give Chris what she needed.

He looked toward his bedroom but couldn't face going in there. He'd left that bed empty for so long. None of the women he'd been with over the last few months knew where he lived, much less saw the inside of his bedroom. He'd gone to their places, or to hotels. Even before he'd been signed, and released a CD, it had been years since he'd invited a woman back to his home. There was something almost sacred about that, and he really didn't know why. Perhaps he was waiting for someone who would stay; someone he wanted to stay.

He could almost see Chris walking through the bedroom door wearing one of his t-shirts. It would come down to mid thigh and practically swallow her. He could see her pulling her hair back in the low ponytail she'd always favored, walking right up to him, standing on her tiptoes and wrapping her arms around his neck. He imagined the kiss that followed the devilishly sexy smile she'd give him. He could almost feel her lips on his, soft and moist, tongue slipping through his lips to tease him. He felt himself harden slightly from just thinking about kissing her.

No, he couldn't let this happen. He couldn't get wrapped up in his fantastical thoughts of her, not anymore. He wouldn't ruin her life; he couldn't be that selfish. He loved her and wanted her, just as much now as back then. But things were different for her. She was married, had two great kids and an awesome career. She had built the life she'd always wanted and it didn't include him. She was only involved with him now because it was her job. He had to keep telling himself that. Even if she did still have feelings for him, the lifestyle he led would not be one that she would want to be involved in. She couldn't travel on tour all the time with kids. Plus, she'd have other clients who would need her here.

He sat up and rubbed his face. He was doing it again. He'd put himself in her life in a way that he couldn't possibly be. It was times like these that he felt the urge to use again. He could just forget everything for a few hours and feel nothing. He still had contacts that could supply him with the heroin, cocaine, acid, or whatever he wanted. Instead he did what he always did when he felt the urge to use. He grabbed his guitar and his notebook and began to write. He didn't know it at the time, of course, but the song he wrote that night, *Torn*, would become one of his most famous pieces of work.

On Tuesday morning Christina got out of her car and took a deep breath. She greeted Jorge as she walked up to her office. She had carefully planned for what she would say to Joe. She would stand firm, ready for every conceivable response that he could come up with. She was ready to ask for a leave of absence, not forever, just for a little while. Six months to a year would be good. She would leave as soon as Steven Lily was released. What she wasn't ready for was a visitor in her office. As usual, Andrea wasn't there when she arrived, and Alex was waiting patiently in front of Andrea's desk reading a magazine. There were two cups of coffee sitting in front of him. When Christina came around the corner he looked up. She stopped where she was looking surprised, then a bit confused.

"What are you doing here?" she asked.

"We had an appointment today, remember? I know I'm a little early, but not that much," he responded, standing as he spoke. He stretched out an arm holding one of the cups toward her. Her face was blank at first before the memory flooded back. She had completely forgotten they had a meeting to discuss the final scheduling and itinerary for the tour, and the requirements for the tour buses. All the final details needed to be nailed down. He'd be leaving the first week of December, shortly after Thanksgiving.

"So, we did. Come on in," she said unlocking her office door. Gratefully, she took the coffee. "Thanks," she said as she took a sip of the steamy, delicious beverage. She would have to wait a while before setting her meeting up with Joe. She didn't know how to tell Alex about her decision. He would think it was just because of him. She didn't know if she could get him to understand that this was what she needed for her family, and for herself. He had probably served as a catalyst to something that was going to eventually happen anyway.

"I just wanted to run through the final schedule and things like that with you, and to see if you have any questions. I also wanted to make sure I have a list of essentials you'll need on the road." She walked behind her desk and sat down, motioning for him to do the same. While he sat across from her she rummaged through her desk drawer looking for the file folder with the information she needed to give him.

"That's cool. Sarah is meeting me later to help me finish shopping and packing. She's been bugging me for a list to guide the process, so this will make her happy. Hey, I want to apologize again for just showing up on Sunday. I know it was inconvenient for me to be there, and I probably took advantage of your hospitality."

"Well, you did do the dishes, so I'm not that mad at you." Christina smiled.

"Have you thought anymore about Thanksgiving? I told my mom you were going to be by yourself and she insisted you come over," he told her.

"Tell her I really appreciate the invitation and will seriously consider it, but I can't commit to anything just now."

"Okay, that's fair. I'll take a maybe. Just in case you decide it's a yes, though, here's the address. Food will be served around 6:00 so show up if you get hungry." He handed her a slip of paper with the address of his mother's house on it.

"Will do," she said taking the paper and placing it beside her computer monitor. "Now, let's make the list of things you'll need for the tour and what you'd like to have in your bus. Remember, the bus will practically be your home for over a month, so think about the things you really want or need to have. No request is too small, and if we can physically get it in the bus, you should be able to have it."

They spent about an hour coming up with everything he needed to buy before leaving and what would be provided for him on the bus. He wanted to make sure there were plenty of Pop-Tarts, Easy Mac and peanut butter and jelly. She chided him about having the diet of a nine year old. He agreed that somewhere deep down there was a nine year old boy whose only control left was over his diet. He said to throw in some granola bars and apples to add a health factor, if that would make her happy. She laughed in a carefree manner. He laughed with her.

After he left, she got to work on making the arrangements for the bus. She would be in the office tomorrow, but she wasn't sure who else would be working. Many people took off the day before and the day after Thanksgiving. She normally did too, but there was no time with a tour starting this close to the holidays, especially since she had taken the day before off. Andrea and Nick would be gone too so that left her today to get most of what needed to be done accomplished. Wednesday would be for paperwork.

Chapter 22

Wednesday morning Christina got up early with her family and helped Todd load the car and gave her kids big hugs and kisses. They would be back on Saturday or Sunday. It wasn't even a full week. She'd been away from them longer than that before. She wasn't sure why she felt the need to hug them tighter and longer before they left this time.

"Mommy, you *have* to let go of me," Kate said. "You're squishing my pigtails and it hurts."

"I'm sorry sweetie. Now, be good for Daddy and Grandma. Help with Jack, okay?" She smoothed her little girl's hair and fixed the pigtails.

"I will, don't worry," Kate said as she climbed in the back of the mini-van and buckled her seat belt.

Todd handed Jack to Chris as he loaded the last suitcase in the back. She gave him a quick twirl with his legs dangling below him, making the little boy laugh with delight. That was the best sound in the whole world. She gave him a loud round of kisses on his cheeks and then buckled him into his car seat. Once he was situated, she turned to Todd.

"You got the oil changed, right?" she asked.

"Yes, and I filled up with gas, and I checked the tire pressure, and I made sure the spare is in good shape, and I made sure I had the jumper cables. Everything is fine, Chris," he said trying to reassure her. He rubbed her arms warming the chill bumps that had emerged.

"And you have plenty of snacks and juice for the road?"

"Yes, honey. I have everything. What's going on with you? Come on, Max!" he called to the dog who jumped in the back of the van.

Max always accompanied the family to Michigan. Todd was really good about arranging the luggage so that Max would have plenty of room to lie down on the road. Her husband put his arms around her and hugged her close.

"I don't know. I guess I'm just being a nervous mom. Of course you'll be fine. Call me when you get there," she said breaking the embrace reluctantly. "Tell your family hello for me."

"I will. Kids, tell Mommy bye-bye and that you love her," he said over his shoulder as he got in the driver's seat.

"Bye, Mommy! Love you!" both kids chorused from the back of the van.

"Bye! Love you too!" she returned to them. She leaned in the door and kissed Todd. "You'd better get going if you're going to pick up your mom and beat traffic. I love you. Be safe."

"I love you too, Chris. Don't worry so much. We'll be fine."

He gave her one last kiss before putting the van in reverse and backing out of the driveway. They all waved to her as the van pulled away up the street. She waved back and stood in her place in the driveway for a long time after the van was out of sight.

She took her time getting dressed for the day. The office would be practically empty so she chose a casual outfit. She wanted to get things wrapped up with her two remaining clients so she could start convincing Joe that she was ready for and needed a break. She arrived a little after 10:00 AM. She'd packed a lunch and brought some of her favorite CD's so she could work straight through.

Andrea's desk was empty and so was the intern pool. Shaking her head, she looked at the state of the cramped space. It was a wreck! The pool consisted of 15 or so desks smushed together in a space that was barely bigger than a cubicle and had all the charm of a crowded warehouse. The interns had left papers strewn about along with empty pizza boxes and plastic Solo cups. It slightly resembled a college dorm room. Apparently, there had been a late night work fest last night and housekeeping had missed the area. She would make a call and get it taken care of.

She entered her office and hung her coat on the hook behind the door. Winter was setting in. The wind had picked up and the chill was definitely penetrating the first layer of clothing. She crossed her office to the small area in the corner where her CD player was. She popped in the latest CD's by Jaymay, Landon Pigg and Gavin Mikhail and returned to her desk. As the first notes of *Sea Green See Blue* sounded she began to relax.

Soon, she got into a rhythm and began to work. By the time the last CD's ended nearly three hours had passed. She surveyed her work and was pleased. She'd confirmed the arrival time for the bus and had made sure the necessary essentials were on board. She'd reserved a bus equipped with satellite TV and radio, among other essentials. The kitchen area had a small stove, sink, microwave and refrigerator. She'd gone with a smaller kitchen in order to get the bus with the bigger bathroom area. Neither was huge, but by bus standards, they were decent. She called ahead to the first three clubs and made sure the dressing rooms were set and ready.

She emailed the list of things needed to the club managers. Alex was definitely new, she thought. He'd barely requested anything. He only wanted to have bottled water, "whatever was available" in his own words, chocolate Pop-Tarts and a few towels in order to dry the sweat after the shows. She'd scoffed at the Pop-Tarts, knowing he requested those just as a joke for her. Well, if he wanted Pop-Tarts; she would make sure he had a vast supply Pop-Tarts. She knew that as his popularity grew so would the list.

By the time that happened though she would be well into her leave of absence unless she decided that staying home was not for her. In reality she was terrified at the thought of a leave of absence. She found much of her identity in her career and if she left it, she was afraid that part of herself would also be left behind. That really frightened her. She loved her kids and adored spending time with them, but she also really loved the job. There just didn't seem to be a way to do both and be equally as good as a mom as she was as a music rep.

She didn't see Alex as needing her services much longer. He might need some tips on handling the press and dealing with interviews, but he was already pretty much set. His album was released with good ratings, and he was all ready to start touring. She'd arranged for him to open for some pretty cool bands that were very hot these days, not always an easy feat. He was sailing through the local radio interviews already.

She was curious to see how he'd do on a TV interview so she'd made a few calls and booked him a spot on Good Day Atlanta for the Monday after Thanksgiving. It would be the perfect way to send him off on this regional tour. She called the show's program director and confirmed his time slot and arrival time. She would begin working through his tour manager while he was on the road.

That would signal the beginning of her departure. Once the manager took over, there was really very little left for her to do. That suited her just fine. Things were better between them since they'd had a chance to talk, but she was still uneasy.

At 4:00 she called it a day and went home. There was no point in going in tomorrow since nothing would be open. She would be in early to watch the sales during Black Friday though. She watched all her clients on that day, especially the newest ones.

The CD sales reported on Black Friday would be a pretty good indicator of how the CD would sell during the holiday season, and sometimes beyond. It had become slightly less reliable since the invention of I-Tunes and MySpace, but it was still worth taking note of.

Tawney Blount's album had been out since summer and was still doing quite nicely on the charts. With her new song being released on radio this week there should be a spike in her sales as well. Christina already missed working with Tawney. She'd handed over the folksy singer to her new team the Tuesday before. She was funny, and full of energy, but she was also an artist whose creativity over-rode almost everything else. Keeping her focused on one topic was difficult, but tolerable.

Christina changed into black yoga pants and a long sleeved blue t-shirt when she arrived home. With her shoes kicked off as soon as she reached the bedroom, she was already feeling more relaxed.

She made herself a peanut butter and jelly sandwich and poured a glass of wine. She shook her head at the combination, but hey, who was watching? She pressed the button on the answering machine. There was one message from Todd saying that they had arrived safe and sound and that he was looking forward to her call the next day. She smiled and entered the living room.

With time to kill and no one to interrupt her, she pulled a book from the bookshelf. She lay down on the couch and began to read. She was so engrossed in the book she gave a little jump when her cell phone rang. She didn't even bother to look at caller ID figuring it was Todd or the kids.

"Hello," she said.

"Hey," said the voice on the other end. Her heart skipped a tiny beat. She told herself it was because she'd been expecting to hear Todd's voice, but heard Alex's instead.

"Hi," she said quickly, maybe too quickly. "What's up?"

"I was just calling to see if you had made up your mind about dinner tomorrow."

"You are persistent, Mr. Lily."

"Well, actually it's my mom. She really wants to use the good china and says there's no point unless company is coming. Apparently, only special guests like you get the good plates."

She laughed. "That's kinda sad for you and your sister, huh?"

"Tell me about it." She could visualize him rolling his eyes.

She thought about it for a few seconds. She didn't have anything planned for herself. She'd been invited to join Andrea and her family, but Andrea's uncle Bart made her a little uncomfortable. He always tried to engage her in a political conversation, and he *always* took the other position. Every conversation with him was a battle and he never let her get out of it. She was truly not up for that.

"Okay, okay," she sighed. "You and your mom win. I'll come to dinner. What should I bring?"

"If memory serves me correctly, you cook just about as well as you sing." He was only partly kidding.

She laughed out loud. She was a horrible cook. Once she'd tried to make broccoli and rice for him and burned both so badly his apartment smelled singed for weeks. He'd banned her from preparing anything that required heat.

"Hey, watch it," she joked back.

"You don't have to bring anything, but if you really feel the need to bring something how about a bottle of wine."

"Done," she paused for a bit. "I guess I'll see you tomorrow at 6:00 then."

"Six it is. Do you still have the address?"

"I do and I'll enter it in my GPS before I even leave my driveway."

"Alright, good night."

"Good night, Alex," she said.

She clicked the cell phone shut and put it on the table. How different things had become! When she first started working with Alex she'd been sure it would never work out, and now here she was having Thanksgiving dinner with him and his family. It was a little weird, she knew, but it felt okay. At 10:00 she closed the cover of her book and went upstairs. She took a bath and then climbed into bed. Sleep came easy; there was no need for Ambien.

Her dreams took her back to their first Thanksgiving together. There had not been enough time off from school to go home. Christina's family was almost seven hours away and his was five and while he could've made it home, he didn't want to leave her alone. She didn't have a car and flying was out of the question. So, they'd decided to throw a Thanksgiving dinner at his apartment.

A couple of other people they knew were staying at school as well. They went to the store and bought the smallest turkey they could find. Still, it was 13 pounds and more food than the group would ever eat. Knowing her cooking handicap, she purchased ingredients to make a tossed salad and they had boxed pies and ice cream for dessert. He bought what he needed for squash casserole. Neither of them had a clue how to make dressing so they went with some that was already prepared by the store.

The afternoon had gone well. The friends arrived around 3:00 and football was immediately turned on. After making the rounds to see if the guests needed anything else to drink while the food was finishing up, she went into the kitchen to find Alex hard at work on the casserole. She stepped in behind him and wrapped her arms around his waist, hugging him. She'd felt the hard smoothness of his back as she'd pressed her cheek against his shoulder. He'd turned to her smiling and kissed her lightly. He'd told her she'd better go back in the living room or he'd end of burning to apartment down from a lack of concentration. She'd obliged but told him to reserve some concentration for her later.

She'd flashed her eyes at him as she left the kitchen. He'd clutched his heart pretending to be spellbound.

As dinner ended Alex and one of the other guys picked up their guitars and played for the group. A fire pit had been dug in the backyard and they'd all sat around a makeshift campfire drinking beer. The impromptu sing-along had been so much fun; they'd laughed and danced and were completely carefree. After everyone left she'd begun cleaning up the mess. She'd put the leftovers in the refrigerator, thrown away all the empty bottles and cups, and loaded the dishwasher. As she was wiping down the counters, she'd noticed Alex leaning in the door frame of the kitchen smiling at her.

"What?" she asked as he stared at her.

"Nothing," he shrugged.

"Why are you staring at me?"

"You just look so damn sexy when you concentrate."

Her eyes narrowed and she turned her head slightly. "That's weird."

"You know what's weird?" he asked as he playfully lunged for her. He scooped her up in his arms as she squealed with delight. "It's weird that you're still in the kitchen and fully dressed."

She'd thrown her head back and laughed, tossing the sponge in the sink as they headed for the bedroom. After they'd made sweet lingering love and were drifting off the sleep, she thought she'd heard him say, "It should always be like this."

It had been a wonderfully perfect day. 'This is why I stayed,' she thought to herself. 'When it's good, it's so good.' She snuggled in closer and smiled. No one else in the world had made her feel like this. Tingles spread through her entire body at just the mention of his name, or the sound of his voice. This had never happened before. She was head over heels in love and though she knew this ride was dangerous, she wasn't getting off. His hands brought forth beautiful music from deep inside her, much like they did his guitar. He made the song come alive in her.

She was so tired of playing it safe and barely living. He'd brought her back to life, warmed her with his fire. She'd not realized how tepid she had become, how meaningless life was since her father died. He'd been dead almost half her life, yet she had just recently come out of the stupor from losing him.

Her father had filled her with life, filled her soul with energy, let her know it was okay to take risks. She remembered being scared of riding her bike without the training wheels when she was six. He'd given her the confidence she needed to try, and keep trying even after falling many times. She had lost that part of herself when he passed away. She'd watched the cancer strip his body down to nothing, and even though it had never beat his spirit, his death had still sapped every bit of the carefree little girl out of her. From then on she began to play it safe, afraid to let herself love someone as much as she loved her dad. She had never wanted to risk losing something so precious again. Until Alex. He'd filled her empty shell of a heart and brought it back to life. True, his fire warmed her soul, but like with any flame, it could burn. She'd felt that outside the library, but it hadn't been enough to make her give up feeling alive again.

Chapter 23

After her run the next morning, which felt a bit weird without Max, Christina proceeded to clean her entire house bottom to top. She started in the kitchen and downstairs bathroom. After vacuuming the living room, and emptying the vacuum chamber twice from the dog hair, she moved upstairs, collecting an armload of kid toys along the way. She stripped the sheets from all the beds, loaded the washer, and then set about the massive task of straightening up the playroom and her kids' bedrooms. After about an hour, those three rooms looked as if kids were just an idea around the house. She already knew her efforts would really be short lived though because the minute they returned home, they would pull down the toys and recreate the mess all over again. That was okay though; it felt good just to have it clean for three days.

Once those rooms were done, she turned her attention to the upstairs bathrooms and finally the master bedroom. She'd found it difficult to sleep without the quiet whirring of Todd's sleep apnea machine so she rummaged through the closet until she found a small table top fan. After putting away the clothes that were piled up on the dresser top, filing away anything important, trashing what needed to be thrown out, and making the bed with fresh sheets, she allowed herself a nice long bath. It felt good to accomplish so much in just a few hours.

Her dream had left her remembering a time she thought she'd forgotten. Her cleaning was a way to keep the memories at bay. Maybe, she thought to herself, maybe safety, security and stability was what she'd needed all along. She had all that here, and she was happy. She told herself that and tried hard to believe it.

After the six mile run and the two hour cleaning extravaganza, she was tired and a bit sore. Relaxing in the hot water with her favorite music playing softly in the background, Christina read her book and enjoyed just being alone. It was a rare moment when she was alone. She could count on one hand the times she'd been completely on her own for more than a few hours since Kate had been born. It felt nice. Following her bath she luxuriated even more by wrapping herself in her thick white terry cloth robe, stretching out right in the middle of the king size bed and promptly falling asleep.

At the same time Alex was busy getting his mother's house set up for the evening's dinner. Sarah's husband Dave helped him bring in chairs and card tables from the garage. They set them up in the breakfast area so the kids would have a place to eat. Then they moved the living furniture around maximizing the small space to accommodate more chairs and to provide opportunities for easy conversation. He had decided long ago that his mother needed a bigger house. She loved to entertain guests, but the sardine box sized rooms made that difficult. If he made it big and could afford it, he was buying her something larger. After all, it was the least he could do for everything she'd gone through with him.

He set out what seemed like a million candles all around the house. His mom liked to create a warm, cozy atmosphere which, unfortunately, often translated into someone's knocking over a candle and spilling wax on the carpet, or worse, on themselves. Luckily, no one had burned the house down yet. He went into the kitchen and was immediately put to work making a tower of plates separated by napkins. He stacked plate, napkin, plate, napkin twelve times. His Uncle Martin was coming, along with his wife and their three kids. His mom's neighbor Renee and her son Donovan were also joining the festivities. Not a bad group, he thought. A good mix of ages and backgrounds should make for some interesting conversation.

At 4:30 he went upstairs and took a shower. He took extra time getting ready. He tried to tell himself it was just in honor of the festive occasion, but he was lying. Walking from the bathroom into his childhood bedroom, he felt very much like he had in high school getting ready for his first real date. He'd had a towel wrapped around his hips, just like now, and was agonizing over what to wear. He really didn't think girls understood how much pressure guys felt to look good on a date. But this is not a date, he reminded himself.

Turning toward the mirror he saw a slightly larger version of that same fifteen year old boy staring back at him. He had been much scrawnier then. His body hadn't filled out, and his torso hadn't caught up with his legs and feet. He'd been the dorkiest looking fifteen year old on the planet. Eighteen years later he stood examining the figure peering back at him, now broader with well defined muscles, and better proportions. Yet, he still felt like that geeky fifteen year old who was so scared he couldn't impress the girl.

The guests began to arrive at 5:45. Martin, Betty and their kids got there first. Dave returned after a quick trip back to his house for additional serving spoons. Sarah had stayed through the day to help out. Renee and Donovan arrived shortly after 6:00. Lynda began laying out the food so people could fill their plates buffet style. Alex checked his watch at 6:15; Christina had not arrived. He hoped she was just trying to be fashionably late, but knew she liked to be early anywhere she went. At 6:30 he began to worry that she wasn't coming at all, maybe she had changed her mind. He tried to suppress it, but a disappointed feeling settled in his belly. The guests chatted easily and then lined up to serve their plates. As he filled his and sat down to eat, the doorbell rang. She was here.

He stood at the door and breathed in deeply before opening it. As he caught sight of her, the breath caught in his throat. She was looking slightly back over her shoulder revealing a profile that showed a well defined jaw line curving down to a long slender neck. She turned at the movement of the door and smiled at him through upturned lashes. Her bright cornflower blue eyes reflected the light from the porch so that they glowed like two blue flames. Her cheeks were flushed red from the cold. Late November was unusually cold this year. Even in the Deep South, temperatures were barely reaching 25 degrees. She held a bottle of wine in one hand and a serving bowl of something in the other. He could have stared at her forever.

"Hi," she said brightly, but with just a hint of nervousness.

"Hi," he answered and for a moment was unsure of how to proceed. They stood facing each other awkwardly for a few seconds before he said, "I'm sorry, come in!" He moved aside allowing her to step over the threshold. "Uh, oh. What did you make?" he asked as he took the bowl from under her arm. "Are you sure you want to serve this to unsuspecting strangers?" he teased.

"Ha, ha. You're funny," she chided him back. "It's hard to mess up Jell-o. Sorry I'm late," she said as she set the wine down on the front hall table. She unwound the scarf from around her neck, and offered no explanation as to why she was late. He didn't know that she had had second thoughts about coming to the dinner. Even though they had reached an agreement about keeping things on a 'just friends' level, with no mention of their past, she still felt uneasy. She'd sat in her driveway for a good twenty minutes before actually starting the car and beginning the drive across town. "It's just dinner," she kept repeating like a mantra the whole way there.

"Well, if anyone could mess up Jell-o, it would be you. No offense, of course," he kidded back. "Let me take your coat. Everyone has just started loading their plates. You're just in time." He took her coat and hung it on the coat rack. Then he took in the whole vision of her. She was wearing a gold long sleeve top with a moderately deep V-neckline. The beaded material that edged the V continued down the middle of the blouse. The gathering slightly below the bodice drew attention to her shapely figure. The curve of her breasts was accentuated by the soft folds of the fabric, creating a subtle but definite aura of sexiness. Dark blue jeans rode low on her hips, and a wide brown belt and brown Jimmy Choo heels completed the outfit. Her hair was loose and slightly windblown, giving her a tousled look. "Wow, you look…" he struggled for an appropriate word. "Amazing" was all he could come up with. The fact was she was the closest thing to perfection he'd ever seen.

"Thanks," she said. "You look really nice too," she said taking in the blue sweater and jeans. He almost looked preppy, but with the sleeves pushed up to his elbows revealing the lower portion of his tattoo, he still had that edge.

The fragrant aromas from the house were almost overpowering. The smells of turkey, dressing, casseroles and the hint of pumpkin pie that was just coming out of the oven blended together to create one delicious scent. That, coupled with the coziness of the candle-lit home lit created a warm and comfortable ambiance. Her unease settled down somewhat as Alex led her into the dining room and made the introductions. Lynda and Sarah got up from their seats to give her a hug, genuinely glad to see her. Christina had been afraid of what they might think of her presence at the dinner. Even though Alex had told her that Lynda had insisted Chris join them, she feared they might think she was playing Alex for her own selfish motives. Perhaps that's what she thought herself, subconsciously.

She piled her plate with the scrumptious looking holiday fare and took her seat at the table. Alex brought her a glass of the sauvignon blanc that she'd brought. Martin asked her about her role in Alex's career and this opened the flood gates of conversation. Talk flowed easily among the diners. She shared stories of the most temperamental stars she'd represented. They were actually able to guess a few of them based on her description of their asinine behavior. In fact, it quickly turned into a game. She described someone she'd represented, and they tried to guess who she was talking about. For a couple of her more elusive clients, she gave multiple choice options. Frequent laughter erupted as well as gasps of shock at the outrageous conduct of some stars.

Then the attention turned to Alex. They all seemed to feel the need to put him in his place, just to keep him humble. Lynda offered up a story she swore she would tell the press if he ever decided his "butt was bigger than his britches". Lynda was a dyed in the wool southern woman prone to use colorful southern phrases.

She shared the memory of Alex around the age of seven deciding he wanted to be Elvis. He'd dressed up in an old butterfly collared shirt that he'd found in the back of her closet, wrapped a white belt around his waist and got her shawl to use as a cape. He'd talked her into painting sideburns on his face with her liquid eyeliner pen. He'd then spent the entire afternoon singing renditions of Elvis songs, mostly with made up lyrics, and hip thrusting all around the house. By the end of the story they were howling with laughter.

Sarah disappeared for a few minutes and came back with a photo of Alex from his early high school days when he had gone through his "The Cure" phase. He was dressed in all black, hair dyed jet black as well, and this time the eyeliner rimmed his eyes in thick black lines giving him an appearance somewhat reminiscent of a raccoon on crack. Christina was surprised to see how rail-thin he had been in high school. She dabbed her eyes with the edge of her napkin as the tears of laughter stung her eyes. Through it all Alex was a good sport. He took the teasing in stride, and even offered some hilarious commentary about himself, making everyone laugh even harder.

After dinner, the guests settled in the living room for pie. There were three different kinds of pie; pumpkin, pecan and apple. A fresh pot of coffee had been brewed and Chris took a cup. She talked with Betty about their kids and the struggles inherent in working while trying to raise them. The evening had gone perfectly and any hint of her earlier discomfort was gone. The food was scrumptious; even her Jell-o got an approving nod, though she was sure they were just being nice. The conversation had been pleasant and funny. This Thanksgiving was shaping up nicely. It certainly beat sitting at home alone eating a turkey sandwich and watching reruns, or enduring Andrea's uncle Bart for three hours.

When she and Betty had finished their pie and coffee, Christina picked up their plates and went into the kitchen. Lynda was there beginning the process of putting the place back together. Dirty plates, silverware and glasses were strewn about the countertops and bowls and pans of remaining food lined one side of the wall. Lynda was rinsing off dirty dishes and loading them into the dishwasher. She gratefully accepted Christina's offer to help her tackle the mountain. Sarah came in a few minutes later and began putting the food into smaller storage containers so the big pans could be washed as well.

"Lynda, I can't begin to tell you how wonderful dinner was!" Christina complimented her hostess.

"Oh honey, please!" Lynda said with her typical southern drawl. "I am just so glad you decided to join us. When Alex said your whole family was going out of town, and you were spending Thanksgiving alone, I told him he'd better get you on the phone and make sure you were comin'. I wouldn't hear of you spending the holidays by yourself. After all, you are responsible for the take off of his career."

"I don't know about that. He's immensely talented, and he got himself signed. All I've done is help him look good. I don't know if I can take credit for his success, at least not all of it anyway," she replied as she dried off a plate.

"Well, all I know is that Alex is lucky to have you with him through this. I know things were once pretty bad between you two and he feels real bad about that. I know he believes he's blessed to have you by his side during this project," Lynda replied.

"It's good you two were able to put the past behind you and work so well together," Sarah chimed in. "I mean, you must feel pretty comfortable now if you're able to spend a holiday with him instead of your family."

"I'm sorry?" Christina asked confused, turning to face Sarah. "I don't really understand what you mean by that."

"What I mean is you're spending Thanksgiving with someone who was once a very strong part your life while your family is far away. You and Alex must have patched things up," Sarah answered.

"We came to an understanding. We work together now, but our lives are very different. We agreed that being friends would be much easier than being at odds over things that happened over a decade ago," Christina tried to explain.

"So, Alex is cool with that? Just being friends?" Sarah asked as she placed the leftovers in the refrigerator and closed the door behind her.

"Sarah, honey, that's enough. Chris is our guest." Lynda tried to divert the conversation to a safer subject. "Would you like an after dinner drink, Chris?" she asked.

"No, thank you Lynda," Christina answered. "Sarah, why wouldn't he be cool with us being just friends?"

"Oh come on, Chris. Isn't it obvious?"

"Isn't what obvious?" Christina felt her heart starting to beat faster in her chest. She wasn't sure where this was going, but she didn't think she liked it.

"You're married. You've moved on. Look at Alex. He hasn't," was all Sarah said.

Christina stood there motionless; drying cloth in one hand, fork in the other. She felt as if the floor were spinning out from under her. What was Sarah trying to say? Alex hadn't moved on? She'd seen him with several beautiful women. Chris had suspected earlier that he was still dealing with lingering feelings, but was he in love with her? It couldn't possibly be. He'd felt bad about the past. That's why he'd written those songs years before and come to her house the other week. It couldn't be anything more than that. She leaned against the counter to regain her balance, letting the fork slip out of her hand. It landed with a slight plink on the countertop. She gaped at mother and daughter in complete silence.

"Chris, darlin', say something," Lynda whispered.

At that moment Alex came breezing into the kitchen holding up the game Scattergories. "Hey, who's up for a little fun?" he asked before stopping dead in his tracks. The smile slipped from his face as he found the three women staring at each other. His mother and sister looked as if they'd just broken some bad news to their best friend. Christina looked shocked, as if she'd just seen a ghost. "What's going on?" he asked cautiously. Christina turned in his direction, the dazed expression still on her face. "Mom, Sarah, what's going on?" he practically shouted as he moved to Christina's side. He put a hand on her arm, and she instinctively flinched away.

"I'm sorry, but I really need to go. Thank you for dinner. It was delicious," was all Christina managed to whisper as she put down the drying cloth and backed her way out of the kitchen.

Alex continued to search his mother's and sister's face for answers. What had he interrupted?

"What did you say?" he hissed under his breath. Then he turned to follow Christina through the hallway. By the time he caught up with her, she was already putting her coat on. "Chris, wait. Please tell me what's happening? What's wrong?"

She looked into his eyes with an incomprehensible look on her face.

"Are you still in love with me?" she asked flat out.

No need in beating around the bush. He didn't answer. He stood there helplessly pleading with her without a sound.

"Your silence says it all," she said as she turned the doorknob and walked outside. She'd only taken a few steps when he was in front on her again.

"What do you think, Chris? Don't you know I'm in love with you? I've never stopped being in love with you."

"I have to go," she said curtly. She stepped around and began to move past him making a hasty retreat to her car.

He stepped in front of her again. This time he took her by the shoulders firmly so she couldn't move away from him. "I have been in love with you since the day I met you. I know I acted stupidly, I know made some horrible mistakes and I know I needed to change. And now I have changed. I made my life better. I cleaned up, got a real job, bought my own house and poured myself into my music, and it's brought me back to you." He tried to run his hand down the side of her cheek, but she jerked away, smacking his hand and backed up about ten feet. A light snow had begun to fall and the flakes danced in between them.

"I'm married!" she shouted at him. "I have been for eight years! What's wrong with you? It's too late for us, Alex. Can't you see that?"

"Christina, we were brought back together for a reason, and it wasn't just the music. You can't possibly say you haven't thought about this, haven't thought about me, in all these years. For God's sake, you still wear the charm I gave you for our first Christmas!"

"We were young and stupid back then. We both made mistakes and we both got hurt, but Alex, I took my life in a different direction and I am happy where I am."

"If you are so happy with your ideal life the way it is, why are you here? With me? Tonight?" he asked.

"Your mother invited me so I wouldn't have to be alone on Thanksgiving!" she responded incredulously, her arms spread wide as if the answer should be obvious.

"Seriously? Is that what you're telling yourself? You're here because you didn't want to be alone on Thanksgiving? Why did you choose to spend it with me, instead of someone else? Why aren't you with your family, Christina?"

"Because I am working on *your* tour, Alex!" Their voices carried through the quiet night.

"It could've waited until you got back. No, you stayed behind because you wanted to! You stayed behind because for a few days you wanted to be free from that life. Admit it!"

"Admit what?"

"Admit that the perfect life that you've created for yourself is not so perfect after all. Admit that you are bored being married to an accountant, even if he is the greatest father in the world. Admit that you work with rock stars because you need excitement in your life. Damn it, Chris, admit that you're still in love with me too!"

He moved forward within inches of her face. He grasped her arms in his strong hands and lightly shook her as if to wake her from an unusually long slumber.

"I've changed. I made myself a better person because of what I did to you. I finally have the chance to prove that to you, can't you see that?"

"What do you want from me, Alex?" She struggled against his grip as the tears slid down her cheeks. He fought to hang on to her.

"I want you to look me in the eye and tell me you're not still in love with me. Tell me you haven't thought about me over the years. Tell me you haven't wondered what it would have been like if things had worked out between us. Tell me the tension that's been hovering between us is imaginary. If you can tell me that you're one hundred percent happy and in love with Todd, that he's the only one for you, and that I have no place in your life, then I'll let you go without a fight. If you can't tell me that, then I am going to fight like hell for you, for us." A hint of desperation mixed with the resolve in his voice.

She stopped struggling and became perfectly still. She dropped her head to her chest and began to sob. He wrapped his arms around her and held her for a moment, snowflakes wisped around them. Just as he leaned down to kiss her, he felt her stiffen. She pulled away and stared, blue eyes to green ones. All trace of emotion had left her face and her eyes, alive with feeling moments before, were blank.

"I'm not in love with you Alex. Let me go." With that she pushed his arms away from her and walked past him to her car.

He didn't even turn to see her drive away. He stared blankly, as flurries of icy flakes swirled around him, too stunned to move. She was gone. It was over.

Chapter 24

Christina pulled out of the driveway and sped off down the street. She couldn't tell which was blurring her vision more, the unseasonable snowfall or the tears streaming down her cheeks. She made her way to Interstate 285 and headed west toward Marietta. When she reached GA-400, she made another decision and turned north toward Roswell instead. The River Park was her favorite spot in all of metro Atlanta. She could sit right next to the Chattahoochee River and watch the water for hours.

Water had always been a soothing element. The never ending flow of the river often helped calm her down when she was upset. It helped her realize how small she was in this great big world; how she would wake up the next day and the river would still be flowing. Life continued on, no matter what circumstances were thrown her way.

Parking her SUV, Christina ignored the sign stating the park closed at sundown. Blinking through the drifting snow, she went to the edge of the dock and lay down, feeling the cold wood slats, dampened from the snowfall, under her back. They were hard, but comforting at the same time. She tried to breathe, but found it difficult to get the cold air into her lungs. It felt as if a fifty pound weight was sitting right in the middle of her chest. This wasn't happening, not again, she said to herself, shaking her head. Her mind involuntarily brought her back to the last time she'd walked away from him.

It had been a blustery late March day. She'd made her way to the park in the middle of campus. Choosing a spot near the bank of the lake, she lay down her blanket. The sun was making its way across the horizon, casting rays of slanted light through the trees. As she sat down, she pushed windswept strands of hair away from her face. She wrapped her arms around her knees and rested her chin upon them.

She was moving into her second trimester. Recognizing the seriousness of the situation, she knew she had to make some decisions soon. The easiest thing to do would be to move back home and finish school there. She could live with her mom until she had enough money saved to get a small apartment for her and the baby. But she really liked it here, and she was very close to finishing her degree. She could get a part time job now and save as much money as possible until next fall. Then she could move out of the dorm and get an apartment nearby. College town rent was cheaper than rent prices back home, she was sure. The university had a great day care program for student and faculty use. She could student teach in one of the nearby schools. The timing put her due date so she'd only miss four weeks of class. She was sure her professors would be flexible.

Christina heard Alex's feet shuffling across the grass before she saw him, but she'd already known he was approaching even before she heard his footfalls. Being able to sense his presence was something she'd developed throughout their relationship. She wasn't sure why she'd agreed to meet him. He still didn't know about, hopefully didn't even suspect, the pregnancy. She prayed he didn't notice the ten pound weight gain, although she was sure she could play it off if necessary. Alex was not going to be a part of this baby's life, she'd decided. He was not going to be a part of her life.

Keeping her eyes locked on the lake, she didn't turn to look at him, afraid her frail resolve would fail her. He didn't ask for permission before sitting down beside her on the blanket. He'd lost weight and she could see, even in profile, the dark circles under his eyes and the slight tremor in his hands. They sat in silence for what seemed like ages. He seemed frightened to talk. She put up her black wall; for her there was nothing to say. She almost predicted the words he spoke before he opened his mouth. She'd heard it all before. Most of it anyway.

"Chris, I need to apologize to you," he began shakily. "I was a fucking idiot and I wouldn't blame you if you never spoke to me again." He paused before continuing. "I know you don't want to hear this. I know you probably wish you'd never met me, but I am so sorry I hurt you. I said atrocious things to you, things I didn't mean, things that shouldn't have been directed toward you. I know I've probably used all my chances up with you, but God I really need you now. I've totally screwed up my life, and I don't know where else to turn. I need help. I want to get clean, I want to get better, and I need you," he said wiping away a tear that escaped his eye.

Oh my gosh, she thought to herself, he's crying! It wasn't the first time, but this felt different. Her heart ached to reach out to him, but she stopped herself from taking him in her arms. She couldn't afford to get sucked back in now. It was no longer just her heart at stake, but one day their baby's heart would be broken by him too. That was something she could not, would not, let happen.

"I want you to know," he continued, "that I've already kicked one bad habit. It's gone for good, and has no hold on me anymore. I realized how much I lost when I gave up on us and tossed you away. You're the one for me, Chris. You always have been and that scared the shit out of me. But what scares me more is knowing that I may never have you back in my life. Knowing I gave up the one good thing that's ever been given to me is almost more than I can bear. I'll do anything, Chris. I'll join a program and get clean, but I just don't think I'm strong enough to do it on my own." They were still staring straight ahead, not chancing a glance in the other's direction. He slid his hand across the blanket in her direction and brushed her knuckles. "Please take me back. Please love me again. I need you. I can't do this without you… I love you."

There they were. Those three words. I love you. A dead weight dropped into the pit of her stomach. She cut him off there. He had finally said the three words she'd longed to hear from him for so long, but it didn't even matter anymore. She refused to go through this again.

"You're going to *have* to do this without me, Alex," she said in a trembling voice and saw him stiffen. "I'm going to say this one time, and one time only. I don't ever want to hear your voice or see your face again. Don't call me. Don't show up at my dorm, or find me here. Don't sing to me, or bump into me by chance on campus.

It's too late. It's over. It's *so* over. I'm done." With that she stood, picked up her backpack and walked away, leaving him sitting on her blanket. She never even looked at his face. She couldn't have, or she would've ended up in his arms. If she'd met his eyes, her weakness would've overtaken her will. She didn't see him drop his head and collapse into himself. It nearly killed her to leave, but it was something she had to do.

That night she miscarried. She'd refused the overnight hospital stay. She didn't have the medical insurance to cover it. Plus, no one knew she'd been pregnant, except her doctor. It would be a little difficult to explain to her mom why she had a tremendous bill for no reason. The nurse told her the baby had been about eight inches long. She asked what would happen to it and was told the hospital would cremate it unless she wanted to make other arrangements. No, she said, and left as soon as she was released.

Climbing straight into bed, she stared at the ceiling for hours. She willed herself to feel something, anything. She prayed for tears to come, but none did. There was nothing left; no anger, no sadness, no relief, nothing. She was utterly numb and she remained that way for longer than she imagined was possible.

She didn't remember much after that for several months. Life just took its course and she went through the motions. The sun came up every morning and it set every night; through it all she managed to breathe. There didn't seem to be much else she could do. A similar feeling settled over her now.

A flash of headlights broke her away from her thoughts. She sat up from her supine position on the dock, rubbed her eyes and looked toward the car that had parked at the end, blocking her way out. A police officer stepped from the vehicle and reminded her that the park was closed. She apologized and rose to her feet. Getting back in her vehicle, Christina started the engine. She started driving and headed toward the only place she knew to go.

Chapter 25

Alex lay on his couch in a near state of shock. He couldn't believe what had happened. He'd convinced himself that he'd rather have Christina in his life as a friend, or at least a colleague, than to not have her at all. He never really knew if that had been true, but it had been worth a shot. Try as he might, he couldn't stop replaying the scene of her standing in front of him, tears glistening on her cheeks, snow swirling around her head. Life as he knew it was over. He'd been given a chance to make it up to her, and blown it. Even when she told him she didn't love him, she'd been breathtakingly beautiful. Watching her tail lights fade in the distance, he'd felt a sinking in the pit of his stomach. The feeling was, unfortunately, all too familiar.

He had no idea where things would go from here. She would most definitely remove herself as his rep. He wouldn't contest. In fact, if it became an issue he would ask for someone else to take over. He couldn't bear the thought of making her anymore uncomfortable than he already had. It was his fault she was upset. Well, his and his sister's big mouth. He'd walked back into the house after his confrontation with Chris and stared at Sarah. She'd tried to apologize, but it was something that needed to be said. He'd just stared at her blankly before going to the hall to retrieve his coat and keys. He left without a word to anyone. There was really nothing more to say.

He turned on the TV hoping to find something to take his mind off of Christina. But after deducting that there was nothing that could accomplish that impossible feat, he turned it off and grabbed his guitar. He tried to play songs he'd already written. He tried strumming something new. Nothing was working. Nothing was helping. Setting the guitar down on the floor beside him he leaned his elbows on his knees. Putting his head in his hands he took a few big deep breaths trying to clear his head. The old urge to use was creeping up again and tears came before he realized it. There was nothing he could do. She was lost forever, again. His mind returned to the last time they'd talked by the lake.

Alex had left a note on her door asking her to meet him there. He didn't expect her to show, but was relieved when she did. She'd beat him and she looked very pale and tired, as if she hadn't slept or eaten well in a while. Yet, he thought she looked heavier, but couldn't be sure. The oversized sweatshirt she wore hid most of her frame. It was a warm day, too warm for a sweatshirt, but the wind let the chill hang on a little longer. Sitting next to her, he could feel that something was different. He was afraid to tell her what he needed to say, but thought he might die if he didn't.

He'd been sober for three days and was trying very hard to control the tremors that plagued his hands. The situation petrified him, but he knew he couldn't continue his life the way it was going.

When Christina ended it for good and walked away, it was as if he'd watched any chance at happiness walk right along beside her. He sank into a deeper depression than he'd ever been in before. Deeper than all the times Audrey had walked out on him, deeper than after his dad left. The detox and sobriety was not something he could maintain on his own. He knew putting that kind of pressure on her to help him stay clean wasn't fair, but he'd been clueless about what else to do. With her he'd felt happiness that he'd never felt before. If she had been by his side, he was sure he could overcome the drugs and they could overcome their past. Once that chance had evaporated, he was left helpless. He went on a five day binge and stayed high almost the entire time.

When he finally managed to drag himself out of his stupor, he packed whatever would fit in his suitcases and drove home. He never returned to school. His mom and sister had driven down later and cleaned out his apartment.

It took nearly two years for him to reach the bottom of his self-dug well. The intervention staged by his friends and family was what he needed. His cry for help had finally been answered. He spent a month in a treatment center the first time and two months the second time. Two more years passed before he felt even remotely human, much less normal.

Eventually, he'd found a steady job that wasn't great and had no future, but it was stable and he could get by. He began to rebuild his life, but the entire time Christina had been in the back of his mind, just lingering. The eternal "what if?" never went away. He had begun to think it never would.

As he lay there starting up at his ceiling fan that was coated in a good half inch of dust, he thought he heard a soft knock at the door. He really didn't want to have another conversation with Sarah. He wanted to forget the night ever happened, but he knew his sister too well. She'd never let him bury this. They'd always been close, despite their age difference, and their relationship was too important to both of them to let anything or anyone stand in the way. Plus, if he left his sister on the doorstep in the freezing cold snow, she would never let him hear the end of it.

Heaving himself off the couch, he made his way toward the door, not bothering to turn on any lights. Other than the dim light above the stove, and the streetlight streaming in through the window, the room was dark. He felt dark right now and that's what he wanted to be engulfed in.

Turning the door knob, he paused for a moment trying to figure out what exactly he'd say to Sarah. He was angry with her for opening her giant mouth, but nothing she'd said had been a lie. He couldn't stay mad at her for saying something that would have come out eventually anyway. She'd just been the messenger. He pulled the door toward him and looked out into the night. His heart stopped and he froze as he realized it was not his sister.

"Hi," she said. "Can I come in?"

Alex stood motionless for a moment waiting for his brain to register that Christina was standing in front of him. She stood there, bundled in her coat, hair slightly disheveled, eyes red and puffy, looking like she'd seen better days. Completely shocked, he moved to the side to let her enter. He gave his head a little shake as she moved into the entryway to make sure he was really seeing her and not hallucinating.

Closing the door behind her, he turned in her direction. She was already facing him, head held high, as if she were ready for round two. Standing ten feet apart both of them seemed afraid to move, afraid the delicate balance would be broken and they would both be sent hurdling into a never ending chasm. Her face was stained red from the tears that were still flowing down her cheeks, and her eyes were bloodshot. She looked fragile, almost breakable. Unable to keep up the façade, her shoulders drooped and she let her head fall forward. She broke the silence first.

"You were right," she said and then stopped as if afraid to continue.

"About what?" he asked in a voice that barely registered as a whisper.

"I am still in love with you. I always have been," she said, raising her eyes to meet his.

She had no chance to say anything more. He moved across the space that divided them, and it seemed to take forever to cross those meager ten feet. He took her face into his hands and his lips finally claimed the place they had been yearning for so many years. His mouth eagerly swept across hers. Heat flooded through his body and everything around him went hazy. Nothing else in the world existed. She had come back to him.

The passion grew too intense for either of them to control. There was no hesitation. For eleven years they had been deprived of each other. He clumsily unbuttoned her coat and slung it to the floor. She unwound her scarf and let it fall. The hallway wasn't very big and in their haste they knocked over the small foyer table. He heard glass shatter from one of the picture frames, but couldn't have cared less. He lifted her up and felt her body's response to his. He felt her quick breath on his neck as he tangled his fingers through her hair. She was still sobbing quietly. Though her tears had stopped falling, her breathing was rapid and shallow.

He reluctantly released her lips, only long enough to pull her shirt over her head. He could feel the shudders of emotion through her body and this fueled his desire even more. She moved her hands down to the edge of his shirt and began to gently tug. She ran her hands underneath along the smooth wall of his chest. He lifted his arms and pulled the sweater and undershirt off letting them fall near her coat. She dropped her mouth to his chest and moved her tongue along the path her hands had traveled seconds before, she leaving a trail of fire behind. He pulled her back to face him, almost dizzy with his desire. He had to make sure before this went any farther. He could still back away if he had to.

"Chris," he whispered, "are you sure about this?" It came out nearly as a whimper and he was terrified of her answer. If she changed her mind and said no, he was sure he would go mad, but he would do as she wished.

"Yes, Alex. I'm sure," she said with heavy breaths. That was all he needed to hear. He picked her up and carried her into his bedroom; the room he'd never let anyone else share before. It didn't feel awkward to have her there. It felt right. It felt as if she belonged; the integral missing puzzle piece that was finally found.

They struggled to remove the remnants of their clothes. He fumbled with the hook of her bra. The filmy gold fabric floated gently to the floor.

As it did, the intensity of the situation flooded through her. She was here, with him, and about to do something she'd promised never to do. This is it, she thought. This is what I've been missing for so long. The volts of electricity coursing through every place he touched her awakened something inside that had been asleep for so long. She didn't care about the consequences right now. She wanted him; she wanted to feel him move with her and in her. Her heart was beating nearly out of her chest. She wasn't sure how she'd ended up here, but she knew this is where she belonged. She noticed she was holding her breath and made a conscious effort to breathe.

She pulled the belt on his jeans through the belt loops and let it drop away. She tugged at the button and quick removed that obstacle as well. While she worked at freeing him from his barriers, he moved to help her remove hers. He pulled the button on her jeans open, dragged the zipper down slowly and yanked the tight denim over her hips.

Standing there together, almost naked save the thin material of boxers and bikinis, they looked deeply into each other's eyes. Together they read the mutual desire that burned inside them for each other. Unspoken words moved between the two. Apologies for the hurt, forgiveness for the pain, and the yearning to begin again were all communicated without either of them uttering a sound.

In that one glance she saw everything she'd seen that first time they'd been together. She saw the man he had once been, the man he was, and the man she always knew he would become. If she left forever after tonight, she would leave with no regrets. This man whom she loved, who loved her back, was all she ever needed to know.

She felt the involuntary responses of her body to his touch. The passion she'd denied herself for the past eleven years was being reignited to its full force. It was a power she was sure she couldn't stop, didn't want to stop, and was eager to experience. She closed her eyes as his tongue performed a deceptive dance just inside her mouth, as if tempting her to come out and play. He put his hands on the sides of her face and smoothed her hair back. When she opened her eyes she found his gaze and locked in.

He gathered her up in his arms and they tumbled ungracefully on the bed. The heat returned and their bodies melded into one another. He moved his hands over her hips bringing them to meet at her belly button. Together they traveled to her breasts, cupping each as he brought his fiery kiss to each of them. He tickled her nipples with his tongue and she felt them stiffen in to small peaks beneath his caress.

She let out a soft groan and dug her nails into the flesh of his back. She pulled him to her urgently. It had been long enough. She couldn't take it another moment. He used his knee to separate her legs as he slid inside her. She cried out as he did. The familiar sensations returned. It was as if the lost key to a locked door was finally found. Everything felt right. There was no chance of keeping it slow, no chance of pacing. Sweat formed on their bodies as the speed and intensity increased. Like caged lions finally released from captivity, there was no tenderness in their actions. They couldn't seem to get enough of each other. It was raw and fierce and exactly what they both needed.

Alex buried his head in her shoulder feeling her damp hair across his cheeks. He had dreamed of this, of her, and she was here. Her body was delicious and he remembered her taste from before. Her smell set off a firestorm of memories and he found it difficult to hold himself back. He groaned her name in a ragged breath. He could feel her body tense as her legs tightened around his and her whole body shuddered. His head reeled as her mouth devoured his neck and when she sank her teeth into his shoulder, he nearly lost control. It was enough to drive a man insane.

Unable to hold back any longer he laced his fingers through hers, held her arms captive overhead and allowed himself every pleasure her body was offering. They came together in a drenched heat; then he collapsed on top of her. Neither had the power to move as they breathed rapidly, perspiration slicking their bodies. She slowly extracted her arms from his and wrapped them around him. The passion for each other that had been missing so long had returned as if they had never been apart.

They lay there trying to catch their breath for what seemed like hours until he gently propped himself up on one elbow and looked at her with concern. Unsure of what he would find, he saw her eyes closed, face relaxed with an almost dreamy smile on her face.

"Hey," he whispered tracing the edge of her face with his fingers. He needed to memorize every line, every curve, afraid if he turned away or closed his eyes for a second, he'd wake up and she'd be gone. She had only grown more beautiful over the years, but in the dim streetlight filtering in through the window she looked twenty again. Fresh, delicate and deceptively innocent. To look at her no one would know that she was capable of the actions that had just taken place.

"Hey," she whispered back.

"Are you okay?"

"For now I am. What about you?"

"I couldn't be better. I just want to make sure…"

"Shh…" she stopped him with her still sleepy smile and pulled him back to her. He laid his head on her chest and gave in to the sensation of her fingers as she stroked his hair. Each movement left small tingles behind. "Let's not talk right now," she whispered. They fell asleep, tangled in a web of limbs. They awoke and made love two more times during the night. With the initial urgency gone, these times were slower and sweeter, but just as passionate as the first. No words were spoken because none were needed. Their bodies knew each other and what was desired. Time had not allowed them to forget.

Chapter 26

Christina awoke a little before dawn and stretched, realizing she was alone in the unfamiliar bed. It took a little while for the memory to come back to her. He was still in love with her, and despite her best attempts to forget him and move on, she was still in love with him. Things were very different now, yet remarkably the same. They were still not free to love unabashedly. This time though it was she who was not available. She gathered the quilt around her naked body and padded softly through the hallway into the empty living room. Not hearing anything at first, she thought he'd left. She wondered if she should plan a hasty retreat. Then she heard the faint strumming of a guitar.

She found him in the small room off the kitchen that was probably meant for a dining room. He'd turned it into a space for his music. The window overlooked a wooded area that dipped down to a small creek. It was a very peaceful setting. She could see why he'd chosen this spot to do the majority of his work. He was sitting on a high back stool wearing only jeans. His bare torso and feet looked more suited for a late spring morning than early winter. He was playing something she thought she recognized. It wasn't from his CD though; she'd memorized that. She finally placed the song as "It's Been A While" by Staind. She crossed the room and sat down in front of him watching him while he played. His eyes met hers, but he continued with the song. She let herself be captivated by his voice and the power of the song. When he finished he put the guitar on its stand beside him and looked at her full on.

"Good morning," he said lightly.

"Good morning. I love that song," she said quietly.

"Me too," he whispered back.

"You know, the first time I heard it I thought about you. I still do every time." She pulled her knees in and wrapped the quilt tighter around her body. "Aren't you cold?" she asked. "It's freezing in here."

"Come sit with me." His voice was barely audible. She moved from her position on the floor and sat in his lap. Resting her head on his shoulder as he wrapped his arms around her, she settled in and let the heat from his body warm her. She felt his hands running slowly over her hair. She heard him breathe in the scent of her.

"Chris, we should really talk about this," he started to say.

"Shh," she held a finger to his lips as she looked in his eyes. "Not right now. Let's not ruin the moment with words. We can do that later."

"So, what do you want to do?" he asked.

"Just hold me right now, okay. Just hold me and watch the colors with me," she whispered as she leaned back against his shoulder. They watched the sun come up through the window. The room's light slowly changed from shadowy grays to wispy blues. Vibrant pink and orange crept over the edge of the trees signaling the beginning of a new day. A light fog had settled over the woods, and the snow from the night before had left a light coverlet on the leaves. The snow would be gone before noon. It was cold, but not cold enough to sustain snow.

Birds began to hop along the ground looking for their breakfast. The world was waking up and before long they would have to as well. For a while they sat together watching one of many sunrises that had that inspired many and touched the lives of all who witnessed them.

"I love this time of day," she whispered. "There's this moment between the night and the day when the world is still. There is no noise, no anger, nothing but fresh potential. Every day is brand new. It doesn't matter what happened before. The dawn will always come."

She reluctantly lifted her head from its resting place and brought her arms around his neck. She rested her forehead against his and turned slightly so she could still look out the window. A faint pink haze created a soft glow among the dark trees. "Do you have rehearsal today?" she asked softly.

"Yeah, I'm supposed to meet the guys around 1:00," he answered quietly.

"Can you cancel or postpone?"

"Probably, why?"

"I just want to stay here with you for as long as possible."

"How long will that be?" he ventured.

"I don't know," she sighed. "Things were just so wonderful last night.

"But, aren't we just putting off the inevitable?" he asked pushing her up slightly so he could see her face. Her silence answered his question. "Hey, are you hungry?"

"Hungry? That's not exactly what..." she started looking a little confused.

"Well, I just thought we shouldn't discuss matters of such importance on an empty stomach," he said as he tucked a lock of hair behind her ear and traced his index finger along her jaw line. "You've probably forgotten that I make delicious pancakes."

She smiled at him. He seemed so much like the guy she'd fallen in love with all those years ago. There didn't appear to be even a trace of the Alex she'd chosen to leave behind. "You're right. I had forgotten that. Now that you mention it, I do feel a little hungry."

"So, why don't you go get back in bed and I'll make us some nice fluffy pancakes and coffee. After we eat, we'll get down to the serious business at hand." He lifted her lightly to her feet.

"Okay," she agreed and started moving back down the hallway. She turned when she reached the bedroom door. He was still gazing after her, and he smiled as she glanced at him.

She gingerly climbed back in bed and smoothed out the sheet and quilt. She'd made up her mind about what she wanted to happen before she left the river the night before. She was sure he would feel the same way, but not that he would agree to what she would propose. She'd confessed that she still loved him, that she had never stopped. She wanted to assume by his reaction that he felt the same way about her, but needed to hear him say the words before she would allow herself to believe it.

She took a moment to look around the bedroom. It was a typical guy room. The real estate friendly beige paint that was there when he moved in had not been changed. There were no pictures of any kind hanging on the walls or sitting on dresser tops. In the left corner of the room was a stereo and next to it a tall tower full of CD's. She estimated 150 in that tower alone and knew there were probably at least that many more in other parts of the house. The one thing she knew about musicians is that they kept their inspirations close at hand and drew from just about any source they could. The furniture was a medium brown wood, simple and clean. It looked like a set from Ikea. The linens were cream, pillowcases to quilt. She was pretty sure this room had never known a woman's touch. For someone so full of life, his room seemed awfully dull.

He came in carrying a tray with two plates full of pancakes with strawberries on the side. Two steaming mugs of coffee also sat on the tray providing balance on either side. She sat up and propped against the pillows, sheet tucked around her chest and under her arms. They ate in near silence save her comments on how wonderfully delicious the food was. When the food was gone and the last of the coffee drained, Alex moved the tray to the floor. He turned to her taking her face in both of his hands. His eyes locked on hers and searched to the depths of her soul.

"Last night you told me you loved me, that you never stopped," he said never taking his eyes from hers.

"That's true," she whispered.

"So, what are we going to do?"

"I don't know, Alex. I really don't. I have so much to think about. So many decisions to make." She tried to turn her head, but he wouldn't let her.

"When will your family be back?"

"Not till Sunday."

"Then, you're mine until that time. No work, no practice, no tour prep, just us." He brought his lips to hers and gently rested them there. "What happens then is completely up to you. But I will tell you that I am going to do everything in my power to convince you to stay."

"I was hoping you would say that," she breathed. She leaned in and kissed him lightly. He moved his mouth down to her neck, gently caressing her throat with his tongue. She closed her eyes as the shivers moved from the delicate place where his tongue was tracing designs all the way to her toes. They made love and then they slept for a few more hours in each other's arms.

That Friday was spent in much the same way. They showered together, and she praised him for keeping his bathroom clean. Afterward they made love again, just one of many times. He gave her a t-shirt and boxers to wear as he put her clothes in to the wash. He was finishing up their lunch preparation when he saw her walk through the hallway into the living room. She was wearing his t-shirt, hair damp from the shower and pulled back into a ponytail. His breath caught in his throat as he realized how many times he'd dreamed of her just like this and now she was really there, in the flesh, and it was not a dream. He felt overjoyed, but terrified at the same time. He had let his fear of loving her drive them apart the first time; he wouldn't make the same mistake twice. Yet he knew that deep down the potential for getting hurt was much greater this time around. He remembered those nights of praying for just one more day to spend with her and realized that one day would never be enough. It would have to be all days or no days. He had until Sunday to make her realize that all days was the choice she needed to make.

In between making love they talked in ways they should have done earlier in their relationship. They shared stories, both good and bad, to fill in the full picture of the other. He told her about rehab and how that had been tremendously tough and how he still had to fight urges, but had been successful at resisting for nearly nine years. He told her about the relationships he'd tried to have after her and how they had all been doomed to fail from the beginning.

She told him about Kate and Jack and how they were the center of her world. She confessed her ambivalence about keeping her job and staying home with her kids. While she loved both, her kids definitely came before the job. It was no longer important to her that she could take off whenever she wanted to see whomever she wanted to see in concert, wherever she wanted to go in the world. That perk didn't hold nearly as much value as watching her toddler pedal his tricycle without help. It sounded silly, she knew, but it was true.

She told him that Jack was her adventurous one. He was a lot like her dad. He was flying down the hill on his fire truck toy and swinging upside down on the jungle gym before he was a year and a half old. Kate was very cautious and logical, like herself.

Except, what was happening now was anything but cautious and logical, Alex pointed out. He was sitting behind her, arms draped over her shoulders. Though he couldn't see it, he could feel her roll her eyes.

He kissed the nape of her neck and teased her that throwing caution to the wind had never felt better, had it? They were half sitting, half lying on the couch together. She playfully slapped his arm, lifted her arms to his neck and leaned her head back. He dropped his head lower and kissed her. The kiss began playfully, but became serious pretty fast. After making love on the couch, they moved to the bed and fell asleep for the night. He lay behind her in the spoon position and stroked her hair as she drifted off to sleep.

"Chris," he whispered.

"Hmm?' she mumbled back.

"I love you," he said without hesitation.

"I love you too," she replied. "I love you, too." This day could not have been more perfect.

Chapter 27

Before dawn Saturday morning Alex awoke to find himself alone. The room was freezing so he threw on a sweatshirt and jeans and moved into the hallway to turn the heat up. It was barely 5:00 AM. What was she doing awake at this hour?

Moving into the hallway, he found her staring out the living room window into the woods, fingers moving over the charms on her bracelet. She was lost deep in thought. Not wanting to startle her, he gently cleared his throat. She turned half way around and smiled softly at him. Her hair tumbled in soft curls down her back. He moved in and hugged her from behind, resting his chin on the top of her head.

"What are you doing up? Come back to bed," he said gently.

"I usually go running or workout in my basement at this time. I think I'm on semi-auto pilot. I woke up, but I don't have any of my running gear. I guess that's a drawback to unplanned overnight stays."

He grinned and pulled her closer to him. She was shivering slightly through the thin t-shirt. "So, you'll just have to start planning better," he said half joking. She turned toward him and the look on her face startled him back into the present. "What? What is it? You look so serious all of a sudden," he said searching her eyes.

"You said yesterday that you would try until Sunday to convince me to stay. Well, I have already made up my mind. I don't need to wait until Sunday to tell you what I've decided."

Her jaw was set with a firmness he'd seen only once before. That was when she'd left him for good, cut off all contact and, as far as he knew, never looked back. He was holding on to her by a string and she was about to cut it and break away forever. He was terrified of what she was about to say, but knew there was no sense in postponing it.

"So, what decision did you make?" he asked with great trepidation.

"Todd is a good man, and a great father. He loves me, and he loves our kids very much. I want them to experience growing up with their dad. We didn't really get to know our fathers, Alex. That's what makes this even harder. Kate and Jack have that opportunity and I will not take that away from them," she began.

Alex felt the well sucking him down. He didn't like the direction this was going. He steeled himself for the rejection and got ready to spend his last day with the love of his life.

"But, the thing is, something that has been asleep inside of me for a long time woke up when you came back into my life. I've never felt more passionate or more alive than I feel when I'm with you. I'm tired of living in the safety zone. I've been there most of my life, afraid to take a risk, never really experiencing life, just existing in a secure little bubble."

"What are you saying?"

"I'm saying I don't know how we'll work it out, but I want to give this a shot with us. I am crazy in love with you Steven Alex Lily, and I want us to be together."

He felt the air rush from his lungs as he let out the breath he was holding and he pulled her close and crushed her to him. The tears flowed freely from his eyes as he held her. The constant tension, the weight of years of regret he'd been carrying around was finally lifted. He had been waiting for so long to hear those words. He would finally have the chance to give her everything she deserved. He would be different this time around. He didn't know what he'd done to deserve a second chance, but he would not mess it up this time. There was nothing to stop his feelings. He was completely exposed and he didn't care. She loved him and wanted to be with him. He didn't need anything more in life.

"Chris, I will make you so happy. We'll make it work. We don't have to make those decisions right now, but I'll do whatever it takes to make the transition easier for you."

"And my kids," she added.

"Especially for the kids. This won't be easy for them. When are you going to tell Todd?" he asked with a hint of urgency. He tried not to be impatient, but he'd waited eleven years to hear her say those words and he didn't want to wait much longer. It was complicated though, and he knew it would take time.

"I've been awake most of the night thinking about that," she said moving to sit on the couch. "The holidays are coming up and I really don't want to spoil those for the kids, especially for Kate. Jack is still young enough that he won't remember, but Kate will. The first leg of your tour leaves next Wednesday. I was thinking I'd tell Todd before then and come with you for the first week or so. That will give me some to figure out where I'll go, whether I'll stay in the house with them, or find a new place to live. It'll also give him a chance to process it all. But, I think I'd prefer to break it to the kids after Christmas."

"What are you going to tell him? That you want a divorce, take a break, what?" Alex sat down in the chair across from her and put his elbows on his knees mirroring her position. He took her hands in his and traced gentle paths around her palms.

"I'm not sure yet. Todd and I have always been honest with each other, and I owe it to him to come clean about us. I'm going to tell him about our time here. I'm going to tell him how I feel about you," she took one of her hands and wiped away the tears trickling down her cheeks. "I do love him, Alex. He's such an amazing man and he doesn't deserve this. But the love I feel for him is not the same kind of love I feel for you. He's my best friend and a wonderful companion, and this is going to tear him apart."

"I'm so sorry I've put you in this place. I never wanted to cause you grief," he said head dropping to his chest. Once again, because of him, she was hurting, but this time it was different. She'd be with him in the end, and he could finally make her happy. "What do you think he'll say?"

"He's going to be upset. He'll probably try to convince me not to go. But I think ultimately he'd want me to be happy, and I know he wants what's best for Kate and Jack. He won't be supportive at first, but eventually he'll come to terms with it."

"Do you think he'll tell them while you're gone or try to retaliate?" He was afraid for her. He didn't know Todd very well, but what if he tried to keep her kids from her when she came back? He wouldn't be able to handle it if she lost her whole family, her whole way of life, for him. Her kids were her life. He knew they meant everything to her.

"No, Todd's not like that. He's a good person. He wouldn't want to damage their image of me any more than I'd want to damage their image of him. We'll explain that I'm going away for business, which is true, and then when I get back we'll sit down and figure things out. Plus, I haven't been on tour since Jack was born so he'll probably have his hands full keeping up with both of them for a week."

"Chris, are you sure this is what you want? It's going to be really tough for them, and for you. I love you and I want us to be together. I'll stand behind your decisions and support you in any way I can, but I just want you to be certain before you do anything." He pulled his head back up and met her gaze. This time she took his face in her hands and pulled in close.

"I have never been surer about anything. I fell in love with you the first time we spoke all those years ago. It was tough for us back then, and it will be tough for us now. But, we've both grown up and changed. I think we can handle these feelings better. It'll take time to sort this out, but know that I'm coming with you and we'll be together in the end."

She rested her forehead on his as she spoke. They didn't bother going to the bedroom.

Around 9:00 they untangled themselves, showered and decided to actually go outside for a while. They drove to the DeKalb Farmer's Market where they enjoyed a breakfast of freshly baked pastries and international coffee. The DeKalb Farmer's Market was located just minutes from his house and was a sensory experience all its own. After eating they browsed the market, picking up produce, rice, spices, wine, bread and seafood from all over the world. Over 100 countries were represented in the produce department alone. Alex picked up an ugly fruit and tossed it to Christina. She added it to the cart already piled high with the rest of their items.

She meandered down the tea aisle and picked up a cinnamon tea she'd only been able to find in England and had missed. She put three boxes in the cart. Alex laughed a little saying he came here every week and they could pick it up whenever she liked. It started to sink in that might become their weekly ritual, and it made her smile.

After shopping they returned to the house where Alex attempted to teach her how to make a seafood curry dish. She managed the prep work of washing and cutting the vegetables and fruit, as well as putting the water on to boil for the rice. He guided her hands through the motions of mixing the spices and infusing the rice. He steamed the vegetables with the mussels and shrimp in a white wine sauce that smelled heavenly. She spooned the rice into bowls and he covered each mound with the seafood vegetable mix. Together they savored every bite and she joked that it was the first meal she'd cooked in years, that hadn't burned beyond recognition. They made a good team she said, laughing as she sipped her wine.

Christina took over clean up duty once they were finished with lunch. While she was putting the leftovers away and cleaning up the dishes she heard his guitar singing. It blew her away every time she heard him play. To possess that kind of raw talent was amazing. That was what made him so special and would help him stand out in the industry. He was completely self-taught and he was better than most artists who'd studied professionally. When they were ready to go public with their relationship, she would probably have to release him as a client, in which case she would choose her replacement carefully. She had never been romantically involved with a client before so she wasn't clear on how Mastermind would handle the situation.

She began to think about her role at the company. Before her family left for their trip, she'd been ready to take her leave and stay home with Kate and Jack for a while. That wouldn't be an option once she and Todd separated. Alex's career wasn't stable enough to provide for them and both kids, plus she would never ask him to do that. She would talk to Joe after she returned from the first week of the tour. They would discuss her options. She would need something that was compatible with Kate's school schedule, although she knew she could count on Todd to help with that.

She would also like something that had flexibility for her to travel with Alex when she could. He would be touring off and on for at least a year to promote this album, and while she knew she couldn't go with him for the whole tour, she would like to be with him for part of the time. So many things to work out! Just thinking about it raised her anxiety level, but then she stopped and listened to the mystical music he was playing and she reassured herself that everything would work itself out.

She walked into the music room from the kitchen, leaned against the wall and watched him play. His back was to her and she could only see his arms. His left held the neck of guitar strong while the fingers of his right strummed and plucked the strings. The feel of the music brought back the fresh memories of how he'd used those fingers to bring forth music from her that she hadn't known was still there. He'd made her body sing the first time they were together. Their music was stronger than ever this time around. She smiled to herself as she walked around and sat down to listen. Everything would work out. As long as they had the music and each other they would be fine.

When he finished practicing, they went for a walk around his neighborhood. The chill had returned to the air as the sun began sinking behind the horizon. It was barely 5:00, but looked more like 7:00. The neighborhood was quiet and cozy. He asked her what she thought of moving in here. "I don't think you'll be here for much longer. Once things take off for you, you'll probably want to move into a bigger place," she answered.

"But until then, what do you think?"

She stayed quiet for a bit. "I really do like it here, Alex and if it were just me I would love to move here. I don't know if I'm ready to progress that fast yet though. It's the middle of the year. I don't want to yank Kate out of school," she said looping her arm around his waist.

"I didn't mean tomorrow," he said putting his arm around her shoulders to shield her from the wind. "I know you don't want to uproot your kids any more than necessary. Whether you guys move in here, or I sell and move up closer to you, it doesn't matter to me. I just want to be near you as much as possible. I want to get closer to you, and not just physically."

"You sure are saying all the right things lately. Why are you so great?" she asked tilting her head up to look at him.

He stopped walking and brushed a loose strand away from her eyes. "I'm just a guy in love. If that makes me great, then I guess it's you who makes me that way." She smiled and he bent to kiss her lightly. "Come on, it's getting cold." They turned and walked back to the house. They finished the leftovers for dinner and snuggled in to watch a movie. Afterward they made love and fell asleep intertwined with each other. She felt a hint danger in being here, but it also felt good, and real. He'd brought her back to life.

Chapter 28

Christina thought she heard her phone ringing but ignored it, figuring it was just her imagination. It couldn't be any later than 2:00 AM. Who would be calling her at this hour? She was snug and warm wrapped up with the man of her dreams. She rolled over and rested her head on his smooth chest breathing in his scent as she did. He had always smelled wonderful, natural, no cologne needed. A salty sandalwood blended with soap. If they could figure out a way to bottle it, they'd make a fortune. Her phone sounded again but she continued to ignore it, refusing to allow anything to interrupt her time with him.

She kissed his chest lightly to rouse him from sleep. She led her fingers across the path of his muscular abs and down under the sheet. They were both fully naked which would make her plan much easier to carry out. She began to kiss, nibble and lick his chest. She heard him groan sleepily, but with pleasure. He moved his left arm down from over his head and found her legs. With the arm that was underneath her he flipped her onto her back, parted her legs with his knee and slid in. He nuzzled down by her neck leaving alternating traces of and fire and ice in his wake. They moved together naturally, fluidly. Their technique had been perfected.

Her phone rang again and he lifted his head. She brought his attention back to her telling him to ignore it. She'd call whoever it was back later.

"Good morning," he said huskily against her throat. "That was a fantastic wake up call, even if it is much earlier than I would ever plan to wake up."

She laughed playfully. "I was hoping you'd think so."

Before she could say anything else the phone beside his bed began to ring. Groaning, he reluctantly broke away from her and rolled over to answer it. Propping up on one elbow he gave the traditional greeting and waited for a response from the person on the other end. He turned back and looked at her with the strangest expression. All the color had drained from his face. "What?" she asked. "Who is it?"

"It's for you. It's Andrea."

She looked momentarily like a deer stunned in the headlights. Her heart stopped beating for a moment and she was unsure of what to do next. Part of her wanted to tell him to hang up, but she knew that would do no good. It must be really important for Andrea to track her down in the middle of the night. Trying to play it off like this was a business meeting wouldn't work either. Ready to face whatever came, she reached out to take the phone. She was completely ready for anything Andrea had to throw at her, except what actually came.

"Andrea?" she asked tentatively.

"Chris, what are you doing? I've been trying to call you all night," her assistant said urgently.

"What is it, Andrea? What's wrong?" The tone in her assistant's voice was scaring her.

"It's your family. There's been an accident. They've been trying to get in touch with you since yesterday."

"Accident? What kind of accident? What are you talking about?" she demanded.

"They were driving home from Michigan yesterday when the car skidded on some ice. They're all in the hospital, Chris." Andrea explained.

The room suddenly felt depleted of oxygen and began to swirl violently. She leaned back against the pillows in an effort to steady her spinning head. She vaguely felt a hand on her arm, but had no idea who it belonged to. She tried to recover her senses enough to find out more information.

"Where?" was all she managed to say.

"They're at Northside Hospital in Cherokee. You need to go there, right now!" Andrea added with emphasis.

She dropped the phone from her hands and struggled to not vomit on the spot. She heard someone talking to her, but couldn't place the voice or where it was. She knew she needed to get up right away and go. She threw the covers back and jumped up, a little too fast as her head was spinning and she lost her balance. She tripped backward and ended up back on the bed. The hands were on her arms and the voice was there, more insistent than before. The hands started shaking her, lightly at first and then with more force. Something snapped and she jolted back into her body. Alex was in front of her with the most frightened expression she'd ever seen.

"Christina! What is wrong?" he practically shouted in her face. His eyes searched hers frantically for the answer to his question. His grip softened as she met his stare. Fear turned to concern as he moved his hands from her arms to her face.

"My family's in the hospital. I have to go. I have to go. I have to go right now," she cried as she tried to stand.

Tears clouded her vision as she look for her clothes. He helped her gather her shirt and jeans and handed them to her. She'd already managed to get her bra and panties on. She took the clothes and dressed hastily. She was searching for her shoes under the bed when she saw that he was dressed as well.

"What are you doing?" she asked as she slipped her feet into her heels. Her belt was lost and she couldn't take any more time to find it.

"I'm coming with you," Alex said, keys in one hand, coats in the other.

"No, you're not!" she insisted as she pushed her way past him taking her coat as she did.

"Yes, I am! Chris, you are in no shape to drive right now. I'll just drop you off. I won't stay if you don't want me to, but I am not letting you get behind the wheel." He blocked her path to the front door and forced her to look at him. "You know I'm right," his tone softened.

"Okay, fine," she conceded. "Let's go."

He opened the door and they bustled out. They rode in silence. The blackness of the hour surrounded them. The only light available was from the overhead street lights and the cars sporadically passing them. He kept glancing at her as he drove. Tears were flowing down her cheeks. At one point he tried to take her hand. She let him, but didn't grip back. "It'll be okay," he whispered. She remained rigidly silent.

Traffic was light and they moved through the city and up to Cherokee County with no obstacles. They got to the hospital in under an hour. She was out of the car before it was fully stopped. Parking on the street, Alex put the car in park and had to run to keep up with her. She was already at the information desk when he caught up. They were directed to the third floor of the hospital where they were met by Dr. Jermaine Solomon.

"Mrs. Hampton, I'm Dr. Solomon. I'm in charge of your husband's case and I'm working with the pediatric specialist who's in charge of your children's cases." They shook hands out of perfunctory habit. "Why don't we have a seat and I'll catch you up. Sir, I need to ask your relation to the family," he asked turning his attention to Alex.

"Oh, I'm just a…friend. I drove Christina up here," he answered. It sounded really lame, but he didn't know what else to say.

"Is it okay with you, Mrs. Hampton, if he joins us for this, or would you rather keep it strictly family?" Dr. Solomon addressed her.

"No, it's fine." She had a thousand questions running through her mind. Where were her kids? Where was Todd? What had happened to them? What about Max? But she was afraid to talk, afraid she would be sick all over the floor, so she stayed quiet and as still as possible. They took their seats in the far corner of the waiting room. The décor in the room made an attempt at comfort. The chairs were cushioned and there were several pieces of low quality art hanging on the walls. A few fake fig trees dotted the corners of room. But the temperature was cold and the room reeked of anxiety and antiseptic.

"Mrs. Hampton," the doctor began, "your family was involved in a serious accident late Saturday afternoon."

"My kids, what about my kids? And my husband, and mother-in-law? What's happened to them?" She couldn't stop herself, but the doctor put a reassuring hand on her arm. She felt Alex's hand in the small of her back, but the gesture that helped calm her most came from Dr. Solomon.

"Ma'am, your kids are going to be fine. They suffered relatively minor injuries. Their safety seats did their jobs. They are in stable condition and you can see them as soon as we finish here. Jack has a broken leg, but it's not too bad. The car seat protected him quite well. Kate's got a pretty bad bruise across her torso and a couple cracked ribs from her seatbelt, but we did an MRI on both of them to rule out internal injuries. We've been keeping them under close observation just to make sure nothing else surfaces."

"Oh thank you, God!" she breathed out a sigh of relief. But the sense of reprieve was short lived. "And Todd? What's happened to him?"

"Your husband is in serious, but stable condition. He suffered a punctured lung, several broken ribs, a severe concussion and some internal bleeding. He'll need to stay here for a while until we get his lung healed. He's already had surgery for it and we've stabilized the bleeding. He's already showing signs of improvement."

"What about his mother? She was with them. Our dog, Max, he was with them too. What about them?" Christina's head was spinning. Relief and fear mingled together in her heart and mind. She felt Alex grip her hand as he sat beside her.

"Your mother-in-law wasn't with them. She decided to stay behind, but she's on her way as we speak. We got in touch with her already. Your dog is at the emergency vet clinic not far from here. He's in pretty bad shape, but I'm sure they're doing all they can."

She felt the tears return. Her poor puppy. She would go to the clinic as soon as she could. Clearing her throat she asked, "When can I take my kids home?"

"They can be discharged this afternoon, I'm pretty sure. Jack's right leg is set in a cast. He has a fractured tibia. Kate's going to be very sore for quite a while. But ultimately she will be fine too."

"What about Todd? When will he be ready to come home?" She held on to hope that it would be soon.

"Todd will be here a bit longer. I can't say for sure how long though. It all depends on his progress. Would you like to see your kids now? I know they're anxious to see you," Dr. Solomon asked standing up.

"Yes!" she practically shouted as jumped from her seat. They followed the doctor down the hall to a small, but somewhat cozy room. She hesitated a moment before following Dr. Solomon inside. She turned to face Alex for the first time since they'd arrived. He squeezed her hand and motioned for her to follow.

"I'll be right out here. Take all the time you need," he whispered.

Christina turned and entered the room where her two children lay. Someone, a thoughtful nurse perhaps, had moved their beds close together. They were sleeping soundly. Kate's hand was extended from her own bed through the bars of Jack's little crib. She was holding his chubby little fist. Jack was sleeping right next to the bars in an effort to be as close to his sister as possible. The cast on his leg was level with his knee. There were some scratches and bruising on his face, but otherwise he looked okay. Kate's face and arms were also scratched and bruised. The worst of the bruising was beneath the child size hospital gown where the seat belt had held her back forcefully.

She reached out her hand and smoothed her daughter's dark hair away from her face. Sweat tinged the little girl's forehead making wisps of hair stick around her eyes and on her flushed cheeks. Christina laid her hand lightly on Kate's chest and pulled the gown back a bit to reveal angry bruises shaded dark purple and black. She could feel her daughter's quiet breaths and decided against grabbing her from the bed and holding on for dear life. Moving over to Jack she stroked the wispy blond hair and put her other hand on his cast. His eyes fluttered at her touch, but the long lashes stayed down as he slept on. It was barely 4:00 AM. They needed to rest.

Her heart shattered as she gazed upon her children. She had not been there for them through this. She could only imagine how terrified they had been. Nearly twelve hours had passed before she'd known about the accident. Guilt consumed her. Turning to the doctor she asked how long they'd been sleeping. He reported they had finally fallen asleep a little before midnight. They silently tiptoed from the room. Her terror was eased by seeing them and touching them. She asked the doctor what he knew about the details of the accident.

"They were about forty-five minutes north of here, outside Elijay, when the van hit an icy patch coming off a bridge. Your husband was able to keep it on the road long enough to get off the bridge, but the van slid sideways into a tree and flipped twice before landing right side up. Several motorists stopped to help and one dialed 9-1-1. Your husband, despite his condition, managed to stay conscious and tried to reassure your kids that everything would be okay. The paramedics said he passed out as they arrived at our ER."

"Have the kids been alone this whole time?" she asked her voice cracking with emotion. She wasn't sure she'd be able to hold it together.

"No, of course not. In fact, one of the motorists who witnessed the accident stayed with them until they fell asleep. She was very good with them. She calmed them down considerably." Christina swore she could hear the condescension behind his words, or perhaps it was her own conscious chiding her for the fact that someone else, a stranger, was there comforting her children when it should have been her.

"I'd like to thank her. Do you have her contact information?"

"Of course, and I'll be happy to pass it along. Your husband is right down here," he said leading them just a few doors down. "Normally we don't keep children on this floor, but we decided they needed to be near their dad."

"Thank you for that," she interrupted.

"Mrs. Hampton, you must prepare yourself before you see him. He's been through a lot, including emergency surgery. He looks pretty rough."

"Okay." She breathed deeply.

Leaving Alex to wait outside, she stepped inside the small space. A bathroom was immediately on the right making the entryway quite narrow. She walked down the very short corridor to find Todd lying on his back sleeping. A large white tube that was attached to a ventilator was taped over his nose and mouth. The punctured lung was not functioning well enough to allow him to breathe completely on his own.

His face was a mass of swelling and dark blue bruises. The colors blended together to create an eerily bright design on a dark canvas. There was some greenish purple color around the bridge of his nose and under his right eye, and his left eye was ringed with deep crimson that blended almost smoothly into an eggplant cheekbone.

The top edge of the tape holding his ribs in place showed from under his gown. The heart monitor steadily beeped away in the corner and the IV stand held a bag of clear fluid that dripped slowly into the tube leading to the bend in his left elbow. Aside from the shockingly blond hair, it could have been a stranger lying in that bed and not her husband.

Her breath caught in her throat as she took in Todd's condition. She prayed that he looked worse than he really was. Dr. Solomon was talking about the emergency surgery on his lung and how they were able to keep it from collapsing. They'd taken steps to control the internal bleeding around his liver as well. His CAT scan showed no damage to his brain, which was excellent.

Todd was sedated at the moment, the doctor explained. The ventilator was difficult and painful for patients to deal with. This way he could rest peacefully and heal. He continued to fill her in on various aspects of her husband's condition, but all she could do was stare at his face. She wrapped her fingers around his right hand and stroked the inside of his palm with her thumb. Dr. Solomon excused himself to give her a few moments alone with her husband. Sitting down in the chair beside the bed, she leaned her head against the mattress near his shoulder, and let out the sobs she'd been trying to hold back.

Weeping openly with a heaving chest, she tried to give her husband the strength to mend, while subconsciously trying to draw on strength from him to get through this. He'd always given her the confidence and strength to face challenges. He'd never failed her, not once in the ten years they'd known each other. But, she had failed him terribly; she hadn't been there for him through this. She'd betrayed him for her own selfish desire and, though her actions didn't cause the accident, he was paying the price.

After what seemed like hours she sat up and combed her fingers through her hair. She stood up and placed a light kiss on the hand she still held. She walked to the door and found Alex waiting patiently on the other side.

She could see the concern on his face. She could tell he wanted to take her in his arms and convince her they would all be fine, that everything would be alright. But she knew he wouldn't. She wouldn't have let him even if he's tried. She sensed that she was on autopilot and was almost functioning outside her body.

"I need you to do me a favor," she said in an emotionless voice.

"Anything," he replied.

"I need you to call Andrea and tell her to bring my car here. Tell her to have Nick follow her so he can drive her home. Tell her to call Joe and have someone take over whatever needs to be done and tell Joe I'll be in touch when I know more." She stood with her arms crossed over her chest as if holding herself in an upright position.

"Anything else?" he asked.

"I'm going to call my mom and have her come get the kids when they're released. I'm going to stay here. So, I'll need some stuff. If you could go to Target, or anywhere that's open, and get me some stuff like toothpaste and a toothbrush, soap, and underwear, I would really appreciate it." She should have felt strange sending him out to buy her toiletries to stay with her injured husband, but she didn't. The numbness of shock was setting in and she was beginning to not feel anything. That feeling of nothing would get her through the next few days.

"Sure, no problem," he answered. "What size underwear?

"Five."

She wanted to be prepared to wait it out. She walked with him back toward the waiting room. He took her hand in his and looked her straight in the eye. His forehead crinkled with worry. She let him pull her into an embrace. When she pulled away, she rested a hand on his cheek and tried to work up a small smile. "I'll be fine," was all she said. She watched the elevator doors close behind him and gazed at the stranger reflected in front of her. She swore she'd aged ten years in the past half hour. What had she done? She headed back to rooms where her family was recovering. She spent the next hour alternating between her kids and Todd.

Alex returned an hour later to drop off the bag of toiletries. He'd also picked up some more comfortable clothes, socks and sneakers he hoped would fit. He'd had to guess on the sizes. He relayed the message that Andrea and Nick were on their way. She thanked him and they stood together in an uneasy silence. "Do you want me to stay with you until they get here?" he asked unsure of how she would respond.

"If you want, that would be nice," she replied. Nearly all trace of emotion had vanished from her voice.

"Do you want me to get you some coffee while you freshen up?"

"Yes, please," she said. He turned to go. "Alex?' He turned back to gaze upon her. "Thanks." He smiled, and resumed his walk to the coffee machine.

He came back to find her wearing the grey yoga pants and pink t-shirt he'd purchased. The white socks and canvas shoes were matched by the white hoodie she was also wearing. She'd washed her face and pulled her hair back into a long braid. To him she still looked twenty, and the expression on her face was a familiar one he'd seen before. She was hurting, and worried, and like before there was nothing he could do to calm her fears or ease her pain. He was also feeling that he was partly to blame for some of the pain she was feeling now, at least for the guilt he knew had to be eating her alive. It was already gnawing into him too.

"I see the clothes fit alright," he said handing her the coffee. It tasted like motor oil, but it would do the trick. "I thought you might want to be wearing something a little more comfortable if you have to stay here for a while."

"Yeah, thanks for picking them up. I already feel a little better." He knew she was lying, but it was okay.

Andrea and Nick arrived shortly after 6:00 and he made a hasty retreat. This was not the time to get involved in the conversation of why she'd been at his house in the middle of the night while her family was lying in a hospital. He was sure that would come up soon enough, but he wouldn't discuss it here. He gave her a quick hug and whispered for her to call him if she needed him, kissed her lightly on the cheek and left the hospital.

The sun was making its lazy way into the sky, spreading shades of oranges and pinks across the horizon. The mist was beginning to burn off as the day woke up. Sitting in his car, he stared up at the brick building for a moment before letting out a deep sigh. The drive home was long and he'd never felt more helpless or alone in his life. Right now there was nothing he could do for her, and they couldn't be together.

Chapter 29

Christina was sitting by Todd's bed when Andrea came to get her. The nurse said Kate was awake and asking for her. Leaving her assistant with Todd, she ran into the room shared by the two kids and scooped the little girl into her arms. She was sure there were no tears left, but seeing Kate's big blue eyes open and alert made the reserve pools release. Mother and daughter held on to each other as tightly as the wounds caused by the accident would allow. Christina pulled back and gently lifted Kate's hospital gown to reveal the long diagonal bruise from her left shoulder across her torso ending near her waist. It measured roughly three inches wide and was an angry shade of bluish-purple.

"How bad does it hurt, sweetie?" Christina asked tenderly.

"It's not so bad if I stay real still," the five year old said as Christina helped her lie back on her pillows. "But, I had to move some to help Jack. He was pretty scared."

"You're a very good big sister," Christina said as she kissed her little girl on the forehead.

The talking had roused the toddler from his sleepy state. Jack rubbed his eyes and tried to roll over. Unfamiliar with the cast however, he couldn't get his leg swung over enough and got stuck in the position he started from. It took him a minute to realize she was there, but when he saw her, his eyes widened with delight and he gave a sleepy baby squeal of pleasure. She lifted him from the crib slightly astounded at how heavy the cast made him. He was a solidly built little boy to begin with, and the extra bulk and weight made him a little difficult to maneuver.

"Hey buddy," she said taking him in her arms.

"Mommy!" he said happily.

"How's my little man feeling?" she asked as they squeezed in to Kate's bed. Christina wrapped one arm around her daughter while snuggling her son with the other arm.

"Leg hurt, Mommy," Jack said. "I got a cast."

"I see that! It's pretty cool."

"Mommy?" Kate asked. "When can we go home?"

"Well, I'm not sure, but I think it'll be pretty soon," she rubbed Kate's arm as the little girl rested her head on her mother's shoulder. "I called Grandma to come down and stay with us for a while. She's going to help take care of you guys until Daddy is better."

"Can Daddy come home with us too?" Kate asked.

"He'll come home soon, but not right now."

"Daddy sick?" Jack asked softly as he used the fingers on the hand behind her back to play with her hair. It was something he'd done since he was a baby. It soothed him, and her. She left her hair long pretty much because she loved this sensation.

"Yes, baby. He needs to stay here for a little while longer so the doctors can make him better. Then he'll get to come home."

"Go see Daddy?" the little boy asked.

"No, not right now. Daddy is resting so he can get better faster. We need to let him rest a lot right now."

A knock sounded on the door as the nurse came in for the 7:00 AM check up. Christina untangled herself from her children long enough for the nurse to check the kids' blood pressure, heart rate and temperature. She also examined Jack's cast and Kate's bruise.

"Okay you two. Things look pretty good. Breakfast will be here soon. I'll tell Dr. Peters you're up. He's the pediatric specialist."

The nurse smiled tightly at them as she left the room. She seemed sincere enough, but Christina was sure she'd picked up a hint of disapproval in her tone of voice, or maybe in her thin smile. Perhaps

Christina's guilty conscious was playing tricks on her. Either way she was consumed with remorse and shame.

Andrea came back over while the doctor was beginning his exams of the two kids. She gave Christina a look that she knew meant, "We have to talk." Kate's eyes lit up when she saw Andrea. Kate loved Andrea; she always had since her babyhood. No one, including Andrea really knew why. Perhaps it was the fiery red hair. That seemed to draw and hold a lot of people's attention.

Regardless, Andrea and Kate were great friends. It was a great way to distract her while Dr. Peters examined Jack. Kate was very protective of her little brother and if anyone caused him pain, she was ready to fight. Andrea helped Kate read some of the words in her magazine while the doctor gently maneuvered Jack's leg.

"Alright Mom, everything looks pretty good here," he said to Christina as she cuddled Jack in her lap. "I'm going to get their discharge paperwork started. Give them children's ibuprophen for pain and swelling. I could give you a prescription, but the over-the-counter stuff will work just as well."

"How long will he need to keep the cast?" she questioned.

"Probably three to four weeks, but maybe less. Little kids are remarkably resilient."

"Thank you Dr. Peters," Christina said.

"My pleasure. They're sweet kids. If you have any questions or concerns, please call me. We'll need to see Jack back in a week to check on that leg. Other than that, these two are good to go. How will they be getting home?"

"My mother should be here shortly and she'll take them home. I'll be staying here with Todd for the time being."

"Very good," the doctor stated. "I'll let Dr. Solomon know and I'll see you soon."

Her mother arrived shortly before 10:00, just as the discharge paperwork was delivered. Christina signed the papers, hugged her mom and explained to the kids why she was staying.

"We don't want Daddy to be lonely, do we?" They both agreed no. "Ok then, Grandma's going to take you home and spend some time with you. I'll be home a bit later."

She hugged Kate first before wiping baby tears away from Jack's eyes. She handed the toddler over to her mother and waved to them as they walked down the hall. Letting out a deep breath she turned to face Andrea. Nick had left a while ago to pick up some food for them, leaving the two women alone.

"I know, I know," Christina started seeing the questions forming on Andrea's face before she asked them. "I have a lot of explaining to do."

"Chris, what were you thinking? I don't need to ask what you were doing at Alex's house, but I do need to ask you why."

Christina moved to the waiting room and sat down hard in one of the chairs. Andrea followed suit sitting across from her. She paused for a moment trying to put into words everything that had happened over the past couple of days. The pattern on the carpet began to make her dizzy so she looked up. "Andrea, I love him. I always have."

"That doesn't explain why you were there. And what else is it? You don't love Todd anymore?"

"Of course I love Todd!" she whispered harshly trying not to draw attention from the hospital staff. She tried to relax against the chair and attempted to calm herself down before continuing. "That's the whole problem. He's my best friend. He's the first person I want to talk to when something great happens, or when something bad happens. We have a wonderful time together, when we get to spend time together, and he's the greatest dad I've ever known. I guess lately things have just been a little on the boring side. I just don't know how much I'm passionately in love with him anymore."

"So, you decide to have an affair with your client to spice things up?" She could hear the disapproval in Andrea's voice.

"I didn't decide to have an affair, Andrea! He confessed that he was still in love with me. I did some hard thinking and admitted to myself, and then to him, that I never stopped loving him either. I wouldn't risk my marriage and family for a random affair."

"So, what's going to happen with you two?" Andrea asked sitting back with her arms crossed over her chest.

"I had decided to leave Todd. I don't have any idea how it would work. I was going to tell him when they got back, then spend the first week of the tour with Alex. That would give Todd time to adjust to my decision. I could spend the time after returning and before the holidays either looking for a new place for me and the kids, or helping Todd look. But that was before all this happened."

"So, what? Your husband almost dies in a car accident and you've suddenly had a change of heart?"

"Well, I can't exactly go on tour right now, can I? Kate and Jack were both hurt and they need me with them. I would never put anything before my kids." She felt herself becoming defensive and stopped to collect her thoughts for a moment. "Besides, I do love Todd and I want to take care of him. I think you're being a little harsh, Andrea."

"A little harsh? Don't you think you need someone to be harsh with you?"

"Don't you think I'm being harsh enough on myself right now?" she said getting up. She tried not to shout, but found it very difficult. "I have been wracked with guilt ever since you called me this morning. I should have been there with them. Perhaps I could have helped prevent the accident, or at least not let them suffer by themselves like they must have. I should have, at the very least, been at home to get the call the first time." She paced the waiting room fervently. "I should not have been tracked down in someone else's bed. I've been beating myself up about this all day!"

"Chris, I'm sorry. Please try to calm down," Andrea said coming over to her. She wrapped her arms around her friend and held her as she sobbed.

"I'm a horrible wife. I feel like a horrible mother. I am a very selfish person. I guess this is karma giving me instant payback for my actions," she cried into Andrea's shoulder.

"Listen to me," Andrea said pushing Christina back to look closely at her. "You are none of those things. Okay, you're not earning brownie points for wife of the year, but you have been a good wife to Todd until now. You made a bad decision, but you followed your heart. You couldn't have predicted the accident and you couldn't have prevented it. You should feel guilty; I'm not going to tell you otherwise. But, you were here as soon as you found out. You're still here to take care of your husband, your best friend."

Christina covered her face and sat down. She rested her elbows on her knees and tried to collect herself. Wiping her eyes, she sat up and took a deep breath. She looked down the hallway in the direction of Todd's room. He was her best friend and she did love him. Would she have been able to tell him she was leaving if the accident had not occurred? She really didn't know. All she wanted right now was for him to get better.

"What it is about Alex that makes you love him?" Andrea asked sitting beside her.

"I don't know really. There's just always been something about him. He makes me feel... alive, I guess. He kind of puts me on edge, like I don't know what's going to happen next," she replied leaning against the back of the chair. "That sounds stupid, but I can't really describe it. It's a feeling I haven't experienced in a long time, not since we were together before."

"Expect the unexpected, huh?"

"Something like that. Plus, he's a very passionate person. Not just physically either. He feels things deeply and puts his heart and soul into everything he does, every song he writes. That's wonderfully attractive."

"Well, let me ask you something else. What attracted you to Todd when you first met him?"

"He was the exact opposite of Alex," she stated plainly.

"Meaning what?" Andrea delved.

"Todd was a grown up with goals and aspirations. And, he was kind and considerate and stable. He's wonderfully funny, of course which is also extremely attractive, and he brought me out of a very dark place. He showed me what real, mature love was like. I never had to wonder what painful thing was going to happen next because I always knew he'd do what was best for me. That hasn't changed."

"What has changed?"

"I guess I need something edgier. Maybe more passion and excitement. We've been together a long time and we've lost our focus on each other. I miss the feeling that anything could happen at any time. I miss the anticipation of... oh I don't know," she sighed. "They're so different from each other, and there are parts of both of them I don't think I can live without."

"So, what are you going to do now?"

"I honestly have no idea. Roll them into one person," she said.

"Well honey," Andrea said giving her hand a squeeze, "you're going to have to figure it out. And probably sooner than later." Christina managed to give her friend a slight smile and squeezed her hand back.

Nick returned a few minutes later with breakfast sandwiches from the small shop on the corner. Although the air was thick with tension, he knew enough not to ask questions. They ate their sandwiches in silence. Christina picked at hers, not eating more than a couple of bites. She was afraid that if she tried to eat she would throw up right there on the floor.

Andrea and Nick left shortly thereafter. Christina assured them that she would call if she needed them. Andrea promised to get to work early on Monday so they could handle any last minute tour issues. Joe was already aware of the accident and knew Christina would be unavailable. Everything on that end was settled. Nick gave her a quick hug before they left.

"Hey," he whispered, "just thought you might want to know that Alex's CD sold over 50,000 copies during the weekend. Not bad for an unknown rookie, huh?"

"Not bad at all. Thanks, Nick." She smiled back and patted his arm. Turning from the waiting room she headed back to Todd's room. The hardest part was yet to come.

Chapter 30

Christina sat by Todd's bed and took his hand in hers. The ventilator hummed quietly. The noise reminded her of the comforting sound made by his sleep apnea machine and she smiled in spite of herself. That machine was a miracle creation. Even though he was on the leaner side, Todd snored like a bear.

The first time she'd slept over at his house it wasn't so bad. After that though, it got worse and worse. He said the first night he'd barely slept because he didn't want to disturb her. They hadn't slept together many times before their marriage, and they were well into the wedding planning when she discovered how bad the problem really was. She remembered the first night he'd used the machine. It was the first time in many months that they both got a full night's sleep.

She let herself remember back to when she'd first met Todd. She'd been student teaching at Woodland Elementary in Dunwoody, assigned to Mr. Power's fifth grade class. The school hosted an annual career day that the fifth grade played an integral part in. She had helped the students in her class write resumes that showcased their skills and talents. Once the career day booths were set up, the students were to rotate through and "interview" with the different representatives. Todd had been there representing his accounting firm. The firm handled the taxes for the school system and was kind enough to send someone each year to be a part of career day.

It was difficult not to notice him right away when she brought the class through. Her head had snapped back in his direction upon first glance. She was amazed that the school's accountant was so young and handsome. He had been sitting at his table, but stood to greet them as they approached. He was tall, much taller than she'd expected. His blond hair was cut short and he came across as very professional. His eyes looked like pools of dark chocolate and they crinkled slightly in the corners when he smiled. She felt her heart skip a tiny beat and she smiled back at him. He extended his hand and welcomed them to his table. She shook his hand and tried furiously not to blush, but to no avail.

What stood out to her the most was how great he was with the students. He was kind and treated them with respect. He asked them questions on their level, and helped them see how their skills and interests could be applied to the accounting and finance world. The preconceived notion that accountants have no people skills and only crunch numbers all day flew right out the window as she watched him work with the kids.

As they got ready to move to the next table, he stopped her for a minute. He handed her his business card and asked if she would like to get together for dinner someday soon. She said that would be nice. As she reached for his card, she took a chance and made eye contact. What she saw reflected there jolted her to the core and froze her where she stood. She saw her future; kids, a home, a dog, all of it. She saw their lives together. It was the most intense sensation she'd ever experienced. She could barely breathe and had to shake herself back into reality. She was at school, in the gym, with her class, holding a business card. Focus, Christina, focus, she thought to herself. His home number had been written on the back. He told her to call him any time. She smiled and said okay, then turned to rejoin her students. A chorus of "Woo-hoos" arose from the group of ten year olds and the blush came back. It had taken forever to calm them back down once they returned to the classroom.

She lay on her bed in her apartment that night. Was she really going to call him? She wanted to very much. It was the first time since the whole Alex calamity that she'd felt any trace of romantic interest in someone else. Todd was very attractive, seemed very nice and clearly liked kids. If she was going to get involved with anyone, he would be a good one to take a chance on. And that look they shared! Was that real? She'd been fooled before by believing in someone's eyes. But this one was different, she thought. This one rattled her entire sense of self, in a good way. She rolled over and picked up her phone. Taking a deep breath, she dialed the numbers. It rang three times before he answered.

"May I please speak to Todd?" she asked nervously. Her heart was beating wickedly fast in her chest.

"This is Todd," came the reply.

"Hi, this is Christina Malone. We met today at the school." She was almost at a loss for words. This had never been easy for her.

"Hi! I'm so glad you called. I was afraid I embarrassed you in front of your students today. I'm sorry if I did."

"Well, I did have to hear about it all day long, but that's okay," she laughed. "I'd like to take you up on that dinner offer if you're serious."

"Of course I'm serious. When would you like to get together?"

"How's tomorrow night?" she asked nervously.

"Sounds great to me. Where would you like to go?"

She was a little stunned. She'd never been asked when *and* where she'd like to have dinner. The few dates she'd been on since moving to Atlanta had all but been decided by the guys before she even had input. "Um, there's a place on Roswell Square I'd like to try. It's called Mercier. I've never been there, but it looks nice from the outside. They have a patio." She rolled her eyes and bumped her forehead with the palm of her free hand. She sounded so stupid; 'they have a patio'. Most restaurants in the area had patios. Was she sixteen again?

"I'd love to go there. Do you want to meet, or should I pick you up?"

This guy knows how to play his cards right, she thought. With women becoming savvier about their safety in the dating world, many were choosing to meet their dates instead of being picked up at their homes. She agreed with this, and though he seemed like a nice guy, she erred on the side of caution and said she'd meet him there at 6:30.

She arrived the next evening slightly before they'd agreed to meet. He was already there and had gotten a table on the balcony patio. The hostess showed her to the table and he stood as she approached. She was still shocked by how tall he was. He stood nearly a half a foot taller than she did even in heels. She was glad she'd chosen to wear her blue sweater that made her eyes really pop. He kissed her cheek as they greeted and he handed her a white rose. With anyone else she would have thought the gesture was cheesy, but he seemed so genuine.

Todd ordered a bottle of wine. He'd asked her what she liked, but she confessed to knowing nothing at all of wine so he made the choice. They talked easily over dinner. He was 25 and had been working at his firm for almost two years. He'd gone straight into graduate school earning his MBA with an emphasis on finance. He was originally from Michigan, but had lived down here for the past seven years. He came down to go to Georgia Tech, and stayed.

He asked her about her life, and seemed sincerely interested in her answers. He laughed at the stories she told about the students she worked with and thought it admirable that she wanted to teach in the inner city. His mom had been a teacher before retiring. He'd always held them in high regard.

After dinner they walked through the historic square and browsed through the shops and art galleries that were still open. Even though it was April, there was still a slight chill in the evening air. She rubbed her arms to stay warm and he draped his sport coat over her shoulders. She smiled up into the brownest eyes she'd ever seen. She saw in them a warmth and kindness that she hadn't seen in a long time. They ended the evening with coffee at a local coffee house. There was a girl playing guitar and singing for tips. Christina explained to him her love of music, though she was definitely no singer. She pointed out the different chords the girl was playing, the count of the song and how she'd altered the original arrangement somewhat. He asked if she played any instruments. She told him she only dabbled with the guitar and the piano, but that she had played woodwinds in high school.

He walked her back to her car after they finished their coffee. They strolled slowly enjoying the brisk evening air. He took her hand in his and she felt a little tingle in her fingers and up her arm. She tried to blame it on the chill, but she knew better. It felt good to be here with him. When they reached her car, she unlocked the door, put her purse and the rose on the passenger seat and turned to gaze up at him. The flutters returned as he melted her with the softness of his eyes.

"I had a wonderful time tonight, Todd. Thank you," she said trying not to sound like a corny adolescent.

"I did too. Thank you for calling and taking me up on my offer," he smiled at her. "Would you like to get together again tomorrow? It's Friday so I thought perhaps we could have dinner and catch a movie."

"I'd like that," she said feeling the nervousness return.

"Great. Do you want to meet somewhere again?" he asked.

She needed to see if what she saw the day before was real, or just her imagination playing tricks on her. Staring into his velvety eyes, it was all there. The wedding, the honeymoon, the pleasures of the everyday. It was all there, hers for the taking. She just had to take it. "I think it'd be okay if you picked me up," she grinned at him.

"So, I'll call you tomorrow for directions."

"Sounds good to me," she hesitated for a moment unsure of what to do next. "Goodnight then." She leaned in and gave him a hug. As she pulled back he held her firmly, but not too tight. He bent down slightly and brushed his lips softly over hers. They lingered there for a moment, the soft glow from the street lamp bathing them in light. She felt her head spin slightly from the sensation.

"Goodnight Christina. I'll see you tomorrow," he whispered and backed up a foot or so.

"See you tomorrow," she smiled as she climbed into her car and started the engine. He waved as she pulled away from the curb. Her heart hammered in her chest as she drove away. She felt her hands trembling faintly as she checked her rearview mirror and saw him give her another small wave before turning and walking toward his own car. She couldn't stop smiling the whole way home. This guy, this accountant with the kind eyes, may be the one to draw her out of her despair.

They began to see each other regularly after that, and he was always extremely considerate. He asked where she wanted to go or what she wanted to do. He showed that he paid attention and offered suggestions for art exhibits and festivals that he gathered she would like from their conversations. When she returned to college for her graduation he came down for the ceremony where he met her mom for the first time. He was charming, funny and open. He entertained them by telling the story of his own experience with college graduation. He'd tripped over the microphone chord and had fallen right on his face in front of what seemed to be a million people. Her mom laughed so hard the water she'd just sipped shot right out of her nose. That set them all to laughing even harder. By the end of it all tears were flowing down all three sets of cheeks. Chris could hardly breathe and her side hurt. That night her mom said she'd noticed the change.

"I haven't seen you this happy, or heard you laugh so much in years, Christina. This one is a keeper."

"Mom, I couldn't agree more," she smiled.

Less than a year later they were engaged. They married in mid-June after school was over. She had completed her first year of teaching and several of her students attended the wedding. She laughed as Todd tried to dance with them at the reception. His lack of rhythm didn't keep him off the dance floor. The only dance he even came close to hitting the right beat on was the Cha-Cha Slide because that song gave step by step directions. She remembered thinking to herself that she couldn't wait until they had kids so she could watch him do this with them. Everything she'd seen in his eyes on those first two occasions was beginning to come true. Her life was finally beginning, thanks to the handsome accountant who had turned it all around.

Christina returned to the present and looked over at the man who had restored her faith in love. How on earth had she let this happen? This man loved her unconditionally, had always put her needs and the needs of the kids above his own. And how had she repaid his generosity? By falling for the one person who had made it so hard for her to find happiness in the first place.

She stroked Todd's blond hair away from his eyes. It was starting to curl around his temples indicating it was time for a haircut. He was her husband. She had made a promise in front of God and their friends and family. Now that she'd broken that promise she wondered how, or if, he'd ever forgive her. She wasn't even sure she could forgive herself and she knew she didn't deserve it from him. She had taken a chance on him, she'd trusted him with her heart and he'd never let her down. She died a little more inside each time she thought about how she was going to let him down, and how her actions would affect him. The tears reappeared as she put her head against his chest. The drops stained his gown as she cried.

Her mother-in-law arrived a few hours later, the emotion clearly visible on her face. She hugged Christina and took up the vigil by her son's side. Christina gave them some time alone and went to find the chapel. She needed guidance right now and God was the only place she could think to turn.

She called home first to check on the kids. Her mother said they were okay, but that it was very difficult to change Jack's diaper with the cast, and she'd given each of them a dose of the ibuprophen recommended by the doctor. They were resting right now, but they wanted her to come home. Christina said she'd be home soon, in time to read them stories and put them to bed.

Then she went into the chapel, sat down in the front pew and prayed. She prayed first for Todd to get better. She was afraid of what would happen if his condition worsened. She prayed for her kids and her mother-in-law as they worried about Todd. She prayed for her dog that was still in the emergency vet clinic. Then she got down to the hard stuff. She prayed for herself, for forgiveness for breaking her marriage vow, for falling back in love with Alex while she still loved Todd, for being ready to tear her family apart, for guidance and wisdom to know what to do next.

As she sat in the chapel silently weeping she had the sensation of a hand patting her shoulder. A sense of comfort trickled through her body as if someone were trying to let her know everything would be okay. She was comforted by the feeling that she was not alone. When she emerged from the chapel, she was still no closer to a decision, but she felt as if some of the weight had been lifted from her shoulders.

Christina met Dr. Solomon as she walked back from the chapel. He told her that they had taken Todd for another round of x-rays and an MRI while she was gone. His lung was stable and he was beginning to breathe on his own. He was off the ventilator and conscious. Dr. Solomon was amazed at how fast he'd begun to recover as soon as she'd arrived.

Todd was groggy, but he was awake. She rushed to the room to find him in a half sitting position. His mother was there helping him drink from a water bottle. He turned when he saw her and smiled gingerly.

"There she is," he said in a raspy voice. "Hey beautiful, we were starting to think you'd skipped town or something." He was clearly exhausted and the effort to speak was communicated through every word. His eyes were barely open and she could only see slits of brown. What she could see was hazy and unfocused.

The words themselves stung. If only he knew why, she thought. She smiled as her eyes once again filled with tears. She moved beside his bed and took his hand. "You're awake," she whispered. "I was afraid we were going to lose you."

"Sweetie, you'll never lose me," his said trying to smile. He winced as he lifted his hand to her cheek. "I'm here for the long haul." He'd never know how much those words meant to her. "Give me a kiss, gorgeous. I've missed you." She leaned down and gave him a gentle kiss on the lips. She tried to hug him but felt him flinch. She pulled back quickly, afraid to hurt him anymore than he already was.

"I'm so sorry," she sobbed into his arm.

"Hey, it's only a few broken ribs. They'll heal." You should see the other guy," he tried to joke.

"No, Todd. I'm sorry I wasn't there. I'm sorry I didn't get here sooner. I have so much to tell you, but I just…" she stopped. She had no idea what to say next, or how she would even begin to tell him what needed to be said.

"Babe," he said stroking her cheek with his thumb, "you're here now. That's all that matters." She smiled back at him and tried to relax. This was not the time or place for the conversation. "How are the kids? Mom said they were at home with Gloria."

"Yeah, she came down this morning. They're okay. They're tired and sore, but overall they couldn't be better. I told her I'd go home tonight to tuck them in. I'll come back as soon as they're asleep," she explained sitting down in the chair next to him.

"You can stay at home if you'd like. I mean, I'd rather have you here, but the kids need you too. If you want to stay there, Mom can stay with me." Once again, in typical Todd fashion, he was putting the needs of others before his own.

"Are you sure?" she asked as she searched his eyes. "I don't mind driving back later."

"I'm sure. You stay with them and come back in the morning after they're awake." He closed his eyes as he spoke. His breathing was labored and his heart monitor showed an increase in pulse. This is too much for him, she thought. He needed to be still in order to recover.

"You need your rest, sugar," his mother interjected. She was a marvelous woman. Chris couldn't ask for a better mother-in-law. It was easy to see where Todd's training had come from. She was very genuine in her love for Christina, and adored her grandkids. She'd moved down from Michigan shortly after Kate was born so she could watch them grow up. Although everyone tried to warn her about having her mother-in-law living so close by, Chris had found it wonderful. She wasn't obtrusive and never wore out her welcome. She was always willing to watch the kids and let them have sleepovers at her house.

"Alright then, I'm going to go. I'll see you in the morning." She turned her attention to her mother-in-law. "Have them call me if anything changes, okay?" She received a quiet nod in reply. She leaned down to kiss him gently and began to rise from her chair.

His hand caught her sleeve and stopped her. "Hey, I love you," he whispered in a gravelly voice. He was exhausted from their conversation and was just minutes from falling back to sleep.

Chapter 31

Christina pulled into her driveway half an hour later. The sun was well below the horizon and the neighborhood was almost completely dark. As she maneuvered her SUV into the garage, it struck her that she hadn't been home in several days. Thanksgiving seemed so far in the past now. She was almost afraid to go inside. It seemed a bit like trespassing on hallowed ground. Most definitely she didn't deserve to be welcomed back here. She felt a sense of disapproval even in the walls surrounding her.

Taking a deep breath, she treaded lightly up the basement stairs. Cracking the door open slightly she poked her head through and peered around. No one was in the kitchen, but she could hear sounds from the television upstairs. From the jingles she could hear, she was willing to bet the Sponge Bob Square Pants movie was playing.

She put her purse on the kitchen counter and dropped the bag containing her other clothes in the trash. She had no desire to ever see or wear them again. Walking up the stairs and rounding the corner, she found Kate, Jack and her mother all snuggled together watching the adventures of a kitchen sponge living in the sea and playing with a squirrel in a space suit. She ruffled the tops of their heads and moved to snuggle in on the other side of Kate. She really didn't understand the cartoon. If Sponge Bob were a sea sponge that would be more understandable, but her less analytical kids loved it, so it was a regularly viewed movie in their house.

They watched through the end of the film together. She glanced over to find Jack fast asleep. The toddler had had a rough few days and was worn out. Untangling herself from Kate, she lifted the little boy and carried him to his room. Kissing his chubby cheeks, which were the only part of him that still looked like a baby, she covered him gently and tiptoed out of the room.

Kate appeared to be just about as tired as Jack when Christina walked her to bed moments later. They barely made it through one book and the little girl was too drained to read another. Christina checked Kate's bruises again, gave her a dose of ibuprophen, and tucked her into bed. She bent to give her daughter a good night kiss and turned to go.

"Mommy?" Kate asked sleepily.

"Yes, baby?" she turned around from the door.

"I'm glad we're home. I missed you an awful lot."

"I missed you an awful lot too, sweetie. I'm glad we're home too." She smiled, turned off the light, and left the door open a small crack.

She ate the dinner her mother had left for her in near silence. She couldn't enjoy the food at all; it seemed her taste buds weren't functioning properly. Her mother asked how Todd was doing and Christina reported that he was breathing on his own and was even able to talk, although weakly. The doctors weren't sure when he'd be able to come home, but it shouldn't be too long. She scraped the plate into the trash and put it in the dishwasher. Telling her mother she was going to have a bath and go to bed, she gave the older woman a long hug, thanked her for coming down and taking care of them, and walked upstairs.

As she lay in the bathtub full of hot, bubbly water, she drifted back to a time she hadn't thought about in years. She was standing in front of her third grade class on her first day of teaching. She felt out of place and completely unqualified to be there. Eight year olds had never looked scarier. Apparently, this was common on the first day of school for new teachers, or so the veterans in the building had told her. She introduced herself and they played some get-to-know-you games. Many children didn't want to play, or gave fake answers, or called other students names.

By 9:00 AM, she'd wanted to cry. They were only half way through a writing project that was not going very well when lunch time came. She somehow managed to line them all up and get them to the cafeteria without losing anyone, or any of them losing an eye. The twenty minute lunch break was not nearly long enough. She spent the rest of the day just trying not to burst into tears in front of the kids. It has been said that dogs and sharks could smell fear. She was now convinced that 3rd graders could too. If they saw her crack, it would be over and she would have no hope of gaining or keeping control of the class.

The disorder and chaos of the day made her begin to rethink her decision to teach in the inner city. She was a brand new teacher in a school where no one looked like her; neither students, nor teachers. She left right at 3:00 and remembered driving back to her tiny little apartment, dragging herself upstairs, collapsing on her bed and weeping.

Todd had called at 4:30. He was leaving work soon and wanted to see how her first day went. His voice sounded so optimistic and hopeful when he began to speak. She broke down in gulping, blubbering sobs as she tried incoherently to tell him how horribly the day had gone. The kids were wild, and some were really mean. There were a few sweet ones, but she almost overlooked them because of the problems with the others. She wasn't sure she could do this. She was convinced she'd made a bad career choice, or at least a bad school choice. In a soothing voice, he attempted to calm her down, and told her to leave her door unlocked; he'd be there soon.

An hour later there was a soft knock on her bedroom door as it opened slightly. Christina lifted her tear-stained face from her pillow to see a little yellow ball of fur peeking in at her. Todd had brought her the cutest puppy she had ever seen. Sitting straight up, with her arms outstretched, she took the tiny bundle and a huge smile crossed her face. The stress of the day was instantly forgotten. Her once bleak mood was now transformed into one of delight as she cuddled the puppy joyfully. Todd came and sat beside her on the bed and draped his arm around her shoulder.

"Oh, Todd! It's so cute! Is it a boy or a girl?" she asked wiping the last of the tears from her eyes.

"It's a boy. I've had my eye on him for a while and wanted to surprise you with him. I figured this was about as good a time as any," he said tickling the puppy under the chin.

"What kind of dog is he?"

"He's a Golden Retriever mix. A family in my neighborhood owns the mom who is full golden. I've watched this little guy grow up for the last six weeks. I know it's a little early to take him away from the rest of the litter, but I called the vet and she said it would be fine." He paused for a moment. "You sounded so upset on the phone. I knew I had to do something to cheer you up." He stroked her hair as she rested her head on his shoulder.

"Thank you, Todd. I love him already." Her elation was short-lived, though, when she remembered the apartment policy. "But, I can't have pets here."

"That's okay. We'll keep him at my house. It gives you a reason to come over and visit more often," he grinned down at her. What do you want to name him?"

"How about Max? I've always wanted a dog named Max. When I was a kid, one of my friends had this dog named Max that was so cool. He was a curly ball of white fluff and he used to chase us all around her house. Her dad tried to convince us once that Max was really a person who dressed up like a dog for Halloween, but the zipper on the costume got stuck so he had to stay a dog forever. Then he told us that Max's people suit got lost at the cleaner and while he could now unzip the costume, there was nothing else to put on so he just decided to keep on being a dog."

She smiled at the memory. "I loved that dog." She rubbed the puppy behind the ears and made them flop up and down.

"Then Max it is. I like that name. It suits him. Are you feeling up to taking Max to the park? I've a got a leash and a tennis ball in the car."

"Give me a minute to clean up and put on my shoes?" she asked.

"Take as much time as you need," he replied. He helped her up and she reluctantly placed Max in his arms. "You know, things will get better at school. You're a great teacher. You just have to get your bearings and show them whose boss. Find out what they like and determine your common ground. You'll win them over."

"I know it'll get better. It's just a first day reaction, I guess." She pulled on her running shoes and went into the bathroom and splashed some cold water on her face. Looking at herself in the mirror she saw the red streaks beginning to fade. He always knew what to say to make her feel better. She smiled to herself as she realized that the things she'd seen in his eyes when they first met were starting to fall into place. The dog had appeared just as she pictured him. She grinned at her reflection and reconfirmed that this was the man she would spend the rest of her life with.

Christina got out of the tub and dried off slowly. She had forgotten about a lot of their earlier times together. That afternoon had saved her life, metaphorically speaking. She had gone back to school the next day with a sense of renewed energy and spirit. It had been tough, but she'd gotten through that first year, even developing deep relationships with many of the kids. Each afternoon she'd gone to visit Max and that gave her something else to look forward to.

She went downstairs and opened her bag that she'd left on the counter. She took out her cell phone and made her way back upstairs and called the emergency vet clinic to check on Max. He was in bad shape. Since he was riding loose in the back of the van, there had been nothing to stop him from flying when the impact occurred. He had two broken legs and some pretty bad injuries to his internal organs. They had had to remove a part of his liver that was severely damaged. He would be there for a while and there were no guarantees that he would make a full recovery. He was, after all, nearly ten years old and the resiliency of puppyhood was long behind him. She thanked them for their honesty and diligence in caring for him and said she'd be up in the morning.

As she climbed into bed, and was about to shut the phone, she noticed the voicemail message indicator lit up. Hitting the button, she heard the familiar greeting of the automated voice tell her she had three new messages. The first was from Joe telling her not to worry about coming in at all until things were okay. His thoughts and prayers were with her and she could call him if she needed anything. Before deleting the call, she made a mental note to call in.

The second message was from her neighbor John who was also calling to check on things. He'd seen Gloria's car pull up with the kids and found out what happened from her. He'd be over after work the next day to bring the kids pizza and watch a movie if she thought that was a good idea. She would call him back tomorrow and tell him it was the best idea she'd heard in a long time. Her kids loved pizza, loved movies and loved John. She hit delete and waited for the last message. Everything in the room was altered when she heard Alex's voice. She could no longer see as clearly and there was a slight thumping sound coming from deep within her chest. She closed her eyes as she listened to the message.

"Hey, Chris. It's me, Alex. I know you can't talk right now and I definitely don't want to take up any of your time. But, I just wanted to tell you that I miss you already and will be here for you in any way that I can. Call me when you can. I love you." She closed her eyes as she heard his voice. At the prompt she replayed the message. After the second time she heard it, she was prompted again. Press seven to delete. Press nine to save. She simply closed the phone not ready to decide either way. She put the phone on the table by her bed, swallowed an Ambien, laid down right in the middle of the king size bed and pulled the covers up to her chin. In the course of a few days her life had completely turned upside down. All she wanted to do now was sleep.

Sleep didn't come so easily however. After tossing and turning for hours she finally gave up and got out of bed. The clock read 2:45 AM. Bleary from the Ambien, she stumbled into the bathroom where she washed her face and brushed her teeth. She changed into some workout clothes and quietly tiptoed to the basement. Not wanting to disturb anyone, she left the TV off. She started pedaling on her elliptical glider and started up her I-Pod.

It had been days since she'd run, or worked out at all, and her muscles were letting her know they didn't appreciate the extended break. She stepped off and stretched, not wanting to injure herself while she was needed to care for others. She climbed back on and pushed her body to the absolute maximum her body would allow. The music thumped and her feet pedaled furiously.

Working out always gave her time to think and her thoughts drove her back to one of her earliest memories with Todd. They'd been dating regularly for about three months. They had a great time together and he was definitely the most attentive boyfriend she'd ever had. She knew the time was coming to have to make some decisions about where things would go with them, but she tried desperately to avoid it. He'd walked her back to her apartment one night after a hilarious evening at Joker's Comedy Club. He came inside and sat on the couch beside her. She could sense what was about to happen and she tried hard not to tense up and push him away. She wanted to love him fully, to experience him physically, but something blocked her from getting close. The kissing she could handle, but they hadn't made it past that.

Todd reached out for her and drew her in close. She let his mouth find hers and allowed his tongue to sweep delicately around. She breathed him in. He moved his hands gently over her shirt and grazed her breasts, and for the first time she let him. Blood rushed through her veins at a speed only known to Indy 500 racers. She tried diligently not to pass out. He moved the kiss down her neck and the ceiling fan cooled the moisture in the wake leaving her skin chilled. She raised her arms and hugged him tighter trying to push away the sense of anxiety that always crept in when they were this close. As he moved his hands lower and began to pull her skirt down over her hips it became too much.

She tried to keep the room in focus. She tried to keep Todd's image clear in her mind. His hands were caressing her so sweetly, delicately. This was *not* the man who had caused her so much of pain, but all she could see in her mind was Alex and how excruciating things had turned out. She had opened herself to him in ways she had never done before and she'd paid a high price. Involuntarily, she cringed and moved away to the other side of the couch. Fighting the urge to throw up, she began to sob.

"What's the matter? Did I do something wrong?" he asked. His hands cupped her face lifting her eyes to meet his.

"I'm sorry. It's not you. You're doing everything right. It's me." She covered her face with her hands, too ashamed to meet his gaze.

"Hey, it's ok," he whispered.

"No, Todd. It's not okay. I want to do this with you. I want to make love to you and know you. But I just can't right now. I'm just so messed up!"

"You are not messed up, Christina." He cradled her in his arms as she cried. "I can tell you've been hurt in the past. I'm willing to wait until you're ready. Whatever issues you have, you need to work through them on your own and when you do, I'll still be right here."

She dried her eyes and looked at him softly. Seeing the tenderness there she knew he was sincere. "Thank you. I promise I'll get myself straightened out."

"No hurry. Whatever it was obviously hurt you deeply. I know you've probably already heard this, but I don't believe it was your fault. You didn't ask for whatever happened to you. Just know that I will never intentionally do anything that will cause you an ounce of sorrow. I love you too much to make you cry."

She lay against his chest and couldn't believe what he'd just said. He loved her and was willing to wait for her. He loved her. He'd said it with no reservation or hesitation. There were no strings attached, no demons to overcome. He was opening his heart to her. All she had to do was take it. Things would turn around. She could see happiness again in her future and she saw it with him. "Todd?"

"Yes?"

"I love you too. One day soon I'll be able to show you."

"There's no rush. We have the rest of our lives to love each other." He stroked her hair lightly, a gesture that instilled a tremendous sense of comfort in her.

By the time she stepped off the glider an hour later she was drenched with sweat. Her body was exhausted, but she felt better. She took a cool shower and drank a large glass of water. Climbing back into bed at 4:00 AM she finally found the sleep she had been craving.

Chapter 32

Christina called the hospital at 8:00 in the morning and talked to her mother-in-law. Todd had had a rough night, but he was doing better now. He was breathing on his own and from what the doctor said his lung looked even better than the day before. Christina said she'd be up in a few hours after the kids were fed and dressed. Her mother-in-law told her to take her time. Todd wasn't going anywhere and wouldn't be running a marathon any time soon. That Midwestern sense of humor was beginning to shine through in this serious situation. Christina smiled and shook her head wryly as she hung up the phone. She got the kids up, concurred with her mother that changing a diaper around a cast was very difficult, and fixed breakfast for them. The one type of meal she was good at cooking was breakfast. She made animal pancakes; a bunny for Kate and a snake for Jack. The snake was the hardest to make, but she did it with the help of two spatulas and a little luck.

Forty-five minutes later, armed with a large travel mug of coffee, she set out for the clinic to check on Max. She'd promised the kids she'd give the old dog a kiss for them. She'd probably give him several if she was able to. When she arrived, the vet showed her to the area where Max was being kept. Lying on his side in his crate, Max looked up when he heard the door open and his tail thumped weakly when he recognized her.

"Hey there, Max," she whispered tenderly patting his head. "You kinda look like Jack with those casts." The dog had casts on his front two legs which severely limited his movement. "He's gonna be awfully glad to see you when you come home, so you need to get better real soon, okay?" His tail thumped a little stronger in response. After spending some time stroking his fur and whispering sweetly that everything would be okay, she left for the hospital.

The hospital parking lot was crowded for so early in the day. She squeezed into a tight parking space and went upstairs to Todd's room. He was sitting up, eating slowly from the breakfast tray in front of him. His eyes were brighter and clearer than they had been yesterday and his complexion had regained some of its color. He smiled when she came in and she noticed the small crinkles around the corners of his eyes. She hadn't noticed those in years and realized how charming they made him look. She was beginning to notice a lot of things about him that she had forgotten over the years.

"You look much better today," she said as she set her bag down on the floor next to the bed. She kissed him quickly on the cheek as he chewed.

"Yeah, I feel much better today too," he answered after swallowing a bite of what was supposed to be oatmeal. "I'm ready to be one hundred percent better right now, especially if it means getting real food sooner. This stuff is awful."

"At least you can eat it," she said sitting down next to him.

Christina greeted her mother-in-law as she emerged from the bathroom. Deborah said she was going home to rest if that was okay. Christina and Todd both agreed that she should go. Deborah had been awake for the better part of two days and needed to get some sleep. They hugged her goodbye and Christina promised to call later with any news. Christina sat down in the uncomfortable chair beside Todd's bed and told him the kids were doing much better, hoping to ease his worry, knowing he was more concerned for their well being than he was for his own.

"Hey, guess what? Doctor Solomon said I can probably go home later tonight or tomorrow morning. They just have to run a few more tests to make sure my lung won't fill up with blood or collapse again at home."

"That's great! The kids will be so happy to see you. They're pretty worried, you know." She took the tray and put it on the side table. "I went and checked on Max. He's beat up pretty badly, but the vet said the internal bleeding is under control and he should be able to come home in a few days, maybe a week. I guess it's turning out to be a good day."

Various nurses and techs came and took Todd and ran him through the same battery of procedures they'd done yesterday to check on his progress. He and Christina waited for what seemed like hours for the results to come back. While they waited, they watched the movie Deep Impact on TV. Todd pointed out that he hadn't seen the movie since they were dating. He asked if she remembered going to see it at that damp and musty theater near what used to be North Dekalb Mall. Christina was surprised he remembered this. She had completely forgotten. It had been the grossest place they'd ever been, but they ended up really having fun trying to guess what substance had created each of the stains on the floor and seats. She'd never laughed so hard in her life. She realized how much of their lives had escaped her memory and it made her more than a little sad. Lacing their fingers together, they held hands while they watched the movie. Todd caught her looking at him a couple of times.

"What?" he asked after the third time.

"Nothing," she replied. "I was just noticing how handsome you are."

He smiled. "Yeah, the bruises look good on me and the IV bag really adds a special touch. I think I'll ask if I can take it home."

"I'd swat you on the arm if I weren't afraid I'd rip that IV out," she laughed back.

Just as the movie was ending, Doctor Solomon came in and said he would authorize Todd's release that afternoon with stringent instructions for him to maintain complete bed rest. Todd could get up only to go to the bathroom and bathe, with assistance. Christina chuckled and rolled her eyes at Todd's comment that she was going to be his beckon call girl for the next several weeks. He needed to make an appointment and come back in for weekly check-ups for the next three to five weeks and Dr. Solomon stressed to them that readmittance to the hospital may be necessary if Todd didn't follow his post-care instructions perfectly.

They arrived home early that evening. Christina had called Deborah from the hospital and asked her to go to the pharmacy to pick up the prescriptions so they wouldn't have to delay their return. When they arrived, their neighbor John was there and ran to the door to assist in getting Todd upstairs and into bed.

Gloria brought up a tray of the pizza John had brought, along with a salad and a coke and Todd ate while Kate and Jack sat on the bed next to him. While she tried to talk him out of overdoing it, Todd insisted that Christina bring in some of their books. After he finished eating, he read three books to his children, stopping only occasionally to catch his breath. He wasn't as animated as usual, but they didn't seem to mind. Their dad was home and they were all together again.

She watched from other side of the bed where Kate was cuddled on her lap. Todd really was an amazing father. The kids didn't realize how lucky they were, she thought. She hoped one day to help them understand how fortunate they were to have a father who loved them fiercely and was always by their sides. The accident could have turned out so much worse. He could've been taken away from them the way her father was taken from her. Only they would have been too young to truly remember him.

After story time Christina gave Jack a bath and, with Gloria's help, they worked around the cast. It proved to be extremely difficult though since Jack loved splashing in the tub. They had to wrap his leg in a plastic grocery bag and rubber band it closed at the top, but even that didn't stop some of the water from dampening the edges of the cast. Kate's bath was easier, but still very slow. Her bruises looked just as livid as it had when Christina first saw it at the hospital. She knew it would look worse before it looked better and it would take time to heal, as all wounds did, but she wanted to will this one heal faster. Seeing her children in pain broke her heart.

Causing them more pain would be unbearable. She wasn't sure she'd be able to go through with her decision to leave Todd for Alex. She wasn't even sure if it was the right choice for *her* anymore. She was needed here. She was surrounded by loved ones, and even though it would be tough taking care of all of them for the next few weeks, she couldn't think of any place else she'd rather be.

She pictured herself with Alex; lying in his arms, listening to him play his guitar and watching him create beautiful music. It was easy to get caught up in the romance of it all. It was stimulating and exciting and it felt true. It felt right in some ways, but in others it felt completely wrong.

Then she looked around at her reality. Her two children, both injured but okay; her husband who easily could have died, but didn't; her mother and mother-in-law who were sacrificing their own time and energy to help them out. It wasn't romantic in the least, but it was hers, *they* were hers. She wasn't sure she could give this up.

Being late November, it was too dark and cold to go out for an evening jog so she got on her elliptical and again pounded away for an hour. She felt the flood of warmth course through her body as she let herself return to a world filled with Alex. She felt his hands on her body and the heat of his lips on hers. She heard his voice murmur in her ear. She felt his kiss sear her from the outside in. It was a sensation she knew she would never be able to forget, even if she wanted to. Losing focus, she nearly slipped off the machine before she caught herself and pulled herself back to reality. She grabbed the remote control from the inclined platform and turned the TV to TLC. She needed something to take her mind off of her memories of him. The guilt, which receded somewhat when she was busy with the others, came flooding back at the alone times like this. If being with Alex was so right, why did she feel like the lowest level of humanity?

A new show called "The Great Proposal" was on. This show told stories of men looking for outrageously romantic, creative and unique ways to propose marriage to their girlfriends. She smiled as she watched the guy on screen talk about how much he cherished his girlfriend and how they loved outdoor sports and rock climbed together as often as they could. Energetic and adventurous, never afraid to try something new. The guy was planning to propose at the top of a very steep cliff after their next climb. Their family and friends would be waiting at the bottom to celebrate with them when they returned. It was sweet and definitely different. The camera panned to show a view of the cliff they would be climbing. She mused quietly to herself that if the couple could make it past the obstacle of the mountain, they could probably survive just about anything together. He sounded a lot like Todd in his younger days.

It led her back to Todd's proposal to her. It had been early February and the weather was playing its usual games with the people of Atlanta. One day was bitterly cold, and the next the temperature was in the mid-sixties. On this particular day it was warm so Christina and Todd decided to take Max to a nearby park.

They'd strolled to the lake in the center of the park where the daffodils were just starting to peek their green leaves through the pine straw. The boat rental stand was open and canoes dotted the water. Blankets were spread out across the rolling slopes and most had picnic baskets on them. Families were eating together, friends were playing Frisbee, and groups were playing touch football or soccer. Couples and singles were meandering around the grounds, some with dogs and some without. They took Max on the long loop twice. He had almost reached his full grown size and was extremely energetic. He probably could have gone another lap with no problem, but they were ready to call it quits after struggling through three miles of Max pulling at the leash. He had failed that part of obedience training, and it was a battle that they weren't sure they'd ever win. Once he left his puppyhood behind though, he calmed down considerably.

Pleasantly exhausted, they found an empty spot near the water and Todd spread out their own blanket. Max lay down at their feet and promptly fell asleep. Though almost full grown, he was still a pup and tended to snooze quite a bit. She opened their picnic basket and took out the turkey sandwiches with roasted red peppers she'd picked up from the local deli along with potato salad and a fruit medley. She honestly couldn't figure out why anyone not being paid to do it would bother learning how to cook, or even make cold fare like this when it could so easily be purchased already prepared. They sat cross-legged on the blanket and ate as they watched the people brave the canoes.

"That water must be freezing!" she exclaimed as she took a bite of her sandwich. "Those people are crazy!"

"So, I guess it's pointless to ask if you'd like to take one out." Todd said.

"Seriously?" she asked as her head turned in his direction. "Do you want to take a canoe ride? I mean, I'll go if you want to, but I'm pretty sure Max would tip the boat and we'd all have to be fished out by the park patrol."

"That's true, and then we'd all have to be treated for hypothermia at… where is the closest hospital? Piedmont?" he said shrugging his shoulders. "Oh well, I guess we'll just have to stay on dry land today."

"A wise decision. That's why they pay you the big bucks," she joked.

"Hey, did you pick up dessert too?" he asked nonchalantly. He brushed the crumbs from his fingers and put his plate to the side.

"No, I forgot. I'm sorry. We can stop on the way back to your house and pick something up if you want."

"That's okay. I brought something. It's tucked in the bottom of the basket. Here, hand it to me and I'll get it."

She furrowed her brow and peered suspiciously at him as she handed over the picnic basket. She hadn't seen him put anything in the basket, but then again she hadn't watched it the whole day. He rummaged through the left over containers of food and pulled out a small white bakery box. He handed the box to her and told her to open it. She slowly broke the seal and peeked inside.

"Mexican wedding cookies?" she asked looking up slightly confused. They were delicious, but she couldn't remember telling him that she had any special interest in them. Her confusion turned into surprise as she saw him drop to one knee on the ground beside her. He was holding another small box, this one of burgundy velvet. He opened it carefully. She gasped as her hand covered her mouth. Inside was a two carat emerald cut diamond ring set in platinum.

"Christina Ann Malone, from the day I met you I knew you were the one for me. You bring passion and energy to my life that I didn't know was missing until you came along. I want to experience that passion and energy every day from now until forever. Will you make me the happiest man on earth and marry me?"

She didn't even pause to think about it. "Yes!" she squealed and threw her arms around his neck. They held each other tightly and laughed and cried together. Then they grabbed a confused Max and pulled him into the embrace. It took them a few moments before they realized people around them were cheering and clapping. It wasn't an extreme or outrageous proposal, but it was sweet and romantic and she couldn't have pictured it any better.

Todd stood and shouted at the top of his lungs, "She said yes!" and jumped up high in the air.

This fueled the crowd even more. She giggled at his excitement. As he slipped the beautiful ring on her finger, complete strangers came up, hugging them and offering congratulations. That night they went back to his house and she spent the night for the first time. Because of her emotional issues, they had waited a long time to engage in intimacy, but now she was ready. There was no trace of the anxiety that had plagued every other attempt they had made to make love. She knew that he loved her deeply and that he wouldn't cause her pain. She knew this was what she wanted. For the first time, she allowed him to fully explore her body and she permitted herself to do the same. They'd come to be so comfortable with each other that now physical intimacy felt so natural, as if they were meant to hold and touch and caress each other for the rest of their lives. They made love tenderly and she fell asleep with his strong arms wrapped around her. It had been the best day of her life. She felt like she had finally found the place where she belonged.

When she returned to their room, she was surprised to find him still awake. He had a book on his lap as if he'd been trying to read but had given it up for the less exhausting task of watching television. He smiled at her as she passed by on her way to the bathroom. She quickly showered, changed into her nightgown and climbed into bed beside him.

"Do you need anything before we go to sleep?" she asked.

"No, everything I need is right here beside me," he said as he reached out and stroked her arm. "Chris, I need to tell you something."

"What is it?" she asked with concern. He sounded serious all of a sudden. The jovial attitude he'd displayed since returning from the hospital had vanished.

"I was so scared during the accident. When the van flipped I honestly didn't know what to do. I just kept thinking I had to save the kids and Max, and then I started thinking I'd never see you again. I saw our lives flash before my eyes and I realized how much I've missed you over the last few years. I miss us. I've never been really good with words, but I hope you'll understand what I'm trying to say. The only thing that kept me alive, once I knew the kids were being taken care of by the EMT's, was thinking about how much I love you and that if I were given a second chance, I'd spend the rest of my life getting us back on track."

She turned to look at him and saw the tears streaming down his face. It was one of the few times she'd seen him cry. Other than the birth of their children, he had always been the picture of complete strength and stability. Seeing him so vulnerable and exposed, she realized there was much more to him than she had given him credit for.

"Todd, you've been nothing but wonderful to me since we met," she started. She was about to come clean. He needed to know. But he stopped her.

"But I haven't given you everything you need. When I get better I'll show you just how much I've missed you. Until then, I hope you'll settle for some pretty amazing kisses." He pulled her to him and she saw him wince with pain. She tried to protest, telling him he needed to rest, but he put his finger to her lips to quiet her.

He tilted her chin so their eyes engaged and what she saw turned her entire world upside down yet again. She saw them traveling to exotic places, experiencing new adventures, as an older couple playing with their grandchildren and then as a wrinkly, white haired pair sitting on a porch sipping sweet tea, their hands, spotted and nearly translucent, joined together with fingers loosely laced as they rocked contentedly in their chairs. She saw, in essence, everything her life would become and underlying it all was an undying love. Their love would change over the years, turn into something deeper, ebb and flow, but it would never fail them. When he broke his gaze he bent his head and kissed her deeply. Every fiber of her being reacted to the kiss. Its warmth seemed to reach her toes and she melted into his arms, never wanting it to end.

As they fell asleep that night she felt completely torn. What she had with Todd was changing. What she had with Alex was new. Confusion and exhaustion overcame her mind and body. She didn't feel strong enough to choose between them. She was afraid that whatever decision she made would be the wrong one. Out of self defense she slept. A deep, mercifully dreamless sleep.

Chapter 33

Tuesday arrived with a barrage of things for Alex to do. He began with a phone-in radio tour of all the major stations in Atlanta. He made a short appearance on Good Day Atlanta as well. His first TV interview didn't turn out to be as nerve-wracking as he thought it would be. He started off by playing his first single live. The hosts praised his debut album as soulful, heartfelt and inspiring. Then he called in a few more interviews to stations in cities where his tour would be stopping first.

While Michael, his stand-in rep, was excellent at his job, it didn't feel the same without Chris. But, he went through the motions, answered the questions from callers and whatnot. He was glad that most of the day didn't consist of face to face interviews because he wasn't sure he'd be able to pull off more than one appearance. The camera added a new element he was unfamiliar with, but he sailed through with no problems. He tried to stay upbeat and positive. He tried not to think of, or worry about, Christina.

Still, he missed her terribly. It had only been a couple of days since he'd seen her and already he felt the emptiness that lingered in her absence. He knew the odds of her coming with him on the road were slim to none with her family in their various states of injury, but in his heart he still held out a glimmer of hope. At least they would be together when he returned from the tour. The kids and her husband would be healed by then, the holidays would be over, and Alex could start building his life with her. He was solid enough in their love for each other to know that, in the end, everything would work out.

He had spent Monday looking at houses in the area where she currently lived. The move would be easier for Kate if she didn't have to change schools. Being the new kid was tough, he remembered. His mom had moved them a lot after his dad split. Rent was always increasing, or there was a better opportunity in another town. He had been the new kid more often than he ever wanted to be.

His house search turned out to be fruitless though. He kept running into the same obstacle. Even if he tried to move into a nearby neighborhood, he wouldn't know if it would be zoned for the same school. He then decided to try to work out a touring schedule that would allow Chris and the kids to come with him on the road as much as possible. He wanted to get to know her children and love them as much as he loved her. He'd played with them a lot at Todd's birthday party. They seemed like sweet, fun kids. What he ran into there was not having any idea how to schedule a tour, or even where to start. His itinerary had been handed to him, planned out by Chris and his manager. All he had to do was practice, record, shop and pack for the time away from home.

Feeling very helpless, he'd given up, grabbed his guitar and began writing new songs. They would work it out. Chris could handle the scheduling and could help figure out the living arrangements. It kind of scared him to realize how much he was already relying on her, not just professionally but personally as well. In such a short time she had gone from being constantly on the periphery of his mind to being the center of his universe. This time though, he was not running away. It would be hard, but they'd find a way to manage it. It would take work, but this time he wasn't going to let fear conquer his life.

Alex was in rehearsals from 11:00 in the morning until well after 3:00 the day before the tour began. Afterwards he had a final review session with Michael. He ran into Andrea on his way to Michael's office which shared a wall with Christina's office. She gave him a sympathetic look and stopped him in the hallway.

"Hey," she said hesitantly.

"Hey, Andrea," he responded. They stood there for a minute unsure of what to say next. "Have you talked to her lately?" he ventured.

"Yeah, this morning. Todd's home from the hospital. He's going to be okay. The doctor said he'd never seen anyone start to heal so quickly from injuries that serious. The kids are home too. It looks like everyone will make a full recovery. Well, except for Max. He's still at the animal hospital in pretty serious shape, but even he will be home before too long."

"How's Chris holding up?" he asked with his hands in his pockets and eyes searching the floor.

"She's staying strong for her family right now. But Alex, she's a mess. We talked in the hospital. She's being torn apart with guilt."

"I know she is. I can't even imagine what she's going through." He stopped before continuing. If Chris and Andrea had talked, then Andrea must have a good idea of what was going on. "She told you everything then?"

"Yes, Alex. She told me."

"What did you think?"

"Well, at first I was angry with her for having an affair when she already has what most people dream of. But, after she explained it to me, I feel less judgmental."

"What do you mean?"

"She loves you Alex. She has for a long time. However, she still loves her husband. That fact hit home even harder when she saw him in the hospital. She's faced with a difficult choice and I wouldn't want to be in her shoes. The best advice I can offer you is to just give her some space right now. She has a serious decision to make and doesn't need anything else to muddy the waters." She checked her watch. "You'd better go. Michael is a stickler for punctuality."

"Thanks, Andrea."

"No problem. Good luck on the tour." She patted him on the arm as she walked past him. "Hang in there."

"Thanks," he said as he turned to leave. Difficult choice? Serious decision? He thought she had already decided. Was she having second thoughts? He couldn't blame her if she was. But it had to be the trauma of the accident. Once things settled back down, she would make her way back to him.

He spent his entire meeting with Michael trying to convince himself of that. But by the time he left he had only determined that he needed to speak to her. He couldn't take Andrea's advice. He'd let her go once without a fight, and he wasn't going to make the same mistake twice. Going to her house was out of the question. There was no guarantee she would answer the phone, but he had to try. He'd keep trying until she picked up.

Alex started dialing Christina's cell number minutes after arriving home. A few times he hung up before her phone began to ring. He hadn't figured out what he would say. Finally, he decided to just let the words flow on their own. The last time he dialed he let the call connect. She answered on the third ring.

"Hi," she said in a low voice.

"Hi. How are you?" he asked.

"I'm okay. What about you?" She sounded a bit flat, drained of all energy.

"I'm fine. I miss you. A lot. What's going on over there? How is everyone?" He'd go with the safe questions first.

"All in all, they're great. We were very lucky. Jack's got a cast on one leg and some scrapes; Kate's got a nasty bruise across her chest and she's pretty sore, and Todd is home under strict orders to rest."

"Are you there taking care of them by yourself?"

"No, my mother and Todd's mom are here helping me out. They'll be here for a while. My mom is staying the week."

"That's good that you have some help." He was at a complete loss for words.

"Alex?" Her voice was practically a whisper. "Why are you really calling?"

"I just wanted to check on you. Tell you I'm thinking about you, and that I love you. You don't have to answer. I know it's not a good time."

"You're right, it's not, but I feel the same way."

"We pull out tomorrow. Any chance you'll be there, at least to see us off?"

"I don't know." She paused for a moment. "Are you nervous?"

"Yeah, I'm nervous. I'd be less so if I knew you'd be with me, but I understand there's a lot more going on right now."

"Thank you for understanding. I can't ask for anything more than that."

"Okay then. Well, I guess I'll go. Call me when you can. I miss hearing your voice. I miss holding your hand. Hell, I just miss you," he finished.

"Okay. I'll talk to you soon."

"I love you, Chris. Never forget that."

"I won't. Goodbye," she whispered.

"Goodbye," he said as the line went dead. He clicked his phone closed and sat resigned in his chair. There was nothing more he could do.

At her house Christina closed her cell phone too. She was standing on the back deck trying not to cry. It was very cold and the wind was whipping through her hair, but she felt none of the chill. She simply felt empty and alone. The chilly air around her mirrored her emotion. Collecting herself she went back into the house. The warmth of fire radiated throughout the entire downstairs area. She heard laughter from the living room and walked around the corner. She saw her kids playing a game with their grandmothers and she felt the warmth return to her soul as well as her hands. Just a couple days ago they were frightened and lonely, lying in the hospital dealing with injuries they had never experienced before. Now they were giggling and having fun. The resilience of children never ceased to amaze her. In fact, her kids blew her away every day.

After getting everyone into bed and making sure Todd was as comfortable as possible, she fell asleep next to him and dreamed. She saw herself in a field surrounded by daffodils. They were her mother's favorite. She remembered that her dad would bring the cut flowers home weekly in early spring. In the fall her parents spent hours planting bulbs and in the spring they tended the yellow and white blooms next to the mailbox and along the path to the front door.

Her parents never cut any of the blooms from the yard. Her mom said she wanted the neighbors to enjoy them as much as she did. So her dad would stop by the florist every Friday to pick up a fresh bouquet for the house. Their gentle fragrance wafted through the house daily from late February until the end of March. She had watched her mother breathe in the aroma every time she walked through the kitchen. Gloria had been especially happy and almost wistful each time she inhaled the flowers, as if the fragrance of daffodils could cure any ailment in the world. Christina had always derived great comfort from the fragrance and the sight of them. The flowers were special for her mother and father, a symbol of their love for each other. Some of this specialness had rubbed off on her too. She wondered why she had never planted them in her own yard and made a mental note to do so next fall.

In her dream she saw a man on the other side of the field walking in her direction. He appeared to glide rather than walk. He was tall and lean, much like Todd. However, as he got closer she saw he was much different. His nearly black hair contrasted with his fair complexion and his crystal blue eyes gleamed with an intense light. Her heart felt light and gave a little jump upon recognition. A wide smile spread across her face and as he reached her she lifted her arms to embrace him.

"Hey, Dad," she whispered. He looked exactly the same as he had before he'd gotten sick. Her theory that after death people return to their most attractive state seemed to be true. There was no trace of the cancer, or the effects of the chemotherapy, to be found. He looked strong and healthy, like he was ready to take on the world.

"Hey there, pumpkin." His answer was slightly muffled through her hair.

"Where am I? What are you doing here? Are you an angel?" Tears glistened in her eyes as she held onto the first man who'd broken her heart.

"I was sent by God to give you counsel, but I'm not an angel. You've got yourself in quite a jam," he said taking her elbow and looping her arm through his. "Let's take a walk and tell me all about it." He patted her hand gently. Father and daughter began to move slowly through the field of flowers.

"I don't even know where to begin, Dad. Everything is such a mess. I don't know which end is up anymore. Is it possible to be in love with two men at the same time? Can I make a fair choice?" She rested her head on his shoulder. It felt solid and firm, as if he were still alive and with her in the flesh, not just part of her dream. She realized how much she missed her dad and wanted to stay with him forever.

"I feel kind of responsible that you're in this mess, sweetie," he said as they strolled through the field of flowers. The blooms swayed gently in their wake. "I wasn't there to help you through everything with Alex the first time around."

"What are you talking about, Dad?" she asked quizzically. "You died long before I met Alex. You couldn't have helped me through it."

"I've been watching over you and your mother since I passed." At her shocked expression he continued, "You've never been alone. You didn't think I went away forever, did you? I've been with you always, just as I said I would."

"If you've been able to reach us all this time, why *didn't* you come earlier? Why now?" she asked as she turned to face her father. It was like looking into a mirror. They had the same dark hair, the same piercing blue eyes. Only his eyes were lighter and reflected the darker blue of hers. Her eyes searched his for answers to questions she didn't even know how to ask.

"You haven't asked for help until now, Christina. You've been strong and you've held your head up through some pretty tough times and taken good care of yourself. You're resilient and recovered in ways beyond your years. You have a lovely family and you've made a nice life for yourself. But now you've gotten yourself involved in something too deep to get out of. God heard your prayers in the chapel. I was sent to help you make the right choice." That explained the sensation she'd had of someone's hand on her shoulder.

"But Dad, I don't know what the right choice *is* anymore. I thought I did, but now I'm not so sure. Do I leave a good man who loves me and would do anything in the world for me, including make it his second chance wish to rebuild our relationship, to be with someone for whom I feel such supreme passion, someone who also loves me and expresses it so eloquently?"

"That is a hard choice. Are you sure they are both who they seem to be?"

"I think so. Alex has become everything I knew he would become, maybe even more. Then there's Todd who has always been wonderful. He's sweet and funny and at one time we were extremely happy with each other. Things haven't been the same between us for the past few years, but I can see that getting better."

"Are you sure you're looking at the right things?" he asked.

"What do you mean?"

"Which is more important? Can you build your life on passion with Alex? Can you live the rest of your life not experiencing that passion? Will it last forever, or will you be right back here in a few years? Can you work hard to change your future with Todd and get that passion back? You need to be happy, for yourself. Kate and Jack need to see you happy. Which man makes you happier?"

"They both make me happy in different ways. I was fine until Alex came back into my life, or at least I thought I was. Now I don't know if I could handle living without him again. He helped me remember who I used to be. But, I also don't know if I could handle not having Todd there every day. His presence gives me strength and calms me more than anything else. I don't know if I'm ready to risk that for something as uncertain as Alex." She stared at the daffodils as they bent easily in the breeze. That same breeze caught her hair and made it tickle her ear.

"Don't forget though, it's okay to take a chance. But the outcome may be something totally different than you expect it to be. Taking a risk doesn't always mean taking a leap," her father said as he hugged his daughter close to him. Suddenly she felt twelve again and as she clutched on to him she knew it would be the last time she'd ever get to hold him. She never wanted to let him go. She'd missed her dad every day of her life for nearly twenty years. Then she watched in awe as each daffodil transformed into a small fuzzy yellow puppy with a musical note on its collar. She picked one up and felt it nuzzle her palm.

"If this is a clue it doesn't really help, Dad. I don't understand."

"You will, sweetie. You will." He held her face cupped in his hands and fixed his gaze on hers. His eyes conveyed the message before he spoke the words. "If it's worthwhile, it's worth fighting for. Don't let him get away, Christina. You will regret it for the rest of your life, and even beyond."

"Which one? I don't know which one," she said as the tears spilled over the brim of her lashes.

"Yes, you do." He kissed her cheeks softly, backed up and faded away.

Christina stood there holding the puppy, watching the others scamper around her. Unrestricted, unpredictable, unbridled passion or consistent, lifelong love? Could she have both? Would the passionate love last forever? Could the lifelong love regain some of the wildness she craved?

The puppy nuzzled her palm, and as it did she felt a tingle start in her toes, spread upward through her body, and expand into a warmth that felt like a huge hug. The light bulb went off in her mind and she smiled. Gently, she unhooked the music note collar from the puppy's neck. She kissed the puppy on the nose before putting him down. Turning the music note over and over, she gripped it in her hand. Then she let it slip through her fingers watched it land on the ground with a soft plunk. Her dad was right. She *had* known all along. If she let him go she *would* regret it for the rest of her life. Her choice was made.

Christina awoke from her dream with a peaceful sense of calm. She glanced over at Todd who was still sleeping and she got out of bed, careful not to wake him. It was barely after 6:00. She still had time. She went to her closet and hastily dressed. Quickly washing her face and brushing her teeth, she finished getting ready and threw her hair back into a ponytail.

She returned to her closet and rummaged until she found her duffle bag. It should be big enough to carry what she needed. Her heart beat wildly as she thought about what she was going to do. Would she be sorry for it later? Only time would tell. She had to keep herself from dashing down the hall and out the door.

She gathered herself together and emerged from the closet a few moments later and quietly went to Todd's side of the bed. Gently she sat next to him and nudged him awake. He groggily took off the sleep apnea mask and tried to sit up. She put her hands on his chest to stop him.

"Don't get up. I have to go into town. I need to take care of something at work. When I get back, we need to have a long talk," she whispered.

"Is everything okay?" he asked sleepily.

"Everything is fine. You rest." She kissed him on the cheek and rose to her feet. She turned at the door to see him put his mask back on and fall serenely back to sleep. She smiled even though she knew that when they had that talk life as they knew it would be forever changed. But that was as it had to be. For the first time in months, she was finally clear-headed. She checked on Kate and Jack, kissing them both gently on their foreheads. In order for them to be happy, she needed to be happy too.   She knew they would suffer in the short term because things would be tense for a while. Her future wasn't the only one at stake. Theirs was too and that meant the world to her.

As Christina pulled out of the driveway, she noticed the last of the morning's muted color changing into bright sunshine. Today was a new day. It was the first day of the rest of her life. She would not take it for granted, not one little bit.

Chapter 34

That Wednesday morning the tour bus arrived, gassed and ready to go. It was barely 10:00 and, besides the driver, Alex was the first one there. He boarded and looked around at the vehicle that would serve both as his transportation and his home for the next month. On the right side of the bus was a long upholstered bench that served as a couch and apparently folded out into a bed.

Across from that was a very small kitchen area with a sink, stove, microwave and mini-fridge. There were three cabinets above the appliances and two small drawers on either side. He was pretty sure there wouldn't be any big meals cooked here. He opened the cabinets and was pleasantly surprised at what he saw. One was loaded with plates, cups and other dishes. The other two were stacked with all of his favorite snack foods, cans of soup, boxed mac and cheese, cereal, bread, peanut butter, jelly and many other comforts of home, including enough chocolate frosted Pop-Tarts to last five years. He grinned and shook his head at the sight of them. She's messing with me, he thought. The mini-fridge was also stocked with milk, juice, butter, and bottles of water.

There was a button on the wall of the bus next to the mini-fridge. He pressed it and a 42 inch flat screen television dropped from the ceiling between the couch and the kitchen. Nice, he thought. He wondered what kind of channels they'd be able to pick up on the bus, but then concluded it must be equipped with satellite or something of that nature.

After examining the kitchen area he moved toward the rear of the bus. There was a small dinette table with bench seats next to the bigger couch and another small couch across from the table. Above this second couch was a stereo/CD player. He noticed there were small speakers throughout the bus. Hmm, surround sound. Nice touch, he mused.

He passed a small closet-like bathroom on the right and an alcove with two bunk beds on the left. To the side of the bunks was a small dresser for clothes. The alcove closed with an accordion style folding door. At the rear of the bus were two very small rooms. One contained two additional bunk beds, a dresser and a small TV. The other room contained a full size bed, a dresser and TV. He assumed the room with the full bed was for him and the bunks were for his band members. In times like these it paid to be the headliner. At least he wasn't stuck across from the bathroom.

Alex put his duffle bag on the bed and began to load the dresser drawers. Instinctively he left each drawer half empty, his clothes pushed to one side. He was almost finished when he heard someone coming up the stairs of the bus. He moved out to see who it was. His spine tingled when he saw her. She had come.

Christina was wearing dark blue jeans and a green sweater that hugged her curves. Though pulled back, her hair had a slight auburn tint to it and was shining in the sun light that streamed through the bus window. She took her sunglasses off to reveal the bluest eyes he'd ever seen and that still shocked him every time he saw them. He didn't know how it was possible that she looked more stunning each day, even now when she looked utterly exhausted. The dark circles under her eyes did nothing to diminish her loveliness. If anything, they gave her a vulnerability that made her even more beautiful. She smiled a tired smile when she saw him. It took all of his strength not to engulf her in his arms and crush his mouth to hers. Instead he simply smiled back and said hey.

"I trust everything on the bus meets with your approval," she said. Her voice, shaky and nervous, betrayed the outward confidence she was trying to project. The air felt thick around them. She put the sunglasses on top of her head and put her hands in the back pockets of her jeans. He noticed she was holding her breath.

"Everything's great," he said with a pause. "I'd hate to be the guys stuck across from the bathroom though. They'll have to draw straws for those beds," he joked, hoping to ease the tension that had developed around them.

"Everyone else should be here momentarily. All your equipment will be stored under the bus, but I've arranged for your acoustic guitar to be boarded with you. I hope that's okay," she said maintaining a slight distance.

"That's…great," he stammered. He glanced out of the window. His heart skipped a beat when saw a duffle bag so full it was barely able to zip sitting on the ground beside the bus. Unable to stand being so far from her anymore, he moved closer and enveloped her in his arms. He felt her arms wrap around his back and they held on to each other for several moments. "I can't believe you're here," he said. He ran his hand over her hair feeling its soft, silky texture. He pulled back to kiss her and then saw the message as clear as day in her eyes. They had always been able to speak to each other without ever having to use words.

"You're not coming, are you?" he asked.

"No, Alex I'm not. Can we sit down?" she asked as she motioned toward the small couch. She waited until he was settled before continuing. "There are things I need to say and I really need you to not interrupt me until I'm finished."

He nodded slowly and took her hand. Her face had taken on a serious expression as she began to speak. Her voice was warm and soft. However the words that followed were anything but.

"I have loved you since the day I met you. I always have and I always will. But, when I'm with you I end up feeling lonely. I feel empty and cold and alone. It's like trying to hold a music note. It's a fleeting moment. It can't be done forever." She stroked his hand and took a deep breath before she continued.

"When I look into your eyes I see everything about you. I see the man you once were, the man you've become and the man you will one day be. I love everything I see there, but all I see is that man. I see nothing of myself. When I look into Todd's eyes I see us; him, me, what we were and what we will become. My life is completely dominated by you when we're together. It's an overwhelming feeling and at times, now and back then, I've lost part of myself. When I'm with Todd, there's room for me. I feel needed and loved and safe. There's a tenderness I experience when I'm with him and the kids that I don't feel anywhere else or with anyone else. I love that feeling. I almost lost it and I don't ever want to take that chance again." She paused as if searching for the right way to say what she needed.

"You make me feel very special, and I do feel loved, passionately loved, when I'm with you Alex. I've never experienced the level of intimacy that we have with anyone else, but it ends up as a vacant feeling. Fire that intense tends to burn too hot too fast. I don't want to spend the rest of my life on edge wondering when it's all going to end. While a part of me will always love you and will never forget you, my life and my heart belong to Todd. I forgot that for a while. I forgot all the precious things he's brought to my life. At one point we had it all, and over time we both let each other down. I need to find a way get that back."

"So, what about us? Are you just going to let this go and run away? I need you too, Christina. I need your soul and your spirit. I need to feel your arms around me. I need your presence. I need you by my side." He placed his forehead on hers and breathed her in. She was leaving him again. He was reliving that day on the blanket when he was sure his life was over. The circumstances were different, but the devastation in his heart was the same.

"No you don't. You've made a life for yourself without me. I was just lucky enough to play a small role for a short time." She stroked his cheek with the back of her hand. The gesture was meant to be comforting, but it just deepened his despair.

"A small role? You're the reason I'm here. Everything I've ever done was only possible because of you." This could not be happening. He wanted to refuse to believe it. He shut his eyes and tried to block out her words.

"That's not true. You're immensely talented. You got yourself signed to a recording contract without my help. You don't need me to get you anywhere. If it hadn't been me, Alex, there would have been someone else. Your songs are amazing and I am humbled to know that I inspired such works of art. But, you *will be* fine and you'll continue to create masterpieces. One day you'll find someone who can give you everything you need, everything you want, without restriction. And I'm not running away from us. I'm running back to him, and our life. *My* life. It's where I belong. I guess I've always known that. I just lost my focus for a while."

Alex couldn't believe he was going to lose her again. The blood beat in his ears and he felt like the bus was spinning. He put the heel of his palms against his eyes and tried to concentrate on breathing.

"Does he know about us?"

"Not yet, but he will. It'll be difficult for him to hear, but I'm confident that we can work through it. If I'm wrong, I'll spend the rest of my life trying to prove to him that we deserve another chance. My battle is only beginning. I have a lot to be sorry for and it's going to take time and effort to earn his trust back, but I'm willing to put in all that it takes."

He felt the tears sting his eyes. She was leaving him and there was nothing he could do about it. He realized almost at once that she was never really his in the first place. He felt his heart break more and more with each passing moment.

"Please don't do this. Please stay with me. I can't believe everything we've been through means nothing to you." He knew he sounded pathetic begging her, but he had no idea what else to do. He looked up to see the tears streaming down her face as well.

"It means everything. Alex, you and I will always have each other, even if we're not together. We are joined by bonds that transcend this world. This was not an easy decision for me. I love you both so very much, in such different ways," her voice cracked from the emotion. "There was a time when all I wanted was to hear the sweet words of love we shared last week. But there was also a time when I felt a level of pain I never knew existed before. It took a long time and there were days I was sure I wouldn't survive, but I got over that once and vowed never to go through it again. But, the pain came back. Only this time it was caused by almost losing the one person in the world I know I can't live without. That's my husband."

He stood up and crossed his arms. His heart felt weighted down and he was sinking with it. "Well, I guess that's it then." Her mind was made up and there was nothing more he could say. "We'll still see each other at Mastermind I guess," he said reaching for straws. When she didn't answer the next reality set in. "You're leaving Mastermind too, aren't you?" That's what was in her bag. It wasn't filled with clothes to live on a tour bus as he had so stupidly imagined. It was filled with the stuff from her office.

She nodded, eyes downcast.

"Why? You're so good at what you do," he said. Leaving him was one thing, but she was giving up her career too.

"I need to be home; with Todd and with our kids. I can't rebuild my marriage if I'm here. I need to be stable and consistent and I can't be that with this job. I've already talked to Joe and placed myself on indefinite leave of absence. I tried to resign, but he refused to sign the paperwork. This was as close as I could get. Besides, you know it'll never truly be settled between us if we are in the position to see each other. There would always be the same temptation we gave into before."

"But, don't you see that you're giving up even more of yourself?" he asked.

"It's just a job. It's not who I am."

"I don't believe that," he said and paused for a moment. "You're leaving; in every capacity." His face was as blank as his heart was beginning to feel. It was college all over again. Only this time, she was the one who was removing herself from the situation completely. The tremendous crushing pressure in his chest was beginning to overwhelm him. He wanted it to bury him. Death would be almost welcome now. He knew he needed to say something. She was staring at him with an expression of deep concern on her face.

"I'm so sorry," she whispered.

"I guess we just always had bad timing." He shrugged in an effort to pretend the situation wasn't as dire as he knew it to be. He knew the gesture wouldn't fool her. They could read each other like a book. She'd always been able to see right through him.

She stood up and took a few steps toward him. "Or maybe it was perfect timing. I wouldn't change a thing about our past or how our lives turned out. I wouldn't have my marriage, or the kids or my career if I had not loved you first. You made my life possible, Alex. I know this is not what you want to hear, but I've never regretted loving you, not even for a second, and I never will. I don't regret the few short days we spent together. They were wonderful and perfect, fairytale-like. I want to be able to teach my daughter that there is a kind of love out there that makes anything possible. You helped create that love in me and through all of this I can let Kate know how wonderful love is."

She paused and then continued. "I have something for you," she said taking a small box from her sweater pocket. "Open it after I leave. I can't be here when you see it." She leaned in and kissed him, a lingering kiss full of sweetness. With her forehead resting lightly against his and one hand stroking the back of his hair, she said her last words to him. Words he'd never, in a million years, be able to forget. "You are a magnificent person. I do love you, more than you'll ever fully know, and that's why I have to leave."

Turning away from him she walked to the door of the bus. He didn't see her turn to watch him as he continued to stand there, head down looking at the box. She descended the steps, hoisted her bag on her shoulder, headed straight for her car and never looked back.

He waited a few moments before he chanced moving. Holding his breath, he was sure if he could just stay still long enough he'd wake up to find this was all just a terrible nightmare. After a while though he knew it wasn't a dream. She wasn't coming back and he exhaled. Slowly, with trembling hands, he opened the box. Icy chills ran through his body as he gazed at the box's contents. Inside he found the circle charm with the star cut from the middle. The one he'd given her for Christmas so long ago. Love much, Live well. There was a small note folded behind the charm. A tear slid down his cheek as he picked the charm up and held it in his palm. He carefully opened the note and read, "Always Remember Where You've Been."

Chapter 35

Two and a half years later

Christina arrived home with Kate and Jack around 4:00. Max greeted them at the door, tail wagging. It had been a hard recovery for him. He'd been in the clinic for three weeks after the accident. They released him when the internal bleeding had stopped completely and one of his casts was ready to come off. The arthritis in his hips had progressed significantly and gave him problems.

They had stopped their morning runs and traded them for afternoon walks and weekly cortisone shots. The white fur around his face had spread through the rest of his yellow coat. He had been around a long time and Christina wasn't looking forward to the day he would finally leave their family. He wasn't the only one moving slower these days though. Christina was approaching her ninth month of pregnancy and it was all she could do to keep up with her students and her own kids.

Christina had gone back to teaching the fall following her affair with Alex. After staying home for the rest of that school year, she'd realized that a huge part of her identity *was* in the work she did, whether it was representing clients, teaching or being a bank teller. Working was an integral part of who she was. Returning to teaching had been a very natural transition. It had been difficult at first, having to learn new standards and assimilate the latest trends in education, but she was good at it and it was a good move for her and her family. She had been able to get a position teaching third grade at the school Kate attended. Jack was in Pre-K there now, which made the logistics of transportation much easier.

She'd also remembered the daffodils. She had planted bulbs each fall following the fallout. She found a sense of calm and reflection from the time she spent in the yard. The scent of the flowers wafted through her house now during early spring and it helped her keep the memory of her dad alive. He had not visited her since that dream, although there were times in the aftermath when she'd felt his presence. It was enormously comforting to know she wasn't going through it alone and that he was with her, even if she couldn't see him.

Christina had told Todd about Alex as soon as she got home that day. Her mother-in-law took the kids to her house so they could have time to talk some things out. She answered every question with full honesty. If there was any shot for them to make their marriage work, she had to come completely clean. He took it exceptionally hard, as she knew he would. After many hours of anger and tears from both of them and a million apologies from her, they decided to give marriage counseling a try. Todd had admitted that not all the problems were caused by her affair and eventually came to see how she had ended up in Alex's arms. Both had gotten so caught up in their careers and the kids that they had not made enough time for each other. The romance of their beginning had been abandoned by both of them. Neither wanted to end the marriage, but he was devastated.

She had even offered to move into the guest room while they worked things out. He had agreed to that. There were times when she was sure they weren't going to make it. She had even begun to look for a new place to live. She'd cried herself to sleep many nights, but after three months he appeared in the door of the guest room and asked her to come back to sleep in their room. That simple gesture made her happier than she'd been in a long time. That first night they held each other without talking.

Through counseling and learning how to communicate better, they had been able to save their marriage. It was a hard road that they tackled one day at a time. They worked on it more everyday and she never took for granted the second chance she had been given.

Rebuilding the trust was hard, and they had been extremely fragile for a long time. They were stronger now, but there was still a lot of work to do. They learned how to interact as a couple again, and not just as parents. They found time to spend together away from work and the kids. They found the intimacy, and eventually the passion, that they had let drift away before.

Joe finally let her resign from Mastermind with the promise that she would leave her Rolodex and not go to another production house. He also let her know that the door was always open if she ever wanted to return. Being away from Mastermind and back in the classroom made it possible for her and Todd to spend the quality time together that they had let slip away. She also got to spend more time with the kids in the way she always wanted to. There were no more late night meetings, long audition sessions, traveling out of state to meet with clients, or missing holidays.

They weren't exactly ready for the pregnancy that happened in mid-August, but it actually served as a means of strengthening their delicate bond. However, with the new baby coming in a few weeks they knew there were more challenges ahead. They couldn't let themselves fall back into the same old patterns that had almost destroyed their family.

Kate and Jack brought their homework to the kitchen table and got started on it right away as Christina got started on dinner. She and Todd had taken cooking classes together as one of their "couples" activities. She discovered that cooking was not as hard, or as tedious as she once thought it was and they had created some fabulous meals together. Like anything else, it required a lot of attention but once she got the hang of it, it had turned out to be quite fun.

Tonight would be a modest menu: spaghetti and meatballs with salad and bread. Baby Meredith made Christina crave pasta and bread more than anything else. She'd never been much of a carbohydrate fan until this pregnancy. That had always helped keep her slim. She had had to stop running in her seventh month so to counteract the carbo-load she ingested every day, she walked twice a day.

After a moment of awkwardness trying to get situated in the chair, she managed to sit down to help her daughter with her math sheet. Kate was now in third grade, but wasn't in Christina's class. However, it helped to know the material. Learning how to teach the new state curriculum had been tough, but she had taken on the task whole-heartedly.

Kate was working on multiplication, division and fractions and seemed to understand the concepts pretty well. Christina helped Jack color the letters of the alphabet with the corresponding crayons that his sheet called for.

After half an hour the phone rang and she heaved herself up and waddled across the kitchen to answer it. She checked the caller ID and saw that it was Andrea.

"Hi Andrea," she said slightly out of breath as she held the phone to her ear with her shoulder. She stirred the sauce with one hand while shaking in oregano, followed by basil, with the other. "What's up?"

"Hey, I know this might be weird for you to watch, but I just thought you'd like to know that Alex is being interviewed on Entertainment Tonight. It was filmed about a week ago and it airs tonight. I totally get it if you don't want to watch it, but I think you should."

"I'll see." She wasn't sure she wanted to watch him on television, or if she even could watch him. She hadn't seen or spoken to him since the day she left him on the tour bus. That had been by design. She was a bit unsure that the flame had died completely away. "Hey, how's it going over there? Are you adjusting to your new role?" On her recommendation Andrea had been promoted to Christina's old position. She knew the job and many of the contacts already. She didn't go in as the head of the department, but she'd risen fast.

"It's hard to get to work on time, but I have this new assistant who is a real ball-buster. She doesn't stand for tardiness."

Christina laughed out loud. "How ironic! And Nick, how's he doing?"

"Good. He's got his third client and he's getting better with each one."

"Well, tell him I said hi and to call if he needs any advice."

"Will do. Hey, do you think you'll ever come back here? Joe asks about you all the time."

"He asks me about it all the time too. I get a call at least once every other week begging for my return."

She lowered the heat on the sauce pan and put the lid on top making sure it was vented to let out steam build up. The aroma of the sauce began to permeate through the kitchen.

"No, I think I'm done with Mastermind and pretty much the whole music business. Jack, do not snatch those away from your sister! Hey, I need to go. We're having a small crayon crisis at the homework table."

Kate was using some of Jack's crayons to fill in her social studies map, and he was not too happy about it.

"We need to get together soon, okay? Baby Meredith is almost here and you know that means no more free time for a while."

"Okay. We will. Plus, I'll be up there as soon as the new little one makes her appearance. Give the kids a kiss for me and tell Kate I'll come up and take her shopping soon. Bye, Chris."

"She'll be thrilled. Shopping with Aunt Andrea is the biggest joy of her life right now. Bye, Andrea," she said. Replacing the receiver on its cradle, she turned to referee the crayon situation.

At 7:30 the dishes were done, baths were taken and Todd was reading the kids their bedtime stories. Having a few free moments, she tenuously turned on the television and flipped until she saw Mary Hart on the screen. She figured there was no time like the present to see if it was truly over and done with. She watched for a few minutes and then he entered the set. He looked different. His hair was longer than before, he had some new tattoos and he looked thinner, but his eyes were the same. The show played a montage of photos and she noticed one new tattoo in particular. On his forearm there was a red heart that was torn across the center. She swore the rip was in the shape of a C, but it could have been her imagination.

She barely heard the interview about the success of the second album and the upcoming world tour. Christina had heard the new album and was even more impressed with it than she had been with *A Little Chunk of my Soul*. It was clearly influenced by their time together, but had blends of other experiences too. He'd even done a cover of Everything Changes, by Staind. The message behind the song was clear and she was pretty sure it had been added for her. Something was being said about extending the European leg, but she wasn't really paying attention.

What she focused on was the necklace he was wearing. As if Mary was reading her mind, the next question brought her full attention back to the show.

"Steven, the name of your second album is *Love Much, Live Well* and the cover has the same emblem as the charm on your necklace. I've also noticed that you wear the necklace a lot. What's the story behind it? I know there has to be one."

She was perky and clearly fishing for a juicy tidbit of gossip that she could break wide open. The gleam in her eyes clearly showed how much she wanted to get the scoop. He smiled and Christina felt herself smile with him.

"Yeah, there's a story behind it. Isn't there a story, and a woman, behind everything?"

"We've seen you with so many beautiful women on the red carpet. Which one of these ladies is behind the necklace you hold so close to your heart?"

"Well Mary, the woman behind this necklace has never been on the red carpet with me. But, she's with me all the time."

"Ooh, a secret love. Is the world ever going to meet the woman behind the charm and the music?" Mary was positively itching to get the story. Christina rolled her eyes.

A mischievous grin crossed his lips. "If I tell you about her it won't be a secret love anymore now, would it?" Christina felt her smile creep back. He sure did know how to keep people on the hook. "Let's just say that the woman behind this charm means more to me than anyone else ever has, or will. We will always have each other even if we're not together." Damn, he stole my line, she thought.

"The timing was wrong?"

"No, I think it was actually perfect timing." Another theft.

"So, why do you wear the charm if it's a constant reminder of something that didn't work out?" the talk show host inquired.

"Let's just say it helps me remember where I've been."

Christina smiled one last time and hoisted herself off the couch. She rubbed her belly and sighed peacefully. Taking one last look at the man she used to love, she turned off the TV and reflected on the moment. She examined her surroundings and thought about what she had almost given up. With no regret and no lingering desire, she walked upstairs and climbed into bed. Todd came in after getting Kate to sleep and cuddled up next to her.

"Hey there," he said nuzzling her neck and rubbing her swollen belly. "Everything okay?" he asked, noticing the strangely serene expression on her face.

She turned over to face him and she looked intently into his dark brown eyes. She saw her life and his love reflected back at her. She brought her hands to the sides of his face, smoothed his hair and kissed him deeply. As she pulled back, she whispered, "Everything's great."

Kara Householder was born and raised near Atlanta, Georgia. She obtained a B.S. in Health Science from Georgia Southern University and attended Georgia State University for her Master's degree in Early Childhood Education. Kara has been teaching since 2002, presently teaching in Marietta, Georgia and she lives nearby with her husband and son. *Torn* is her debut novel. She is currently working on her second novel, *Witness.*

www.KaraHouseholder.com

2424795

Made in the USA